THE
MASTER
OF DECEIT

SEARCHING FOR ANSWERS

ROBERT JOHN DELUCA

DEFIANCE PRESS
& PUBLISHING

Master of Deceit

First Edition: 2020

Printed in the United States of America

10 9 8 7 6 5 4 3 2 1

ISBN-13: 978-1-948035-43-9 (Paperback)
ISBN-13: 978-1-948035-44-6 (ebook)

Edited by Sean Cowie
Cover designed by Spomenka Bojanic
Interior designed by Debbi Stocco

Published by Defiance Press and Publishing, LLC

Bulk orders of this book may be obtained by contacting Defiance Press and Publishing, LLC. www.defiancepress.com.

Public Relations Dept. – Defiance Press & Publishing, LLC
281-581-9300
pr@defiancepress.com

Defiance Press & Publishing, LLC
281-581-9300
info@defiancepress.com

Other books by Robert John DeLuca

Fiction

The Pact with the Devil
Justice for a Texas Marshall

Non-Fiction

Beatles, Books, Bombs, and Beyond
The Perfect Pro Football Coach
Tackling the Perfect Pro Football Coach

To: John B. DeLuca and Richard L. Whitehead

My father and father-in-law, both of whom toiled tirelessly as government employees for decades, always putting forth maximum effort to return to the good citizens an excellent work product in exchange for fair and reasonable compensation.

"The art of pleasing is the art of deception."

Luc De Clapiers

Prologue

The oldest son of Texas real estate magnate, Travis Nelson, is struggling to find himself after the untimely demise of his overbearing father during a violent cartel shootout in Mexico. As the former president of his father's company, Matt Nelson is lucky to have avoided prosecution when Travis's unsavory dealings sent his entire empire up in flames. In the aftermath of the disastrous scandal that followed, Matt and his mother have cobbled together a small management company, which pales by comparison to the industry dominant Mesquite Development Company lorded over by Travis. Matt wonders if it is time to abandon his desk jockey lifestyle and join his brother, John, who operates a covert corporate security operation. As he ponders his alternatives, it is inevitable that Pamela, his party-hearty sister will lend a hand whether he asks for help or not.

Author's Note

The Master of Deceit is the second in the "Nelson Family Saga" series, of at least four books. *The Pact with the Devil*, the first, was published in 2016. It is available through Amazon and most booksellers as an E-book or paperback.

1.

The man was swallowed up in a pitch black abyss. He could scarcely make out anything in front as he slowly paddled his kayak through the muck, marsh grass and palmetto scrub. There was no breeze, and the putrid smell of the rotting bog filled his nostrils. An owl's staccato hoot high up in the lodge pole pines echoed through the South Carolina night. Instinctively he froze, stopped paddling, and strained to hear anything out of the ordinary. Stealth was critical to his mission. They must not know he was coming. He was alone, and only he could pull this off. Any slip-up could destroy everything. He fought the urge to move faster. Get in and get out, but he dared not rush, even though every extra minute raised his chances of being discovered. He had to succeed. Failure was not an option.

The twinkling of a solitary boathouse light appeared a short distance away through the gloom. He was relieved as he'd found the right place. He eased the craft in gently as the keel scraped along the mossy bottom and shuddered to a stop. His guile and training had gotten him safely across the murky water from where his SUV was hidden. So far, so good.

He glanced at the luminous dials on his watch. He was on schedule. He felt around his camo jacket to be sure everything was where it should be. The plan was simple. Move cautiously to the objective, grab what he was after, and get out as quickly as possible. Seeking one final reassurance, he ran his hand along his belt and felt the bulge of his Glock. On this mission, there would be no reason to need it. Yet, just having it gave him a boost of confidence. After checking and re-checking, he was ready. He listened one more time. Nothing. It was showtime.

He took a deep breath as he grabbed the gunwales of the kayak and slowly rose up. A warm bead of sweat trickled down his blackened face. As he carefully lifted his left leg over the side, without warning the little boat rocked, teetered, and flip-flopped totally over. Water rushed in from all sides, leaving him confused and disoriented. It was several seconds before he realized that he was underwater and upside down in the smelly swamp. Apparently, he had misjudged the depth at his landing point. He must not panic, as he had been trained. Preserve silence. The mission! The mission! At all costs the mission must not be jeopardized.

Such noble ideas were fine in training, but as he struggled to free himself, he quickly realized that without air, more than the damn mission was at stake. Right the ship pretty quickly or become gator food. Screw stealth! He squirmed, scrambled, grabbed at the bottom, thrashed, and twisted. Finally, somehow, he freed himself from that blasted boat. A few more seconds upside down in total darkness, underwater, and he might not have made it.

When his head burst from the murky muck he gulped and gasped for precious air, standing in waist-deep water. The irreverent owl applauded his flailing performance with a series of discourteous hoots. When his panting and wheezes finally caught up to his breathing, he slogged towards dry land and rolled himself up on the slimy bank. He lay there completely still, hoping against hope that his splash landing had not given him away. He was sure anyone nearby would not have confused his frantic escape with an alligator mating ritual. His cover might well have been blown. If so, he would shove the boat back out and paddle away as fast as he could. Abort the mission and face the consequences with his handlers. Admit that he had failed.

After a few minutes of straining but hearing nothing, his fears eased, and a measure of confidence returned. He would gamble that no-one had heard him. Soldier on. He dragged the kayak up onto the bank and began to creep towards the large house some fifty yards through the underbrush. He had to be careful where he placed his feet, just as he'd done dozens of times hunting wild turkey back in Texas. An errant twig snap could be a dead giveaway. His confidence was growing now that he was in a more familiar element. He watched his steps closely. In fact, so much so that in the darkness he smacked his head into the gnarled trunk of large oak tree. *Ouch!* he stammered under his breath. Stars other than those above were suddenly visible. He was stunned and dropped to a knee to let his head clear. *Where did that come from?*

After a few more steps, he could make out a building through the shadows cast by dozens of Spanish moss-laden trees. He knew it would be a substantial structure, typical of beach homes along the South Carolina coast near Kiawah and Seabrook islands. The stately bay home was on a secluded spot overlooking an estuary that offered protection from ravages of the unpredictable nearby Atlantic. It consisted of two stories with a wide wooden porch completely surrounding the ground level. Out front, a long gravel driveway led to an asphalt two-lane country road some two hundred yards away. The place was just the sort of out-of-the-way beach retreat a wealthy Charleston businessman might choose.

His trainers had assured him that such an upscale property would have a security system, although probably not outside motion detectors, which would be tripped so often by deer and other local wildlife as to make them unpractical. Dogs, however, were another problem. Although there might not be canines patrolling the grounds, he must plan for them just in case. As he thought about it, this wrinkle had given him some pause. Mission success aside, he was reluctant to injure or destroy an innocent animal, even a vicious one protecting his home. What was a dog lover doing in this spot? From his pocket he removed a foil packet containing several chunks of raw red meat laced with a powerful anesthetic that would send doggy into dreamland, but not harm him permanently. He pitched this bait into the grass in the backyard where a roving Fido couldn't miss it.

Overcoming the security system would be the most daunting obstacle he would encounter. Short of a forced entry, there was no way to ignore it. He hoped at least that the system would be of simple design that didn't do much more than create a racket to scare away potential intruders. He knew that when tripped, even a basic system would notify a central monitoring base, in some faraway place like Bangladesh, and the police would be promptly alerted. Given the remoteness of the house, however, once the locals were on their way, he calculated that he'd still have half an hour or so before they would show up, affording him enough time to do what he came to do. Nonetheless, it was critical that he get in and get out as quickly as possible.

It was well after midnight, and the interior of the house was entirely dark. The mission had been intentionally planned for a mid-week night when they could be reasonably certain the owner would be at home in Charleston and not at his beach hideaway. The place looked empty. If anyone happened to be there, they were in bed. He tried to control his breathing as he crept slowly out of the shadows towards the side door entrance. He stepped lightly across the wooden floorboards of the porch, fearful that any wayward squeak would give him away. His heart was beating rapid-fire, but, so far, no dog, no light, no alarm, no problem. His intense concentration aside, he could not help but notice the malodorous swamp stink he carried with him from his kayak scuttling. Phew!

Getting this far was supposed to be the easy part. Things were going to get more complicated; he must gain access. If all else failed, he could enter forcibly, although it would be far preferable to pull this thing off without being detected or damaging property. He had spent long hours with instructors learning how to pick locks. It was time to see what he had learned.

He brightened and could not help but smile. He'd caught a break! The door lock was the exact $22.95 Kwikset model he'd worked on in training. The house had been fitted with economy version over-the-counter lock sets. There was apparently no reason to overspend on door locks at such a remote location, where someone could easily smash a window to get in. He glanced at his watch. It was 1:05 AM. He should be inside within ten minutes, tops. He got out his tools and began carefully tapping, nudging and lifting the tumblers.

He was confident he'd defeat this piece of metal in short order. After half an hour of picking and twisting, though, his blood pressure began to rise. He tried to stay calm, but the damn lock just would not pop open. He had been piddling away for a while when he checked his watch. Holy cow, it was almost 2:00 AM! He'd been at it for an hour and still wasn't in! He wiped the sweat from his brow and plopped down against the wall next to the door for a moment to rest and regroup. It had been so simple during training. What was the problem? He was already busting his timeline. Scrap the mission? Of course not. What he lacked in burglary skills, he made up for in determination.

And then, all hell broke loose.

2.

His heart jumped as scrambling, scratching, and growling sounds caught his attention from the back of the porch. There was no mistaking the commotion, a four-legged beast was rapidly headed his way. So much for the snooze meat bait. He moved to react, but his body was stiff and he had trouble rising up from his seat on the porch floor. He was still sprawled on all fours when a ferocious growl was accompanied by the sharp pain of dog teeth sinking into his ankle. He knew not to scream but could not suppress a muffled, "Yee Ouch!" that would be heard by anyone nearby. Not only was the animal's bite excruciating, it would not let go. He had to stand up rather than roll around on the floor with the enraged creature. As he struggled with the dog fastened securely to his leg, he saw shadows and a light coming from the front of the house. His heart jumped again. There were car lights in the driveway. *Holy shit. Someone is here!*

He rapidly surveyed his limited options. He wanted to bolt back into the woods but couldn't with that damn dog on him. He still had to get to his feet. In an effort to stand, he grabbed the cursed doorknob to use as leverage. In doing so, he fell against the door. Guess what? It flew open. All his work and the damn thing wasn't locked! Why hadn't he tried to open it? He was so surprised that he tumbled into the house and ended up flat on his face. If there was any good news, it was that the dog had finally given up his lunch and let go. He was able to kick the door closed before the irascible mutt could follow him in. Great. *Now what? I am finally in, but there is someone out there. They'll be in here in a minute.*

Luckily, from his study of the house plans, he had a good idea of the layout of the house. He was lying in a mud room between the kitchen and the garage. He glanced up through the glass in the door and saw an approaching light outside, which was surely a flashlight. Either move quickly or be spotted. Just as the doorknob started to turn, he ducked into the rear stairs that led up to the second-floor bedrooms. He scrambled up, trying to be as quiet as possible. Just as he reached the upstairs hallway, he heard voices from below. They were muffled, but one was a man, who said, "Mid Coastal Security." He must have tripped a silent alarm somehow and the security service had come out to investigate. Now he was trapped. If they searched the whole house, they'd find him.

He was fresh out of clever moves. He must have missed the day of training that dealt with these situations. What would his brother, John, do in this mess? Where could he hide? How about the closet? They'd never look there. *Right.* Not for at least five seconds! Still, there was no choice. He ducked into the closest bedroom and jumped into a closet, shutting the door behind him. He prayed they would not do a complete search of the house, but if they did, he was toast.

Crouched there in the dark with a minute to gather his thoughts, it suddenly struck him that while his "mission" was important, it was not worth risking his or someone else's life. He would give himself up before any kind of violent confrontation with the law. He was certain to be arrested and booked. He hoped John would know someone to bail him out?

It didn't take long for him to discover that his "secret place" was the wife's closet. As bad as he reeked, this place was even worse. The clothes carried a perfume fragrance that made him nauseous. To complicate matters, it took everything he had to suppress a whopper of a sneeze. He might as well call them to his hiding place. In a way, he almost found it amusing. He had a wonderful wife from whom he had never dreamed of straying. Now he felt like a cheating lover about to face the consequences when the lady's husband suddenly came home. Just another reason never to be unfaithful.

And, of course, there was the bigger question. He also wondered what he was doing there in the first place, playing like a super-secret spy of some kind. Was this what he really wanted to do? He had been a real estate executive since college, running a company on a nine-to-five basis. This kind of stuff was what his brother, the ex-Marine, did for a living. After their father had been lost, his company had been toned down and cut way back. Collecting rents and managing properties was a lot less exciting than building new projects, and he had become bored; but was this stuff really right for him? At the moment, it sure didn't seem so.

On the other hand, he always admired John, who had gotten out of the service and started a corporate security company that operated all over the world and had lots of exciting and often perilous assignments. He wanted to prove to his brother that he had what it took to pull off one of those jobs. John had given him a chance and put him through some pretty rigorous training.

His first mission on his own should have been simple. Paddle your boat across a pond, gain access to an empty, isolated home out in the woods, search an office for certain documents, get out, paddle back, and report for work at 8:00 AM the next morning. No bullets, no danger.

Well, it really hadn't worked out that way so far, had it? First, he dumped the kayak, and then he struggled trying to open the door, not knowing the door was actually unlocked. Next, a dog took him down, and then he cowered in a boudoir closet. It was pretty conclusive so far that John's brand of corporate security was not the life for him. The vaunted mission was destined to end as an utter failure. When he got out of the slammer, he'd head back to Houston as soon as possible and resume his position behind his large wooden desk, where his biggest decision would be where to go for lunch. He'd have to admit failure to John, but that seemed the least of his worries at the moment.

That smell was driving him nuts. "Ahh, ahhh, shoosh!" He was barely able to keep it in. He had been cooped up for over hour an hour. How much more could he take? And then suddenly, he could feel there was someone out there. A switch flipped and rays of light flickered under the door. And then he heard panting and whining. That rotten dog. Of course, he would lead the security people right to him. His jig was up. He was sure they were standing outside the door right now with leveled sawed-off shotguns. He quickly decided to take the initiative and give himself up before some trigger-happy recruit made him Swiss cheese.

"Okay! Okay!" he blurted. "I am giving myself up. I am coming out. Please don't shoot! It is all a misunderstanding. I give up." He slowly opened the door, expecting to get blown away at any second. His eyes were blinded by the bright bedroom lights and he couldn't focus for a few seconds. Where were the security guys with big, bad guns ready to blast him? The room was empty. No-one seemed to be there. Maybe they were hiding just around the corner, waiting to see him before they pounced but, when he looked, there was no-one in sight. He sensed movement at his feet and quickly glanced down. Standing there, rapidly wagging his tail, was a ten-pound-tops, brown-and-black miniature Yorkie with a blue bow in his hair. The dog was clearly looking for affection and not a battle.

What the heck?

And then he almost jumped out of the window when, from around the corner, a figure burst in, brandishing a baseball bat.

"You stand right there, mister, or I am going to bash you good. Don't you dare move!"

On a day of astonishments, yet another one had just occurred. He looked through the door at a teenage girl in bare feet wearing a pink Grunge tee shirt and baggy, gray sweatpants. Her spiked hair was a kind of aquamarine green. She could not have been much over five feet tall. Her pale complexion provided a stark contrast to her steel-blue eyes, which were burning holes into him as he stood there with his mouth open. She was brandishing a wooden Louisville slugger over her shoulder and looked very capable of using it.

"Who, who are you?" was all he could think to ask.

She continued to glare and ignored the question. "This is my house. I live here and you broke in," she answered, and then looked down to where the tiny dog had begun to rub against his smelly trouser leg. "Latte. Get away from him. Right now!" she commanded, but the little pup merely looked up at her and didn't move.

"Look," he began, trying to find the right words for this peculiar situation, "I am sorry. You are right, I should not be here."

He started to take a step forward but froze when she screamed, "Stop right there! The security cops are downstairs. They will be right up!"

Now, that was one he really doubted. If they were anywhere around they'd have him cuffed and tied by now. He replied in what he hoped was an even and steady voice. "Let me try again. What is your name? I am Matt, and, as a matter of fact, I have a daughter about your age, who, by the way, is a big Grunge fan herself."

The girl hesitated to answer, but then seemed to soften. "I am Sabrina. I don't live here, but come out every so often. My uncle owns the place."

"So, your uncle; that would be Kenneth Moore?"

"Yeah, he's the dude. He likes to bring his girlfriends out here to get them drunk and have sex. He thinks I don't notice. He is a real jerk."

"If you don't like it here, why do you come?"

"I don't have a choice. He doesn't give a rat's butt about me, but my mother is dead and he has to be nice to me and take me places or he won't get cash out of my grandparents' trust. Even though he is my mother's brother, she couldn't stand him either, when she was alive."

"I am sorry, Sabrina. So, he just leaves you here all by yourself?"

"Yup. You got it. I don't mind being alone, and Latte is pretty good at protecting me. He gave you a run for your money out on the porch a while ago."

Matt was incredulous. "That? That was the dog that attacked me?"

"Yes, sir. He's something, isn't he? I watched you roll around on the video camera from my uncle's office." The little dog looked up and seemed to take it all in with a curious doggie smile.

Matt's eyes rolled back. What a great spy he was. "Where are the security guys? I know they were here. If you saw me, why didn't you tell them I was here?"

"I dunno. I told them there wasn't any problem. Maybe only a deer or something. They took a quick look around and left. You didn't look like a bad guy to me. I was so bored watching you try to get in when the door was already open and then Latte took to you. He was only playing out there on the porch. He is a pretty good judge of character. Just look at him make up to you now."

Matt was astounded, but she had even one more surprise for him. "But, still…," he began. She cut him off. "And I figured you were here to steal something from my ass-wipe uncle, and I wanted to help. Why are you here, anyway?"

Matt smiled. This was unbelievable. "Well, yes, I did want to look through his records."

She shrugged. "No problem. Follow me." He did wait until she finally decided to lower the slugger. He followed her down the stairs to her uncle's office.

Matt sat at his computer and fired it up. John's firm had been hired by the owner of the software company where Ken Moore was the senior vice president. The owner was suspicious that Moore was stealing firm secrets and selling them to competitors. John was trying to obtain proof. Immediately, of course, Matt's access was blocked by demand for a password. He was stuck.

He was about to start searching and copying whatever files he could find when Sabrina reached around him and typed in "IAMASTUD." The desktop immediately appeared.

"Thanks," Matt responded.

It took only a few minutes for Matt to confirm that this guy had been stealing secrets. He copied several key files on a flash drive and then transmitted them back to John's mainframe using his iPhone. They were in and out of Moore's office in less than ten minutes.

Sabrina stood there with a canary grin as Matt thanked and re-thanked her. She assured him that she would not divulge a peep to her uncle. He'd tried not to leave fingerprints or DNA trace possibilities in the office. It was almost 4:00 AM when he finally headed through the woods towards the kayak. Sabrina had settled back in the house and was about to text some friends. There was a knock on the door. Matt stood there looking more than a bit sheepish.

"What's up now, Matt?"

"Ah, Sabrina, I had a little accident with my boat. I think there is a hole. It doesn't float."

She looked out at him and smiled. "No problem, Matt. Drag it over here and throw it in the back of my pickup. I'll take you back across."

Matt, what a super sleuth!

3.

An assignment had been successfully completed. Matt Nelson had bungled his way through and somehow came out with the critical information they were seeking. He should have been pleased, as John would be, but he was a realist and knew how close he had come to a complete disaster. He continued to ponder whether this was the life for him.

As the oldest child in the family at thirty, Matt had always been more cautious than his siblings. Perhaps it was because he had to "pave the way" in some respects for the others. He was grudgingly allowed to stay up until 9:00 PM as a grade-schooler. His two-year-younger brother, John, and sister, Pam, had no trouble moving it to 10:00 PM or later. Matt got his driver's license at age sixteen, but he was actually closer to seventeen. Pam had her learner's permit at fifteen and a half. Matt was an excellent, if not quite superior, student. He made the first team on the high school football team, but not until his senior year. He rose to student council vice president, but not to the top job. He was never in trouble. When the guys managed to get that six-pack of beer in junior high out in the woods, he sipped a little and acted high, but really didn't drink much. When he tossed "dead soldier" empties out of the window, they went "clunk" instead of "clink." He didn't like Ferris wheels, and it took all the courage he had when swimming with friends to leap off the twenty-foot limestone banks into the cool Blanco River in the hill country. He had many friends and was universally well-liked by his peers and teachers.

From very early on, the youngster idolized his handsome and successful father. At times, he did not seem to be aware of the aloofness and coldness Travis had for his family. Despite having had major issues with his own father as to where he would attend college, the man did not hesitate to push his oldest son to Texas A&M, where he had gone. That decision turned out quite well for Matt, who met Ellen, his wife-to-be, on campus. In fact, he saved her life in a brilliant rescue when the two of them got caught in the middle of the ill-fated collapse of the traditional Aggie bonfire log structure just before the football game with the University of Texas. Had it not been for Matt's quick thinking, both he and Ellen would have been crushed in the midst of huge cascading logs.

In addition to the two sons, there was Pamela, who was just now turning twenty-one. While both boys had always been hard workers, serious-minded, and determined to succeed, Pam had been a party girl first and occasional student only when it became absolutely necessary. She was always more than willing to enjoy the advantages of a wealthy father who clearly favored her over any of the other members of the family. Remarkably, the young lady surprised everyone, especially herself, and was scheduled to receive her undergraduate degree from Sam Houston State University in a few months.

Diane Nelson, who was in her early fifties, had endured a long and tumultuous marriage to Travis Nelson. It became clear early on that her husband would always hold his company and business interests above any real concern for his family. Travis was convinced that he fulfilled his fatherhood obligations simply by providing an abundance of physical things. They lived in a magnificent home in the exclusive Tanglewood section of Houston and were kept well supplied with cars, clothes, camps, trips, electronics, equipment, and whatever else they wanted. He paid scant attention to the boys and even less to Diane. Only Pam seemed able to divert him on occasion from the sacrosanct Mesquite Development Company.

Each family member reacted to Travis's indifference in his or her own way. Matt, who looked up to and adored his father, was willing for a long time to accept his supercilious attitude and fall in line with his every command. On the other hand, John rebelled, and disappeared just as soon as he could. He would tolerate none of his arrogant bs. Pam reveled in her role as the favored one, and Diane became increasingly depressed and sought refuge in alcohol. The presence of a loveless marriage did not seem to bother Travis, as long as his "model" family remained intact for image purposes as a complement to his reputation in business. It was critical that he maintain a favorable image with lenders and other members of the Texas real estate and affordable housing community, and his "beautiful" family was important to this process.

After graduating from college, Matt was thrilled when his father brought him into Mesquite Development. The company was involved in developing low-income affordable housing using federal tax credits. It is an extremely competitive and highly technical business. To be successful, a company must be able to secure its share of tax credits, which are in high demand and of a very limited supply. Matt eagerly jumped in with both feet and learned the business from the ground up. By doing so, he became a very valuable asset to the company.

It was certain that his father appreciated the contributions that his son was making to the company, but when one day his father announced that he was naming Matt the new president of the company, virtually everyone was shocked, Matt included. Matt was highly regarded by all, but the move seemed premature by at least a year or two. Travis Nelson, however, knew exactly what he was doing. Matt was bright, likable, and presented a good image, and was developing a good sense for the very complicated affordable housing business. What Nelson wanted, and what he got, at least for a while, was a complete yes man in the president's office. As chairman and controlling stockholder, he alone made every significant decision for Mesquite Development. Who could be a better president than his own son, who idolized him and was loyal to a fault? At first, the scheme worked very well, especially when the company was experiencing record profits and earnings year after year. Matt also understood that he had a lot to learn and, until he did, he was content to occupy the president's office on his father's terms; which, by the way, included generous compensation and benefits.

It was only when the company fortunes began to turn down that Matt began to realize how isolated he was from the real decision-making. When his father concocted an ill-advised deal with a vicious Mexican cartel boss without consulting him, it was the last straw. That situation opened his eyes to a general pattern of questionable and sometimes outright unethical business practices that were routinely followed by his father. Matt became increasingly uncomfortable in his position.

Finally, one day, he marched in and confronted his father about his lack of communication and decision-making. His father completely ignored his son's concerns. Instead, he pressed Matt about where he stood on torpedoing a competitor's development project, which Matt had already flatly refused to do. Matt glared at his father and resigned on the spot. Sadly, Travis Nelson watched his son storm out without another word. Ironically, that confrontation was the final time he ever talked to his father, who disappeared shortly thereafter. With Travis Nelson gone, many of the questionable business practices of the firm soon came to light. The company, a leader in the affordable housing business, was barred from ever actively becoming involved in the development and construction of tax credit projects in the future. In fact, Matt and his mother, Diane, who had gotten involved in the company after her husband left, were fortunate not to have been pursued by the Drug Enforcement Agency and other authorities. The once-exciting and dynamic tax credit development industry standard-bearer was wound down and converted to a passive property management company, hardly a shadow of the robust organization that Travis Nelson had ruled over.

4.

By the time Matt arrived back at his flea-bitten motel room after Sabrina dropped him near his SUV, it was close to 6:00 AM, and the sun was about to rise. The undertaking had exhausted him both mentally and physically. He knew he'd better try to get some sleep before he hit the road back up to John's place in northern Virginia. He also crucially needed a shower after his muck bath. All that said, his success had generated a natural high and sleep did not come easily. After tossing and turning in the motel bed, he gave up after only a few hours. By 10:00 AM, he was up, showered, dressed again as a normal civilian, and ready to hit the road.

Matt had plenty of time to reflect as he drove back north along I-95 through the Carolinas and up into Virginia towards his brother's facility just outside of DC. It was a good nine-hour trip of over five hundred miles. He would arrive well after dark. He had transmitted the files from Kenneth Moore's computer to John, who had immediately turned them over to his analytical crew. In this case, a drone-driven laser weapon manufacturer engaged John's firm to investigate their suspicions that the senior vice president of marketing had become a little too friendly with some of their competitors. In no time, they were able to confirm that Mr. Moore had indeed been very unfaithful to his employer. Several corporate secrets, including weapon system design data, had been conveyed to third parties from the Far East. The fruits of Matt's mission had solidly corroborated their worst fears. Mr. Moore had deposited a cool six figures into his personal account for his efforts. John's client understood that the information produced the way Matt had gotten it could never be accepted in a court of law. On the other hand, the firm would have no trouble dealing with the thief on a one-to-one basis. The man's larceny would ruin him. He would never work in that industry again. Also, John and Matt were assured that their little sojourn to his bay house would never be reported to the police. The last thing Moore would want was to call more attention to his predicament.

Curiously, Matt had turned out to be quite a hero in his brother's eyes. Despite having encountered and blundered through almost every conceivable problem in the clandestine effort, he had succeeded beyond anyone's wildest hopes. John was exceedingly pleased (and surprised) with his older brother's performance.

Growing up, Matt worked very closely with his father. John, on the other hand, had given up on his father. As soon as he graduated from high school, John was off to join the Marines, where he became a member of the elite Force Recon group and distinguished himself during a combat tour in Iraq. After leaving the Corps, John and a military buddy parlayed their experience and contacts to form a corporate security firm, Marsea Consultants, Inc. He saw the rest of the family infrequently, and almost never communicated with his father.

Matt, who tended to be somewhat laid-back and conservative by nature, nonetheless admired the boldness and fearlessness of his war hero younger brother. Even when Matt was doing fairly well in the Texas real estate business, he still wondered if there was more to life that he should be pursuing. His wife and two children, of course, had to come first, but maybe there was some part of John's exciting profession that could be a fit for him. In fact, that was exactly why he had just gone solo on the Kenneth Moore caper. He had discussed his interests with John, who was at first, frankly, dubious about his laid-back brother becoming involved in the types of assignments he confronted on a daily basis. Not only did John face situations that could be downright dangerous, sometimes he was forced to tread on the very edge of the law for his clients (e.g., breaking and entering). John was a bachelor. If ever he were accused and convicted of a crime, at least the consequences would impact him and him alone. Matt had his family to consider. Matt's restlessness did not abate, and he badgered his brother about giving him an opportunity. When it became clear that Matt would not be dissuaded, John agreed to discuss the matter with his partner, Harvey McClung, an ex-Navy SEAL. If John hoped that Harvey would give him ammunition to discourage Matt, he was disappointed.

John walked through their facility in northern Virginia and found Harvey at a computer workstation in a back room intently studying weather pattern data in Madagascar. The Marsea facility consisted of 15,000 square feet in a gray metal, non-descript warehouse building in an unassuming suburban office park in Lorton, Virginia, just up the road from the Quantico Marine Base and ten miles south of Washington, DC, proper. There was a secure chain-link fence surrounding the half-acre site with a weathered sign at the front gate stating CONSOLIDATED PACKAGING. By design, there was nothing outwardly exceptional about the complex, which looked like thousands of other small, tired businesses. There was little to indicate from the outside what really went on in the building. The interior was divided into one-third office space and two-thirds shop, storage, and parking for several tactical vehicles.

John walked up to his partner, who continued to peer intently into the screen. "Harvey, what is so interesting on that computer? Are you on the Playboy channel or something?"

Harvey snickered, but didn't look away. "No, unfortunately I am not, but even if I were, I understand that the girls wear clothes now, even in the magazine. What the heck is this world comin' to? If we need to head to Africa on that mercenary job, I am just boning up on what it will be like over there. It sure does not look like Aspen."

John smiled. Harvey had one of the driest senses of humor he had ever encountered, yet he was incredibly cool when the heat was on. John had never seen him lose his composure, even in the tightest situations. Harvey always had your back.

"Say, Harv, I was wondering…"

Before John could get to the point, Harvey interrupted, "Hey, I am all for it. Get him over here. Let's see what he can do."

Without John even finishing his sentence, somehow Harvey already knew exactly what was on his mind. John was not surprised, which spoke to a major reason their partnership had been successful. Each man was a perfect complement to the other. "A lot of help you are. I thought I could rely on you to discourage him, but no, you are on his side," John responded with a mock sense of indignation.

"He went with us to rescue your father in Mexico and did really well. We can always use another reliable hand. We should at least give him a try. I think when all is said and done, Matt will discover that a nice, cushy desk in Houston is a hell of a lot more comfortable than a pup tent on a mountain in Africa."

And so it was decided; they would bring Matt over and put him through some training. If things worked out, they might even send him out on a real assignment. During a couple of weeks of training at their facility, Matt did well. The Moore assignment popped up, and they decided to give him a shot.

Neither of them realistically felt he had much of a chance to succeed. Now the son of a gun had delivered far beyond their wildest expectations. What the heck do they do with the desk jockey now?

5.

Matt was shaken out of his daydream by the vibrating of his cell phone in his upper shirt pocket and the stirring rendition of the "Aggie War Hymn" from his ring tone. Matt was a proud graduate of Texas A&M University in College Station, Texas. He had been driving steadily north on I-95 for nearly four hours when John reached him.

"Where the heck are you?"

Matt glanced out of the window and confirmed that he was somewhere in the middle of North Carolina, not too far from Raleigh-Durham. He started to answer when it dawned on him that his brother's question might well be another test. Never, never give away your position. You don't know who might be listening. He hesitated for a moment and then confidently replied, "Why, I am on the road."

There was hesitation on the other end. Finally, John came back. "Very good, old brother. I was sure you were going to blurt out your exact location, including the mile marker. Even though we are not in mission mode, it is still good practice to be vigilant. There are a few bad boys still kicking around that have it in for Harvey and me. You passed the test."

Matt, who had never been imbued with an excess of self-confidence, needed positive reinforcement from time to time. Coming from his brother, it was especially meaningful. Of course, he couldn't let on so easily how pleased he was to receive a compliment. "Hey, what did you expect? I learned from the best."

"Well, you got that right. Say, Senior Sleuth, Harvey and I have been talking. Our client was extremely pleased with what we were able to provide him from your mission. In fact, not only does he have some additional work for us, but said he was going to add a bonus into our fee. Let me tell you, Matt, that never happens. Be assured his good favor will also make its way into what we pay you. You deserve it. Neither of us were sure you had what it takes for this business, but you certainly removed any doubt."

"Thanks. I appreciate hearing that, John." *If they only knew how much I screwed up and almost blew the whole thing!*

"Okay. Let's go a little further. When you arrive here, and after you catch up on some shut-eye, Harvey and I are going to buy you the biggest steak we can find. It may not measure up to Texas standards, but I promise it will be all you can handle. You have been after me for some time about getting involved here, and now we would like to discuss the very possibility with you."

Holy smoke! They want me to join their team. I have been after that for years.

"We know you are still the president of Mesquite, which has been far, far toned down since dad had it. You have mentioned to me on several occasions that all you do these days is ho-hum routine property management, and that mom is perfectly capable of running it herself, especially after being there two years after dad checked out. You need to think about that company and how independent it really is. Also, of course, you need to consider Ellen and the kids. After what our family has been through over the past few years, she might well prefer her husband stick to real estate in Texas rather than chase all over the world with his half-crazy brother. Anyway, think about those things and let's see what we can come up with. Let's not talk about it now. We'll have plenty of time when you get here. Drive safely," John concluded, and was gone.

Matt's head was spinning. He happened to glance down at the dashboard and gulped. He was up to almost ninety-five miles per hour! *Slow down, boy. Slow down.* The conversation was like a shot of adrenaline, and he immediately lost his weariness from the difficult events of the past twenty-four hours. After slowing down to a more reasonable seventy miles per hour, his "mine monster" kicked in on overdrive as the mile markers whizzed past. *I really can't believe what I just heard John say. I have had dozens of conversations with him to let me get involved. He has always tried to discourage me. What is it? Little brother protecting big brother? If it weren't for Harvey, I wouldn't even have gotten this chance. And look how well I did! A bonus, no less. That never happens. Maybe I have been cut out for this business all along...*

Or am I? Who am I kidding? I was so sure hiding in that closet that I was going to jail. How many things went wrong at that house? I was so lucky. And who would have thought a teenager would pop up to lead me to the info? What might have happened to Ellen and the kids? We have a nice lifestyle with enough money to raise the children and take occasional vacations. The money with John, I am sure would be great, but how much do we really need? And there is the danger factor. I certainly understand what it's like to grow up without a father, one way or another. I'd have to be an idiot to sacrifice what we have now to join a bunch of ex-SEALs and Marines. That is not really me.

Or is it? I went with John and Harvey on the escapade to Mexico. It was certainly dangerous enough. I proved I could handle a gun besides my Remington 1100 bird hunting shotgun. I came through that just fine. I don't remember ever being scared during that whole thing. In fact, it gave me a rush, and it was great to be a part of John and Harvey's team. When Dad was around, as bad as things got, at least we were doing some challenging and exciting new development projects. Now, though, all we can do is collect rents and make sure the plumbing isn't stopped up. It is a fine business, but not exciting at all. Mom can handle it just fine without me there every day. She will probably try very hard to discourage me from joining John, as any mother would, but at least I know the company won't crater without me. It might even improve.

Of course, there is Ellen to consider. I am so very lucky we discovered each other that horrible day back at A&M among the falling logs. She is the perfect match for me and a wonderful mother of our children. I cannot, and will not, simply ignore her feelings. Actually, though, I already know how she will respond. She will grill me up and down to be sure I have thought of everything and all the implications of a move. She will want to be absolutely sure that I have determined that it's what I want to do. Once that is done, she will give it her blessing and encourage me to follow my dream. She is so incredible. I love her so much.

Hell, I damn well know I can do it, and it is just what I need. Stand by for the new Matt Nelson. Goodbye, reluctant astronaut. John and Harvey, I've decided. If you guys want me, I'm in! I'm in!

Even if Matt had not been so tired or so preoccupied by his conversation with his brother, based on his being so new to the corporate espionage business, it is unlikely that he would have noticed the dark-blue Honda Civic with heavily tinted windows that had remained several car lengths behind him since shortly after he crossed the North Carolina line.

6.

With the strength of his conviction and his mind firmly made up, as quickly as he had risen, all of a sudden Matt came crashing back to Earth. He could no longer deny the fatigue he had been ignoring. He saw the exit sign for North Carolina State Highway Route 64 and the city of Rocky Mount. It was promptly followed by another sign promising the Nash County Rest Area just a few miles ahead. As near as he could calculate, he still had over two hundred miles to John's place. He had better stop and at least get a cup of coffee or maybe even grab a little sleep. It made no sense at all to rush back along that congested high-speed highway in such a groggy condition.

He took the off-ramp for the rest area and glided to a stop in a parking space a hundred yards from a small, painted concrete block building that contained the restrooms and vending machines. It was just starting to get dark, and there were only a half-dozen other cars in the parking area.

As he stepped out of his SUV, a cool rush of air hit and revived him from his stupor. He closed the door, clicked his remote to lock the vehicle, and walked towards the building. As he approached the restroom area, he noticed an elderly couple with a chunky little white Spitz in a designated area. He was heartened to see that the animal was securely on a leash and smiled at himself for even noticing. The men's facilities were all the way at the back, as always seems to be the case. He entered the men's room through a heavy door and promptly rid himself of three hundred miles of build-up. The place was musty, damp, and reeked of disinfectant. He washed his hands out of habit, but wondered if they had been cleaner before or after. He moved back outside, where now it was completely dark. The vending machine area, however, was well-lit. It was a sign of the times that the machines had been secured with sturdy wire mesh to keep vandals from abusing the machines in an isolated location.

Seeing nothing the least bit appetizing in the array of culinary options, he quickly dismissed the "delicious" food choices and settled on some plain, old black coffee. He inserted his two dollars and watched a thin cardboard cup tumble down and fill with a stream of brown liquid that passed for coffee in those parts. When he grabbed the filled cup, he had to keep shifting it from one hand to the other to keep from getting burned, it was so thin. He almost forgot to snatch his two quarters in change from the machine.

As he walked back to the SUV, he noted that the Spitz and family had left, and there was only one other car in the entire parking lot. The area around the building was very well-lit, but the light declined significantly off into the parking lot. It struck him as strange that the dark-blue vehicle with tinted windows had been parked on the other side of his SUV away from the rest-rooms, especially when there were so many closer empty spaces. He didn't see anyone around. Still juggling the hot cup, Matt fished his keys out of his pants pocket and pressed the button to unlock his door, which answered with the standard metallic "click." He decided to set the hot cup down for a moment on the pavement until he opened the driver's side door. It was this impulsive, insignificant action that no doubt saved Matt Nelson's life.

Just as he bent over to set the coffee down, he heard a thunderous boom and felt a hollow echo pop in both ears. He jerked up and looked towards the back of the SUV, where there was a wisp of white smoke. The acrid smell of cordite filled his nostrils. His eyes didn't focus for a moment, but then he gaped in disbelief as a dark figure materialized with a large handgun pointed directly at him. Somehow, the first shot had missed, and now the assassin was about to shoot again. Transfixed, even at a distance of perhaps fifteen feet, Matt looked directly into the killer's coal-black eyes, which showed only a steeled determination to finish the job. Matt was transfixed by this sinister person. He shivered all over. Was it time for him to die?

In thinking about it later, Matt had no recollection of what happened next. Apparently, consciously or otherwise, he dove to his right just in time to avoid a second shot that blasted through his open door but, somehow again, miraculously missed him. Sprawled on the rough asphalt parking lot surface, his instinct to survive took over. He crabbed, rolled, and scrambled to his feet and ran directly back from his vehicle into the open part of the rest area. Terror filled his heart as he raced across the grassy surface with the killer not far behind. Another shot rang out, just missing him but splintering a young pine tree to his left.

Matt tried to get his bearings, but wasn't sure where he should go. He might try to sprint back to the restrooms, but this pursuer could easily find him there. Maybe he could escape out the back of the rest area, although as far as he could see, there was an eight-foot chain-link fence running the length of the property. Surely, more cars from I-95 would be entering the rest area soon, although so far none had.

He kept running and tried to stay in the shadows, away from the site-lighting lampposts. Soon his nose told him that he was near the designated doggie area, which did have a wire fence around it with individual metal posts hammered in the ground every ten feet or so. He hesitated; which way to go? He could hear the person trudging not far behind him. He couldn't stay in dog town or he'd be done for, for sure.

With no other choice, he sprinted towards the restroom building. He was about twenty feet from the building when another shot ripped into a trash can barely a foot away from him. Matt was terrified and running out of options. The shooter would be on him in a minute. He had no way to defend himself. No gun, knife, or even a broomstick. He burst into the men's restroom and searched desperately for a janitor's kit or anything he might use to fight back. There was nothing. Now he was trapped; the killer would find him there very shortly. He was out of choices. All he could do was jump into a stall and get up on the commode so that his feet were not showing. That might fool the guy for about two seconds, but Matt was desperate.

He waited there for what seemed like an eternity, certain the shooter would find him standing on the commode where he could not miss. Despite his circumstances, it occurred to him that, for the second time in twenty-four hours, he was trapped and holed up, waiting for the very worst to happen, although the worst in this case was really the worst. Scared? Damn right he was scared. Why did the person want to kill him, anyway? Did Sabrina tell her uncle about his raid and this was retribution? John had assured him that would not happen. The cold-as-death look in that shooter's eyes made him shiver. He knew John would take care of Ellen and the kids. Things sure didn't look good.

And then he heard the restroom door creak open very slowly. The killer was now in the room with him. The reek of the disinfectant was never stronger. The fluorescent lights over the sinks hummed and blinked spasmodically. He heard footsteps in the room, but could not see through the stall door. He might try rushing the person but, frankly, he was shaking too much. He closed his eyes and made a silent prayer. Maybe the guy would miss him?

Well, he didn't. Matt took a deep breath and was preparing for the very worst when a deep pitched voice directed, "Okay, you in there, that last stall.

Come out now! And with your hands high in the air."

Matt cringed and continued to shake with terror in his heart but realized he might as well come out. Maybe he could reason with the person. "Okay, Okay, I am coming out. PLEEZE don't shoot me," he pleaded. "There must be some mistake. Just go away. I'll never tell on you. Honest."

Quivering like an aspen in the fall, Matt fumbled with the stall latch. Once he had it open, he pushed the door and stepped out into the flickering light with eyes closed expecting at any second to be blown away. But, when that didn't happen, he dared open his eyes and looked squarely into the stare of a huge African-American North Carolina State Trooper who had drawn his service revolver but quickly holstered it when he saw there would be no reason to use it. His name tag said "Sergeant Johnson" and he looked massive in dark pants, light-blue shirt, and drill sergeant hat. "Mind telling me what's goin' on here?" He asked.

"Thank you, Lord," was all Matt could muster.

Matt was so relieved it took him several minutes to regain his composure. The sergeant took him outside towards his patrol car with light bar blazing and accompanied by at least four other similar police vehicles. There were several officers milling around. Matt was taken over to a nearby picnic bench where they sat him down. Someone even brought him a cup of coffee from the vending machine. (Great.)

"Okay, now, sir," Sergeant Johnson began, "Why don't you tell us what happened from the start. How about your name, where you are from, and what you are doing in North Carolina?"

Matt took a deep breath, sipped the brown liquid, coughed, and began in as measured and low-key tones as he could muster. He was tremendously relieved, but still very shook up. "My name is Matt Nelson. I am from Houston, Texas, and I'm here to pursue business interests. Here is my identification; driver's license, etc. I was just passing through on I-95 when I pulled off here for a cup of coffee."

"So, how did you end up in the men's room hiding on a commode?"

"Honestly, Officer Johnson, I really am not sure exactly what happened. I drove in and parked."

"Is that your SUV over there?"

"Yes, it is."

"It is registered to a John Nelson from Lorton, Virginia."

"It belongs to my brother. I was on my way back to his place when all this happened."

"Okay, go on."

"I got out of my vehicle and went in to use the restroom. I then bought a cup of coffee from the vending machine and walked back to the SUV. I unlocked the door and bent over to set down my coffee while I opened the door. Then I heard an explosion. I looked up and saw a horrible-looking person in black pointing a big handgun at me. After that, I really don't know what happened. I know I panicked and took off running. I seem to remember being at the dog park and the person was shooting at me. I ended up in the men's room and tried to hide. I honestly thought you were him when you came in there."

"We will want a full description."

"Sure."

"Why did this, eh, "person," want to kill you?"

"Officer, I have no idea. I have never seen him before. I have a wife and family in Texas. I manage properties for a living. I am not used to this kind of stuff. I was amazed, though, that no other cars came in here."

"Well, that was probably because the person dragged a "Closed" barricade across the entrance. I guess that was so he could have some privacy while dealing with you. In fact, that was what brought us in here. We knew something was up. This area was not supposed to be closed."

"But, why me?"

"You tell us. There is one possibility for such an apparent random hit as this. It has happened to travelers around here before. Believe it or not, some of the local gangs have connections to Mexico. They seem to like to flex their muscles every so often. If they can get in quickly, make the hit, and get out, there is little chance we can find them on the interstate. Have you ever heard of the Surenos group?"

"No, never."

"Judging by what we found out there, I think you were very lucky, Mr. Nelson. The bullet hole in your door was most likely made by a .45 at close range. It makes a big hole. Also, how do you feel about dogs?"

"Ah, well, I guess they're okay, I suppose. Why do you ask?"

"We'll have to do a lot more crime scene investigation to be sure, but it looks to us that when this perp chased you through the dog park, he encountered a few problems. We found some blood pooled on the ground next to one of those iron fence posts, which can be pretty sharp. It looks like your person impaled himself on that post. Also, it seems as though he very likely slipped and lost his balance when he stepped in some dog poop laying around over there. That probably caused him to fly into the post, so it could be that your tail was spared because of dog bombs laying around."

For the first time in quite a while, Matt actually smiled – saved by a pile of dog shit!

At that moment, the melodious Texas Aggies war hymn erupted out of Matt's pocket from his cell phone. It was probably John, or maybe even Ellen. As he reached to answer, he looked over at Sergeant Johnson and saw a dark frown cloud across his expansive face. "What the hell was that?" Sergeant Johnson demanded, pointing to Matt's hand reaching into his pocket for his phone.

"Sorry, Sergeant Johnson. I can let it go and call them back after we're through," Matt apologetically responded.

The big man continued to glare. It was remarkable how a businesslike conversation had deteriorated so quickly. "Was that the Texas A&M song I just heard?" Sergeant Johnson, the big man, growled.

"Why…… yes, sir, it was."

The sergeant looked up at one of his colleagues who had been standing there. "You know those damn Aggies whupped UNC bad in the Liberty Bowl in December. I'm not over it yet. Book this guy, Fred, and throw away the key!"

In his thoroughly dazed condition, Matt did not know if the sergeant was kidding or not.

7.

As the United Airlines jumbo jet climbed out of Dulles airport for the three-hour flight to Houston, Matt Nelson sat back, squeezed in a middle seat in the coach section of the cabin. A lot had happened over the past few days, and he was still trying to sort it all out. Although the man had him concerned for a moment, the North Carolina State Trooper had been joking when, after hearing the Aggie fight song, he commanded Matt be booked. As it turned out, Matt was so exhausted that he spent the night in a local hotel and continued on to John's the next morning. The extra time was also needed for the North Carolina authorities to fully debrief him and take his complete statement concerning the events of the attack. So far, no information had been established about the assailant, who had disappeared along I-95 minutes before the troopers arrived. Without any other apparent motive, the police had no choice but to conclude it was a random act of violence that probably had been carried out by a local gang preying on passersby on the interstate. Thank goodness no-one was injured, except possibly the perp himself.

Matt had a long conversation with his brother from his hotel room that evening. John offered to immediately drive down to Rocky Mount. He was worried about the Surenos, which had infiltrated parts of the southern US, including the Carolinas. He explained to Matt that technically, a Sureno is a foot soldier for the Mexican Mafia. Even though the cells and groups are widespread, most inter-relationships among them eventually tie back to the Mexican cartels themselves. Their activities are characterized by murder, human trafficking, the drug trade, and a wide range of illegal activities. The Surenos brand emerged as a national gang of the United States that often sport blue or gray as clothing colors. John hoped that the attack on Matt was a mere coincidence, and had nothing to do with their father. His instincts, however, told him otherwise. Their venture into Mexico relating to Travis's disappearance last year had brought them into direct contact with cartels. It was possible that the hit on Matt (or maybe they confused Matt for John) was somehow connected with those events south of the border. Surenos would stay well-focused on his radar and advised Matt to do the same.

Matt calmed down considerably and assured John that he didn't need to rush down to North Carolina. They could talk when he arrived in Lorton the next day. Matt kidded that in order to recognize him when he arrived, just look for an SUV with a large bullet hole in the driver's side door. That would be him. John's reaction was swift. He demanded Matt's insurance information. At least the conversation ended on that light note. Matt collapsed into bed.

It was not quite noon on the day after the attack when Matt rolled up to the front gate of Consolidated Packaging in his "holy" SUV. The front gate immediately rolled open. John and Harvey came outside as he pulled into a parking space. Matt jumped out and underwent the standard greeting ritual of fist and chest bumping with both men. "Good to see you, bro," John began. "You've had quite a time. You make the hard stuff look easy, and then you make the easy stuff, like driving home, look hard."

A low whistle interrupted their conversation. "Ooooh! Man, look at that hole!" Harvey exclaimed, as he bent over and placed his finger on the large, jagged exit hole where the attacker's bullet had ripped through the metal. "Let me look inside to make sure there isn't any blood on our interior upholstery. That little ding is going to cost you, boy. All our people have to be personally responsible when they use company vehicles. No exceptions. When we get that door fixed, you'll be lucky not to owe us money for the past three days."

Matt smiled. It was so good to be around these guys again.

The Marsea owners made good on their promise and within the hour, the three of them were seated for lunch at a favorite local steakhouse. While John and Harvey were ebullient in their praise, Matt was surprised to find himself subdued and quiet. Even after the second round of sixteen-ounce drafts, he was puzzled by his own reticence. This was a festive occasion after a very successful mission and his joining their team, which was something he had secretly hoped would happen for a long time. Heck, he'd been through a lot over the past few days. Who wouldn't be exhausted? He'd surely get with the program.

Not one to beat around the bush, right after they'd ordered their steaks (Harvey ordered his "bloody," by the way), John got right to it. "Okay. Harvey and I have talked long and hard about it, and over my stringent objections…, I am just kidding. We would like very much for you to join our team at Marsea Consultants."

"Absolutely, Matt," Harvey chimed in. "Your performance on the South Carolina assignment was excellent. We also got to work with you under fire and in tough circumstances in Mexico, where you were cool and had our backs. We could not have asked for more. Obviously, you are a little green yet, but only experience can help that, which will come in time. Our staff, whom you worked with before going to South Carolina, had good things to say about you, too. We will set up a compensation package that I am sure you will be very satisfied with. We really want to have you come aboard. So, what do you think?"

All of this was music to Matt's ears. In fact, he could not believe what he was hearing from two men he respected so much. Men who had put together an incredible company that did exciting things all over the world and who were very well-paid to boot. It was a dream. They were absolutely sincere in wanting him for his abilities. There was no brotherly favoritism stuff, but, he hesitated.

"Matt?" Harvey queried, as he began to hoist his big beer in a joyous toast.

Matt didn't speak. The wheels were obviously spinning in his head at breakneck speed. Here it was, what he had always wanted.

It was his brother this time "Well, Matt, are you with us?"

Still, Matt said nothing. The two Marsea partners looked at each other. Harvey's beer suddenly came crashing down on the table with a resounding thud and foamy splash.

When Matt finally spoke, he could hardly believe his own ears. "Harvey. John. I really don't think this is for me. I am kidding myself to assume I can run with pros, who have been doing it for so long. I am a desk jockey, pure and simple. Like everyone these days, I hide in my computer, emails, and texts. I am not brave. I have to realize who and what I really am. I love you guys and your team, and all the excitement you generate. It was a rush to sneak into that Carolina place. I have never felt more invigorated afterwards. My self-confidence was at an all-time high. It was great. John, your call hinting about this on the way back up here put me on cloud nine. I was so thrilled and happy. I couldn't wait to get up here and get measured for my Kevlar vest. I knew I wanted to do it. All I had to do was convince myself I could do it, which I did."

John asked, "Well, then what happened? Was it Ellen? I thought she might be a problem."

"Maybe a little, but not really. She is an incredible person and desperately wants what is right for me, even if it might interrupt our family somewhat. As long as she was sure that I had considered everything and still wanted to go forward, she'd support me all the way, even with my crazy brother."

John grinned.

"No, I think it runs a bit deeper. I am just not sure that I am capable of succeeding in your business. Let me give you a few details about my sleuthing into the Moore place. First of all, as I paddled in and finally reached the shore under cover of darkness, I tried to be as quiet as possible. Then, as I got out of the kayak, it rocked and did a one eighty. I was trapped underwater. After thrashing around, I was able to scramble out. Boy, the swamp water smells."

John looked at Harvey and Harvey looked at John. "Those boats are unstable. That comes with experience. So, you got wet. So far, I don't see much of a problem, unless you blew your cover," John responded.

"No, no-one heard me. I did regroup and moved slowly through the woods to the house, which we assumed, or hoped, would be empty. I did toss the sleep-inducing meat strips in the yard, even though I didn't see or hear any dogs around. I crept up onto the porch and got a break. The lock on the door was a very simple and standard one, exactly the same as I had trained on here with your staff. I got out my pick set and got to work."

Harvey: "Good, so far."

"Yes, except that an hour later, I was still not in." John: "That's not too good."

"Then, I heard ferocious animal noises around the corner. It was a dog who came flying at me. He was hardly sleepy. He grabbed my leg and we were rolling around on the floor when I saw headlights in the driveway. Now, I am about to panic."

Harvey: "What kind of a dog was it?"

"I was not really sure. Some mongrel English breed, I think. It was determined. I was fighting as hard as I could."

Harvey: "Was it a Bullmastiff, Shepherd, or a Bulldog?"

"Er, no, I believe it was a Yorkshire."

Harvey blinked. "A what?"

"A Yorkshire terrier?"

John's and Harvey's eyes met. They tried very, very hard to suppress their widening smirks. It was tough to keep it together.

"So, anyway, in fighting off this beast, which had my pants leg, I fell against the door where I had been working for an hour. It fell open and I tumbled inside. The dog let go and remained outside."

John: "So you mean the door…"

"Yeah. It was unlocked the whole time."

While Harvey turned to chug his beer to keep his amusement as much under control as possible, John tried hard to play it straight, although the mirth in his watering eyes was not hard to spot. "Then what did you do?"

"I ran upstairs and hid in a bedroom closet. I did hear voices, at least one of which was a security firm. There must have been an alarm."

John: "Well, didn't they search the house and find you?"

"No, they didn't. In fact, they left."

John: "What? Why didn't they search the whole place? How did you avoid getting discovered? Or were you?"

"No, they didn't find me, but Sabrina did. She's a sixteen-year-old with green hair wearing a Grunge tee shirt."

John: "Sabrina? Grunge tee shirt? Who the hell is Sabrina?"

"Hold on! Hold on!" Harvey could suppress it no longer. He leaped up from the table, yelled at the waiter to bring three more, and ambled off to the men's room with a huge baloney-eating grin on his face. "Green hair?" he chuckled.

When Harvey returned and the table was restocked with full brews, Matt continued his story to his table mates, who, despite their best intentions, found themselves virtually howling in their suds by the time he finished up with the hole in his boat.

At first, the inwardly morose Matt hardly shared their fun, but even he, after a while, began to see the hilarity in his adventure. Even he had to chuckle a bit when he thought back about the vicious Yorkie. Nonetheless, he came right back down to earth when he said, "So, you see what a screw-up I am? I blew that simple little deal ten ways to Sunday. How can you even consider me for a part of your team?"

Sensing his brother's angst, John immediately switched to a serious mode. "Look, Matt, you are new to a lot of this stuff, but let me assure you that things never, ever go exactly as planned. There are always screw-ups. That is why we try so hard to allow for every contingency. What counts is that no-one got hurt, and you succeeded beyond anyone's expectations. You were sharp enough to react and adjust to changing conditions. You should not let yourself get down over a very successful mission. Come on, get with it."

Matt could see his point. He, himself, reached that very same conclusion driving up I-95, but that was before the rest area attack. "Yeah, I can probably attribute my bungling to inexperience, but I guess what really drove things home to me was the rest area incident. I have not been able to get the look on that guy's face out of my mind as he stood there in the dark with that huge handgun pointed at me. Cold, hard, grim, and ugly. But for the grace of God, I would be a dead man. And then he chased me up the hill into the dog park and the restroom. I stood there on that commode in that filthy place waiting for him to come in and execute me. I figured I was a dead man. And you know, as terrible as that was for me, what I have thought so much about is what my death would have done to Ellen and my two kids. In a way, you and I grew up without a father. I don't want that for them. I know I can cut it with you guys. I am just not sure it is the right thing for me to do. For those reasons, I am just going to have to pass on your wonderful offer."

John smiled and reached over and hugged his older brother. Harvey caught the waiter's attention and ordered another round.

8.

Diane Nelson sat at her desk and stirred her chamomile tea, as she began to prepare for the day ahead. It was not yet 8:00 AM. She always arrived at the office early so she could organize her thoughts and prepare for whatever came her way. She had been running the company for less than two years and was just now getting comfortable that she could handle almost any situation or crisis. She had Matt to step in whenever he was needed, but more and more she was able to figure things out for herself. After two decades of staying at home and being kept as far away from business matters as possible, it had taken her a while to get into the swing of things and rekindle her self-confidence.

Of course, the company today was far, far different than in Travis's days, when he personally made every significant decision and ran it as an absolute dictatorship. The business itself was dissimilar as well. The Mesquite Development Company had been replaced by the Mesquite Property Management Company. Through the years, Travis Nelson had built the development company into an industry leader in the field of affordable housing using government tax credits to provide his equity financing. The company had amassed an impressive portfolio of multifamily properties spread all over Texas.

Each year, with Matt mainly carrying the ball, the company would add another property to its list. He had become well versed in the development process, especially when dealing with low-income housing tax credit financing, which is extremely technical and requires a thorough knowledge of the nuances of the business. After locating and tying up a suitable site, an exhaustive feasibility analysis is necessary, which, assuming it is favorable, is followed by a several-hundred-page application to a Texas state agency to apply for an allocation of tax credits, which are always in short supply. The credits are handed out on a very competitive basis. Perhaps three proposed projects go begging for every one that receives an award. Nonetheless, Mesquite Development had received an allocation for several years running. With credits in hand, the project had then to be lender-financed, constructed, and leased up to sustaining occupancy, a process that could take two years or more.

The development business, however, is very risky, and it's easy to stumble along the way and plummet into financial problems. For years, the Mesquite Development Company under Travis Nelson prospered and was generally recognized as an industry leader in that niche business.

And then, almost without warning, everything tipped over. Travis was gone, leaving no-one to fill the void of the only decision-maker the company had ever had. Due to a special arrangement, which Travis had implemented simply to gain precious competitive scoring points for his tax credit applications which were granted to WOB's (Woman-Owned Business) applicants, the ownership stock of the company was actually held in Diane's name, even though they knew that without its "dictator" the development business would soon crater (and it did). After Travis disappeared, together Matt and his mother worked hard to hold together whatever they could. Matt came back from his short exile after his resignation and re-assumed the duties as president.

Diane left her idle Chablis afternoons behind, put on a business suit, and took over the day-to-day operations of a company that was teetering and about to spin, crash, and burn.

When all the flames were finally extinguished, Mesquite Development was history. In a desperate attempt to sustain something, Matt and Diane were able to cobble together from the ashes one small part of the Mesquite operation. Through the good graces of some understanding clients, hard work, and a whole lot of good luck, they somehow preserved the property management portion of the business. Unlike the exciting, sexy, and dynamic development business, where you build brand new, gorgeous, shiny projects every year, property management is restricted to the humdrum daily operations of the ongoing finished properties. You lease the units, collect the rent, cut the grass, paint the units, make reports, fix the commodes, talk to the residents, make reports, clean the pool, fix the roof leak, make reports and make reports. Property management is a vital, yet least appreciated and least glamorous, aspect of owning real estate. Needless to say, compensation levels in management are far less than on the development side. So far, they had done well and the company was gradually growing. After her long sentence as mother/ wife, Diane was blossoming with restored confidence she never knew she had. Matt, on the other hand, was virtually bored to tears.

Diane looked up and saw Sandy Springer walk into her office. Sandy was their administrative assistant, who had previously been her husband's secretary for many years. In her mid-fifties, Sandy was attractive, professional, and extremely efficient. Like all of them, she had taken Travis's disappearance hard, but was more than willing to stay on with the new company, even at a reduced salary. Sandy was worth her weight in gold.

"Morning, Diane. Your eight-thirty has not shown up yet. I lay you two to one he never shows at all."

"You may be right, but if he wants his last paycheck, he'd better make an appearance. Let me know if and when he graces us with his presence. I'd like you to be in here when I speak with him."

"Sure," she replied, as she turned around and went back to her desk in the outer office.

Well, that really wasn't a surprise, was it? If I were getting terminated, I guess I wouldn't be too anxious to face my bosses, Diane mused, as she sipped her tea and sat back. She now had a few minutes to relax. Their regular Wednesday morning meeting wasn't until nine. Matt was flying back from DC. His plane was due to land at Houston's George Bush Intercontinental Airport at noon, which would put him at the office in the early afternoon. She was anxious to hear how things had gone with John. She'd had several conversations over the phone, but she knew those were edited for "mother" reports. After thinking about Matt and then John for a moment, she found herself reflecting back about their father, long marriage, and often turbulent relationship. *Had it always been rocky? There must have been some good times...*

As a Vanderbilt student, she remembered being instantly smitten when she met the handsome, confident Texas Aggie at a fraternity party. Apparently, he must have felt the same because for the balance of their respective senior years, he kept in touch and even managed to haul himself all the way from College Station to Nashville on several occasions just to see her. Perhaps fate was at work because after graduation, he ended up taking a job in Houston, which was a short hop on Southwest Airlines to Amarillo, where she had returned to work for her father's oil company, Duschene Drilling. Even better, Diane's daddy immediately took to Travis. The fact that they were both Texas A&M grads didn't hurt, and they also spoke the common languages of oil, gas, and real estate. In fact, they got on so well that when Travis needed some cash to go off on his own, Mr. Duschene was quick to open his wallet for what he correctly anticipated to be his new son-in-law.

Unfortunately, the marriage didn't click, and was probably doomed from day one. The two were very different individuals with widely divergent needs. Moreover, it is doubtful that Travis could make a success of any marriage. He had always been married to his job. Not much else mattered to him. If you couldn't benefit him or his business, Travis Nelson had little time for you. That, unfortunately, included his wife and family.

And, of course, there was his inevitable roving eye. Philandering was almost second nature to him. He needed his ego boosted, and pursuing other admiring women was one sure way to do it. Understandably, Diane also needed attention and occasional stroking. She had always been the center of things in the well-to-do Duschene household. Her parents coddled her, and there was little she wanted she didn't get. It was off to Vanderbilt, sororities, and the works. She could not stand to be ignored. At first, she was sure she'd made the perfect catch in handsome Travis Nelson. They looked so good together. The first few months proved to be the height of their relationship, which began a long, downhill toboggan ride after that.

As is so often the case, at least from Diane's perspective, their decaying marriage endured mainly because of the three children. Travis knew the score, but he had everything he needed—a trophy wife and a nice-looking family, along with the freedom to make other liaisons as often as he chose. His family lived in a splendid home in the Tanglewood section of Houston and did not want for anything that could be bought with money.

Diane was well aware of Travis's wanderings. At first, she was heartbroken by his infidelity and turned to alcohol to drown her sorrows. Through the years, she took pride in her children and did her best to support them under difficult circumstances. Pam was now in her twenties, even though she sometimes acted like she was ten years younger. She was the only child left at home, but would also be gone in the not too distant future. Her tempestuous marriage hurt, but Diane had come to grips with most of it. In fact, every so often, she caught herself chuckling about the situation. She wondered how surprised uber-businessman Travis Nelson would be when the divorce lawyer she had been meeting with for a while finally confronted him. Just maybe he would be shocked to find out that his tipsy little trophy wife had some teeth of her own. She never got to find out. Suddenly, Travis was gone. So much had happened.

Abruptly, she snapped back to reality when a chunky, young, dark-skinned man in his early twenties sauntered right into her office. He had scraggly, black, unkempt hair, a round face, wide nose, and deep-brown eyes that seemed watery and glazed. He wore a deep-blue Dallas Mavericks basketball shirt and jeans that sagged to the point that they might fall down at any moment and bunch around his threadbare running shoes.

Diane gulped, stared, and tried to quickly regroup. "Er, you must be Rico Corona?"

"That's right. Gimme my paycheck."

Diane sat up and hesitated before she spoke. Where was Sandy? She had asked to be told if and when this man arrived. It wasn't like her to stray from her desk. This guy was a little scary and he looked agitated, like maybe he was on something. She had asked that he come in because he had been on their payroll as an assistant maintenance man on a property in Pasadena, a community just south of downtown. After less than a month, he had turned out to be a totally unacceptable employee. He was short-tempered, hard to get along with, frequently late, and showed very little aptitude for the work. When he happened to be "working" just outside a window where a young female renter was taking a shower, the property manager quickly called Diane and recommended that he be fired. Diane immediately agreed.

Unfortunately, while Diane was making great strides in the management business, she had not had a lot of direct personal contact with employees, especially in the field. By necessity, a property management company is very heavy in employees, since the staff needed on a typical property is usually at least six or seven. To do her job properly, she felt she needed to understand the field people better. Mr. Corona's dismissal presented an opportunity.

She had attended and took copious notes at a Houston Apartment Association seminar on proper personnel practices, especially termination of employees. It is easy to get sued if you are not careful, she remembered hearing. To make matters worse, this man was Hispanic, making him a minority and an EEOC concern. In light of all these things, she decided to have him come into her office for his exit interview. In person, she could be sure the correct steps were followed, the file was properly documented, and she would learn in the process. Of course, all that was before the dreadful man showed up in her office. Where was Sandy?

Finally, she came to grips and knew she had to take control of the situation. "Certainly, Mr. Corona, I will have it for you in just a moment. Won't you please have a seat? I have a few questions for you," she asserted in a desperate attempt to take charge.

The man, who it was now very clear was under the influence of something, just stood there teetering forward. He stared at her, but did not respond.

"Please, sir, if you will have a seat, I'll find your paperwork. Please. Right there!" Diane urged, pointing at one of the chairs facing her desk.

The man did not respond, but seemed to be looking around the room at her family pictures, mementos, and favors from outings or dinners that had been left behind by the former occupant of that office. He stopped when he got to a photograph on a shelf of Travis at a golf tournament. He leaned in and looked closer. After what seemed like forever, he scowled at Diane, who was huddled in her chair as far away behind her desk as she could get. He finally spoke. "Are you married?" and then, pointing to the photo: "Is that your man? 'Cause I know that dude."

Now Diane was really concerned. She frantically searched the top of her desk for his check but couldn't find it. Then she remembered that Sandy had it. Where was she, anyway? She just had to give him his money and maybe he would leave.

"Mr. Corona, I must ask you to leave, right now, or I will call security. Please leave! I will get your check on the way out."

If the man heard her through his stupor, he made no indication. In fact, he asked again in a loud and demanding voice, "Who is that dude in that picture?"

Diane was now in full fright mode. She squeezed around the far side desk and bolted for the door. She had almost made it when a rough and calloused hand with filthy fingernails seized her arm hard and spun her back towards her desk, knocking her off her feet onto the carpet. She was sprawled out on all fours when she heard the office door slam with a thud and a "click" of what could only have been a switchblade.

9.

The two men in business suits, complete with stylishly appropriate ties, huddled to one side of the entrance of a meeting room on the eighth floor of the Harris County office building in downtown Houston. A steady stream of people filed past them with an occasional nod or smile. The monthly board meeting of the newly created Southeast Texas Unified Partnership was about to take place. Board members, employees, prominent local politicians, and numerous other interested parties were on hand. The meeting had been allotted two hours, from 6:00 to 8:00 PM, but few in attendance expected the time would be sufficient. There was important business to conduct that evening.

The taller of the two men spoke in hushed tones to his colleague, who was eager to absorb every word from his senior cohort. "We have been waiting for this day for some time. I am sure all is going to go well and end up the way we planned. We have done our homework, and the voting should be just as we expect. I have been in this business for a long time. Politics is just a matter of understanding where the real power lies and being able to work deals. We know who we can count on, and who we cannot. Just keep cool, and things will play out the way we rehearsed. Now, before we go in there, do you have any final questions? Is there anything that is bothering you?"

The other man took a couple of steps away from the entrance and motioned his associate to follow. With more privacy assured, he whispered, "No, David, I am as ready as I will ever be. I have wanted this for a long time. There is no way I am going to blow it. But, there is one thing. Henry Francesca, who represents the barrio districts near the ship channel, I know he is against me. Obviously, he wanted one of his own, a Hispanic, to get the job. If that couldn't be, the last person he'd vote for would be an African American. Won't he be trouble?"

"Just take it easy, Dwight. You are right on about that. African Americans and Hispanics have been competing in this city for decades. Of course, Henry would prefer to have someone from his constituency in the job, but he is no dummy, either. He has been around, and knows how things work. Yes, he will give you a hard time, if he can, for show purposes; but in the end, he'll be fine. He knows that if he plays ball with us now, he'll definitely expect us to back him on the next thing coming along. We have talked long and hard about it. Henry will not be a problem in the end. Just remember what I told you, and if he starts busting your balls, it is just for show. Do not lose your cool, under any circumstances. The only real uncertainty is that University of Houston professor. It is hard to know where she is coming from, but she is just one vote. We don't need her. Now, let's go in there and get it done. Hey, just a second. Let me straighten your tie."

Without another word they entered the large room, which was set up with a raised dais facing several rows of individual chairs. When full, over two hundred people could be accommodated. That evening, almost all of the seats were occupied. The two men sat about halfway towards the front and on the end of a row, where it would be easy to get up and come forward when requested. There were seven people sitting on the dais; the board of directors and founders of the newly created "super" housing authority. The diverse mix of backgrounds, ethnicity, and walks of life of this group reflected an obvious attempt to draw a representative cross section of the area's political, racial, and economic interests. The elderly chairman, Wilbert S. Hobby, was from a wealthy Houston family that had been prominent in local politics for decades. Presumably, he stood for the old-line wealth. The most reverend Edward Pike was a senior Baptist deacon at a church with a huge African-American following on the near north side. Edwin Smith was a senior vice president at Shell Oil. Kathleen Barnes was a professor of Sociology at the University of Houston. Henry Francesca represented a heavily Hispanic district on the east side of Houston in the Texas state senate in Austin. LeRoy Boden was an elected Harris County county commissioner. Eloise Quimby was a member of the Houston City Council, and a vocal advocate for the local LGBT community. After everyone was seated and the Pledge of Allegiance recited, the gray-haired, ruddy-faced chairman pulled his microphone directly in front of him, cleared his throat, peeked down furtively at his notes, and called the meeting to order.

"Ladies and gentlemen," he began with a surprisingly deep, clear, and stentorian voice for such a frail and angular-looking man. "Tonight, we are on the threshold of a unique and potentially wonderful accomplishment, not only for our city and our county, but also, and most importantly, for the citizens of southeast Texas. Due to the long and tireless efforts of many individuals"—he paused for just a second to glance down into the crowd towards where the two men were sitting—"we are about to give birth to a unique and unprecedented partnership between the city of Houston and Harris County with the creation of the Southeast Texas Unified Partnership. The State of Texas has enabling legislation that allows for not only the creation of typical city and county housing authorities, but also for the establishment of 'super' or regional housing authorities. While both Harris County and the City of Houston already have excellent housing authorities, which will not be affected by our actions, we have created a new and unique super housing authority that will allow us to serve the housing needs of all of southeast Texas in a manner never before seen. Further, I would be very remiss if I did not acknowledge the role played by the Department of Housing and Urban Development in this historic undertaking. As you know, of course, HUD funds housing authorities. We couldn't do it without our friends from HUD."

He paused to let that sink in, and there was a rift of amused laughter through the crowd. "So now, enough patting ourselves on the back. Let's get to work." He picked up a piece of paper in front of him and read, "Agenda item 1A."

David Gamble eased back in his seat and half-listened as the board started down the inevitable list of boring agenda items. He was here for only one reason, which would come later on in the evening. The board would announce the name of the first executive director of the brand-new super housing authority. The executive director was in fact chief operating officer, or really, the president of the new entity, who would run it on a day-to-day basis. The board would meet regularly to review progress and set policy, but the ED was responsible for getting things done and making them happen. Since this brand-new entity was backed by three heavyweights: the City of Houston, Harris County, and HUD, there was every likelihood it would become a significant player very quickly.

Gamble, in his mid-fifties, was a political junkie of the first order. He was born and raised in Houston and was an honors graduate of Rice University, after which he obtained his law degree at Southern Methodist. He easily passed the Texas bar but had no interest in grinding it out and getting lost in a large law firm. He did not have the elite River Oaks stamp or Hobby family wealth, but his folks were well-off enough that he could take his time figuring out what to do with his life. He did pro bono legal work for several non-profit groups, such as Goodwill Industries. It wasn't too long before he had made numerous influential contacts across the local socioeconomic and ethnic spectrum. He made sure he got around, playing golf at the toney River Oaks CC, eating barbecue in the Fourth Ward with African Americans, and smashing piñatas in a northside barrio. He was delighted when the mayor and head county judge approached him about finding the right person for the critical executive director position for the new super housing authority.

Sitting rather uneasily next to him was Dwight Lamar, a thirty-five-year-old African American who had been born and raised in the poverty of deep East Texas. At first, Gamble felt it would be easy to find someone for this new high-profile position, but his search had proven more involved than he had imagined. As an astute observer of local politics, he knew how difficult it would be to find someone who passed the smell test for both the city and county. They had already run a national search without finding any candidate acceptable to both factions. The two groups had to coexist, but they never agreed on much of anything. A potentially satisfactory candidate for one would not meet the minimum threshold of the other. Despite scouring the landscape far and wide for months, David Gamble had been unable to find anyone he thought might win over both sides and then, luckily, he had stumbled on Dwight Lamar only a few weeks ago.

Dave Gamble discovered that there was no level playing field for finding a qualified candidate. Each side demanded to have his guy and imposed certain implied, if not spoken, limitations. There was also the practical reality that a housing authority in the south, especially one that covers extensive, poor inner-city neighborhoods, could not have a Caucasian executive director. Right or wrong, it just wouldn't work. The new hire must be either an African American or Hispanic. Asians were coming on strong, but had not quite commanded a critical mass of influence yet.

He proceeded to interview several city and county employees without success. A woman would have been terrific, but no qualified candidate surfaced. The official kick-off date for the super HA was fast approaching. Gamble was worried. He had no-one to recommend running it.

Gamble was playing a round on the public golf course in Memorial Park with clergymen from some of the poorer districts in the community. The discussion that day eventually led to the Katrina storm in 2005 and the terrible devastation it had wreaked on New Orleans, where one of the preachers in the foursome called home. As the golfers waited patiently for the group in front of them to finish a par three, the Crescent City transplant mentioned a fellow named Dwight Lamar. Lamar, he said, had done valiant work on the mayor's staff correcting the abject conditions in the storm's aftermath. He had established an excellent reputation working tirelessly among the poor and homeless. In fact, he had even dealt directly with HUD during those dark days to develop a housing voucher program, which became the basis for a model that was adopted around the country. Unfortunately, when all the dust cleared, Lamar's boss, the mayor of New Orleans, was indicted and convicted for accepting kickbacks. He eventually went to prison. Lamar was never implicated, accused, or even suspected of anything. Still, as an employee of the city, despite his wonderful work during the crisis, he was terminated along with all of the mayor's key employees. The minister believed that Mr. Lamar ended up somewhere in East Texas.

Impressed with what he'd heard, David Gamble sought out Dwight Lamar, whom he discovered was located only fifty miles away in the Golden Triangle of Beaumont-Port Arthur. After a quick drive over and a lunch, he was encouraged enough to bring the man to Houston for interviews. During those interviews, he somehow managed to impress both sides with his knowledge of the public housing business, likability, intelligence, and quick wit. His impressive credentials included an accounting degree with honors from Tulane University. Refreshingly, he had no history or baggage with either of the two key SETUP sponsors. He was single, and relished the opportunity to help build the new organization.

There was, however, one possible tragic flaw: he was an African American. The Hispanic crowd would just have to accept that situation. Lamar had hardly avoided this tinderbox subject during his interviews. In fact, he had been candid and open about the need to bring harmony among the races, especially the black and brown communities. He even made points with Senator Francesca. No one seemed at all concerned with his proximity to the mayoral scandal in New Orleans. Gamble felt there was a good chance they would confirm him. Take Dwight Lamar or find someone else to do your hunting. The opposing factions so far ruled out anyone else who might have fit.

Dwight Lamar's candidacy to run the new super HA would be put to an up or down vote that evening by the Board of Directors. David Gamble knew he had put forth the best and most acceptable candidate available, given the diametrically opposed politics of the city and county, not to mention the unspoken snarled web of racial preferences. Gamble, however, was not naïve. He understood that, although his guy looked pretty good, he really didn't know him very well. Given the politics, the vetting process was not as comprehensive as it might have been. He had been desperate for a body. There were holes in Lamar's background. Only time would tell exactly what kind of executive director the man would make.

The meeting droned on for over an hour. Finally, Gamble could feel the moment approaching. Chairman Hobby reached for and again dragged his microphone directly in front of him, creating an ear-piercing screech throughout the room's sound system. Everyone winced.

"Will Mr. Dwight Lamar please come forward to the podium?"

10.

During the heyday of his development company, Travis Nelson maintained his headquarters in an attractive, contemporary, glass-and-granite four-story office building nestled among the pine trees and hardwoods on Memorial Drive, just outside the beautiful city park of the same name. The importance of conveying to his lenders and financial partners that he was doing well was not lost on Mr. Nelson. A visitor to Mesquite Development back in those days was greeted by a block-oak-paneled and tastefully appointed reception area and a conference room complete with soft lighting, Mexican tiled floors, and pieces of expensive, genuine art. His own spacious office included a group sitting area, fully stocked bar, and expansive picture window offering a relaxing view of the park's lush forest greenery and Buffalo Bayou slowly rolling by. Travis was not afraid to spend dollars where it showed.

Diane and Matt, however, quickly realized that their remaining slice of the business did not need ostentatiousness, and even if it had, there was no way they could afford such lavish digs. They relocated a few miles to the north where the 610 Loop crossed I-10 into a much more spartan, single-level office-service center that was perfectly suitable and cost a fraction of the rent Travis paid. The preponderance of folks who visited their offices were tradesman and contractors who required no more impressing than timely payment for services rendered. They also greatly reduced their home office staff to just the bare essential data processing, accounting, and a few other administrative people. Besides Matt and Diane, the only managerial staff at the main office were two area-level property supervisors who were responsible for ten properties each. The preponderance of employees was based out on the properties, and except for occasional meetings and training, remained in the field. Since management fees were not especially generous, a successful company in that industry had to be run as efficiently as possible. Controlling overhead and operating expenses was very important. Unfortunately, they were soon to discover that it was a huge mistake to spare security personnel in exchange for a little austerity.

When Sandy walked out of Diane's office after discussing whether or not the terminated guy would show, it dawned on her that she was supposed to get his final paycheck from accounting. It had completely slipped her mind, and with the guy due in, she needed to get it right away. She didn't want to add anything to what could be a bad scene if he did show up and his money wasn't ready. She also smiled to herself. She had a great admiration for Diane, who had come into the company after all those years at home. Diane was turning out to be a great person to work for, and they got along famously.

The lady was a quick study, but every so often she did something that was a little bizarre—like having this fired guy come to her for an exit interview. Forget the management classes; that just didn't make sense. Diane was still learning. She'd better get that check and not leave her boss hanging out. She got up from her desk and headed down the hall to personally pick it up.

It took several minutes for the head bookkeeper to locate the paperwork sent in by the manager of the property where the man worked. After the dictatorial days of Travis Nelson, Matt and Diane had gone to great lengths to recast the management company as a comfortable, low-pressure, and friendly workplace. Everyone knew their job and could be reasonably expected to get it done without a lot of browbeating by supervisors. Under Travis, Sandy would never have left her post as his Praetorian Guard to personally grab the man's check. Now, though, she took time to chew the fat for a few minutes with the accounting supervisor, whose daughter had just had another baby. The pictures were (of course) adorable.

It had been almost fifteen minutes since she'd left when she walked back to her desk with the check in hand. She glanced over and noticed that Diane's door was shut, which was a little unusual. Maybe the guy had shown up? She was just about to get up and knock when the outside door to the reception area opened and in strode Pamela Nelson, of all people.

Pam was the youngest child of Travis and Diane, and was prone to disappear and reappear like Houdini at the most unexpected times. After giving absolutely no indication that she cared anything about school whatsoever, other than as the consummate party girl, amazingly, she was about to receive her bachelor's degree from Sam Houston State University in Huntsville, Texas, about a hundred miles north of Houston. Sandy had found a kindred spirit in Pam, and it was not unusual for Pam to stop by every so often just to visit for a few minutes. While Travis had largely ignored his family and closest associates, the two exceptions had been Sandy and Pam. He relied heavily on Sandy to keep his business affairs in order, and their relationship had been strictly related to office matters. On the other hand, he also had a soft spot for Pam, who was able to manipulate his attention in her own best interests. It might have been this shared special "favored nation" status that bound Sandy and Pam together.

Sandy gave the young woman a stern look, and without further pretense or greeting, offered, "Okay, so who is he, and what did he do to have you ditch him this time?"

Pam took a deep breath and instantaneously took on a dramatic look of indignation and dismay. "Huh? What do you mean? Are you talking about a man? Such a put-down. I am so insulted! No 'Hi, Pam, how are you?' Right away with the heavy hard stuff. I just might turn around and walk right out of here." But try as she might, she couldn't keep it up. The frown morphed into a big grin. She walked over to Sandy and gave her a big hug.

Pam was a beautiful child, and now that she had progressed into woman-hood, it was clear that she had inherited the special good looks of both her parents. Her lithe but sturdy athletic build and searing blue eyes were from her father. Her blond hair, soft facial features, and "proportionate" figure were undoubtedly passed down from her mother. As a teenager, she never lacked for attention from her male classmates. Pam was drop-dead gorgeous, but sometimes acted as if she were unaware of her effect on the young men around her. Perhaps as a spin-off from her attractiveness, Pam owned an irrepressible independent streak. She was determined to do her own thing and refused to follow the crowd. At the same time, she was hardly "way out" there and did not try to be different just for the sake of it. While she wouldn't dress exactly as her mother would have liked, she never went with the frizzy purple hair, skintight short skirts and halter tops route. She was not quite a rebel, but certainly not a conformist, either. No-one could guess how she might show up dressed on any particular day, but in truth, she kept an eye on fashion trends a lot more than she would have admitted. It didn't take her long to realize that her dad's bucks were pretty darn good when it came to buying stuff. She had a big advantage over most kids. How about an open line of credit at all the finer shops in the Galleria? Why not spend his money and look nice?

She had been active in extracurricular activities at St. John's School, an expensive and exclusive private school in River Oaks, as long as they did not involve academic matters. She was a natural at cheerleading, but was definitely not math club material. Being very cute, laid-back, and approachable, Pam Nelson did not lack for attention from boys. In fact, she had several boyfriends during her high school years. She tended to go with someone for a while, inevitably become bored, and send him packing. She would play the field until the next acceptable guy wandered in and repeat the process all over again. She never had what could be called a serious relationship in high school.

Despite her average grades, she scored well on the college boards, confirming that she possessed excellent innate ability but suffered from a lack of interest and willingness to put forth effort on day-to-day schoolwork. Nonetheless, her academic credentials were good enough to gain acceptance to Sam Houston State University in Huntsville, not quite halfway up the interstate due north from Houston towards Dallas.

The home of the Bearkats had an enrollment of some 16,000 students on a two-hundred-acre campus in a rural setting. The school was the second-most well-known institution in the city. The Walls Unit of the Texas Department of Corrections likely received more attention than did SHSU. When a youngster in the Lone Star State misbehaves and their parent tells them to "straighten up or you will end up in Huntsville," they are not usually referring to the university.

As things turned out, Sam Houston was the right choice for a bright but academically indifferent party princess, even though there were long, silent gaps during the semesters when Travis and Diane began to wonder if their daughter was still alive only two driving hours away. At first, her academic performance gave them little reason to believe they'd ever see her in a cap and gown under a mortarboard, but as was always the case with Pamela Nelson, never count her out. After a seasoning period, she seemed to realize that the Bearkat school had a lot to offer. She could have a great time and, with a minimum of effort, make progress towards her degree.

Of course, with Pam, don't ever try to predict her actions, because she will fool you every time. In the middle of the summer break between her sophomore and junior years, she suddenly met Mr. Right, who was a Mexican foreign national, of all things. With only a brief notice to her mother, she left the country with him. Diane understood her daughter well enough to not try too hard to dissuade her. A strong push on her part could have sent Pam off into the unknown, never to be heard from again. At least Diane convinced her wayward child to stay in contact, which she faithfully did. About the time her father disappeared, apparently Mr. Right became Mr. Boring. Once again, she surprised everyone by returning to school and was now set to collect her sheepskin.

"When is the big day, Pam?" Sandy asked. "I want to be sure I am there to see you walk across the stage."

True to form, Pam responded, "Well, it is in early June. I am not sure of the exact date, but I am thinking of not going anyway. A couple of thousand kids. Can you imagine anything more dreadful than sitting there listening to all those names? I am probably just going to have them mail it to me."

At that moment, both women's eyes jerked over at the closed door to Diane's office as a muffled scream and loud crash caught their attention.

"What was that? Is my mother in there?"

"Oh my God! Yes, I think she is!" Sandy yelled, as she dashed over and grabbed the doorknob, only to find it locked.

Inside the office, Diane crawled on the floor towards the left side of her desk and the window. She was totally consumed by terror. The ugly man who had knocked her to the floor stood there for a moment and watched as she trembled with fear. He held a switchblade with a long, gleaming blade in his calloused left hand. In two steps, he was on her before she could get close to her desk, phone, or anything to defend herself. He seized her roughly by the arms, yanked, and twisted her to her feet. In doing so, she hit a large lamp on a coffee table that smashed to the floor with a resounding crash. At the same time, Diane let out a loud, ear-piercing scream. Her attacker slammed her up against a built-in bookcase and pressed his body against hers. He then raised the razor-sharp blade up to just under her chin. With his other hand, he covered her mouth.

"No more of that, lady, unless you want me to use this little thing. Can you keep your mouth shut? I have some questions for you. You need to decide if I have to get rough or not. So far, I have been nice to you. Will you keep quiet or not? No more screaming." Diane could not help but look into this monster's glassy eyes.

He did not look like he was capable of rational thought. She shivered with fear. His arm across her mouth was extremely painful. He had an iron grip. She could not get away from him, especially with that knifepoint at her throat. She had to co-operate. There was no choice. With tears streaming down her face, she nodded her head as best she could.

"Okay! Okay! I'll be quiet. Please move your hand, you are choking me."

The man remained transfixed and said nothing. Finally, he slowly lowered his arm away from her mouth, but did not remove the knife from under her neck. She gasped for air and continued to quiver from head to toe.

"Now listen to me. I want some information and I want it fast," he demanded in a gruff and urgent voice.

"What? What?" Diane pleaded. "Anything. Anything. Just let me go. You are hurting me!"

"No lies or you will be very sorry! Where is your husband? I want to know that right now. I know you are in contact with him. Tell me this, or I will be forced to use this knife. You will be very sorry if you don't tell me. He cannot protect you now. The truth!" Diane gulped. What could she possibly do now? Her husband was dead and gone. That was all she knew. There was no other information. "He is dead. He is dead and gone. I have no other information. Please believe me!" Diane shuddered.

The man's scowl became more intense. He slowly raised the knife to where it was about to prick the skin under her chin.

"So, you refuse. You are protecting him. Have it your way."

At that very moment, the office door burst open. Pam rushed in with Sandy close behind. Neither woman could believe their eyes when they saw Diane pinned up against a bookcase by an ugly, dark man in a Dallas Mavericks shirt with long, unkempt hair holding a huge sharp knife under her chin. Sandy reacted immediately by turning and rushing out to call for help. Pam, on the other hand, stood her ground. Her mother was in big trouble and needed help right now. She looked around and spied her father's favorite putter sitting next to the door. Without hesitating, she grabbed the metal golf club and leaped at the man, who was still staggered by the sudden intrusion. Pam used all the athletic grace and strength in her body to swing the shaft directly at the head of the horrible creature. Metal struck skull with a sickening "whomp."

"Let her go, you asshole!"

She didn't have to ask twice. Rico Corona, or whatever his name was, was staggered by the home-run blow delivered by this young woman. He released Diane and dizzily slumped down, just able to catch himself on the edge of Diane's desk. Even in his now foggy state he knew it was time to regroup, especially as he watched Pam raise the golf club again. He had just enough time to glare one last time into Diane's eyes as he brandished the blade and now started for Pam, who froze at the sight of razor-sharp steel but held her ground. Then, just when it seemed that he might run the weapon into Pam, he dashed out the door and was gone.

When the police arrived just a few minutes later, they found mother and daughter locked in an embrace and wailing their eyes out.

11.

David Gamble watched his candidate stride confidently towards the podium at the front of the large room. There was a hushed silence among the gathering. The main event was about to start, which was why they had bothered to show up. Despite his flourish of feigned confidence, a rush of panic washed though the seasoned politico, who always had all the answers. A few seconds ago, he was absolutely certain that Lamar would sail in. Now he wasn't so sure. It was a stark reality. In dealing with the government, there were no sure things.

He reflected for a moment to consider the big picture. He snickered to himself about how Americans look down at the stern and strict autocratic governments of socialist countries, when our own mammoth and ponderous tangled web of the federal government is hardly any better. While there were legions of dedicated employees, a prevailing attitude of lethargy was all too obvious in many aspects of government service. There was little excitement factor associated with the daily grind. Workers went through the motions to put in their time and cash a paycheck.

Gamble was amazed at the overwhelming involvement of the federal government in housing for the less fortunate. The numbers were staggering, with massive annual financial outlays in every state. He tended to agree with the think tank experts who believe the fed's involvement is far overblown, should be curtailed, and left primarily to the individual states and private industry. The unwieldy Department of Housing and Urban Development's very existence has been challenged time and again on Capitol Hill. Yet, despite numerous cases of documented inefficiency and waste, the cabinet department plods on.

The department had grown so massive and unmanageable that a pervasive indifference infected many levels, which encouraged inefficiency and waste: billions in false claims during disasters, expensive pork barrel projects currying local favor but benefiting few. Millions upon millions of improper payments. Huge unneeded or misdirected subsidies. Out and out costly misjudgments and mistakes. In a sense, our government housing programs were banks waiting to be robbed. Gamble knew our society was chock full of brilliant and devious operators of questionable morality who saw rampant opportunity to feast upon the mammoth broken system in their own interests. He'd heard of many a slick operator reaping personal gain from the slow-moving, ponderous system. As he considered these issues, it never dawned upon him that he was about to become an unwitting facilitator to just such an arrangement.

Everyone, including Gamble, who was involved with the SETUP arrangement knew that it was a tenuous undertaking at best. The city and county had never agreed on much of anything in the past, and now they were expected to co-operate in the co-ownership and management of a shared venture. Gamble had his doubts if it could work, simply because of the nature of the operational organization that was being created. A housing authority was typically state-chartered as a non-profit for the purpose of providing safe, clean, and decent housing for those in need. "Need" as defined by HUD meant poor. Despite being created by a state, however, a housing authority must operate within the purview of the federal government's housing watchdog. The reason is simple: HUD pays the bills. Gamble just didn't see how the SETUP housing authority, which would be sandwiched between three huge bureaucracies—two local and one national—could survive, never mind prosper. Usually in Texas, a housing authority belongs to either a city, "municipal," or a county, "county." In the case of the Southeast Texas Unified Partnership (SETUP), a unique and special category had been authorized, which merged together a city, Houston, (municipal) and a county, Harris (county). This arrangement had not been tried previously. Gamble did not want to think about the confusion that would ensue when a city, county, and HUD all tried to agree on a single project. Slip-ups, disagreements, and misunderstandings would reign supreme. He even had a small pang of guilt having led his "wonder candidate" into a potential calamity. Of course, what he could not have known was that the wonder candidate, Dwight Lamar, was counting on exactly that situation when he decided to get involved.

Background chatter in the large room disappeared as the nattily attired African-American man walked confidently down the aisle between the rows of onlookers. The audience was truly excited to meet the prospective head of the foundling agency. Dwight Lamar approached the podium and eased into a wooden chair behind a table so he faced the board members but had his back to the assembled crowd. He unbuttoned the top button of his suit jacket, leaned slightly forward and smiled at the elderly chairman. Bring it on, he thought. I'm ready.

"Good evening, Mr. Lamar," Mr. Hobby began. "It is nice to see you again."

"Likewise, Mr. Chairman," Lamar responded in a deep, clear, and enthusiastic voice.

"Now, of course, everyone in this room knows why you are here, although many of the folks have not met you personally. Tonight, the idea is to let them get to know you, and also to give the board members, all of whom you have met in private chambers, a chance to ask any additional questions they might have. As you know, we are all excited about this unprecedented City-County-Department of Housing and Urban Development partnership and are anxious to hear your thoughts. So, unless you have any objection, we will proceed by letting each director question you one at a time. Does that approach seem all right?"

Lamar nodded. "Yes, sir."

"Okay, then I will start," Mr. Hobby continued. "Tell us, Mr. Lamar, what you would do to keep any public housing under your control in as good and attractive physical condition as possible. I am sorry to say that even in our fair city, there are public housing projects belonging to the city's housing authority that are far below standard, especially the one along Allen Parkway, just before you enter River Oaks."

What a cracker, Lamar thought. He's worried about those poor minorities messing up his exclusive high-priced estates; but still, a softball question. "Mr. Hobby, it has long been my strong conviction that it is much easier to develop and build beautiful new affordable housing than it is to keep it up afterwards. Property management is one of the most important aspects of the real estate process. I place special emphasis on upkeep, including planning for regular and periodic capital upgrades and, sir, let me tell you this. I am not the type of leader who is bound to his cool and relaxing office. I am out on my properties virtually every day. I want to know firsthand what is happening on them."

Hobby smiled. The man had moxie. What a terrific answer. He looked to his left and nodded to the Right Reverend Edward Pike, an African-American Baptist minister. Clearly, the clergyman was delighted to see a fellow man of color sitting there. He was not about to give him a hard time.

"Mr. Lamar, I am very happy to see you sitting there," he began in an even and almost patronizing voice. "Oh, and off the record, where did you get that tie? I just love it."

"Well, Reverend, you might have noticed it has a red background, with blue and maroon diagonal stripes on it."

"Yes, I can see that. So?" Reverend Pike prattled on. He didn't seem to get it. Then he burst out, "Oh! Oh! Now I see. Red is for the UH Cougars, blue for the Rice Owls and maroon is for Texas A&M. Am I right?"

Lamar patiently chided back, "Well, almost. Maroon is for the Texas Southern Tigers." Lamar had done his homework. TSU is a Houston-based historically black university. A ripple of amusement went through the crowd and Reverend Pike was delighted. Lamar had no problem fielding his question about offering faith-based programs on his properties.

Next came Eloise Quimby, the council member from the city of Houston. Ms. Quimby was a full-bodied person whose squiggly black hair tended to flop across her brow when she spoke. Between her constant gestures to sweep the locks back in place and reset her thick granny glasses back on her ruddy nose, it was sometimes hard to understand what she said. That was hardly the case today. She fired it right out, both barrels directly at him. "Sir, what do you think of gays and lesbians?"

No beating around the bush there. He had to be very careful. A satisfying answer to this woman might court disaster with someone else later. He chose his words carefully. "Personally, ma'am, I have no problem with others who may have chosen a lifestyle somewhat different from my own. As long as they stay within the canons of common decency and the law, they are no different from anyone else." He decided to go for it. "And if your next question is, would such people be acceptable as residents on my properties, the answer is a categorical yes." He wasn't sure if he'd won her over, but he had certainly defanged her a bit.

After Ed Smith from Shell Oil quizzed him in some detail on numbers and financial responsibility, the mic was handed to Professor Kathy Barnes, who taught Sociology at the University of Houston. As is often the case, academics can seem distanced from the world of reality. "Mr. Lamar, I am sure you are very familiar with Torstein Veblen's work, The Theory of the Leisure Class. Aren't you?" she inquired.

Lamar smiled and nodded, even though he had absolutely no idea what she was talking about.

"Good. Well, then please explain to us how Mr. Veblen's concepts on envious distinction might apply to some of the residents on your properties." Several muted guffaws and snickers could be heard in the crowd. Let's see how he handles that one?

Lamar sat there for a moment as he decided how to respond. He thought about making a joke about being absent that day but didn't think that would go over. He could only do one thing and hope to slide by—fire back with his own double talk.

"Well, Professor Barnes," he began in slow, measured, and thoughtful tones, "You know that Mr. Veblen lived several centuries ago. Many of his ideas and principles have just not proved to apply to society today. In my years of working with low-income folks, I have never found his ideas to be relevant." Then an inspiration. "Most of our tenants are at the working-class levels, while he dealt mostly with upper-income people, the leisure class, who didn't live in affordable housing. So, I guess I would say his ideas don't apply very much." He finished trailing off to the point of being almost inaudible.

It is fair to say that there were few in the room that could have challenged his dodgeball answer, but the prof was having none of it. "Oh, come now, Mr. Lamar, surely you don't believe that." She then continued to take him from post to pillar while ranting about a long-dead, obscure German sociologist. He sat there and took it like a man. He was defenseless. The very good news was that every other member of the board found the exchange amusing. He lost no points with anyone else.

Nonetheless, he was happy when the last board member lined up against him, even though it was Henry Francesca, the hard-line Hispanic who was clearly upset that his own nominee, a brown man, was not sitting there. Francesca did not disappoint. He came out guns blazing.

"Mr. Lamar, I understand that you spent a lot of time in New Orleans during Katrina and the aftermath. Is that correct?"

"Yes, sir, that is correct."

"Okay, then I am sure you must have some idea of the racial and ethnic mix of that city, since you worked there for some time?"

"Yes, I would say that I do."

"Good. Then, Mr. Lamar, would you kindly break down for all of us here tonight the approximate allocations by percentage of the three primary ethnic groups in New Orleans?"

"I can try. This is not exact, but I would say it is about one-third white, 60% African American, and about 5% Hispanic."

Francesca then raised his elocution level to make a point. "Wait a minute, sir, did I hear you say 60% African American, but only 5% Hispanic?"

Lamar looked up at the man with perhaps the very slightest hint of contempt and stoically replied, "Yes, that is what I said."

"I thought so, and I am also sure that you are aware that the percentage of Hispanics in Houston and Harris County are much, much higher." For a moment, Lamar thought the man was going to come right out and accuse him of favoring blacks over browns, but he stopped just short of that. Instead: "Based on your past experience, do you consider that a problem, Mr. Lamar?"

Dwight Lamar knew this was his big test. It was pass or fail right here. If he blew up and responded the way he would like, he might as well catch the next bus back to Beaumont. He knew the man was overplaying his hand for the crowd, and it was very unfair for him to be cast in that light before he even took over. He had to swallow his pride if he wanted this job. For the most part, he'd been able to suppress a desire to snap at some of these inane questions. There was probably a lot of sympathy for him among the onlookers, but they couldn't help. Only the group on the dais counted.

"I certainly did not have anything to do with the ethnic racial mix of New Orleans," he responded in a tone that barely disguised his simmering angst, but then recovered. "During my entire career in affordable housing I have never, ever, showed favoritism on the basis of skin color or national origin. I don't plan to start now. If my candidacy is deemed unacceptable for this position for some reason because of the ethnic mix of where I worked during one of the worst disasters this country has ever faced, then so be it. I am more than happy to move on." With that he got up, turned, and walked back to his seat, where David Gamble was beaming. A funny thing happened during that short walk. Some two hundred people stood up and gave him a hearty round of applause.

All that was fine; but now the proof was in the voting, up or down, for his hiring. Chairman Wilbert Hobby then polled each member of the board, and it was no contest. What had they been worried about? Every person was a yes so far, with only Francesca and the professor remaining. Lamar glanced down at his shoes when Francesca's vote was requested. Then the crowd inexplicably clapped and buzzed. His Hispanic adversary had voted yes in favor of him. Despite himself, Dwight Lamar broke out in a big grin. It only lasted a second, however, as the last vote was called. The professor voted a resounding no. He would not forget that woman.

12.

The oscillating fan whirred and tinkled as the bent blades nicked the rusty wire cage frame. A steady blast of tepid air gushed through the tiny kitchen, but had no noticeable effect in reducing the oppressive heat that swallowed up the place. After all, it was well above ninety degrees outside, and probably closer to the century mark in the direct blazing sun. Even though the worst summer hot weather was still a few months away, June in east Texas could still be sweltering. If Louella May Rivers noticed the heat, she didn't let on. It was almost noon, and she had to fix lunch for her children, who were always hungry. She stood over her greasy two-burner cooktop and swirled around a plum-size lump of lard that sizzled and disappeared in a frying pan. She had floured some nice catfish filets ready to toss into the pan. She was lucky to have the fish, which Mr. Jones had given her last night after catching them on a cane pole in the river. As she swirled the fish around with a fork, she found herself smiling. That conniving Mr. Jones couldn't fool her. He was definitely after something besides just being nice. But what the heck; her five kids needed to eat, and she hadn't seen the father of her youngest in months. She guessed that a little romance now and again wouldn't hurt her none.

As she stepped away from the stove, she brushed the perspiration out of her eyes and moved to the open outside door of her two-bedroom apartment. She peered between the rows of single-story buildings to see if there was any sign of her brood. They needed to come home for lunch. School had just let out for the summer, and the kids were still wound up with nervous energy. No telling where they might have gone. There was no sign of them, so she turned and went back into the apartment where her oldest, nine-year-old Leroy, was curled up on the threadbare couch thoroughly engrossed watching Family Feud or some other addictive daytime game show on their fuzzy black and white TV. "Boy, get your butt up and go find your sisters and brothers. It's time for lunch. I need to get them fed so I can get off to work on time. I've already been late once this week. I can't afford to lose my job. Then we'd all be in a real fix."

"Aw, Momma. Can't I just wait until this show is over?"

His mother glared down at his supine body in a way that told him she meant business. "No! Get moving, right now. Scat."

The boy knew he'd better move, and he did, but at his own slow pace, still glued to the tube. Finally, he was out the door.

With the messenger properly dispatched, Louella May set the table with five plastic plates she took down from one of the two cabinets built into her kitchen. She had sliced some fresh tomatoes, which she put out, and then added a half-bag of Doritos. She thought there was a half-gallon of milk in the fridge and maybe even a popsicle each for dessert. Certainly not the most nutritious meal for a growing group of youngsters, but it was the best she could do.

As much as they drove her crazy as a single mother, she loved them all deeply. She smiled as they filed in one by one. "Hey, Dwight, leave that frog outside!" she instructed her seven-year-old, who always seemed to have two or three things going at once.

"But, Mama, if I do, he'll get away!"

"Dwight!"

"Okay, okay," he relented as he ducked out the door out of sight of his mother. He slipped the frog into his pocket and came right back in, passing the cursory inspection of his mother who was now busying doling out the fried catfish.

The kids gobbled their food and were anxious to rush back out to play. She caught sight of Dwight checking his pocket while he was eating. His frog caper wasn't fooling her, but she decided to let it go. It was so easy to be on those children for everything all the time. She appreciated how lucky they were to have even what little they did. On the other hand, she understood sadly how far behind they were compared to most, especially the white folk in town.

Louella May lived with her family of five, ages four to nine by three different fathers, in the sixty-four-unit Oakvale apartment complex operated by the City of Sparta Housing Authority. Sparta was located in the region commonly referred to as the "Piney Woods" or the "Big Thicket," which runs north and south from the Gulf of Mexico to Texarkana and east to the Louisiana line along the Sabine River, which forms the state border. The vast expanses of local forests provided lumber for the wood products that served as the area's primary economic driver. Huge logging trucks rumbled by at all hours of the day and night. With few large cities, most of the local residents lived in small towns and subsisted at below nationally recognized poverty levels.

Louella was born and spent all her life in Sparta, the Panola County seat and economic hub of the surrounding towns and settlements. While there was some oil and gas production, it was minimal compared to the western part of the state. The city's population had remained stagnant at 5,000 or so for the past century, as was the case in the late 1980s when Dwight was growing up there.

Dwight, his mother, two sisters, and two brothers, shared an apartment in the public housing project located on the city's north side. The good news was, they were able to live there virtually rent-free; even their utilities were covered by the funding from HUD. The bad news was that, free or not, the living conditions were woeful. Even then, HUD's minimum property standards, which were obviously ignored, did not permit more than four people to occupy a two-bedroom place. Surely, not six. There was one central room to serve for living, family, and dining requirements. It abutted the tiny kitchen and single bathroom with two dingy bedrooms down a short hallway. Both routine maintenance and needed capital improvements had been ignored throughout the complex. Paint was chipping on both interior and exterior walls, plumbing stop-ups were everyday occurrences, and roof leaks were widespread throughout. The grounds were comprised of mostly open, bare dirt with a few scraggly weed patches here and there. The designated children's playground consisted of old, rusting swing poles with no seats or chains and was just a few feet from a green oozing fractured sewage pipe. Conditions were awful, but this was East Texas in the 1980s. Everyone was poor. Expectations were not high among those who were clearly born disadvantaged.

Louella did have reason to take heart, though, because some progress was being made. As dismal as some things remained, they were still a lot better than when she was growing up. Equal rights, nationally, was gradually gathering steam, although there was still a long way to go, especially in backwaters such as Sparta, Texas. She had been just a child when the Sparta Housing Authority came into being as a regretful example of the way such matters were often handled before equal civil rights became an outright mandate. In the 1940s, when the first public housing authorities appeared across the country, there was considerable sentiment among some folks that these organizations were just another way to pander to people who were not oppressed but just lazy. Few small towns across America embraced the concept, and many simply ignored or refused outright to establish a housing authority. Over time, however, increased pressure from Washington and the ultimate lure of free government grant dollars compelled most municipalities to address the housing issue for the people truly in need. One of the primary reasons for local resistance was the bizarre notion that such places would create instant slums by attracting undesirable folks to a community.

In many cases, a simple solution was used to address this problem. Cities would create two clusters of physically separated housing units, often on either side of the tracks. Minorities and other deemed undesirables were restricted to one side, which was as far away from the nicer parts of town as possible. The other housing, closer to the better areas was reserved for needy white folk. Effectively, this approach established de facto segregation with separate white and black complexes. Of course, Oakvale, where Dwight lived, was far across the tracks on the worst side of the city. Louella Mae always knew the whites had it better, but was happy she could at least house and feed her brood at all.

It gets hot in Texas, especially during the summer months. There is a standing line that: "It never got hot until we had air-conditioning." Just try to live without it. While it may be true that complaining about the heat probably only makes you feel worse, it is unfathomable that Dwight and his family were forced to live in such crowded and cramped conditions without any cooling system other than a rusty electric fan. Louella and her neighbors occasionally heard rumors that the bureaucrats at HUD in Washington's were aware of the need to address the abject poverty in rural America. In fact, one of their own, Texan Lyndon Baines Johnson had gotten the ball rolling with several pieces of social legislation. Funding for critical capital improvements was supposed to be on the way. Finally, HUD began to recognize that in a place like steamy Sparta, air-conditioning was a basic critical need and not a luxury. Of course, no-one was much surprised when funding did finally trickle down, that every white complex became fully air-conditioned before any of the black property units were upgraded.

Even as a youngster, such things were not lost on Dwight Lamar. He had often walked by the Fountains, which was the public housing project on the white side of the tracks. He could not get over the constant mechanical noise he heard from the outside air-conditioning units. Those folks were cool.

Where are those machines for us? Dwight wondered.

After finishing his lunch, Dwight paused for a moment before chasing after his siblings in the blazing heat. He heard his momma speak to Leroy, who was on his back glued to the tube. "Now listen, boy. I've got to skedaddle to work at the poultry plant. I'm on the late shift today. I won't be home until after midnight. You see that those kids get their supper. You hear me, Leroy? You're the oldest. There's chitlins in the refrigerator. Open a jar of applesauce. One chocolate cookie for dessert, and get them to bed no later than ten. Have you got that, boy?"

Dwight heard no acknowledgment from his older brother, but his mother appeared and stepped out of the door. She saw Dwight standing there looking up. She smiled. "Now, Dwight, don't you be causing trouble either." She reached over and gave him a hug and then marched her bulky frame out between the buildings towards the main road. She knew Dwight wouldn't cause any trouble. He was different. Maybe, just maybe, he'd have a chance to escape this hellhole.

13.

Sure enough, Louella Mae had been right about her third child; he was different. While he was never confused with being a "good" child, he was exceptionally bright and clever. Often, trouble and bad circumstances followed him around, but rarely was he implicated or held responsible for the mischief. He had an uncanny ability to avoid getting caught or even accused. In fact, he was praised by adults as the level-headed one who "fessed up" on the other kids, even when he had been the real instigator.

The hubcap game was a good example. Back in the eighties, most cars still had the clamp-on hubcaps that were pounded on the wheel hub with a balled fist or rubber hammer. The roads were especially bumpy in the Texas Big Thicket, where there were sparse allocations of tax dollars for highway funds. It should have been no surprise that all the money went to the big cities. None was left for East Texas. The rough surfaces were tough on hubcaps, which had a way of coming loose and rolling away without warning. A lost hubcap usually didn't mean just one replacement. A set of four had to be purchased because the one you lost was never in stock.

It didn't take Dwight and his pals very long to realize that there was an opportunity for them in this lost wheel cover situation. Dwight organized teams of kids to search for lost hubcaps, walking up and down the sides of the roughest and most heavily traveled roads. It wasn't long before they had built up a good supply of metal disks that had bounced off cars traveling through the area. Dwight then approached an auto mechanic on his side of the tracks who readily agreed to pay him fifty cents for every one he could bring in. He made sure, of course, that his teams never got too close to the negotiations with the mechanic. Dwight cheerfully paid each kid who found a hubcap a shiny quarter and then pocketed one for himself. For a while, things worked out pretty well.

The problem was that the supply of hubcaps was unreliable. After their first big sweep, they were lucky to get two or three each week. Dwight decided to apply some poor folks' economics and manipulate the supply and demand curves a little better. The answer was obvious. After a little practice, he became skillful in removing a well-seated hubcap from a parked car's wheels in just a few seconds. Once he had it down pat, he then held training sessions for his teams. No longer would they have to wait for the hubcaps to bounce off, but would become proactive in snatching them.

He also knew he had to be very careful where and when he had his boys operate. The local Winn-Dixie grocery store was a perfect spot, especially at night. He realized that many customers were local residents. If they began to complain, he would be shut down quickly, and the cops would watch that parking lot like hawks. Winn-Dixie was only good for a few per week. He encouraged his teams to hit white folks, if they could, since they drove better cars and could afford to replace the missing hubcaps. He remained obsessed by the Oakvale vs. the Fountains, black-white unfairness. Dwight Lamar possessed a powerful memory. He just didn't forget things.

The best place he found to nab hubcaps was at Catfish Charlie's on the outskirts of town on the heavily traveled SH-78. Most of the traffic passing through consisted of transients headed east toward Shreveport or west toward Longview. Catfish Charlie's was known far and wide for delicious food and drew hundreds of hungry patrons from all over the area who couldn't wait to enjoy their special lemon pepper catfish. Dwight's crews could snatch a half-dozen hubcaps on a Saturday night in the restaurant's big, dark, gravel parking lot. In most cases, the diners came out after a hearty meal, jumped into their cars, and were miles and miles away before they ever noticed a missing hubcap. At that point, they weren't sure where they'd lost it.

Business was so good that Dwight decided to push the envelope. Try as he might, he could not get that skinflint mechanic to pay him more than a half a buck per item, so he decided to try a new approach at the Dairy Queen, also on SH-78. People tended to be in a hurry on the way through town and usually stopped for a quick creamy treat. He would concentrate on women who were alone. When a lady pulled in and left her car to go up to the window, one of his henchmen would sneak up and remove one of her hubcaps. Dwight would sit there in plain sight at all times in front of the store, enjoying a cone himself. Hopefully, when the lady came back out with her cone, she'd notice the missing wheel cover and be shocked.

An extra-polite Dwight would ease over to the woman, who was probably wondering what she was going to tell her husband. The glib young man would schmooze her a bit and sympathize at how bad the roads were around there. He would then ask her what make and model car she was driving. What a coincidence! He would tell her he and his friends found all kinds of hubcaps in the weeds by the side of the road every day. He thought it was possible they might have one to match her other three. If she could wait a few minutes, he would run home and check. If she agreed, he disappeared around the corner where his younger brother, Devon, was hiding with the lady's hubcap he had just removed from her car. They would wait five minutes exactly and then after carefully checking that the coast was clear (remember, this was before cell phones), Dwight would reappear with the "matching" hubcap. She assumed it had come from Dwight's supply of random finds. He readily agreed to let her have it for two bucks, less than half of what an auto parts store would charge. He would then snap it on for her, and often even get an extra fifty-cent tip. He figured that some of the women suspected they were being duped, but two bucks was still cheaper than having to try to find a match. They were happy to be on their way and were delighted with the helpful, polite, and soft-spoken young man. And his profit? How about two twenty-five net for his time. Not bad. Dwight had used his new approach four or five times with good success. In one case the lady had left when he returned, but so what? He still could peddle her hubcap.

It was a boiling Friday afternoon in Sparta. The huge stands of pines and oaks were breathlessly still, with no hint of a cooling breeze. He had been sitting in front of the DQ for almost an hour waiting for the next scam candidate to pull up. It was sweltering, and he was just about to pull up stakes when a light-blue Ford Fairlane 500 pulled up. A twentyish blond woman in shorts and a halter top jumped out and headed up to the window. Dwight went into business mode and scratched his right ear. The signal given, Devon darted out of the bushes, eased over to the Ford, nabbed the left rear cap, and disappeared in an eye blink.

The woman soon returned to her car, anxiously licking a strawberry sundae before the heat melted the whole thing. She paused and fumbled around in her purse for her keys. She happened to glance down and noticed the ugly axle core and five lug nuts where her shiny hubcap should have been.

"Oh, no!" she exclaimed to no-one in particular. "Where the heck did that go?" She took a couple of steps towards the back of the car, hoping against hope that she'd find it laying on the gravel. No such luck.

Right on cue, Dwight walked over and with a sincere look of sympathy allowed, "That is too bad, ma'am. The roads around here are something terrible. People lose hubcaps to potholes every day. We find them in the weeds."

Surprised, she looked over at the well-groomed and polite young black boy who was slurping his own cone. "I guess so, but my husband is going to be furious. This is the first time I have driven his new car. That wheel is so ugly without the cover. Is there anywhere nearby I can buy a replacement?"

Dwight smiled. "Well, that is certainly a beautiful car. Is it a new Fairlane 500?"

"Yes, a 1991."

Dwight hesitated, and then in an almost apologetic tone offered, "I am not sure where you could get one around here, but if you don't mind one that is not quite brand new, I think I have one just like it at home that we found last week. I live right over there," he said, pointing in the air. "I could run home and look."

With little to lose, she readily agreed. "I guess I could wait a few minutes. If I can avoid my husband blowing his top, it will be worth it. Do you mind?"

"No, ma'am. I'll be right back."

He turned and disappeared around the back of the store where his brother was waiting. Dwight grabbed the shiny Ford hubcap from Devon and waited until five full minutes had passed. He then slowly walked around the corner and quickly checked out the scene. The lady leaned against her car while finishing up her sundae, and there was now a pickup in the parking lot. Assuming the coast was clear, which turned out to be a big mistake, Dwight strode purposely towards the lady, who smiled at him. When he was just a few yards away, a large man popped up from the other side of the Ford. The guy was well over six feet tall and had leather suspenders holding up his well-worn jeans. His thin white tee shirt accented his ripped torso and bulging arms with USN tattooed prominently on his swollen bicep. His black-and-red plaid lumberjack cap was scrunched down over his unkempt blond hair that squirted out underneath. He did not look happy as he moved rapidly toward a startled Dwight. "Gimme back my hubcap, you little thief, or I am going to beat your butt into this parking lot!"

Dwight had to think fast. This monster was about to whip his ass but good. A lesser con artist would have split right then, taking his chances on being able to outrun the ogre, but that wasn't Dwight's style. The man was almost on him when he held the hubcap up and out in front of him. "I am so sorry, sir. Here you are. Here is your hubcap back. You need it for your beautiful car."

The charging man snatched it roughly away, but was so surprised by Dwight's willingness to give it up that he pulled up short of smashing into him.

"So, you think you could get away with stealing my property and then taking advantage of my wife? I know your game. I am still gonna bash you, but good."

Dwight smelled the man's breath, which gave off the telltale effects of several hours in a local gin mill. A drunk Paul Bunyan! But still he courageously (or foolishly) did not give ground facing this raging hulk.

"Sir, I am returning the hubcap to its rightful owner. I found it behind the DQ on the ground."

"Yeah? It was there because you put it there."

"Nope. I was out front here the entire time. I was eating my own ice cream when she pulled in. How could I have taken it back there? Ask your wife."

The man hesitated. "Kaylyn, is that true?" he demanded, glancing over at the woman who was placidly standing by. Obviously, confrontations like this one were pretty common with her hot-headed husband.

"Ah, yes, Frank. He never moved from when I got here until he tried to help."

"Okay then, smart-ass, how did the hubcap get back there?"

Dwight was ready. "Well, I am not sure, but I reckon it might have snapped off and rolled back there; but more likely, there's your answer," he calmly replied, pointing down the street at Devon, who was hightailing it in plain sight about a hundred yards away.

"That little son of a bitch," Frank slurred, as he watched the kid disappear around a distant corner.

"Come on. Let's get out of here, Frank. If we don't hustle, we're going to be late for Paw Paw's birthday," the lady ordered. Her large husband shrugged, banged the hubcap on, and exchanged keys with her. He got in the Fairlane and left with his tires eating up a long, dusty scratch in the parking lot.

"Well, I guess I'm in the truck," she said, as she withdrew a dollar from her purse and handed it to Dwight, who still hadn't moved.

"Thank you, ma'am." As he watched her drive away, he thought, "*that one was a little too close,*" but the greenback still felt good in his pocket.

14.

Even though the public housing situation in Sparta had not fully responded to the legally mandated edicts for racial equality that began to take hold in Texas after the imposition of President Lyndon Baines Johnson's "Great Society" legislation in the 1960s, the public schools were mostly fully integrated when Dwight Lamar matriculated through them during the early 1990s. In fact, his closest association with white folks came at school, where he realized that it was in his best interest to pay attention, perform well, and get along with everyone. He knew he would have to set aside his deep-seated inner bitterness if he was going to lift himself out of the circumstances of his birth. Demonstrating openly rebellious behavior, which had become so popular within the black community, would get him nowhere.

He was blessed with a sharp intellect, and routine schoolwork came easy to him. He was a continuous member of the honor roll and eventually graduated from Sparta High an impressive tenth in a class of two hundred and thirty-five. By the time he was a senior, he stood five feet ten inches tall and weighed in at just over two hundred pounds. As a chubby youngster, he was the subject of fat jokes on the playground. As he matured, his body became sturdy and compact. The teasing of his youth stopped, but he never forgot it.

He strived to always present a neat and well-groomed appearance. He kept his hair short and closely trimmed and was never tempted to adopt the raging styles of the day, such as afros, or dreadlocks. He avoided team sports, where he could not control his own outcomes. He did, however, play the two-headed drums in the marching band. In time, he gradually emerged as an exemplary student and a leader among African-American students that made up about a third of the school's student body. He was well-regarded by most everyone, including the principal, who liked to use him as a shining example of how well racial harmony was doing in his school. Dwight was elected vice president of his senior class. He tried very hard to come across as affable, agreeable, and well-spoken to everyone. This attitude caused resentment within the smoldering African-American community whose causes he sympathized with but refused to champion publicly.

Dwight had few close friends, and those kids around him tended to be more of a retinue, or in the vernacular, "posse." He had a sixth sense about certain things, especially schemes to make money, such as hubcaps and even newspaper routes. Not only did he have one route, he had five spread all across town. He developed a network of kids to do the physical delivery, while he handled the billing and relations with the distributors. His personal cut was always more than proportional. He understood the need to be sociable and made sure to show up at parties, at least for a while, but was never seen drinking alcohol. There was no steady girlfriend, and he rarely dated except on the big occasions, such as Homecoming and the Spring Dance, when he always had an attractive lady on his arm. He encouraged the generally held belief that he was shy among the opposite sex.

Dwight worked hard to cultivate his public visage as an intelligent and well-regarded young man. There were a few occasions growing up, however, when a more candid peek into his true makeup came close to bubbling up. In truth, he was hardly reluctant around girls. He had observed several black men from the projects side of town who had been sent to prison for rape and improper conduct with women. As a black man who wanted to move easily within the white community, he clearly understood that any hint of a romantic association with a white girl could instantly destroy him. It was much easier to stay away. In order to satisfy the robust urges of his manhood, he had to look no further for company than several young ladies right there in Oakvale. Some of them were older, in their twenties, and even had children. A bottle of Boone's Farm wine and a stroll along the secluded Sabine River bluffs did wonders to keep his hormones in balance. In general, he attempted to maintain his access to both sides of the tracks, which, on some occasions, was very difficult. During his freshman year in high school, he was taunted by a white boy named Eddie Zorn, who was from one of the wealthier families in Sparta. His father owned the John Deere dealership in town. The boy had a reputation of being a bully and antagonist when it came to African Americans. One morning, Dwight and a friend had just come out of a hamburger joint in downtown Sparta when they ran into two girls they knew from English class. They stopped on the sidewalk to gab for a moment. Just as they were leaving, one of the girls touched Dwight innocently on the shoulder, smiled, and moved on.

Zorn happened to see the exchange between Dwight and the white girl from across the street. Enraged, he ran across and stepped directly in front of

Dwight and his friend. "I saw that, Lamar!" Zorn screamed so that everyone nearby would hear him. "You keep your black claws off our white women! You understand me, boy?"

Dwight stopped and glowered at the loathsome jerk blocking his way. The kid was a head taller than him but probably weighed less. He could toss him in the gutter with no problem. Although he was very tempted, he understood how that act would be interpreted. Seething underneath, he managed to mumble, "Yeah, okay, Zorn," and walked around the lanky kid on down the sidewalk. He'd not forget that confrontation. There would come a day when he'd get even.

Back in those days, other than going to the movies on a Saturday morning, Boy Scouts, and Little League baseball, kids had to make their own fun. One of the more favored spots that drew kids from all over the city was the high and sandy bluffs that overlooked the muddy Sabine River that flowed from somewhere up in Arkansas all the way to the Gulf of Mexico. From the Sparta side you could see into Louisiana, which to many was a mysterious foreign land. It was great fun to hike along the bluffs, start a campfire, skip rocks into the river, sneak beer or cigarettes, or just check out who else might be around. It was spring, and Dwight's second year of high school was just about over. The early rains had been especially heavy and the ugly brown river was boiling and running high. After several dreary days cooped up inside because of the weather, when the sun came out on a Saturday morning, half the kids in town set off for the bluffs. Dwight sat on a large shale ledge that overlooked the turgid mocha ribbon, just hanging out with a couple of his cronies. The conversation had been about the chances of the Texas Rangers in Dallas and the Astros in Houston. Dwight had little interest in Major League Baseball, but the talk got him thinking about some kind of a scheme he might set up to charge people money who attended local sporting events that were free. Like high school basketball; maybe his guys could go in early and save all the good seats. Would it be worth it to parents of players on the team to pay fifty cents or so for those seats? Hmmm…

The group was relaxed and enjoying the rare nice weather when, all of a sudden, a large rock came skipping across just in front of them and splashed into the river. It didn't hit them, but came pretty close.

"Hey! What the hell? Who tossed that?" demanded an indignant member of Dwight's group.

They all looked over and standing tall about fifty yards away upriver on a dirt mound was none other than Eddie Zorn with a smirk on his face. He was standing with a group of white kids. He bent over and picked up another rock to heave in their direction. "Let's see how well you can dance, Lamar!" Zorn yelled.

The kids had become so used to moving around the bluffs that they often lost sight of just how dangerous it could be. As Dwight watched, he was startled to see Zorn lean back to throw from his spot across from them and, without warning, wobble and lose his balance. He started to slip and frantically grabbed at a girl next to him, which caused them both to tumble, slide, and careen down the slope right into the swollen, rushing river. To the horror of all who watched, they splashed in and went under.

Dwight was as shocked as anyone, but he quickly recovered. He leaped up and scrambled down to the muddy water's edge. The swift current swept both kids towards where he stood. He grabbed what he hoped was a sturdy tree root, dug his feet into the mud, and leaned as far as he could out over the rampaging flood. Two heads were bobbing and rapidly approaching him. He tensed and stretched. It would have to be quick. They were moving fast, and he wouldn't get a second chance. He was able to make out Zorn's ashen complexion and thin, gaunt face. The kid was terrified, and struggling for all he was worth to dog-paddle to shore. His pleading eyes met Dwight's as he hung there with his arm outstretched. Dwight's eyes met those of the frightened young boy. The current brought Zorn to within his grasp, but Dwight remained rigid. Their hands missed. Zorn sailed by and their eyes locked again. A slight smile curled on Dwight's lips. They both knew. So sorry, Eddie.

Seconds later, the girl came within reach. This time Dwight stretched his arm and hand out as far as he possibly could and, thank goodness, somehow managed to grab her wrist and hold fast. With a herculean effort and drawing upon strength he did not know he had, he battled the incredibly powerful flow and was able to drag her to shore. Several people clambered down the bank to help lift her out of the water and carry her back up the hill where a Rescue Squad vehicle was waiting. An exhausted and totally wasted Dwight crumpled on the bank.

Despite the valiant efforts of several professional first responder groups, Eddie Zorn's body was never found. A number of eyewitnesses testified that

Dwight Lamar had done all he humanly could have to save the boy. On the other hand, he had become a local hero for having grabbed the girl. It was headline news in the local paper, and there was even a special assembly at the high school to honor him. Once again, Dwight Lamar had come out just fine, doing things on his own terms. No-one realized that he had been hiding in plain sight. Even then, payback was sweet.

15.

As he walked block after block along St. Charles Avenue through the Garden District of New Orleans, a drab-red trolley car rumbled past him on the tracks laid in the middle of the street. Had he known about the trolley earlier he would not have had to lug his suitcase all the way from the bus station to the campus. Still, the young man enjoyed the sights drinking in the size and opulence of the perfectly preserved historic mansions. They were like nothing he had ever seen in East Texas.

And just that quickly in a few blocks, the street scene changed from magnificent residences to street after street of tiny white clapboard shotgun houses, similar to where he had grown up. His first impression of the dramatic contrasts in huge southern Louisiana city on the winding banks of the mighty Mississippi was never to leave him. The metropolis was unique in many ways. It owed its very existence to a complex network of dams, floodgates, and spillways, since a large portion of the land area was actually below the normal level of the great river. Somehow, up to that time, the city had avoided major flood disasters, although most agreed, it was just a matter of time. How prophetic. Let the good times roll!

Dwight Lamar had no shortage of college alternatives as a senior in high school. He was an excellent student with exemplary board scores and numerous extracurricular activities to his credit. He also had first-rate recommendations from his teachers. Diverse enrollments were beginning to become popular goals on many campuses. As an exceptional minority student, had he been in a more mainstream and visible location, he would have had many offers from across the country, including even from the haughty Ivy League schools back east. As it was, he was pursued by historically-black colleges, such as Grambling, Tuskegee Institute, Texas Southern, Alabama A&M, and several others, even though he had little interest in pursuing those opportunities. His choice of a college or university would be determined by two basic criteria. First, obviously, was cost. Even though he had proved himself skillful at raising pocket cash, his mother had no ability to fund one dime towards his education. In fact, he had actually been able to help her to keep the family afloat. He needed to go somewhere where he would receive a full financial ride. The second requirement was that the college had to be highly regarded, offer an extensive curriculum, and be located in a large metropolitan area. Dwight wanted to grow. A small black college in a rural southern town was not for him. As things turned out, at the urging of his social studies teacher, who was an alumnus, Tulane University in New Orleans rose to the top of his list. When a very generous award letter arrived in the mail, the deal was done.

After his long walk, he reached the uptown campus and easily found Warren House, a 1920s vintage three-story, red brick residence hall virtually at the center of the tree-lined and beautifully manicured campus. He walked in and was warmly greeted by a young lady, obviously a student, sitting behind a table, who handed him his welcome packet and directed him to the second-floor. He found his room, twisted the key in the lock, and opened the door. It was a double occupancy room with about four hundred square feet. His roommate had already arrived, and his gear was strewn on one side of the room. To many, the space would have appeared musty, tiny, cramped, and confining, but to Dwight Lamar, compared to where he'd come from, it looked like heaven. A thin boy with curly, dark hair and thick glasses rose up from one of the desks to meet him. They shook hands. It was no surprise to Lamar that his roommate was also African American; after all, this was still the Deep South before the turn of the century in the 1990s.

The eager new student was determined to extract from the university everything and anything it had to offer to distance himself from his dreary past. As his undergraduate years unfolded, he had less and less contact with Sparta, including his own family. He kept in contact with his mother, but seldom went home. During his junior year he did return for the funeral of his older half-brother, Leroy, who had been murdered during a drug deal gone bad at that very Dairy Queen where he had pulled off his hubcap scam.

After much deliberation, Dwight decided to major in accounting, since he had already caught on that most things in life ultimately depend on numbers. The course work came easy to him, and he was not reluctant to put in the extra grinding hours needed to succeed in that major. He also knew that jobs in the accounting field were plentiful for new graduates. As an accounting major, he became a member of the Tulane Accountants' Society, which met from time to time. The group had speaker events on topical issues within the industry, or sometimes just met socially for drinks or dinner. Membership in the group was open to undergraduates, graduate students, and Tulane alumni. At one of those functions, Dwight met a tall, thin, and outspoken, but very affable master's candidate graduate student, who had been working for private corporations in the communications field for several years after graduating from Tuskegee. Despite their age difference, they became casual friends. Little did either of them know at the time that the graduate student, Ray Nagin, would go on to become the mayor of the city of New Orleans during one of the worst disasters ever to hit an American city.

Dwight also became a member of, but avoided active participation, in a black advocacy campus organization called Men of Color (MOC). As always, Dwight was sympathetic to issues of racial injustice, but did not want to be seen as an outspoken proponent for fear of negatively impacting his acceptance within the white community. He saw no reason to rush a fraternity. In general, he enjoyed the ambiance of New Orleans and was not reluctant to take a break from his studies to visit the French Quarter from time to time with fellow students. As in high school, he was determined to maintain a respectable image and stay out of trouble, in a city where the unsuspecting could become easy prey.

Although the young man from Sparta, Texas, was an unusually driven person who had some definite ideas about where he was headed in life, at times even he was compelled to take a detour. One bright spring day with billowing, white clouds overhead and a gentle breeze off the river, he had just purchased a tuna salad sandwich and a carton of milk, intending to grab a quick lunch on a bench under an oak tree canopy not far from the student union. He took his first bite and was fumbling through his cost accounting book when he heard some muffled sniffles and unmistakable weeping coming from the other end of the bench. He had been so preoccupied when he sat down, he hadn't even glanced over to see who was sitting there.

When he did, he discovered a diminutive young lady wearing a Tulane tee shirt, cutoff jean shorts, white tennis shoes, and sporting wire-rimmed glasses. She noticed his stare and looked away while bringing a tissue up to her watery and sobbing eyes. Dwight Lamar, an inveterate stoic and realist, was hardly the sympathetic or sensitive type, especially when it came to the opposite sex, and a white girl, no less. There was usually nothing in that equation to benefit him. If anything, she had all the makings for complications and trouble with a capital "T." All those issues aside, something about this girl was different and caught his attention. Totally out of character, before he had time to reconsider, he struck up a conversation with the helpless-looking waif.

His weak trial balloon launched, "Hey, what's the matter? Did you get a "C" in English Lit?"

The girl looked over at him and revealed stunning, deep-azure-blue eyes. She swallowed and tried hard to force a smile. "No, that's not it. I am sorry to have disturbed your lunch. It's just that no, I am really sorry, I'll just move to another bench." She began to pick up her books.

He startled himself by saying, "No, please don't do that. You are not bothering me. Stay right there. Please."

She looked over at him again and now he noticed her petite nose and perfectly shaped mouth with a tinge of red lipstick. Her soft, chalky skin was just beginning to show the effects of what would surely become a gorgeous bronze tan. Her Tulane tee was tight enough to reveal a well-developed upper body, entirely consistent with her short but shapely crossed legs. Her lustrous sandy-brown mane hung carelessly over one shoulder.

"Are you sure?" she questioned, and then broke completely down into sniffling and sobbing.

Totally out of character, Dwight took her breakdown as his cue to slide towards her. "Hey, hey. It can't be that bad. Nothing is. I'm Dwight, who are you?" Dwight inquired tenderly as he pulled out his little plastic wrap package of Kleenex that he always carried in his pocket and handed her a couple of tissues.

"Thanks...... Dwight. I am so embarrassed. It is just that adjusting to being away from home has been much tougher than I thought, and now this had to happen. Oh, and I'm Karen, by the way."

"It is okay, Karen. You can tell me if you want to. What happened?"

"Well, I guess I have to talk about it to someone. I certainly wouldn't discuss it with my roommate. She's such a jerk. How do they pick roommates around here anyway?" Karen responded, as some of her grief turned to anger.

"I sure don't know about that one, Karen, but try me, if you want."

She hesitated, with the emotion building to a crescendo. "I just talked to my mom back in Poughkeepsie. That's in New York, by the way. She told me, she told me (sniffle) that Evelyn died, and I wasn't even able to be there when it happened. We were so close! I am just miserable. It is probably the worst thing that ever happened to me!" Karen wailed, as she completely lost it again.

Dwight desperately wanted to hug and console her but even here on an enlightened college campus out in the open, it would not look too good. "I am so sorry. Who was Evelyn? Your sister? An aunt? Dear friend? Who?"

"No, Dwight, none of them. Evelyn was my kitty, and she was sixteen years old, and I wasn't there. Boo hoo!"

Now that admission did stop Dwight in his tracks. A cat? A friggin' cat, like the ones we used to tie to railroad tracks or weight down with rocks before we chucked them into the river? A cat? She is bawling over an old cat? You have got to be kidding me. Boy, some of these folks from up north are strange; but I guess that is why I came here, to find out stuff like this. A useless cat? I still can't believe it. Well, now he had a choice to make; cut and run, or hang in. There was just something about this girl. In for a dime. In for a dollar. "Oh, Karen, that is so sad. I know just how you feel. I lost a puppy once. I was devastated."

She blew her nose and wiped her eyes and looked over at him with a fabulous, mournful, and vulnerable gaze. "Really? Then you do understand what I am going through. Tell me about the puppy, Dwight."

So, there he was, having to come up with a quick completely made-up puppy story, which really wasn't too tough. Maybe he should have said frog? In any event, there was something special that clicked between them that day, which led to Cokes at the U, study dates at the library, movies, concerts, football games, and a lot more under the covers. Dwight was taken with this pert little New Yorker, so much so that he violated many of his hard and fast rules of the road. He took some consolation that the progressive, wide-open Tulane campus was a far different place than the tiny town of Sparta. Also, chances are that he wouldn't see many of the college people ever again. And what about her then?

16.

Occasionally, a college romance ends up in a "happily ever after" marriage, but, by far, most fizzle out long before the sheepskins are ever distributed. Dwight always viewed his connection with Karen in the latter category. Sure, he'd been smitten by the attractive young lady, but he never expected that their relationship would extend one day past graduation. She was a sweet and lovely person who was fun to be with and gave him a very pleasing outlet in bed. Perhaps the old adage about opposites attracting was in play. He was very demanding and even rough with his partners, whom he seldom ever saw again. Sex for him was a release he needed from time to time, but from which he sought few other entanglements.

Karen, however, was special and truly different from any other woman he had dated. For reasons that were unique to her personality, she understood Dwight Lamar and accepted him as he was. She rolled with his moods, his taciturn periods, and even the occasional eruptions of his deep-seated anger, which he tried desperately to keep hidden. She enjoyed his intelligence, his dry humor, and self-deprecating charm.

As the Tulane years clicked by, Karen was not smitten, she was deeply in love. Although she was an admitted hopeless romantic a good part of the time, she knew she must be sensible and realistic about the future. Her family in upstate New York was initially thrilled when she called and told them about the wonderful guy she'd met. She extolled his virtues on such things as being an accounting major and dean's list student. The level of her excitement was perceptible to her parents over the phone. They were happy for their daughter, and eager to meet Mr. Wonderful. As concerned over-protective parents are inclined to do, however, their enthusiasm was guarded. They cautioned her about getting too involved too quickly with anyone. She mustn't let her studies suffer. Naturally, she assured them that she was in firm control and not to worry.

Her parents had asked on several occasions for a picture of Dwight, which she kept forgetting to produce. It was also just pure coincidence that when her parents traveled all the way from upstate New York to the Tulane campus for Parents' Weekend that Dwight had gone home to Sparta. In reality, he was holed up in his room studying. He had no desire to attend the lousy Tulane football games anyway. Finally, when Karen went home to Poughkeepsie for the summer just before her junior year, the pressure was becoming untenable. She had to tell them about Dwight, whom she fully intended to marry after they graduated. Hopefully, her mom and dad would accept things gracefully and welcome the young man into their family.

To say that her candid sit-down with her folks went badly would be a huge understatement. It was an unmitigated disaster. Her parents, who had long been suspicious, were mortified. They struggled to keep their cool and reason rationally with their daughter about all the practical challenges she'd face in an interracial relationship and, perish the thought, marriage. Karen would hear none of it, and was insistent that love conquers all. Eventually, calls for reason and logic escalated into a shouting match on both sides. It ended with Karen's father prohibiting her to ever set foot on the Tulane campus again. Her slammed door shook the entire house. She did not bother to say goodbye when she left for New Orleans the next morning.

The leaves were fully out, the vivid azaleas were in bloom, and the Crescent City enjoyed a brief spring respite before the weather along the Gulf turned into oppressing humidity and heat of the summer. Graduation was a few weeks away. Dwight, who was set to receive his bachelor of science in accounting with honors, had solid job offers from IBM in Houston and Peat, Marwick, and Mitchell in New Orleans. Karen, a music major, was in her junior year with one more year to go to earn enough credits to graduate. For some time, she had been gently pushing him to commit to their future. In fact, the accounting trainee position with PMM right there in New Orleans would have been perfect. She could finish out at Tulane, and they could be together in New Orleans. She knew enough about her man not to lean on him too hard. He did not react well to that kind of pressure. On the other hand, after three intimate years, she deserved to have some commitment from him.

It was a Sunday morning and they lay tangled up in sheets in the one-bedroom apartment Dwight had moved into near the Tulane campus. While his relationship with Karen was no secret, he still did not relish the idea of anyone seeing him bring a white girl into his dorm room on a regular basis. They had made love last night in a session that was neither tender nor passionate. Dwight seemed to have gone back to his old ways. Things were relaxed at that moment, though. Karen decided it was a good time to press him about their future.

"So, what is your thinking about Houston or New Orleans? I have to register for next semester's classes this week. What should I do?" Karen asked.

Dwight remained silent, almost as if he had not heard her, and then suddenly seemed to snap back from wherever he had been. "Do? Do? Why are you asking me? It is your degree. You can sign up for whatever you want."

"Yes, I guess I can, but I was really hoping to work something that would permit us to be together. Houston is five or six hours away. It would be tough seeing each other. We have had a great three years. I don't want it to end. I think we have been terrific together, haven't we?" Karen responded, giving him an easy out to her questioning and letting him duck the central issue.

"Yes, we have been pretty good. I have never met anyone like you. Somehow, you are able to handle me like no-one else I've ever met. You can sense my moods and seem to know when to just let me be. I've appreciated that in you."

Now she was beginning to get a little desperate. "Well, I sure don't want it to end."

"Karen, everything in life must end sooner or later."

The tears were fast forming. Her voice had begun to crack. "But, but, Dwight, I love you. I don't want to lose you. I want to be with you the rest of my life," Karen sobbed, as she put her arms around his waist.

Dwight said nothing for a few minutes as he listened to her weeping. Then, in a flat, unemotional voice he replied, "Let me ask you something, Karen. In all the time we have been together, have I ever said those words to you? Have I ever promised that there'd be a future for us after Tulane?"

"Maybe not specifically, but I always assumed you felt them for me, for us. You agree we have been so good together. I want a life with you and have for some time. I want to have your, our, kids. You are my life!" She let it all pour out amid tears and gasps.

Dwight's eyebrows went up when he heard *kids*. "Karen, tell me just how all that would sit with your parents and family up in New York. They have already made it painfully clear what they think of you associating with me. I don't see that changing soon. They forbade you from ever coming back to Tulane after you told them I was black. You are lucky that your college trust fund continued to pay your bills. If it were up to mommy and daddy, my guess is that you and I would already have been toast some time ago."

"Dwight, I don't give a damn about them. I think they would come around in time. I talk to them on the phone every so often, but it is *us* I care about. That is the only thing that matters."

"Unfortunately, even though you say you don't care, I do. I have some plans in this world, as screwed up as it is. I am afraid I can't have someone like you by my side. I have been around long enough to know that despite the wonderful goals of the racial equality crowd, mixed marriages still make some people sick. I can't have that holding me back. Whispers can turn into slammed doors for someone moving up the ladder. I am very sorry that is the case, but it is a hard fact."

Karen was shocked as she listened to his reasoning. She could hardly believe her ears. Were these statements coming from the man she thought she loved and wanted to spend the rest of her life with, or some stranger? She knew Dwight ran deep and there was still a large part of him she didn't understand, but to throw her out for his greedy job ambitions?

"I really can't believe what I just heard. Are you telling me that you'd drop me, us, just because someday, somewhere, you might not get a promotion because you have a white wife? Is that what you said, Dwight?"

"Yes, I guess it is, at least a big part of it. I am not sure that I am going to have time to deal with a wife and family, especially in what is still a very prejudiced society."

She unclasped her arms from around him and drew the sheet up to her front. With the most mournful look imaginable she pleaded, "Then what you are saying is that this is the end of us?" With no hesitation, Dwight replied in a stoic, flat voice without the slightest hint of emotion, "Well, Karen, I am afraid that it is. Sorry about that."

A thoroughly shaken and clearly distraught whimpering young woman slipped out of the bed. She hurriedly got dressed, gathered up her things, and was out the door without another word. Dwight looked over at the clock radio. It was already past 9:00 AM, too late to catch a little more sleep. He decided to get dressed and head down to the corner Starbucks.

Dwight did eventually decide to stay in New Orleans and take the position with Peat Marwick, which was a noted training ground for young executives wanting to start with a good foundation and eventually move on to another company, often one of their clients. Neither he nor anyone knew that the storm to end all storms called Katrina would soon turn the city upside down.

In a then "Big Eight" accounting firm, the newest hires in the door, of course, are burdened with huge workloads of what is mostly grunt work. This situation hardly bothered Dwight, who was only interested in getting ahead. Midnight oil was already part of his routine, and he had been in party town New Orleans long enough that local nightlife held little allure for him.

One spring evening almost a year after graduation, he was working late in his cubicle at the PMM offices in a high-rise tower downtown. It was getting on towards 8:00 PM, and he decided that an extra three hours or so was enough additional effort for one day. He tossed his adding machine tapes into the waste basket, slipped on his suit jacket, and walked out of the office. He noted that only a few of his contemporaries were still at it. Most had already given up the ghost.

As he rode down the elevator, he remembered he had skipped lunch and was hungry. He had to pass a little Italian restaurant just down the street before getting his car and driving out to Kenner, where he had an apartment. It was pouring as he left the building and strode purposefully towards the restaurant.

After a few steps, he sensed someone was behind him on the sidewalk. When he glanced back, he did a double take: Karen. Despite the weather, he froze in his tracks and turned to face her. She stood there looking up sheepishly at him with those still gorgeous eyes. She looked tiny, with wet and stringy hair, huddled against the wind and the rain. She clasped her hands around her and pulled tight the light-gray sweater she wore to protect her from the weather. She looked pitiful, but in a strange way, she also looked beautiful. She caught his gaze and gave him an awkward and doleful grin. Dwight, for once, was speechless as they stood there getting wetter by the second. Finally, his surprised and perplexed look morphed into a wide smile. He reached over, grabbed her damp hand, and ushered her towards the restaurant.

After asking for a booth in the back and quickly surveying the place for other PMM people, Dwight took a seat across from the only woman, besides his mother, with whom he had ever had a relationship. For a few moments all they did was stare across the table. Finally, Dwight broke the ice. "Well, Karen, this is a big surprise. How have you been? I guess you are almost ready to graduate." Dwight's initial emotional thrill at seeing his former lover was quickly replaced by his standard talking points.

"Okay, Dwight. I've been okay," Karen mumbled, and looked as if the tears would burst forward any second. They continued to stare at each other in silence until the waiter appeared. Dwight ordered a bottle of Chianti, just as much to get rid of the guy as anything. "So, what brings you downtown in the evening? There's not much college nightlife around here. It is hardly the French Quarter."

She did not reply at first, and then stated the obvious. "What do you think, Dwight? You."

It was the response he had expected, but also feared. He really did not want to go there, so he tried something else. "Oh. Well, how are things in the land of the Green Wave? I've been over there once or twice for accounting society meetings, but really haven't kept up."

Karen took her time in responding. Finally: "I don't know either, Dwight. I dropped out of school last fall. I just couldn't concentrate. When you left, I was, and still am, completely lost. School just didn't mean anything to me anymore. Even my music."

"Oh, Karen, I am so sorry to hear that. I expected to hear that you were finally first chair clarinet in the Tulane student orchestra, which you should already have been. Well, what have you been doing?"

"I was able to get a part-time job at a library a few days a week. I share a room with a couple of girls. You won't believe it, Dwight, but it is actually in the French Quarter. Talk about a partying place."

For the first time, Dwight looked a little closer across the table. What he had assumed were the usual Karen tears was really just a wateriness in her eyes. Her sniffling also seemed to be a bit more than the result of crying. She looked pale, and slight, but that could very well be the low lighting in the restaurant.

"How about your parents, Karen? I am sure they wouldn't be too happy about you dropping out of school. What do they think?"

Now real tears erupted. She picked up a napkin and tried unsuccessfully to dry her eyes. After several deep breaths, she finally reached some measure of composure. "You (deep breath) are right. They were very upset, but then on Thanksgiving Day, my dad had a massive heart attack and died. And, you know, I wasn't even there. I didn't even go home until the funeral. That has always been my pattern with losses like that. I feel so terrible, and my mom is completely lost without him. She wants me to come home, but I just can't think of being around her in that state. Things can be pretty difficult here, but at least I don't have to listen to her grief twenty-four hours a day."

Now, Dwight was truly shocked. He really did feel sorry for the poor girl. "Karen, I am so sorry. I had no idea what you've been through."

The poor woman just looked across the checkered tablecloth at him. She held up both hands and shrugged as if to say, "What are you going to do?"

At that point, both of them recognized that they simply could not continue on this emotional downer. They decided it would be far better to spend the evening recounting old times and mutual acquaintances, which would hardly be jovial, but at least avoided the raw emotional scars. Surprisingly, Karen gobbled down a hearty plate of pasta like she was starved, which maybe she was. A second bottle of Chianti was consumed.

It was after 10:00 PM when they left the restaurant, wobbling a bit. Karen took Dwight's arm, and he showed no resistance. They found Dwight's car in a nearby parking garage. His offer to take her home ended up at a Motel 6 on the trolley line not far from the Tulane campus. Staying so busy at work, Dwight had had little time lately to satisfy his manly urges. Karen's appearance was opportune in that respect.

After making love, Karen quickly drifted off into a deep sleep. Dwight could not get over how slim she looked and, as he got out of bed, was not surprised to see several telltale marks on her arm. The sweet little girl from upstate New York had certainly come a long way, but that was not his problem. Once he was dressed, he was about to slip out the door, but stopped and reached into his pocket for his wallet. He extracted a couple of twenties and tossed them on the dresser. There; at least he had done his part.

17.

As soon as Matt touched down in Houston, he called the office and was upset to learn about the attack on his mother by the unsavory ex-employee. Had he been around, he never would have let the guy come in for an exit interview, but it was too late now. Diane was learning more and more every day. Bringing him in was just not a good idea. At least no-one had been hurt.

The police had arrived and spent a lot of time interviewing Diane, Sandy, and Pam. While they were there, a man was apprehended in the parking lot. He drove in, saw the police cruisers, and tried to drive right out again. The cops thought he looked suspicious enough to pull over. Then, for a moment, the officers believed they had nabbed one of the dumbest perps of all time. His identification and green card said he was in fact Rico Corona. The man was handcuffed and secured in the backseat of a police cruiser. One of the officers went into the Mesquite Management offices to advise the detective who was interviewing the women that they had the guy in custody. The officer, who was very proud of his fine police work, did not have a chance to take a bow. The ladies were taken outside to positively identify the hostile hombre in custody. Unfortunately, they could not. The Rico Corona in cuffs was not the Rico Corona who had attacked Diane. Obviously, what had happened was that the real perp had never been asked for any identification. He was an imposter, and now long gone. The real Rico Corona had shown up, albeit a little late for his exit interview, not knowing the other guy had caused such a stir. Even though he clearly wasn't the attacker, he did have some explaining to do: how did the other guy know about the exit interview? The real guy got his money, and also earned a free ride downtown where the cops would question him a little closer about whether he had any connection to the incident.

By the time Matt finally arrived at the office, the police were gone and all three women were gathered in Diane's office with the door closed. They were shamelessly breaking strict company policy with three glasses and a chardonnay bottle that was almost empty.

"Well, there you are, just in time," Pam cracked, as Matt walked in.

"Yeah, I guess so, but from what I've heard, you three didn't need me here anyway. Heck, I might have gotten punched or something."

"Well, one thing is for sure, overhead cost to hell, we are getting a security guard for this office during the day," Diane announced. There was no argument from anyone.

Diane then filled him in on the false start with the real Rico Corona.

"I'd like to feel bad for the guy, but he was out anyway. From everything I heard, he was a bad actor himself. It will be interesting to see if the cops get anything more out of him about how the other guy knew about the meeting. Say, let's get John on the horn and update him about this. Have you talked to him?"

"Nope," Diane replied, as she picked up her phone. "We haven't had a chance. It's ringing.

Hello? Hey, John, it's me. You are on the speaker."

"Hi, Mom. To what do I owe this intrusion into my valuable nap time? I suppose you have my older brother with you. He should be back there by now."

"Yes, he's here, and so are Sandy and Pam."

"Pam! No kidding? Say, sis, have you made it to your sophomore year yet at that Ag school in the prison town?"

"You know it, John. I expect you to be here for my graduation next month," Pam shot back.

"Enough of that stuff," Matt cut in. "John, we just had a bad incident here we need to talk about."

"Really? Okay, shoot." All jocularity was gone.

Matt let the three women describe to John exactly what happened that morning. He listened patiently, asking a few questions as they described the attack. When they were done, he replied, "Okay, number one. Get armed security in uniform at that office every day."

Diane looked around at everyone. "Done."

"Now, the part that really scares me is the part about dad. As far as anyone knows, he is dead and buried as of a year and a half ago. Why would this guy be looking for him, or think that we have any information that was not made public?"

Matt interjected, "At least they want to find Travis Nelson and apparently not his family, although two of us have had close calls within the last forty-eight hours. I wish we knew who these people were."

"Mom?" John asked. "What did this guy look like? Was there anything distinguishing about him?"

"Well, he was just one ugly man. I dunno. He was dressed kind of weird. He had on a Dirk Nowitzki basketball shirt that you couldn't miss. He didn't strike me as the Dallas Mavericks basketball fan type."

"They are dark blue, aren't they?"

"Yes," Matt confirmed.

"I am afraid that is our answer right there. The domestic gang that is getting more and more widespread and does the bidding here in this country for some of the Mexican bad guys loves to wear dark blue, especially Mavericks jerseys. It looks like the Surenos are now involved, although I have no idea why. We all need to keep on our toes. You all keep your ears and eyes open. Matt, maybe you should call the DEA agent there in Houston. I will check with my contacts. Be very careful, and let's keep in touch. I've got to run. See you all; even you, Pammy," John chided, and then checked off the call.

After Pam headed out to parts unknown and Sandy went back to the outer office, Matt asked his mother if she was up to a little shop talk after all she'd been through that morning. He was especially glad that he was not going to announce that he was leaving to join John. The timing for that would have been very poor.

"Bring it on, Matt. If I go home now, all I'll probably do is open another bottle. I am a lot better off here talking with you."

"As you know, our business has changed a whole heck of a lot since dad was here. The management business is good. We have proved we can make it work and do well."

"Yep. Stop right there," his mother broke in. "Tell me, Matt, why aren't you going to throw in with John? From what you described on the phone, your assignment with him and Harvey went well."

Matt looked at his mother in amazement. "Now, please tell me how you knew that? I thought sure you'd be convinced I was leaving."

Diane smiled, "All I can tell you is that a mother knows certain things. Call it mother's intuition. I am right, aren't I? You are staying?" she replied, with just a very faint hint of questioning in her tone.

"Of course, I am staying. I was thinking of hooking up with them, and then I realized that kind of stuff really isn't for me. I guess I could get the hang of it, but I am afraid I am just a confirmed desk jockey."

"Bull feathers. You can do whatever you want."

"Okay, enough mothering. Here is what I was thinking. As I said, management is okay, but you can handle it darn well by yourself without me. I was on the East Coast for almost three weeks and everything went very smoothly. I mean, we only had one assault."

Diane smiled.

"Management is good except for two things. One is that it is a low-margin business. At 4 to 5% of gross collections, we have to work very hard and have a big portfolio to do well. The other thing is that it is B-O-R-I-N-G for me."

Again, she smiled. "But not for me. What are you getting at?"

"Well, with all of the mess with dad, we are banned forever from trying to develop new projects through the Texas Department of Housing and Community Affairs. I get that; although development for me was my first love. There was nothing like taking an idea and have it become a living and breathing two-hundred-unit housing project two years later. So, here is what I was thinking. The tax credit development business is a complicated one where experience and expertise are at a premium. We are long on both. I think there may be a market for our expertise on a consulting basis. There are plenty of non-profit groups, for instance, that would like to jump in but don't dare. With us as a part of their team, they might give it a try. It would be a low-overhead experiment. I am already on the payroll. I might want to add one additional person as an analyst. After a while, if it doesn't work, we try something else. All the while, I will operate from right here in the office next to you. What do you think, Mom?"

For the third time in the past half-hour she smiled, although this time it morphed into a wide grin. "Matt, I love it. It just might be perfect for you. After all those years with your father, it is a shame to have all you learned go to waste. I think a Mesquite consulting arm would be great. In fact, look at this." She reached over on her desk and held up that morning's Houston Chronicle Business Section. The story read: CITY AND COUNTY HIRE EXECUTIVE DIRECTOR FOR NEW MEGA HOUSING AUTHORITY.

"There's your first client!"

18.

The board meeting of the newly-organized Southeast Texas Unified Partnership (SETUP) at which Dwight Lamar was confirmed as the first executive director hardly made a stir across the city. The event was followed only in the local print media. Houston's daily newspaper, the Chronicle, carried it the next morning way in the back in the Business Section as just one more incidental, barely newsworthy story. There was nothing on the local TV stations. For most people, the concept of a new housing authority was hardly earthshaking or very interesting news. The mere mention of a housing authority often connoted free places for poor people and a whole load of government bureaucracy. Unless there was any hint of a misappropriation of funds, folks just yawned over what some considered one step away from outright socialism. Housing authorities could sometimes get a little coverage when irate tenants picketed projects over broken sewer lines. Even those stories, though, were usually fillers on slow news days. So, the first-ever real City of Houston/Harris County/Department of Housing and Urban Development partnership hatched into being well under the radar.

Dwight Lamar leaned back at his government-issue, drab, gray metal desk with his suit coat thrown over the back of his matching chair. He set down the Chronicle Business Section and smiled. He was sitting in an office that was not much bigger than his dorm room at Tulane. It was a bare white box with painted walls and functional, drab, green vinyl tile on the floors. At the moment there were two metal folding chairs facing his desk to accommodate visitors to his office, although more appropriate ones were on order. His lone two-feet-square window gave him a panoramic view of the bottom portion of one of the concrete buttresses supporting an elevated section of I-10 highway above. The sum total of his SETUP domain consisted of a little less than two thousand square feet of C-grade office space on the fifth floor of a 1950s vintage office building nestled under the freeway in the northern corner of Houston's central business district. His entire staff was comprised of three individuals, two of whom had been "transferred" over from the city and one from the county. He wasn't sure, but after having met them, he guessed that their transfer was an alternative to termination.

Lamar had always prided himself on maintaining an equanimity of composure, despite the fires that might be smoldering inside him. He tried very hard not to tip his hand in any situation. He preferred to be seen as someone who approached every situation with an optimism and a can-do attitude. It might have been discouraging to some to have taken this highly ballyhooed position as executive director of a brand-new mega-housing authority to now find himself mired in third-class digs with no staff.

In truth, his sanguine veneer aside, Dwight Lamar could not have been more pleased at the way things had turned out. If he had stepped into a going concern that had been established by others, his grand plans for the organization would have been infinitely more difficult. Even if his offices had been a bit plusher, he would have had many more visitors and de facto scrutiny. No, he was extremely pleased at the start-up and austere beginnings. He had big plans, which would take a while to unfold, but as of right now he was right on course. Once again, he was hiding in plain sight.

The first order of business for SETUP was to arrange for the services that housing authorities are supposed to provide. He understood that the founding sponsors of the entity from both the city and county hoped that their creation would ultimately take on some major high-visibility projects. To start with, however, he had to get enough organization in place to actually provide some shelter for those who were in need. It would have been nice to jump right into some big deals, but it was way too early, and would have almost certainly condemned the housing authority to failure.

On the other hand, he did face the immediate complication that there were already two fine housing authorities serving much of the market areas where he could operate. The City of Houston Housing Authority controlled thousands of units within the city limits. That HA and the Harris County HA also managed the distribution of several thousand Housing Choice Vouchers, which enabled needy tenants to seek shelter in private complexes and have their rent paid by HUD. Those vouchers were formerly known as Section 8 assistance. In fact, the Houston Housing Authority alone controlled some 17,000 vouchers, and also provided direct housing for some 5,500 residents in twenty-five public housing properties they owned and operated directly.

Lamar liked vouchers. He had worked extensively with voucher programs, especially in New Orleans. It was a universal fact that there were almost always long waiting lists of deserving folks seeking voucher assistance. The persistent problem was not the number of qualified families, but the limited amount of HUD funding available for vouchers. Houston was no exception. In order to agree to the very establishment of SETUP, though, HUD had assured the city and county that additional housing choice voucher funding would be forthcoming for the new entity. In fact, that promise alone was a big incentive for the city and county to promote the new HA. Their own HA's were maxed out with voucher authority. The new entity would provide a back-door way to bring additional HUD voucher funds to the region for the benefit of needy citizens.

Lamar was a voucher guru, and knew that a public housing authority can only provide a limited number of owned properties for housing. The voucher program offered the chance for needy families to rent suites in private apartment complexes using HUD dollars to pay the rent. Vouchers permitted SETUP to get moving right away. To be eligible for a voucher, there were income limits above which a family would not be eligible to receive vouchers. Unfortunately, in most cities, there were long waiting lists for vouchers. No surprise there; free money. With a voucher in hand, a family can rent from a landlord whose property has been determined to be acceptable to the HA, including a physical inspection of the unit. HUD then kicks in all or most of the monthly rent. HUD also pays the HA a fee, which is income to Lamar, to administer the voucher program. The voucher program is extensively used all across the country. In addition, every local HA must undergo an annual audit and review by the HUD, pursuant to which the voucher programs are to be closely scrutinized. Certainly, someone like Dwight Lamar, who was clever and had been around for a while, could find a way to circumvent the system; but would he? Well, not for a few months, anyway.

It was time to get things moving and, with the help of Dave Gamble, he was able to get permission to hire five new employees. It was a mere coincidence that three of them had most recently been working for him in Beaumont. At least none were directly related to him, yet. That would come later. It took a few months, but as promised, HUD did turn loose a healthy Notice of Funding Authority for vouchers worth several million dollars to support SETUP and get it off the ground. Dwight knew numbers, the HUD protocol, and how the system should be implemented. Since he was starting from ground zero and the other two housing authorities had long waiting lists, it only made sense that those people already in line, who had been waiting for a while, would be transferred to SETUP. Dwight was delighted. He had been given the ball and would take off towards the goal line. It was his time to shine.

The new executive director stood at his office door. It was past eight thirty on a Friday night and the office was still humming with activity. There were pizza boxes and Coke cans crammed in overflowing wastebaskets as he watched his team scurrying around the cramped office. The harsh neon lights on the ceiling glared down on the overloaded desks where clerks were frantically re-verifying incomes and processing the applications of voucher applicants. So far, they'd received over two thousand transfer applicants. Dwight was determined to process them all as rapidly as possible. It was unheard of that a housing authority would be hard at work on a Friday evening. Most of the late-working crew had worked for him before. They knew that their efforts would be rewarded one way or another.

"James!" Dwight called to one of the workers sitting in the middle of the room, and whom he had appointed as his office manager. "Could you come in here? I need to speak with you, and bring your list."

A stout man with thick, dark-framed glasses looked up from the stack of paper on his desk. He jabbed his fingers into the collar of his shirt to undo the button and loosen his tie. Dwight insisted that his employees all dress well—the image, the image. "Sure, Boss. I'll be right there."

The man got up and walked into Dwight's office. He closed the door behind him as he knew Dwight would want.

"How are we doing with the apps, James? How many have we finished, and how many do we have to go?"

"We're cranking them out pretty fast. I'd say we have already done over eleven hundred or so. That would leave another eight hundred to finish up all the ones that were sent to us. You know, of course, that even our funding from HUD will run out before the entire list is complete. There will still be a waiting list."

"Yes, I am aware of that. Let me see your list."

The man reached across the desk and handed his boss a computer binder that contained all the names of the people on the waiting lists from the other housing authorities. Normally, the order of processing would follow the priority established by the other HAs, which was basically by application date. Dwight opened the printout and scanned the list. He picked up a pencil and began to check off several names. James was puzzled, but waited for him to speak.

"Okay, so how many names do you think we will be able to accommodate before our money runs out?" Dwight asked.

"I would put it at about fifteen hundred or so."

He then placed the listing on his desk and pushed it around so James could read it.

"Now, read the names I have checked off."

"Hernandez, Garcia, Correa, Martinez, Gomez…"

Dwight stopped him. "Now, do you notice a pattern to those names?"

"Of course."

"Good. Just between us, you need to follow the established date priority as much as possible, but we are merging two lists. That in itself can get confusing. I want to make sure that at least 60 to 65%, say at least 900, of "those type" of names are issued vouchers. Do you get my drift? This is important, and don't just move them up front. That would be too obvious. Work them in. Can you do it?"

James's eyebrows raised slightly, but he was used to working with Dwight. "No problem, Boss. Consider it done. And before you say it, I will. We never had this conversation."

Both men smiled, and James headed back out to soldier on.

19.

Dwight Lamar was excited to be in Houston, our nation's fourth-largest city and a diverse melting pot where people from virtually every ethnicity, race, and heritage call home. It was a perfect place for him to set his master plan in motion. With little geographic and minimal zoning constraints, the metropolis extended to all points of the compass with pockets and clusters of folks with similar backgrounds occurring randomly throughout. Owing to a historical disdain for zoning, affluence and poverty were often found in close proximity. A prime example of this urban inconsistency occurred along the southwest freeway just a short drive from Sugarland, in affluent and fast-booming Fort Bend County. The "Gulfton Ghetto," characterized by low-income, ethnically diverse families in densely populated clusters of apartments, had evolved right across the freeway from the Galleria, one of the city's most upscale retail-office settings. Drugs, alcohol, prostitution, and all that goes with them were readily available. English was the primary spoken language in fewer than half of the households. To be sure, there were worse places in the huge city, but few others encompassed such a wide range of ethnic variety in a single location.

George Nguyen was a gang banger who lived in a small, two-bedroom Gulfton apartment with his mother, Mary, a refugee from Vietnam some thirty years ago. George's father had long ago disappeared. Mary struggled to support her only child by cleaning rooms in a motel across the freeway near the Galleria. Stretching her meager wages to pay all her bills, especially the apartment rent, was a challenge. As difficult as things were, Mary clearly understood that they could be far worse. She had applied for citizenship in her adopted country. During that process, she learned about a government program that gave out vouchers to pay the rent. She eventually visited the Houston Housing Authority and made an application. Unfortunately, the program was out of money, so she was placed on a waiting list with a very high number. After several years she slowly moved up the list, and finally she was approaching the top. In fact, when the new mega housing authority was created, she had moved all the way up to number fifty-seven. Neither she nor George really understood how such programs work, but when SETUP's new voucher funding was announced, word spread fast. For the first time, Mary had reason to believe she might actually get a "voucher paper."

Dwight and his group had been burning the midnight oil and had done a commendable job in processing a huge number of vouchers so quickly. Dwight's experience during the Katrina crisis in New Orleans served him well. His new Houston workload could not begin to compare to those days. Getting a person qualified for a voucher is a big part of the process, but still, once you are approved, you must find an approved place to live.

It was almost noon on a steamy Houston morning. George Nguyen stood outside of a Mini Mart convenience store on Bissonnett Street, a block from where he lived with his mother. He and two fellow gang members were passing around a joint. George was almost twenty, and was getting old for the gang banger scene. He had been thinking about getting a job, but so far, there hadn't been any visible effort. As a tenth-grade dropout, his opportunities were limited. He had slicked-back, greasy, dark spiked hair with a tail at the back. A thin black mustache line was barely noticeable over his upper lip. He was slight in build, but looked threatening in an all-black outfit including biker boots with hobnailed heels. He kept a stiletto in a sheath fastened to his lower right leg. As the joint burned down, one of his buddies suggested heading over to Popeye's Chicken across the street for some lunch. Before they could leave, George's diminutive mother ambled up to them on the sidewalk.

Mary had no illusions about the daily activities of her son. Finding him loafing at a convenience store in the middle of the day smoking pot was not especially alarming. George, however, was surprised by her and quickly "lost" the joint after one last drag. "Hi, Mamma. I thought you'd be getting your rest after working all night. Are you out shopping? What's up?"

Mary looked up at her offspring. As a rule, people from her country were industrious and hardworking. They could not stand to be idle. Yet, here was her child, a school dropout who never worked a day in his life. She sighed. Nonetheless, she loved him just the same.

"No, George. Actually, I was looking for you. I got this notice in the mail today, and I don't understand it. I thought I was very close to getting one of those rent voucher things. Read this," she said, as she handed him a computer-generated tear-at-the-edges notice. It was printed with Southeast Texas Unified Partnership at the top and read:

Dear Ms. Nguyen:

Under the regulations of the Departmental Housing and Urban Development and the State of Texas, we are obligated to notify you where you stand as an applicant of the Housing Choice Voucher Program. We are pleased to notify you that you are now listed as number 613 on our waiting list. Unfortunately, there are not sufficient funds for all applicants to this program. We will keep you informed of your position from time to time. If you desire to have your name removed from the list, please contact us at your earliest convenience at the number listed below.

James R. Luken Supervisor

George was not a good reader, but he got the sense of this letter pretty quickly. "What was your number a few weeks ago?"

"It said I was number fifty-seven. Now I am way over six hundred. I will never get there. I am going backwards. What happened?" she pleaded, with a hint of despair in her voice.

"I sure don't know. Those idiots don't have a clue. They are supposed to have more money now. I am pissed. I am going down there to talk to them in person. They can't treat us that way. You are such a hardworking person." George, who had a low boiling point was getting mad. "Damn those bastards! I'll let you know, Mamma!" he called out, as he stuffed the notice into his pocket, walked over to his Kawasaki Z1 motorcycle, and strapped on his helmet.

"George, please be careful!" Mary called after him as he tore out into the street.

Dwight recognized from the start that a big drawback of his cramped office space was that there was no way to accommodate the lines of people that came to visit them. They would just have to hang on until they found a larger space, which he was already discussing with the board. Dwight was thinking about how they might expand when an incensed George Nguyen stormed into their office and demanded to see "James Luken, Supervisor." The slick-haired greaser was shown into their tiny conference room, which was crammed with boxes of files. At a desk nearby, James calmly set down his glasses, rubbed his eyes, and walked slowly towards the conference room. He opened the door and walked in. For the next half-hour, the raised voice and shouts of the Asian man thundered through the office. Finally, the door flew open and the fuming fellow burst out, never glancing at anyone as he marched out of the office.

James followed him out of the conference room a few seconds later. All he could say to his office staff was, "Whew!" as he walked over to Dwight's closed door, where he knocked and entered. Dwight looked up from a report he had been reading. He had heard the commotion, but it was not his style to get involved in super-charged emotional situations where he might not come out on top.

"That was George Nguyen, the son of a Mary Nguyen, apparently one of the voucher applicants transferred from the Houston Housing Authority. Oh, and he is also a gang banger, and was considerate enough to let me see the stiletto strapped to his leg."

Dwight's eyebrows flickered up. He made a mental note; they needed security—soon.

"This guy's mother," James continued, "was number fifty or so on the Houston list. She just got a notice from us that she is number 613. Here is a copy of the notice his mother got in the mail. He lives with her. He was very upset, obviously. He threatened to go to their local city councilman if it wasn't fixed."

"Who is it?"

"Actually, Boss, it is your old buddy, Councilman Francesca." Dwight smiled, "That is interesting. We really can't have that. What did you tell this fellow, James?"

"Only that I would check on it and get back to him. He could look around and see how busy we were. We couldn't possibly remember every file."

"Good. I'll take it from here. Thanks." Without another word, the "Supervisor" got up and left the office. During the entire incident, his pulse never beat an extra beat. He'd been around Dwight Lamar too long.

Back in his office with the door shut, the executive director hit a speed dial number on his cell. The conversation was brief, with just a short bit of information passed along.

George had cooled down considerably by the time he got back to Gulfton. As he suspected, there were nothing but assholes at that housing authority. He'd never hear back from that guy, who barely seemed to be awake, even when he was screaming at him and let him see his blade. At least he tried to do something for his mother. He walked into the apartment, where she was preparing to go to work. She thanked him, but said she was convinced that she'd never get that voucher thing money. She said she would see him in the morning. Sadly, those were her last words to her only child.

George kissed the old woman on the forehead and headed back out to find his friends. They headed to a local roadhouse a few miles away near the Barker-Cypress Reservoir. After several longnecks and tequila shots, during which he told and retold his buddies about getting a piece of that government asshole, "You guys should have seen him when he saw my blade," it was well after midnight when he staggered alone out to his bike in the poorly-lit gravel parking lot. He never knew what hit him when the tire iron came down to crush his skull. Just another banger wiped out by a biker. Seemed to happen almost every night. Yes, his mother did see him the next morning, but it was in the city morgue. Perhaps his effort was not entirely wasted. As Dwight headed out the door that evening, he told James to go ahead and fund Mrs. Nguyen's voucher.

20.

Dwight Lamar was a deep-thinking and well-organized man. He had been through a lot in his short life of just over three decades and, if he hadn't learned anything else, it was that patience is a golden virtue. Haste and greed had brought down many otherwise well-conceived plans. After the first six months, he gradually maneuvered his new mega housing authority in the direction that would best suit his ultimate objectives. The organization was making demonstrable progress, but remained out of view of everyone except those he could not avoid, namely his board of directors and the HUD staff who were charged with overseeing his operations. A misstep with either group, and his program could be derailed overnight.

He expected, and was not disappointed, when pangs of jealousy and protectiveness erupted from the two existing housing authorities, who were understandably resentful that their domains had been invaded by Dwight's group. He had already "pirated' their voucher waiting lists. Both groups were scrutinizing his every move, ready to pounce on his first misstep. He had no intention of tripping up and giving them a chance to do him in.

HUD, however, presented a much different issue. SETUP was a brand-new animal on the farm and, as a consequence, was in for intense oversight and auditing, at least for a while. Dwight knew that after his group got through a few audits and reviews with exemplary ratings, the scrutiny and attention from the HUD watchdogs would substantially decrease. That was, of course, human nature. Doesn't the teacher expect her best students to receive the best grades? Naturally, she does. Once Dwight proved himself and established a comfort level with the federal watchdogs, he would have more freedom to operate.

Dwight had to be careful during the incubation stage of his new "baby," SETUP. He was determined to convert this opportunity into a big score. He needed to resist the sometimes glaring opportunities that festered within some of the HUD programs. It would be simple to create back door income streams through these voucher programs, as he had used in New Orleans when every-one was desperate for the programs to get up and running again after the horrible flood. No-one cared what happened along the way—for a while—as long as the "po' folks" got housing. For instance, it was easy during the confusion of the Katrina crisis to direct the voucher funds to any of the devastated parts of the city where the locals wanted them the most and were willing to pay for them. Even HUD didn't care as long as poor displaced people were getting back into decent, safe, clean and dry homes.

He knew that the most frequent scam under the voucher program occurred during the tenant recertification process, by falsifying both the number of residents living in an apartment and understating the income level of the families holding the vouchers. More residents living in a unit meant more HUD cash, and holding income levels below program level maximums kept families in the program even after they were making too much money. Therein lies the Catch-22 of many welfare programs. As a needy family's income from employment increases, the government benefits are supposed to drop off. The more you earn, the less Uncle Sam kicks in, leaving a disincentive to improve yourself. Of course, maybe you can have the best of both worlds, with the help of a friendly income re-certifier. Again, these opportunities were rampant after Katrina, and people were willing to pay for them. Eventually, HUD did catch up in Louisiana, but long after he was gone. His old friend and mentor, Mayor Ray Nagin, did go to jail, but he was caught with his hand in a much bigger cookie jar right out in the open. Dwight had learned a great deal at the unfortunate mayor's expense.

He was much too smart to consider such penny-ante schemes in Houston, except from a very self-serving angle. He knew he was walking a tightrope with the HUD auditors, as would any new group. All his programs must be kept squeaky clean and audit-proof. The waiting list jockeying was dangerous enough, but he decided that maybe he could turn the tables and create a situation to ingratiate himself to the HUD folks. His group would play sanctimonious whistle-blower to root out cheaters within the HUD system. He smiled when he thought about personally uncovering attempts to contravene the program and turning them over to the auditors.

Lenny Fogelman was a bright enough man, who, at fifty, had worked in a number of different manual trades in the residential construction industry. He was a bachelor who lived in a small home on the southwest side of Houston. He was rail-thin, with a poor complexion, and teeth that had desperately needed but never received braces. He was shy around women. He couldn't remember the last date he'd had. Overall, though, Lenny had never aspired to be or achieve much, which was fine with him. He was basically content, and didn't care about much other than his Heinz fifty-seven mutt and being able to knock back a few cold ones at the neighborhood watering hole cheering on the Texans, Rockets, and Astros.

Then one day, Lenny noticed a pickup truck on his street that belonged to a home inspector. Maybe that could work for him? He could be his own boss, work at his own pace, and surely, with all his years of construction knowledge, the inspections themselves would be a piece of cake. When Lenny looked into the inspection business, he discovered an even better deal. He could become a HUD-certified inspector involved in the inspection of apartment units for Section 8 voucher tenants. The work was almost all computerized, steady, and reasonably simple. It took him a while to become certified, but once his name was on the right list, a steady stream of work came his way. The pay wasn't terrific, but enough to keep the pup in kibble and him in longnecks, and he didn't have to work that hard. Lenny Fogelman had never been confused with a person who was ambitious.

Lenny had been a HUD inspector for about four years when one morning, he was inspecting units on an apartment property in southwest Houston. It was a humid day and his shirt was sopping wet. He was happy to see that it was almost noon and was just about to break for lunch. As he walked along the sidewalks and emerged from the interior section of the property to his pickup near the leasing office, he noticed two Houston Police Department cruisers parked nearby. He was curious, but not particularly surprised or alarmed. Police calls to some of these apartments was a daily experience. In fact, he was trying to decide where to go to lunch when three uniformed officers suddenly appeared and surrounded him. He was ordered to the ground. He stared in disbelief and tried to reason with them but was looking straight down the barrel of a police .38. One held him down as his arms were roughly wrestled behind him and tightly cuffed.

"Officers! Officers! What is going on? I haven't done anything. I work here. I'm a HUD inspector. Please!"

All he heard from one of the burly cops was, "You have the right to remain silent...." and on through the entire Miranda warning. A crowd of gawking apartment residents surrounded them. He was lifted to his feet and herded into the manager's office. The door was closed behind him. The manager, a woman about his age, was sitting behind her desk. She looked away. He had known her for some time, having inspected many units in her complex. He had even gone to lunch one time with her and a group of employees. A young, sobbing African-American girl was sitting next to her. The police positioned him to stand right in front of her desk.

"Do you know this man?" the police sergeant, asked the manager.

"I do," she replied. "He is a HUD inspector. He has been out here many times to inspect units."

"Has there ever been a problem with him before today?" the sergeant asked.

"Not while he was here, but some of our residents have reported missing items from their apartments after he had been here."

Lenny could not believe what he was hearing. "Surely you don't think… you don't think that I had anything to do with that? That's crazy!" he stammered incredulously. She didn't answer.

The sergeant then motioned to one of the other officers, who handed him two plastic evidence bags, which he held up one at a time. Looking at the tearful young woman sitting next to the manager, he asked, "You are a tenant here, ma'am, are you not?"

"Ye-yes, officer, I live here."

"Do you recognize the items in these bags?"

She looked at them closely. "Yes, officer, I think so. The small one is my pearl ring that my mother gave me just before she died, and the other looks like a pair of my red panties. I thought I'd lost both of them."

"Can you think of any reason both these items would have been stuffed under the front seat of Mr. Fogelman's pickup truck out there?"

She began to cry again, but whimpered a weak, "No, sir."

"That is impossible! It can't be! I've never seen those things or this woman before in my life!" Lenny pleaded.

"Oh, and one more thing before we take him downtown." The sergeant looked at the manager. "Didn't you tell us that this man approached you for extra payments to get an acceptable inspection?"

The manager hesitated but calmly replied, "Well, at lunch he did tell me that we were getting the best inspections 'that money can buy.'"

Lenny cut her off. "I was just kidding! It was a joke. I can't believe…" He tried to continue, but was yanked around and pushed through the door out towards the backseat of a waiting squad car.

In an eye blink, the life of Lenny Fogelman, an insignificant but good and decent man, was quashed. Even if he happened to beat the charges, he'd never do another inspection.

Dwight Lamar contacted the key local HUD co-ordinator and made him aware of unfortunate rumors that had crossed his desk concerning an independent HUD inspector. Dwight's concern, of course, was that none of his voucher folks end up in an unfit unit passed by an improperly motivated person. The HUD man assured Dwight that he would immediately look into the matter. When the suspicions about the man were confirmed based on Dwight's tip, he scored points with HUD people, which was exactly what he had in mind. Framing poor Fogelman required little more than another call to Beaumont to start the ball rolling. Another bug was smashed on the windshield, but Dwight was still cruising right along.

******

Dwight's primary interface with his all-important board was at quarterly board meetings, where he was on the carpet and in the bright spotlight. It took him a few meetings to analyze each of his collective bosses to figure out where their hot buttons lay. He knew he had no chance with the UH professor. It was just a matter of keeping her at bay. She was largely ignored by everyone else anyway. Henry Francesca, however, was another story. The man had plenty of influence on the board and would make a very unpleasant enemy.

Since he was not the Hispanic director's man, if anything, Francesca would revel in Dwight's failure. Clearly, it was in his best interest to earn as many positive points with the man as possible. As an African American, he could never completely win over this champion of the barrio, but he had a trick or two up his sleeve. Francesca's primary opposition to Dwight, although he would never, ever admit it, was his race. Heretofore in Houston politics, the rule had been simple: a brown man in control favored his group, and a black man always catered to the blacks. It was indisputable, almost an unwritten law. No less was expected from Dwight Lamar. The politics had gotten a black man in during this cycle. Francesca would bide his time until Lamar screwed up or left for some reason. The next ED would certainly come from the Hispanic community.

At the most recent board meeting, Dwight stood in front of the group and held forth on the progress of SETUP while the directors thumbed through the reports that had been prepared for them. As they listened and looked at the written material, most of the directors, including Francesca, seemed impressed at the detail and comprehensive nature of the information presented. Francesca was especially interested in the allocation of vouchers from the "borrowed" waiting lists of the other HAs. Dwight sensed that the man would try to flush him out in that area and reveal his true colors, so to speak. Francesca flipped through the report until he found the voucher program section.

The director was a cat ready to pounce on an unsuspecting mouse. He peered closely at the figures presented. He acted confused and then noticed a footnote, which he read and reread. Still not satisfied, he reached into his coat pocket and put on his "cheaters" to read the footnote a third time. Councilman Francesca looked up. He was astonished. Under Dwight Lamar, a black man, over 68% of the new vouchers were given to families that had Hispanic surnames. He simply could not believe it. What was this guy all about?

21.

After making sure things had settled down at the office and his mother was fine, a few minutes before five o'clock, rush hour traffic notwithstanding, Matt headed straight home. He had been away for a while and was anxious to see Ellen and the kids. Their place was a few miles from the office in the leafy-green Memorial area of near west Houston. The homes in his neighborhood were upscale, but not nearly up to the quality or price range of Tanglewood, where he had been raised. As president of Mesquite Development under his father, his ample salary had been more than sufficient to support a several-hundred-thousand-dollar mortgage. After the firm was reorganized and had to rely strictly on management fee revenue, Matt's paycheck shrank considerably. So far, they had been able to afford to stay in Memorial. The allure of a bigger salary had been a significant factor in Matt's pursuit of the opportunity in Virginia.

As Matt waited for the last stoplight on Memorial Drive before the entrance to his subdivision, he reflected on how lucky he had been. Although he had been a part of a cataclysmic implosion of a company that ultimately resulted in the loss of his father, somehow, he had been able to avoid most of the legal entanglements that the entire mess had created. Despite multiple charges and allegations against his father by the US Drug Enforcement Agency and the limited partners who shared ownership in their properties, Matt, who had actually resigned from the company just before everything blew up, had been omitted from the lawsuits and actions the investors brought to protect their investments. While he was now prohibited from ever actually developing properties again, he was at least free to pursue other types of business, such as property management. He could have been ensnared in the legal jumble and banned from any activities in the real estate industry. Prison time had also been a distinct possibility. He'd dodged a huge bullet.

All those work-related horrors aside, however, Matt also knew how fortunate he was to have found Ellen, when they were both students at Texas A&M. They married right after graduation almost ten years ago. His wife was a vivacious redhead whose mercurial temperament proved to be the perfect complement to her laid-back and conservative-minded husband. Ever the optimist, Ellen's basic conviction in life was that if you didn't succeed in something, it was simply because you just didn't try hard enough.

Matt was the inveterate worrywart and reluctant to move until he was absolutely sure of things. Ellen sorted things out as they came, mostly at full speed. She was a workout warrior who went to the gym every morning and then ran four or five miles. A head shorter than her six-foot husband, she kept her body in excellent shape with toned and curvaceous legs, a trim waist, and ample bustline. Her fair complexion helped set off her bright-green eyes, rosy cheeks, and sensuous mouth. As a regular member of the dean's list in college, she was no slouch in the classroom, but she realized some time ago that what she wanted most in life was a good husband, terrific kids, and a warm home. She was prepared to join the workforce if the economics demanded it, but she took pride in making their home as wonderful as possible.

Less than two years after they were married, fate blessed them with their first child, Rusty, who quickly acquired that nickname for obvious reasons. His given name was actually Travis, in honor of his grandfather. If Travis Nelson was pleased at that choice for his grandson, he never gave any outward indication. Rusty was now an active seven-year-old thoroughly immersed in sports and outdoor activities. Gail arrived to grace the Nelson household three years ago. Still a toddler, she was fast developing a personality, which both parents acknowledged in many ways bore a striking resemblance to her aunt Pam. Batten down the hatches if that trend continued.

Matt pulled into his driveway and sat there a minute to admire his charming and comfortable home. It would be a shame if they had to move. Thick landscaping hid from view all but the two entrances to the circular driveway, which were guarded by rough red used brick pillars topped with elegant post lights. Dozens of mature, stately oaks bordered a lush St. Augustine lawn. The house itself was a rambling single-story structure with rough gray lap and gap wood siding with a huge central picture window. Vigorous English ivy and myrtle ground cover filled in the shady patches spreading from the house, drives, and lawn. In all, they had almost an acre of land, and even though their neighbors were quite close on either side, it was impossible to see their homes.

Matt drove into the attached garage and glanced down to unsnap his seat belt. He pushed open his door and was blindsided by a whirling blond-haired three-year-old, whom he swept up into his arms. "Daddy! Daddy! I am so glad you are home. I missed you so much. Mommy said that when you came home I could play Pokémon on your iPad. Can I, Daddy? Can I?" the words rushed out of this little angel's mouth.

Matt grinned and drank in the length of the bundle of energy in his arms. He replied, "Well, I guess so, as long as I get a good report from Mommy about how you have been while I was gone."

"Oh, I have been very good, Daddy. Mommy will tell you that." Matt had hardly set down the little whirlwind, who scurried off to find her mother, when a basketball bounced into his hands. Rusty was standing in the driveway just a few feet away, wildly gesturing for a pass back. Matt grabbed the ball and faked a pass in his son's direction. He then dribbled towards the youth basketball hoop set up on the edge of the driveway. Just before he was about to go in for a layup, he tossed the ball behind his back to the youngster, who immediately chucked up his own shot that rattled around the rim and dropped in. "Way to go, Rus!" Matt yelled. He then walked over and hugged his son and they walked towards the house where Ellen and Gail were waiting on the front step.

Matt gave his wife a warm kiss, and the four of them went inside together. The family's one-hundred-sixty-pound Bullmastiff charged at his missing master before they could even shut the front door. The huge dog's entire body seemed to wag as he crowded in for an affectionate ear rub. The good-natured canine was not to be denied until he received his part of Matt's homecoming and left a big slobber stain on his shoes to prove it.

The family spent a relaxing dinner catching up on the kids' activities over the past weeks that Matt had been gone. The school, social, and fun activities were gushed forth nonstop by the two children. Not surprisingly, though, he did have to dig some for details on classroom progress and any discipline from mom. Matt and Ellen were pleased to let the children ramble on. They knew they could catch up with each other when the little ones went off to bed. It was a school night, so Rusty was in bed before nine. His sister had surrendered about an hour earlier.

It was almost nine thirty before Ellen poured them each a glass of Coco Bon, their favorite red wine, and they settled next to each other on the couch in their family room. Like many homes in the Bayou City, the Nelson's lot bordered on a small stream that meandered through the woods at the back of the property. The architect who designed the home endeavored to make the beautiful outside woodland features as visible as possible from inside. He had wisely inserted a large window that overlooked the backyard and trickling water. The damp, almost swampy ground gave rise to an abundance of plant life, including palmettos, pines, oaks, and many other varieties of vegetation. With a few strategically positioned landscape lights, even after dark their backyard presented an elegant and relaxing forest scene.

As they sipped wine, Matt started to recap his activities and discussions with John in Virginia. He hadn't gone too far, though, when Ellen interrupted, "Wait. First, before you get into that, tell me about your mom and what happened at the office today. Is she okay?"

"Oh, yeah. Okay. Right. Yes, she is fine now, but I guess it was tense for a while. Luckily, believe it or not, the infamous Pamela showed up in the nick of time and literally drove the thug out of the office."

"Who was the guy? Why was he there in the first place?"

"Well, after sitting home all those years, mom has done well in the business world, but she is still learning. One of our properties fired a guy, and she decided to conduct the exit interview herself at the office. It sounds good, but was probably not the best thing to do."

"So that fired guy attacked her?"

"Well, no, not exactly. We thought it was him at first, but then the real fired guy actually showed up later. We don't know who actually attacked her, or how he even knew to be there."

"What did he do?"

"This is the weirdest part of all. He got her alone in her office with the door shut and then threatened her about the whereabouts of my father. It looked like he was going to get rough when Pam and Sandy burst in. Pam swatted him with a golf club and he bolted before the police arrived."

"Wow. That's strange. As far as the world knows, your father died in Mexico. Right?"

"Of course. I have always assumed that was the case. We talked to John about the attack, and he feels it might have been by a US gang that works closely with the Mexican cartels."

"Gee, Matt, after all that stuff two years ago with the cartel, I hoped we'd heard the last from them," Ellen lamented with real concern in her voice.

"Me too. We have already beefed up security at the office and will have an armed guard on the premises whenever anyone is working." He did not speculate about any possible cartel-gang connection concerning the attack in North Carolina. There was no sense unduly worrying her.

Matt spent the next hour rehashing his escapade with John and Harvey, being careful not to make the gang connection. They had discussed most of it on the phone anyway. Then, they were both silent for a moment, lost in their own thoughts and a now empty bottle of wine.

"Okay, then," Ellen began carefully picking her words, "I just want to be convinced of one thing. Are you absolutely sure that the John thing is totally out of your system? I mean, absolutely sure. As much as I love the way things are now, I need you to be happy. You know I will support you, whatever you choose. Am I clear on that? Crystal clear?"

Matt looked directly into the radiating green eyes of the woman sitting across from him, but did not answer. He continued only to stare at his beautiful wife. In fact, he noticed that the third button on her blouse had become undone.

"Matt!" she pleaded. He remained silent. "Matt!" she almost screamed. He suddenly blinked and smiled, "Oh, yeah, sure. That's not my bag."

As she took a second to digest his words, her mouth turned up to form a silly grin. She then reached over, grabbed his hand, and they both staggered towards the bedroom.

22.

A sense of serenity washed over Matt as he lay there in bed next to his slumbering wife. He felt the reassuring shape of her bottom against his legs and savored the sweet, lingering smell of their lovemaking. After being away for a while, it was always good to come home. The juices that flowed in their thirty-year-old bodies seemed to make things especially satisfying after being apart for a while. That was not to say that Ellen was not a willing, co-operative, and pleasing lover, because she was certainly all those things. It just seemed strange to him that the eagerness and satisfaction was always so much higher after he was gone for a while.

Matt was a deep thinker, who was compelled constantly to reflect, re-reflect, analyze, and re-analyze all aspects of his life. He knew that their sex life was an important aspect of their relationship, but it was only one of many factors that contributed to a happy marriage. After the long flight back and the incident at the office, Matt should have been exhausted, but sleep still eluded him. His own personal mind monster continued to thrash around in his head. Despite his repeated statements to John, Harvey, his mother, and Ellen that the executive security field was not right for him, the issue still tormented him. Yes, he had been "Mr. Conservative" all his life. He had always been "Mr. Good," if not "Mr. Great." Vice president, never president. He always took the road well-traveled and not the more perilous and exciting alternative. His risk threshold was limited. Buy blue chip stocks and collect 5%. Stay away from speculation with high potential returns but also high risk of loss.

He often wondered why he had embraced this attitude and general philosophy. It was convenient to duck into the excuse of his family situation. He had a wife and two children to think about. Concern for them came first and, of course, it always would. Hell, even if he were a jet test pilot, he'd never subordinate his job to the welfare of his family. He worried compulsively about everything, or so it seemed. He loved their fantastic house, as did his whole family. So far, two years after the debacle, they had been able to still afford it, but that might change. Would he be able to continue to make the high payments? In fact, he guessed, even if he were single, he would be a paper pusher in an office. That was his nature. Still, there was a restlessness inside him that sometimes cried to be let out. Would he ever answer that cry?

John had never been afraid to take chances. In fact, he thrived on them. Not only did he and Harvey frequently find themselves in dangerous situations, but they had also put all their personal resources on the line in their business with huge financial investments in people and equipment. Their next paycheck was only as good as their next assignment. Their business could turn down overnight and creditors would sweep in like vultures. Ironically, even Pam, as scatter-brained as she was, appeared at times to have more "balls" than he did. She didn't hesitate to follow her heart. Of course, she tended to do that a few times a month, which was a little much.

And then what about his father, Travis Nelson? He also was not afraid to wing it. He started from very little and created one of the most successful real estate organizations in Texas. He had been highly respected in the business community. He had bankers and investors lined up to do business with him. He owned a string of successful properties and was virtually rolling in cash. Matt had been a part of that process, after a fashion. He could not help that he loved and admired his father. He looked up to Travis Nelson, despite the fact that the man kept him on a very short leash. Matt was the "president" of Mesquite Development, but that title was in name only. Every major decision was made independently by his father, often without even telling Matt. For the first few years, Matt marched along as a good soldier, following his father's dictates to the letter. Often, his orders involved some ethically questionable business practices involving competitors. Matt carried on without hesitation. He was just happy to hold the title of president of such a successful company, and was paid a healthy salary as well. A groggy Matt tossed and turned and reached out to find Ellen's hand. Thinking back now, Matt could see that just before he left his father's company, he had become disenchanted with his real role, even if he was supposed to be the top person. He remembered having to swallow his pride when the Durango Deal with the Mexican drug cartel surfaced, and his father sought the counsel of his female floozy office manager, with whom he had been conducting a very obvious affair, rather than talk to him.

The final straw came when his father ordered him to use unsavory tactics against a competitive project. Matt balked, openly refused, and then to his own surprise, resigned on the spot. His father took it completely in stride and made zero attempt to dissuade him, or even encourage him to think it over.

He marched out of that office having made no future plans whatsoever. He remembered being nervous when he called Ellen to tell her what he had just done. What a woman. She was thrilled for him. She encouraged him not to worry, the family would be just fine. How could he ask for anything more?

Soon thereafter, his father's company had come crashing down, and the man who had ruled it mysteriously disappeared. Matt was surprised how much clearer everything seemed looking back at it now than when he actually lived through it. He had been so naive and blind. Travis Nelson had built a terrific company but at tremendous personal cost. His unethical business practices may not have been obvious to outsiders, but they were very much a part of his success. He showed little personal loyalty to the employees that had helped build his company. His marriage vows meant nothing, and he openly took other women whenever he chose. Perhaps worst of all, he completely ignored his family, which he used as a tool to reinforce his pristine business image. He felt that as long as he kept Diane and the kids well supplied with physical affluence, his job as a father and husband was complete. Poor Diane stayed at home and turned to the false sanctuary of alcohol. John had it out with Travis and took off on his own as soon as he could. They never reconciled. Pam was her father's special one and the only member whom he doted upon at all. Pam was able to use him to her own advantage. Her bulging clothes closet was testimony to that situation. That left Matt, who obediently did his father's bidding without question. Unfortunately, just like the warm puppy who approached his father to have his head scratched, he was coldly kicked away.

It had taken years, but Matt finally realized he wanted no part of his father's way of doing things. Dollars and cents success be damned. Still, when the man disappeared, family devotion trumped all, and the entire family rallied together to find him. If it had been his goal to exorcise all possible love from them, on that score he was an abject failure. All, including John, still cared deeply. They literally went to the ends of the earth to find him.

Now there was this other problem—the Surenos gang. If he really wanted something to worry about, that was tops on the list. Until recently, he had been convinced that any interest a Mexican cartel might have in them died with Travis Nelson. The company's total involvement with that unsavory group had been handled by his father. In fact, very few people at Mesquite Development even knew the deal had been made. It ended very abruptly, with the DEA right in the middle. That was over two years ago. What could the Mexicans possibly want from them now? Were they owed money? Was it revenge? The guy in Diane's office had demanded to know Travis's whereabouts. The man was dead and buried, as had been reported in every newscast on both sides of the border. Even the US legal justice system had accepted the fact that he was dead.

The Surenos angle was not something he could afford to ignore. It needed to be investigated. He would contact the local DEA agent, who unfortunately he had gotten to know only too well. He had been very candid with Ellen on almost everything, except for the Surenos attack on him in Virginia. He really didn't want her to worry about that.

Pure exhaustion finally claimed Matt Nelson just an hour or two before he had to get up. He promised himself to soldier on in the morning. After all, the plodder who never gave up; that's who he was.

23.

Matt was anxious to get out and start selling his consulting services. He was excited and arrived at the office early before anyone else, prepared to dig in. He had been in the multifamily and government-assisted development business long enough to be convinced there was a demand for his expertise, especially among the less sophisticated network of do-good non-profit firms. Such groups were committed to providing adequate housing for the unfortunate, but simply did not have the budgets to maintain qualified development personnel on their own payrolls.

He was also aware that in most cases, governmental organizations like the IRS and the Texas Department of Housing and Community Affairs (TDHCA) recognized the bona fide need for the services he would supply and permitted them as cost certifiable project expenses. Although he was personally banned from developing new projects for his own account, perhaps he could harness some of his creative enthusiasm for the process on behalf of clients. He spent an hour or two sketching up a simple organization chart for his effort and even composed a job description for the single analyst he would need at the start.

The new fun stuff aside, he turned to more pressing and sobering matters. He knew he had to contact the local Houston office of the Drug Enforcement Agency and find out all he could about this Surenos group. Always mindful of how close he had come personally to being targeted by them, he nonetheless needed to make them aware of the two recent incidents. The DEA phone call was not an easy one for Matt to make. After all, Travis Nelson's show or not, Matt had been president of an organization that had been caught red-handed doing illegal business across the border with one of Mexico's largest and most vicious drug cartels. Even though he'd largely been left in the dark about the deal by his father, he was lucky to have escaped prosecution when the feds moved in. He had avoided prosecution at least in part because of a side deal he negotiated to help the DEA. Although Matt was very frustrated at the time by his father's lack of communication with him, clearly it was by design. Travis kept Matt on the sidelines about the cartel arrangement, to protect him. Matt truly did have plausible deniability. He didn't know the details of the Durango Deal. All that said, Matt thanked his lucky stars daily.

He knew to leave well enough alone. The local DEA representatives were not pleased to give him immunity, especially when the real big cheese, Travis Nelson, had eluded them and was killed.

Finally, he picked up his phone and called Kevin Forney, special agent in charge of the Houston office. He was immediately put through and with virtually no chitchat, arranged to meet in the DEA offices the next afternoon. Matt had learned about the long arm of the DEA. The Drug Enforcement Administration (DEA) is part of the United States Department of Justice, with a mission that involves the enforcement of the Controlled Substances Act by bringing those persons or groups who violate the act into the formal criminal justice system of the United States.

As was his custom, Matt was fifteen minutes early for the meeting with the drug cop, who returned his punctuality by keeping him cooling his heels for thirty minutes in the waiting room, coffee-less, and flipping through six-month-old copies of the Government Times under the likeness of a vigilant eagle on the plastic Department of Justice – Drug Enforcement Agency logo on the wall facing him.

Matt's trepidation eased only slightly as he entered Forney's office and the man got up from behind his desk with a big smile and warmly shook his hand. "Matt, it is good to see you. How have you been? How's your mother doing?" Matt realized that the guy would probably have greeted El Chapo about the same way if the famous Mexican gangster walked into his office.

Matt crafted his words carefully during the meeting. He knew these government guys would give away nothing but were always alert for any tidbits they could squeeze out of the other side. Matt was there for information, not to reopen any recently-healed scar. "Fine, Kevin, both my mother and I are doing well. Thanks for asking," Matt replied. There was no sense going anywhere near their state of mind about losing their husband and father. Forney's next question might be "Well, how is your dad? Have you heard from him lately?"

After a brief pause, when it was clear that Matt was not going to elaborate on the most basic small talk, Forney asked, "So, what's up?"

"I decided to call you, Kevin, primarily at the suggestion of my brother, John, who runs a corporate security business over in Virginia, near DC. You may remember him."

Forney nodded that he did.

"There have been two incidents recently involving both myself and my mother that I need to tell you about. I suppose that it is very unlikely that either of them relates back to my father's company, but on the off chance they might, John suggested that I run them by you. That whole mess happened more than two years ago. I was convinced we had heard the last of that, but I would like to have your input, if I may."

"Of course, Matt. I am interested to hear what has you concerned. As for the cartels, I have devoted my entire working life to the eradication of those monsters. We have made wonderful progress in some areas, but somehow, they seem to be operating bigger and better than ever. Tell me what happened."

Matt proceeded to give Forney a decidedly edited version of the incident along the Virginia interstate, as well as the attack on his mother at work. He decided to keep the part about the impostor employee's demand about his father to himself. He also indicated that the state police in North Carolina had mentioned the Surenos gang as a possibility. Matt asked Forney if he had any information about that group being active here in Houston.

Forney looked at him with rapt interest. At one point, just after Matt finished his stories, the DEA man's eyebrows seemed to twitch just a bit. "That is interesting, but why do you think the Surenos may be involved? I know the Carolina police mentioned them, but what about here in Texas? Is there a connection?"

Matt thought for a moment. This guy is very cagey. I'll bet he knows things that I don't. Unfortunately for Matt, that assumption turned out to be right on. "I guess it is because of my brother, who knows a lot more about these things than I do. The guy here was dressed in a blue Dallas Mavericks jersey. John says that blue is popular with them."

Forney smiled. "Come on, Matt, there must have been something else. I know we are in Houston, but Dallas is only a couple of hundred miles away. I am sure you can buy blue jerseys all over Houston."

Matt had blown it. He wondered if he should try damage control or just hang on. Before he could decide, Forney tossed his cards on the table. "You know, Matt, we solve things and set cases aside, but we rarely close them tight forever, especially a big one like Mesquite Development. We keep our monitoring information outlets online for quite a while. In fact, I have a copy of the police report on your mother's attack right here on my desk. I was already well aware of it when you called. I was intrigued to read that the perp, or whatever he was, tried to find out from your mother where Travis Nelson is now." Matt hoped his complexion was not as red as it felt. He could not think of anything he could say that would help his situation, so he remained silent.

Forney waited for Matt to respond, but when he didn't, he added, "I also noted in the report that your mother told the guy that he is dead and buried. Right?"

Matt nodded.

Forney continued. "You know, I appreciate your coming here today. If these Surenos guys are lurking around, we need to know about it. You and your family could be in great danger. No-one wants that to happen. The actions we, the collective government entities, took two-plus years ago were long considered, discussed, and deliberated. Nothing was done in haste. Our decisions were final, but can always be reopened. Please do not ever give us a reason to doubt. Am I clear, Matt?" he concluded with strong emphasis and looked the man across the table directly in his eyes.

Matt swallowed hard and responded with a very simple and hardly audible, "Yes, sir."

"I hope so. I really do. Now, let me tell you what I know about the Mexican gangs operating in our area. Ties between Mexican cartels and US gangs are hardly new. US gangs have been big customers for the cartels' products for years and play a big part in US street drug sales. With the direct frontal assault of the cartels by the Mexican government in recent years, many of the larger cartels have been weakened, fragmented, and forced to realign. It has become a logical next step for many of them to create collaborating relationships with the US gangs. New alliances have been formed, and new potential markets have been opened. The gangs who were formerly just buyers have now become junior partners in the whole process."

"The latest Gang Assessment by the Texas Department of Safety estimates that there are more than one hundred thousand gang members in Texas. What is particularly interesting is that the composition and very nature of these gangs is changing as we speak. Inter-gang activities are bridging the racial divide and setting aside long-time rivalries. The drive for profit is actually winning out over many of the traditionally-held beliefs. Gangs that have competed against each other in the past now have relationships with the same cartels."

"The Surenos are a confederation of loosely affiliated Mexican Mafia that originated in California and spread to Texas and even the East Coast. Texas ranks gangs by a scale using three tiers they have devised based upon threat to public safety. The Surenos are at the top of Tier II."

"Great," Matt deadpanned. "I feel so much better now."

"Hey, they could have been Tier I. You might also be comforted to know that they are right in the middle of the current threat level classification, sandwiched between the Banditos and the Mexican Revolutionaries. Here's the worse news; the Surenos are growing at a faster rate than most other gangs. It seems that they are basically Mafia and are into more Mafia-like tactics than just pure smuggling. I am not sure, but I have an idea that you really may have bumped against the Surenos, as opposed to some other gang group. I say that because their activities are more closely associated with violent crimes than the whole scale smuggling activities of some of the others. Your two incidents almost look like paid hits. It is possible that someone way down in the land of the sombreros, desert, and cactus still has it in for Travis Nelson and is willing to contract and pay the Surenos to look into it."

"But why, Kevin? Everyone knows that my father is dead and buried. Even the forensics, the DNA proved it," Matt quizzed the agent. "It doesn't make any sense to me."

The man looked wistfully across his desk. "I know it, and you know it. Right, Matt?"

24.

The stifling humidity and muggy overcast skies had little effect on the raucous horde of people gathered in a circle surrounding a tightly blindfolded diminutive figure crouched in the center. The last glimpse the boy had was of a poorly done blue ink tattoo that said "SM 13" burned into the hand of the man who had tied the rags snugly around his head. He was young, but he knew the meaning of that mark. He was shoved into the mob of rabid people who were chanting, yelling, and screaming at him. There was no question their frenzy had been fueled by a lot of alcohol. They urged him to attack, as quickly and fiercely as possible. He stood there bewildered, not really sure what to do next. He knew that this was a test, which he had better pass or he'd be scorned or worse by his family and all those around him. Someone slapped what felt like a heavy club into his quivering hand. He had no choice but to move forward and attack. It was the only way. He moved unsteadily and after a few tentative steps, he stopped. He must be able to reach from there. He slowly reared back, and then swung his weapon in a wild arc as hard and as viciously as his tensed muscles let him.

He missed everything and almost lost his balance. The crowd howled. He heard several ridiculing laughs, but if anything, their intensity increased. They were out for blood, and he mustn't disappoint them. He charged forward and again whipped the stick savagely in the direction where he thought his opponent must be. This time he connected with a sickening dull thud, which resulted in an even louder bellow of approval from the crowd. Suddenly, his own dormant bloodlust awakened and he moved swiftly in for the kill. Bedlam erupted as his opponent crashed to the ground and was promptly beaten into submission.

The excited group of folks on hand that day had settled in an area that had changed considerably through the years. Decades ago when the city of Pasadena, Texas, was incorporated, community planners had reserved a few tracts here and there for use as urban neighborhood parks. The city, which was just a few miles southeast of Houston on the Gulf Freeway towards Galveston, was the home of some one hundred thousand residents. At one time, the municipality had held the dubious distinction of being the Texas home of the Ku Klux Klan and was widely regarded as the heart of "redneck" culture, or lack thereof. Pickup trucks far outnumbered passenger cars, and there were ten barbecue joints for every IHOP. Recently, however, with the tremendous influx of Hispanics, fueled at least in part by illegal immigration, the formerly redneck bastion took on a decidedly different character. There was now a predominant influence of the Hispanic culture in the still working-class neighborhoods. While not yet a pure barrio, Pasadena had moved steadily in that direction. In fact, now taquerias outnumbered barbecue restaurants.

In general, the more recent arrivals were hardworking and industrious, blue collar hourly wage earners in the major petrochemical plants on the east side of the giant Houston complex. As with most Latin cultures, the family was the focal point of social activity. Family fiestas and get-together parties were everywhere, especially on Sunday, the one common day of rest. Public parks were always crammed with groups sharing family activities. Usually early in the day when it is cooler, men organized competitive football (soccer) games, followed by teams sharing kegs of a cold Mexican beer (cerveza). Kids swarmed playgrounds and ball fields. Extended families claimed patches of space to enjoy aromatic meals of south-of-the-border cuisine. Every inch of the parks was serenaded by blaring trumpets and mariachi music blasting over boom boxes. The day of rest was devoted to family and fun, just as it has been for hundreds of years. Many of the partiers were of Mexican origin, but several other Central and South America countries were also represented. Everyone enjoyed a fiesta: fun, food, and relaxation.

After the thrashing he had dealt out, the young man ended up sitting on the ground, hardly able to catch his breath. He was snatched up by the man who had tied the blindfold. As the cloth was ripped away, the boy was relieved to see a huge smile on the man's face. They both looked down and saw that the paper mache donkey, which had been hanging from a young oak tree, was now shattered into so many pieces it was hardly recognizable. Young children were swarming over the carnage to claim as many pieces of candy as possible. The crowd was cheering and clapping. He had met the test and thoroughly whipped the piñata on his seventh birthday. After it was over, the ordeal did not seem so difficult or terrifying after all.

"Mijo! You have done very well. You attacked that donkey like a fighter and knocked it to smithereens. I am proud of you," the man with the tattoo told the youngster.

"Thank you, Uncle Carlos!" the suddenly now self-confident and beaming youth replied.

After roughing up the kid's hair, the man set his nephew down so that the boy could share in the loot he had created by smashing the donkey. Carlos Garcia was in his mid-twenties and looked every bit the tough hombre that he truly was. Stocky, and standing a few inches short of six feet, his rugged build, hewn through several years of manual labor at the Phillips 66 ethanol plant, was apparent. He wore tight jeans that accentuated his powerful thighs and a black sweatshirt that paid tribute to the fallen Hispanic singing goddess Selena, with sleeves cut off to display his bulging biceps. Besides the small tattoo on his right fist, he had several others up and down his dark but hairless arms. His short, scraggly beard accented his bronze complexion and slicked-back, charcoal hair. Although his high cheekbones and deep-set brown eyes seemed to connote a permanent scowl, he was surprisingly animated when he spoke. His threatening visage had earned him the reputation as a rough customer who had little time for nonsense, although in truth, when the mood suited him, he could be affable and engaging—up to a point.

He tipped back his plastic cup and drained the last of his beer as he watched the young man scramble for the little bits of candy still on the ground. He then walked up to the sunshade tent held up by four aluminum poles that the Garcia family had erected and refilled his cup from the keg sitting in a large galvanized tub of ice. There were sixteen members of the "familia" on hand to celebrate his nephew's birthday. Despite what some may have assumed, not one of those present had come across the border illegally. All were bona fide US citizens. That said, however, they had many relatives living in Mexico with whom they kept in close touch.

Both of Carlos's parents, his three brothers, their wives, and their kids were all either seated or standing around the table under the tent. Everyone was having a good time. The men were in an animated discussion about the just-concluded football game. The women were rattling on about the upcoming school year, shopping, and the like. Kids were scurrying everywhere. The family patriarch, old Celestino, Carlos's father, sat back in a beach chair, sipping his tequila, and taking it all in without saying much. His mother, however, was constantly on her feet hovering over and rearranging the offerings, which she had spent days preparing.

And what a feast it was. Set out on the table was an impressive array of home-cooked Mexican food. There were both chicken and beef tacos with either hard shell or soft corn tortillas. There were several dishes of enchiladas, chicken, pork, beef, or just cheese. You could also have sizzling fajitas with all the lettuce, cheese, onion, tomato, and pepper dressing you could heap on. She had also prepared a bowl of menudo. Red hot jalapenos were everywhere. There were several dozen tamales wrapped in aluminum foil. Of course, big dishes of both refried and charro beans and rice were there for the taking. Spicy salsa was strategically positioned around the table by the gallon. Delicious sweet flour sopapillas and an assortment of cakes and cookies provided dessert. To Mamasita's delight, her family was assaulting the food to the point where, despite the enormous quantities laid out, she began to fret that maybe she had not prepared enough.

Carlos was scarfing down a tamale when he felt a buzz in his pocket. He wiped his sticky hands on his jeans and fished out his cell phone. He quickly read the text and replaced the phone into his pocket.

"You must leave now, eh, Carlos?" a soft, raspy voice rose up from behind him from his father, who had been sitting there watching him check his phone.

Carlos looked down at the old man who had worked hard and struggled his entire life to provide for his family. He smiled. Celestino knew. He was wise. "Yes, Papa. I must go." His father sipped from his tequila and looked up at his son with watery, doleful eyes. "I understand. Please be careful," he replied, and then watched his oldest son walk across the now-empty soccer field towards his truck in the parking lot.

Carlos jumped into his shining, bright-blue-and-silver, one-year-old, loaded Ford 250 pickup. It would take him about fifteen minutes to get to the cantina, which was on Spencer Highway just west of Highway 3. As he drove through the working-class neighborhoods, he thought of his father and his brief but disturbing comment. No additional words had been necessary. The old man knew exactly where he was headed and was concerned. His business was not the best. Maybe he should quit and get out. He wasn't married yet and didn't have kids, but he had been dating that hairdresser for a while now. She just might be the one. On the other hand, just look at this elegant truck. There was no way he could have afforded it on his laborer's pay at the plant. He couldn't drop out now. He had to stay with it. As he turned into the parking lot, he noticed the vehicles of several of the others who had already arrived.

A blast of cold air hit him as he entered the small restaurant and walked to an unmarked door to the left of the bar. The place was almost empty on a slow Sunday afternoon. The bartender was washing glasses and barely nodded to him. He entered a back room that was designed to host parties and family functions but was now arranged with a bare table against one wall and a semicircle of chairs facing it. The room had rough pink adobe finished walls decorated with a Mexican beach scene mural. Six men of Latin descent slouched in the chairs nursing draft beers from frosty glass mugs. The room was quiet, but a few of the group grunted or made eye contact to acknowledge Carlos's arrival. Carlos grabbed a beer from a tray next to the door and took a seat, which had been left empty just to the left of the center table. He sipped his beer but did not speak to anyone. A few minutes later, another man entered and filled the last vacant chair. Everyone was there. Now they could begin.

The mood was somber. Everyone could feel it. These meetings could be and usually were fun, but not this time. Just the fact that the gathering had been called on a Sunday afternoon with no advance notice meant something was up, and it wasn't going to be good. The burly, dark man who wore a checked blue bandanna and leather vest over his bare chest broke the silence from his seat facing the assembled group of men. "Okay, let's get to it. I, as colonel and highest-ranking officer of the Surenos Del Sol chapter, call this special meeting to order. You all have already figured out that if I wasn't pissed about something, I wouldn't have brought you all in here today. You all got it?" he blurted out in a rough voice that underscored his obvious irritation.

Nods and grunts of agreement among the troops indicated they understood.

"I am the leader of this group, and I intend to do my best to make it work for everybody, but I can only do it if I have total co-operation and effort from all of you. We are in a tough business. It ain't for everybody. I know you have heard about all those gangs and groups that have deals worked out with the big, rich cartels. All those assholes have to do is take in street goods from across the border and get rid of it, and they supposedly get paid big bucks. I seriously doubt that they are making the cash we hear about, but that really doesn't mean shit for us. We aren't set up that way. Never was, never will be. If that is what you want, don't let the door hit you in the ass on the way out." The incensed man paused to slurp his beer and let his rant sink in.

"We are very lucky here in Surenos Del Sol to have some major contacts across the border. These people need things done, and we do them. They have paid us plenty. Every one of you sitting here today has gotten your share. We are a brotherhood. We share everything, just so long as everyone is in and everyone performs. There is no place in Surenos Del Sol for non-performers or piss-poor efforts. Our contacts in Mexico can very easily go elsewhere for the jobs they want done, and they will, if we keep screwing up. We cannot afford to let them down. Are you all with me?" he demanded. After the rousing response of sis and grunts settled down, his eyes bored into a man seated directly in front of him. "And what about you, Miguel? Are you with us?"

Despite the intensity of the cantina's air-conditioning system, the man had broken out in a clammy sweat. He fidgeted nervously in his seat and tried to avoid the leader's intense gaze as he replied in a low voice that was barely audible, "Yes, of course, Excellency."

The leader continued to stare at the unfortunate man, relishing his discomfort. "I am not so sure about that, señor. Our trusted brotherhood was given a fat assignment from our compadres in Durango to merely obtain some information about a gringo from Houston. We were, and I repeat, were, to receive $25,000 for obtaining this information, and then," he continued with his voice rising to a bellow, "we would be given an additional contract to eliminate him, his associates and family. Do any of you realize how much dinero could be coming our way? One hell of a lot! One hell of a lot! But now, because one of our trusted soldiers did not perform his duty, every cent is in doubt. We will be lucky to get one peso!"

"For those of you who might have been on the moon, our trusted sergeant here, Miguel, was sent out to a local real estate office to obtain the information from the family of the man our client is seeking. Not only did he fail to get any information, he screwed up the whole thing and was overwhelmed by two women, no less. It gets worse; now the police and even the feds, if you can believe it, may be on our trail. This dumbass may cost us our brotherhood. Speak! Tell us about this mess, señor!"

There was a perceptible sense of discomfort and uneasiness among the Surenos Del Sol members. "Excellency, my brothers, I do not know what to say. The wife of this man, Travis Nelson, said he is dead and gone. I didn't know what to do. I was just about to force it out of her when the girl rushed me. I…"

"Girl!" screamed the leader. "Girl! You are one weak hombre. You are not fit to remain in our brotherhood for another minute. Let's vote on Miguel. Out?" Every man raised his hand and shouted "Si."

The leader nodded, and the men on either side of the trembling man each grabbed a shoulder and physically dragged him out the back door to the alley behind the cantina, where he was tossed roughly on the hot concrete.

When the two returned to their seats, it was Carlos who spoke first.

"Excellency, he is now gone from our brotherhood in shame. Do you want us to take the next step with him to make sure he does not damage us further?"

The leader seemed to consider Carlos's question for a moment and then replied, "Perhaps the answer is yes, but not right away. Let's watch him closely. If he gives any reason to give us doubt, then he will become a part of the next concrete foundation at one of the plants. Comprende?" he said, as he looked around the room, where many of the men were still visibly shaken by all that had happened. "Okay, we still have our contract to fill with the Durango clients. Carlos, I am giving it to you. Find out all you can about this Nelson guy. If you have to kidnap or do worse to a family member, so be it. I know you will not fail us. You have always come through for us in the past. As always, be very careful. You were made the second in command here for good reason."

Carlos looked back at the leader and tried to flash a confident smile, even though he felt himself swallowing hard. *Get out of this nasty business? Hell, I've just been shoved into the big-time.*

25.

John Nelson searched the crowd in the grandstand of Elliott T. Bowers Stadium on the campus of Sam Houston State University in Huntsville, Texas. His plane from DC had been late. It was lucky the Houston airport was north of the city and in the right direction of Huntsville, about an hour's ride away. The plan had been for him to meet his mother, brother, and family at the airport and drive together to the university to witness an event that no-one had ever expected to happen – Pamela Nelson receiving her college degree.

The graduation ceremonies were taking place on the campus at the stadium on a beautiful spring day with blue skies and billowy clouds. East Texas college graduation ceremonies that dared to be held outside were usually 100% doomed to either ninety-degree heat with comparable humidity or torrential downpours. Weather-wise, at least, this one was off to a good start.

John craned his neck to find the group and spotted Matt gesturing at him a couple of sections over and about fifty rows up. It took a few minutes to reach his family. Hugs and kisses were exchanged as he settled into a seat between his mother and Matt. "Sorry about my schedule. I have been really busy and, frankly, I forgot about this until two days ago. I scrambled for reservations. The only thing I could get was late to boot. I tried to get on an earlier flight with no luck. Maybe my company needs its own plane," he said with a wink at Matt, who returned the suggestion with a wistful smile. "Have I missed much so far?"

"Only the valedictorian and salutatorian speeches. Robert Gates is the commencement speaker. He is about to start. There has been no parade of degrees yet," Matt replied.

"Robert Gates. Wow, that is impressive. It is worth my trip just to hear the former Secretary of Defense under both Bush and Obama. Does the princess know that I planned to come? I wanted it to be a surprise."

"I don't think so. I haven't seen or talked to her in a while. Mom, have you talked to her lately? Does she have any hint that John would fly halfway across the country just to see her accept her sheepskin?"

"Hey, you guys know your sister. I haven't heard from her for at least a week. I am sure she'll be surprised to see John."

The former Secretary, who was a college president in his own right, gave an introspective and encouraging speech, especially if you happened to be getting your degree in the next few minutes. While John, Matt, Ellen, and Diane gave him polite attention, Matt's kids felt under no such obligation. The squirming and whining began.

As the clock moved towards noon, the wonderful weather gradually morphed into the inevitable heat and humidity. Mercifully, the conferring of degrees finally began for the two thousand or so anxious graduates. Of course, the doctoral and graduate degrees were announced first before the undergraduates, which came last. Each of them tried to determine which one of the whirling mass of mortarboards down there belonged to Miss Pamela. No-one ever spotted her for sure.

They were approaching the second hour of the degree march when Diane answered her phone. "Oh, hi, Pam. What a big day for you. We have a surprise, too. Say, we are having a discussion up here in the stands trying to figure out which one down there is you. Where exactly are you sitting?" As Diane listened, the initial excitement in her voice flattened into a monotone. "Oh, really. Well, that is a surprise. Okay. Sure, I'll tell them. Yes, the party is still on. Matt's house at four o'clock. See you then. Bye." Diane ended the call and sat there rolling her phone over in her hands. She was silent.

John looked at Matt. Matt looked at Ellen. Ellen looked at Diane. They all knew, and Diane confirmed it. "She had a late-night and is just now getting up. She's not down there. She had her degree mailed, but she will see us at the party this afternoon." No-one was surprised. After all, this was Pam. No-one was particularly upset. On the other hand, Matt's kids sang out with unbridled joy as they got up to leave.

Pam sat on the edge of her bed holding her cell phone as she checked for other messages. She had just hung up with her mother, who was apparently sitting at the stadium watching graduation ceremonies. What is up with that? She never told anyone she would go through the long, boring morning just to be handed a piece of paper. Oh, well, what was done was done. Her head hurt. They had partied hearty last night, and why not? It was graduation time, a signature life event. She would never see most of those kids again. If ever they had a good excuse, last night was it.

Despite Pam's scatterbrained and sometimes wild ways, she was not the type of girl to sleep around. She was no prude, but was usually pretty discriminating… although, last night? Who was that guy? She never even learned his name. At least she threw him out well before morning. Yuck. For some reason, she reflected back to two years ago when she had left school and took off to Central America with a guy who, at the time, she was convinced was "the one." It had been a wonderful few months but eventually, as was her habit, she tired of him and headed back home to Texas, much to the relief of her mother. It also didn't help matters that the guy was a key player in the horrible business deal her father had made with the seedy Mexican drug cartel. Luckily, the guy disappeared from the face of the earth. For a long time, she assumed he was dead, but just a week ago, she had heard from him. He left a voicemail, but she never followed up. She hadn't bothered to tell any of her family about hearing from him.

Of all the Nelsons, Pam was the most affected by the loss of her father. Sure, he doted on her like no-one else in the family. He gave her carte blanche to buy and spend whatever she desired, and she had taken full advantage of that situation, but it was more than just the physical things. In a way, she was a kindred spirit. All the others had his drive and sense for accomplishment, which she sorely lacked, but none of the others were imbued with the unique ability to cruise through life being absolutely assured that whatever happened, you would come out on top. Matt was an inveterate worrier, and John made things happen through his insatiable drive to succeed. Like her father, Pam just knew everything would work out in the end.

As the third and last child in the Nelson family, not only was she the baby, she was also the only girl. It didn't take her long to figure out that by virtue of her birth circumstances, she would automatically receive a disproportionate share of attention. While that was not unexpected from her mother, who was mired in a loveless marriage, it was more remarkable that Travis Nelson devoted far more attention to her than he did to his sons. While as a father his primary and virtually only role in the lives of his sons was to impose discipline, with Pam, he was much more interested in her early development and progress on almost a daily basis. It was as if he had one child.

It was no accident that Pam became extremely spoiled. When things did not go her way, the world would know. Her arsenal contained the full array of weapons from crying-screaming meltdowns as a toddler to slammed and locked doors in her room as a teen. Somehow, her brothers accepted her individuality and selfish behavior without resentment. In fact, the three of them shared an unspoken bond of mutual care and affection. "That's just Pam being Pam" became a brotherly mantra that was applied many, many times through the years.

As Pam evolved into womanhood, it was clear that she had inherited a combination of the special good looks of both her parents. She had the lithe but robust athletic build of her father, along with his searing-blue eyes and distinct, yet soft, facial features. Her blond hair and proportionate figure were undoubtedly gifts from her mother. As a teenager, Pam was always inclined to do her own thing and not follow the crowd. She was not quite a rebel, but certainly not a conformist either. She typically dressed with an eclectic bent, but after a while she began to realize that her dad, forgetting about his issues, was a pretty darn good provider. She could afford to shop at the finer shops in the Galleria, so why not spend his bucks and look nice?

As might have been expected, Pam's scoring on the generalized intelligence and aptitude tests far exceeded her performance in the classroom. She was a consistent "C" student who occasionally brought home an "A" in peripheral courses such as gym or art, but also struggled to pass math, for which she saw very little use in her life. It was all about motivation. If Pam cared, she could probably do well in anything. In general, she was content to move through life at her own pace and, along the way, acquired the ability to take advantage of situations, such as her daddy's money. Pam was an accomplished user and schemer, but she was not a competitor.

She was active in extracurricular activities at the Kinkaid School, which was an expensive and elite private school in the River Oaks section of Houston, so long as they were not academically oriented. Being very cute, laid-back, and approachable, Pam Nelson did not lack for attention from boys. In fact, she had several boyfriends during her high school years. She tended to go with someone for a while, inevitably become bored, and send him packing. She would play the field until the next acceptable guy wandered in and repeat the process all over again. She never had what could be called a serious relationship in high school. At first, her moving a hundred miles up the road to Sam Houston State after high school seemed to be an ideal college choice. "Sam" was not especially rigorous academically, and offered an abundant social life in a very pleasant campus setting. It was also close enough for her family to keep an eye on her.

During the first few years, she barely made it from semester to semester and was seriously unmotivated. She had scads of friends, dated a lot, but just seemed to scrape by in the classroom. When the new, exciting, and mysterious Pablo stumbled into her life, she was off with him in a minute. Of course, that too did pass, but something peculiar must have happened while she ran off with him. When she returned to campus, she discovered a renewed interest in her studies and began to do well, even ending up on the dean's superior academic performance list. She took a couple of courses in criminal justice, which piqued her interest. Although she ended up missing the ceremony, she earned the right to walk across the stage at graduation, which, based on her start in Huntsville, was an impressive accomplishment.

Like many graduates, however, she had little idea what was next in her life. Matt and mom were willing to talk about something with their company, but she had tried that when Travis was around. Boring. She completely ignored all campus corporate recruiters. Maybe something working with people? For the immediate future she accepted a spot at the "Q," which was a large health club in the Galleria area of Houston. She might have to fold towels to start. She really didn't care. Things would work out. They always did.

It was a sunny, clear, beautiful afternoon for the party in honor of the new graduate in Matt and Ellen's terrific backyard. Even the humidity had eased somewhat. The Memorial area featured hundreds of elegant and richly-appointed residences that had been carefully placed within a heavily wooded tract so as to have displaced a minimum number of trees and preserve maximum privacy for almost every lot. The sunlight reflected in the shimmering, crystal-clear blue water of their immaculate swimming pool and the enticing smell of the sizzling fare on Matt's grill wafted in the smoke across the patio and perfectly manicured lawn. Guests mingled about the expansive inlaid stone patio.

A low rock wall, which was just the right height for sitting and chatting, bordered the patio and separated it from the lawn and array of native bushes and grasses. Stately oaks and mature pines provided shade from the intense Texas sun. Guests had their choice of sipping champagne punch from a circulating fountain, drawing a cup from the margarita machine, or requesting something more from an open bar staffed by a bartender in a neat white coat. An assortment of domestic and imported beers was also available. Willie Nelson, George Strait, and other "kickers" were piped in over speakers positioned in the trees above the assembled group. Had Travis still been around, he might have arranged for Willie to show up in person.

The young guy was nervous. All eyes seemed to be on him. Maybe he was too much like his dad and worried about everything. He crouched there out on the back lawn cradling a heavy wooden stick in his arms. His uncle peered at him from several feet away and yelled, "Come on! We're counting on you!" Another man who was even closer reached back and hurled a white object at him. The boy grimaced and swung with all the ferocity he could muster. He completely missed and ended up falling to the ground, where he landed on the seat of his pants. He heard a resounding laugh from the onlookers. Were they mocking him? He got up and brushed himself off. He re-assumed his position and tensed for the next pitch. This time, the results were much different. His bat made solid contact and drove the ball over his uncle's head and far out into the rear of the backyard. He ran to first base and stood perched there with a big grin.

Uncle John ran over to him and, being careful not to spill his beer, snatched the seven-year-old up into his arms. "Great job, Rusty! You drove in the winning run! We won the game because of you. I knew you could do it. I am really proud of you."

The boy looked over at his uncle, whom he had always idolized. The praise was especially meaningful coming from him. "Thanks, Uncle John. I wasn't sure I could smack it. I have only played tee ball so far. Coach pitch is next year."

Just then, they noticed a commotion by the house. The party had been arranged by Matt and Ellen to commemorate Pam's impressive academic achievement. Several of her friends from both high school and college were there, as well as neighbors and folks Matt and Ellen had invited. A large "CONGRATS PAMELA" banner had been hung between two large trees.

Since the party was in her honor, it would have been nice for her to show up, and she finally had, albeit an hour or so late, but that was Pam being Pam. She looked terrific in matching aqua shorts and a halter top that accented her radiant tan. She was swarmed by her friends, many of whom she hadn't seen for some time. She was obviously thrilled to be the center of attention. The adults stood aside and waited for her to work her way through the gaggle of admirers. She gave her mother a big kiss and hugged Matt and Ellen. Then she spotted John and rushed up to him. "What are you doing here, brother? I thought you were busy chasing bad guys around the nation's capital?"

"Well, Pamela, I heard a rumor through my intelligence network that you were about to graduate from college. It was so preposterous that I had to come over here and check it out for myself. So far, after a trip to Huntsville, I still am not sure."

It took a lot to embarrass Pam, but this was one of those occasions. With a very sheepish grin on her face she looked up at him and, in a soft and contrite whisper said, "Oops. I'm sorry."

John could feign injury no longer. His face lit up in a huge smile and he bear-hugged her. "Pammy, you will never change."

With the arrival of the honored guest, the party picked up steam. The drinks flowed, and everyone enjoyed the delicious assortment of chicken, rib eye, pork loin, and burgers that appeared off Matt's marvelous smoking grill. There were copious amounts of coleslaw, potato salad, sweetcorn, and much more. Several apple, pecan, and peach pies provided dessert. From time to time, Ellen would check with the domestic lady they had hired to help out to make sure everything was okay. The food and drink were terrific. No-one went hungry or thirsty.

At one point during the evening, perhaps around ten o'clock, Matt walked up to Ellen and pointed over towards the big oak tree. Virile, hostile, and fearless brother, John, had his arm around perhaps the geekiest, uber-liberal-radical-passionate-environmentalist-scraggly-haired-thick-glassed friend of Pam. From the look of things, the pair had settled a world of issues already and were now more concerned with exploring other areas of mutual interest. Matt and Ellen smiled.

And then it was Ellen's turn to point. Standing next to the pool were the guest of honor and the young man Matt had just hired right out of Rice University as an analyst to help him with his new consulting business. The fellow was a math major who was obviously very bright, but did not come across as a very social sort of guy. Matt guessed that he had probably not had many dates during his four years at Rice. The ultimate party girl, however, seemed to have discovered something of interest in this fellow. God bless them all.

Matt was glad to have gotten John aside for a while to discuss his meeting with Special Agent Forney. They had talked about it over the phone, but in person they were able to go into more detail. John respected the capabilities of the DEA, especially Forney and his staff in Houston. The DEA men were good, and unlike many of their governmental brethren, they were reasonable. Still, they were not to be completely trusted. If Forney ever suspected for one second that the Nelsons had put something over on them, he'd reopen the case in a New York minute.

The Surenos angle was troubling from at least two standpoints. First was the obvious danger that a Mafia-like gang could impose on them. They must be very cautious and ensure they had security around them twenty-four/seven. John suggested that Matt start carrying a gun. Matt had reached the same conclusion. He'd discussed it with Ellen but did not tell the children. John advised Matt if worse came to worst, he should not be reluctant to go back to Forney. The gang threat to their family trumped all other considerations; plus, they absolutely had not put over anything on Forney. They could swear to that in good faith. The DEA likely knew everything they knew. Well, almost.

The other troubling issue with Surenos was that they apparently had information about their father that Matt and John didn't. It was a mystery why they would attempt to extract information from Diane. Surenos was a United States-based Mafia-like gang that had ties to the cartels deep in Mexico. The local Surenos chapter was probably under contract with a cartel to get the information. But why? Travis Nelson was dead and buried, and Mesquite Development was long since out of business. There did not seem to be a ready answer for that.

The festivities began to wind down around eleven or so, which is to say in the singularly Texas tradition, the host and hostess circulated around and thanked those who were left for coming. They were headed off to bed, but everyone was welcome to stay as long as they liked. Naturally, most of Pamela's crew continued to party on. Why, it wasn't even close to midnight yet! John, who was staying there at his brother's house, had already disappeared a while ago, as had Ms. Geek. He had pointed to his phone and mumbled something about an issue back in Virginia. Matt's analyst was still around, however.

As the party continued, a pair of dark eyes closely studied everything that went on. A husky figure dressed entirely in camo lay on a large, flat rock in the middle of the stream that meandered through the woods behind Matt's house. He had been there for several hours, deeply hidden among the foliage trees and shrubs. He remained absolutely still and didn't move a muscle that wasn't necessary. He had been able to crawl to within fifty yards of the patio. He was certain that with all the merry-making and drinking, no-one suspected that he was there.

With his camera, he was able to shoot many stills, as well as a lot of video of the party goers. At first, he thought it was sort of fun to spy on the gringos like this. Having been born poor in the barrio, he had never been around white folks except at the plant. The longer he watched, though, he felt a fire beginning to burn inside him. Just look at all the food and stuff they had. Such a large house! Why did they deserve all that? He thought back to their little fiesta in the park. Maybe he would put the fear of God into them.

Carlos studied the Nelson family in detail, and was familiar with each person before he'd set out that evening. As he watched their antics, he tried to determine which one would be the best and easiest to grab and then break under pressure. He immediately discounted John, whom he could see would be a rough customer. He couldn't take his eyes off Pamela for obvious reasons. He quickly found himself lusting about what he could do to her. Reality then set in hard. He had been given this job by their jefe (boss) because of the other man's screw up. He was not about to repeat the failure by getting distracted. Mano, she was caliente, though! He doubted if Pam actually knew very much. That left Matt and his kids. His kids? Hmm? His goal tonight was strictly to recon and gather information, unless a "can't miss" opportunity cropped up. Maybe it had...

26.

After graciously saying their good nights, Matt and Ellen made their way into the house and down the hall to their bedroom. Both were bone-weary. Throwing a party takes a lot out of a person. Fatigue aside, there is a big psychological let-down afterwards, to say nothing of all the booze Matt had consumed. Both were ready for bed. They shuffled out of their clothes and into their night stuff. After brushing her teeth, Ellen was out the second her head hit the pillow. She never heard the continuing din of the still active party outside her window. Matt was close behind, but he always made one last check on the kids before he jumped into bed. They had put Rusty and Gail down in their rooms around eight o'clock and then returned to the party.

Matt smiled as he cracked open Rusty's door. On his way to bed, the kid would not shut up about how he had won the baseball game and driven home Uncle John's run. Through the dark shadows he could see his little man snoring away with his baseball glove right next to his pillow. He quietly shut the door and eased over to Gail's room. Again, he slowly pushed the door open, not wanting to disturb his little angel. At first, he couldn't quite see her form in the "big girl" bed she had just graduated into. He moved into the room and squinted through the darkness. He still didn't see her. Maybe she had just fallen out of the new bed? He moved around and looked. Nothing. He began to sweat; his heart started pounding. Where was she? Did she go to the bathroom? Maybe to the kitchen? In with her brother? Matt flicked on the light, and to his horror he saw that her window was raised and the screen was torn half out of its tracks. Oh my God! Full panic set in. Someone had taken his little girl! *Those bastards! Those bastards!*

His first impulse was to run back and wake Ellen. He was about to do that when he decided to be sure he wasn't leaping to conclusions. He did not want to scare her half to death for no reason. Wearing only his boxers, he darted down the hall, looking everywhere. He entered the family room, but instead of returning to the party out the back, he ran out the front door and stood in his driveway. Then it hit him. John, I must call John. Where the hell is he?

Carlos Garcia realized that any adult he grabbed would be a problem from a size standpoint. Yes, he'd like to wrestle with that babe for a while, but that was out of the question. He also knew that parents would do anything to save their children, who would also be far easier to handle.

With the party blasting away, he had seen the kids disappear around eight o'clock. They had to be in bed fast asleep. Single-story house on a very private street. Plenty of natural cover. He knew that both parents were out in the back tending to their guests. He might never have a better chance. Once he had the child, he'd contact them immediately, and then they'd readily give him the information about Travis Nelson, and the whole thing would be over very quickly. The kid could go back unharmed in less than twenty-four hours. The cops would investigate, but not with near the intensity if the child were still gone or killed. Tonight was right. He had to move now.

As he anticipated, he had no problem carefully moving without anyone seeing him through the trees and shadows to the planting beds at the bedroom windows in the front of the house. He would have settled for either child, but as it worked out, the window to the girl's room was unlatched, although he did have to twist off the light aluminum screen on the outside. The window raised easily with only a small screech. He waited for a full minute to make sure no-one had heard it and then vaulted into the room. He was on the little girl in an instant. She started to wake, but he put his hand over her mouth and pressed the scented cloth pad on her nose he had brought with him, just in case. She quickly passed completely out, and easily gathered her up and exited through the window. He then sneaked through the woods on the same path he'd used to approach the house. He was in and out in less than one full minute.

John Nelson had been working hard lately. He couldn't remember the last time he had a full day off. In a way, this trip to Houston for Pam's graduation was a chance for a little overdue R & R time. Harvey could certainly handle things at Marsea for a few days. John was also someone who did not do things halfway. Once he arrived at the party, it did not take him long to start ordering double shots from the amused bartender. After all, his rack for the night was only a few steps away in Matt's guest bedroom. What the hell? Well, one thing led to another, and he found himself talking to one of Pam's frizzy-haired ultra-liberal friends, with whom he had absolutely nothing in common whatsoever. Progressive-conservative. Gun control-NRA. Abortion-right-to-life. Democrat-Republican. Global warming-myth. Amnesty-the wall. Hillary-the Donald. Black-white. Talk about opposites. That is, except for one thing; to their mutual delight, they discovered that neither had had "any" for some time. Politics were shoved aside and a deal was made. John's first problem was to escape the party without too many raised eyebrows. That was easily solved by faking an emergency call from Harvey. His co-conspirator went to use the restroom a few minutes later.

As agreed, the pair rendezvoused out the front in Matt's driveway, and then problem number two occurred: neither of them were driving. Why had he let Matt convince him to turn in his rental car in Huntsville? This rather minor inconvenience, however, did not discourage the young lady, who was still very eager. No mission ever went without a glitch, and John went into contingency planning mode. He thought for a moment and then dashed back in the house to the guest room, where he snatched the comforter off the bed. Back out in the driveway, he threw the blanket over his shoulder and grabbed his "date's" boney hand. Together, they headed off down the street to an empty lot with plenty of trees and brush. John was now on point. This mission was going to succeed.

They stumbled into the bushes far enough that they hoped they were out of sight. John opened up Ellen's beautiful antique hand-stitched quilt comforter and threw it down on the pine needles. Finally, time for the good stuff. They had just begun anxiously groping and grabbing when the ever-vigilant John caught a flicker out of the corner of his eye. Could that be a man moving slowly in the dark through the underbrush with something slung over his shoulder? Maybe John subliminally remembered having seen little Gail in her pink PJs, but something sparked in him. Without any warning, he suddenly leaped off his present company, who managed to deliver the world's most ugly frown in his direction, and bolted into the darkness towards the figure. He catapulted through the trees in the shadows and tackled the man, who had been looking in the direction of the party and never heard him coming. The impact was square on the back, causing the guy to slam down hard onto the pine needles and roll the package from his shoulder.

Carlos had been blindsided and was stunned, but he was a street fighter. He pushed up with his hands and tried to get to his feet, but John held fast to his legs. John immediately knew he was in for a fight. Sure enough, the man slammed John on the head with a balled fist, causing him to lose his grip just long enough to scramble out of John's grasp and leap to his feet. Despite his drunken condition, sensing the gravity of what he had gotten into,

John immediately sobered up and switched into survive-and-destroy mode. He glanced over and saw tiny Gail curled up on the ground. She had begun to cry, so at least she was alive. Just seeing her there, though, accelerated John's rage. He glared at the dark, greasy man crouching in a fighting stance three feet across from him. John was hoping it would not happen, but was not surprised when the guy reached down to his shin and drew out a gleaming stiletto from a scabbard he had strapped there.

The greaser now definitely had the advantage, and John was willing to let him make the first move, which he expected would be a leap and wide-arcing attempt to slash him across his upper body or face. This man was a street thug who would not attempt to stab on his first rush. John tensed as Garcia flew at him, swinging his weapon high and wide. The natural instinctive reaction for most people is to raise an arm or elbow to protect your head and face. This tactic, however, almost certainly means you are going to be slashed in the wrist or arm. While not fatal, such an initial wound, with the pain and blood, would greatly reduce the ability of the defender to ward off subsequent attacks. As the man charged, John deftly ducked out of the way of the whiz of cold steel just past his face but brought his left knee directly into the attacker's crotch. The breathtaking low blow staggered the kidnapper just long enough for John to leap upon his back like a big cat. With his right hand, he seized the wrist that held the ugly, razor-sharp knife.

It was now a test of strength on strength. Who could control the knife? John locked onto his wrist as tightly as possible and tried to bang and scrape the man's hand across the rugged bark of an oak tree just in front of them. Garcia, though, was a beast, and not willing to relinquish his stiletto easily. In fact, his superior strength began to prevail and gradually he was able to draw the weapon down in front of him, even though John's hand was still firmly wrapped around his wrist.

John had been in many tough spots before and he was well aware that his strength was no match for some opponents, including this bull. If he was going to prevail, he must rely on quickness and superior intellect. John could feel his grip gradually slipping as their arms struggled downward. Unless he acted soon, the blade would be loose and rammed right back at him.

It was just at that instant when John was about to lose control that he released his hand from the man's wrist. He did it so quickly that Garcia was completely surprised, and his own force drove his arm directly down almost to the ground. John knew the knife was now free and he must act immediately. As soon as he released the wrist of the arm holding the knife, John's other arm flashed up, encircled Garcia's neck with the inside crook of his elbow, and he heaved back mightily. With John on his back, the two of them toppled over backwards, ending up with John on the bottom fighting desperately to keep an iron chokehold on the kidnapper's neck and windpipe. With his free hand, the guy began thrashing the knife towards any part of John that he could reach. In fact, he did slice into his right side near his ribs with one of his thrusts.

The two of them lay there in a death struggle on their backs with John on the bottom and Garcia directly on top of him. It was now a question of who could hold out longer. John was choking the life out of this monster, who had a free hand and was swinging that dammed blade in every direction, desperately trying to impale John. John had never had an opponent who didn't give up once he had him in this chokehold, but this guy just wouldn't quit.

The knife flashed by his face, just missing it. He wasn't sure he could hang on much longer. Sooner or later, the blade would find some critical part of his body. He saw little Gail laying in a heap a few steps away. He just had to hang on. He tried with all his might to increase the pressure on the man's neck, but it did not seem to matter. The blade flashed by and just nicked his cheek. The next flail might get him. If that happened, at least he'd gone down fighting.

He felt his own strength sapping. Now the guy was winning. John squirmed and girded himself for the worst when suddenly, the kidnapper relaxed and went limp. John was exhausted but quickly threw the flaccid body off him. He tried to struggle to his feet but could barely raise himself up.

Gasping for breath, he looked up through the shadows and saw a thin form caressing and hugging Gail to her breast. His head began to clear. "Is that you, eh…?" He then realized he hadn't even learned her name.

"Muriel, John. I'm Muriel, your disappointed date."

"Oh," he replied, trying to hide his embarrassment, even after all he'd been through.

Looking at little Gail he asked, "Is she okay?"

"I think so. She is plenty scared and confused, but she does not look injured. I am going to take her back to the house right now; that is, as long as you are okay."

"Sure. I am fine. I've been through a lot worse." John's bravado was returning fast, but he had to ask, "What happened, Muriel? Did you see it? And what is that awful smell?"

Muriel looked down at the pitiful hulk of a man sitting there with a bleeding cheek. "Well, when you so rudely left me, I decided to see what caught your attention. I have had a lot of men disappear on me, but not quite under those circumstances. I came upon you and at first in the dark with you two laying on each other, I thought maybe you had a better—or, more appropriate—offer. As I got a little closer, I realized that maybe you needed some help, and then I found a cloth laying right there on the pine needles that smelled like chloroform. I knew from my criminology class at Sam—which is where I met Pam, by the way—that kidnappers often use it to immobilize their victims. I figured turnabout is fair play. I picked it up and carefully held it on your friend's nose. He went out like a light."

John could hardly believe his ears, but broke out in a big smile. He could only reply, "No shit. Thanks." But it was too late; the lady had already scooped up the youngster and had disappeared into the woods.

John knew he had better secure the kidnapper before he woke or round number two might ensue. He had just completed doing that when Matt, still in his underwear, burst into the clearing. He was completely out of breath. "John, are you okay? Who is that? What happened?"

"Come here, brother," John replied, as he pointed to the still inert dark figure laying on the ground. He picked up the guy's limp arm and showed him the tattoo on his wrist. "Can you see that in the dark?"

"Surenos! Those bastards," Matt swore. "I guess we were very lucky."

"You got that right, Cisco."

"Say, John. Can that guy get away tied up like that, and is that what I think it is?

John relaxed for the first time in quite a while. "I don't plan on leaving him like that for very long. Yep, I do have him tied up with a brassiere."

Matt looked down at his brother with a weird quizzical expression on his face.

"Well, it was all I had, and she really didn't need it. Field expedient!"

27.

After Matt was sure that John was okay, he was about to head back to the house to check on his daughter, when John grabbed his arm.

"Hold it. Let's think this one through for just a second. Except for a little excitement and a nick or two," he contemplated, brushing a finger against the oozing gash on his cheek, "no real harm has been done. Maybe, just maybe, we can take advantage of this situation and get to the bottom of this stuff about dad."

Matt glanced down at the dark figure clothed in camouflage who had begun to moan.

"Him?"

"Yep, him. Tell you what; go make sure your baby's okay. That is priority number one. I think this asshole had a cloth doused in some kind of Mexican drug. Not chloroform, which does not knock you out like it says in the mystery novels. From what I have read, though, there is some Mexican stuff that makes you lose consciousness and woozy without any lasting effect. Make sure Ellen watches her closely for at least twenty-four hours. It might be wise to have a doc take a look at her too, but I think she'll be fine. He didn't have her long enough to do much other damage.

"When you get back over there, downplay things as much as possible. Nearly everyone has left by now, anyway. Let's not call the police."

Matt interrupted, "Are you sure about that? This turd just broke into my home and tried to kidnap my daughter. He needs to be locked up, maybe forever."

"Simmer down. Take it easy, would you? If we call the cops and they take him in, it is possible that his interest in dad just might come up. Before you know it, Agent Forney will be all over us demanding to find out why this guy thinks dad is alive, and why we have hidden that from him. I can almost guarantee that the DEA and others will re-open the investigation. Is that what you want?"

"Of course not, John, but the truth is, as far as we know, dad is dead and gone. We don't have anything to hide."

"Yes, but it might not look that way to the DEA. We can't afford to take that chance. I think we should have a little session of our own with Mr. Nightstalker here. Is there somewhere we can take him that is private?"

"I am sure that can be arranged."

It took a lot from Matt to convince Ellen that they should not report this incident to the cops. Once Gail fully woke up, she acted fine and was more interested in a midnight snack than any lingering effects of the incident. It is likely that she had never fully awakened and did not realize what she'd been through. A neighbor down the street was a pediatrician. Ellen would call him in the morning.

The remaining few guests posed more of a problem, but Muriel grabbed Pam and took her aside. She asked Pam to blame all the commotion in the woods on her and John. With a wink and a nod, that explanation worked.

With no flashing red lights or blue uniforms on hand, the festivities ended quickly. Matt kissed his wife and told her that he and John had an errand to run. He would see her sometime in the morning but would check in. Ellen rolled her eyes and smiled. Here they go again. All in a night's work in the Nelson family.

John and Matt retrieved a few things from Matt's garage, including zip ties to restrict the uninvited party guest more securely. They never did catch up to Muriel to return her missing article of clothing. Matt pulled his SUV along the street next to the bushes where John was waiting. They quickly opened the rear gate and heaved the groggy man in. A tarp was thrown over him to ensure he was not visible from the outside.

When Mesquite Development was going strong, the company maintained a small metal building to warehouse various items of equipment they used from time to time in the development business. It was located almost directly under the primary approach runway of Hobby Airport in south downtown off of Telephone Road. The locale was strictly a commercial area and was dotted with similar buildings used for storage by small businesses. Rent was cheap, especially with the constant whine of air traffic just a few feet overhead. It was about 5:30 AM when Matt drove into the rough white caliche parking lot and parked next to the building. The first rays of daylight were beginning to glow in the eastern sky. Matt had not been there for a couple of years. The property was deserted and apparently had not been re-leased. He was pleased when the key he'd kept for several years still worked. They had thrown in a wrecking bar to smash the padlock, if necessary.

The damp, windowless building reeked of stale motor oil. A puddle in the corner was a sure sign the roof had some major leaks. Matt was about to ask John if this place would work when the entire building vibrated and shook with the high-pitched shriek of a Southwest Airlines 737 lumbering off overhead on the way to Dallas. John smiled and gave two thumbs up. They dragged their very unhappy guest into the building and tossed him down on a couple of rough-sawn, rotting wooden pallets.

The brothers could see that they had captured a rough customer. The Los Surenos were known for their Mafia-like tactics and would accept almost any dirty job ranging from beatings, extortion, kidnapping, home invasions, and even outright murder. This man had broken into Matt's private home and violated personal family space. He deserved little sympathy as might have been accorded a captive on the battlefield subject to the Geneva Convention or other commonly observed protocols. They had little doubt that given a chance, he might have killed Gail.

It took considerable personal restraint for John to keep his rage in check. He could not let his emotions take over or he might just do him in on the spot, in which case the guy would die with his secrets. Matt was likewise incensed, but knew to follow his brother's lead.

John drew out Garcia's stiletto and held it a few feet from the man's face, where the man could not miss the gleaming steel point. They had firmly secured him with his hands behind his back and his ankles fastened together with zip ties. He wasn't going anywhere, but he could still squirm and thrash. John glared at him, only to have the brazen man return the look with just as much intensity.

"Your name, señor?" John asked in a level voice. There was no answer, just a continued hateful glower. "Maybe you didn't hear me? Tell us your name, asshole."

The guy looked away and remained silent, but suddenly shot his head around and let fly a huge wad of spit that just missed John's leg.

"Chinga tu madre!" he hissed in a vile, guttural tone.

John smiled, but it was not a pleasurable, warm grin. It was an acknowledgment that he had at least gone through the motions of trying to be civil to this beast who had no interest in being co-operative. The gloves could now come off. It was time to bring out the stuff that would get this animal to sing. It was always better, and cleaner, to use respectable conversation, but their friend had chosen his fate. He'd regret blowing his chance in just a few minutes.

"Okay, Matt, Jose here—if I may call him Jose—has just given us the rules of the game. I saw an old wooden door near where we walked in. Could you drag it over here, please?"

Matt went over and dragged it to where the man was sitting. Garcia tried to ignore what the brothers were doing, looking away and feigning no interest, but John could see his pupils carefully follow Matt across the room and back.

"Good. Now, he is going to try to make it rough on us by jumping around. We want to tie him to the door across his chest and legs." They had brought some short lengths of rope. "We need to flip him onto the door on his back, which he won't like. When he starts to bounce around, just back off and let me handle him." Matt nodded, and sure enough, the guy began thrashing all over the place. He did not want to be tied to that door. Matt stepped back for a moment and John moved just to the right of the door. He fingered the stiletto, making sure the guy saw him clearly. Despite his outer cold visage, fear flashed in his eyes for the first time. Then with a flick of his wrist, John flipped the weapon around in his hand and drove the bone handle as hard as he could right between the man's thighs. His wails and screams might well have been heard above the million decibels of the airliner afterburners. Even though his throbbing and pain caused some additional quivering, he offered no resistance as they tied him to the door.

In Iraq John had dealt with more than a few dickhead prisoners on the battlefield. With his own and his men's life on the line, he had little use for political correctness. In fact, when the Bush administration began to take heat for using "enhanced" interrogation techniques, he took that as a sign that his days in the Corps were numbered. Idiots and do-gooders in Washington just didn't understand what they faced in the field. He hadn't actually observed such a situation, but he had it on reasonable authority that one of the best ways to crack a recalcitrant enemy soldier was to simply take him and a buddy up in a chopper to about two thousand feet. With little or no warning, boot the buddy out the open door. It was surprising how co-operative the other formerly tight-lipped man became.

They didn't have a chopper, but they did have a towel and a few jugs of water. If anything, John felt that waterboarding for this dreg of humanity was too easy on him. Still, it would work, and they probably wouldn't kill him in the process. The idea of waterboarding is that the subject feels that he is suffocating and about to drown, when in fact with his head upside down the water cannot actually enter his lungs, which are still full of air. The sensation, though, is immediate and horrible. The subject can actually suffocate if he is left in that position very long. When the coalition forces in Iraq used this technique, they always had a physician standing by to render aid to the subject if things went too far. Unfortunately, in this case, try as they might, John and Matt were unable to locate a doctor to come out to a desolate warehouse at six in the morning. Poor Jose would just have to take his chances.

At John's instruction, Matt slid a concrete block that was laying around under the door so that Garcia's feet were elevated above his head. Even though the man could see what was about to happen, they doubted he was familiar with waterboarding, which was too tame for Los Surenos to use. They preferred ice picks and chainsaws. Nonetheless, even though terror filled the man's eyes, he continued to glare at them but did not try to twist or thrash around. John did admire his courage.

John made one last attempt. "Before we start, señor, have you changed your mind about chatting with us?

"Carbron (dumbass)! Vete a la mierda!" came the staccato response.

"Well, my Spanish is a little rusty, but I think you have indicated a 'perhaps not.' Okay, Jose. Hey, I just made a rhyme! Open wide!" John teased as he raised up a plastic jug of water, they had brought with them from Matt's house and dribbled it on the man's face. At first, most of it ran off, but then some ran into his nasal cavity and caused him to start gagging and coughing. When his mouth opened, John increased the flow. His mouth and nose were soon full of water. At John's signal, Matt held a smelly old rag over his mouth to keep him from coughing out the water. Carlos was now in misery. He felt like a drowning man. He tried holding his breath but that did not work.

"About fourteen seconds, Matt. That is the average before most men give up. Let's see how our little kidnapper does. I'm guessing about twenty seconds. What do you think? Want to make a bet?"

Matt remained deadpan and did not answer. As furious as he was with this man, this stuff was hard to take.

Sure enough, almost a half-minute passed before the man started to scream and beg them to stop—in perfect English, by the way. John let him suffer and gurgle for another ten seconds before he motioned Matt to remove the rag. Together they grabbed the door and tilted it to one side so he could cough and spit out the water. He lay there for several minutes looking as white as a ghost and coughing, wheezing, and hyperventilating. Gradually, some color began to return to his face, but the brothers made no movement to let him up. In fact, they flipped the door so he was on his back again with his feet elevated and ready for session two. "We have plenty more water here, Jose. Shall we try it again, or will you talk to us?"

Now the sullen fire was gone from Carlos's resistance. He was a truly beaten man. His pride was destroyed. There was no reason for him to continue to resist. He knew John was a professional and would kill him. Actually, when he thought about it, there wasn't a lot he could tell them anyway. If he had any chance to get out of this, it would be to talk. In between gasps and heaves, he was able to utter a barely discernible, "Okay, okay."

John looked across at Matt, who reached into his pocket and switched on a small recorder.

"Good choice, señor," John began, as he stared down at the prone figure. "But be assured that if you try any funny stuff, you will be praying for some more water. We are done fooling around. They will find you in here in a couple of months with your own knife stuck between your shoulder blades. Comprende?"

"Yes."

"What is your full name and where do you live?"

"I am Carlos Garcia. I live in Pasadena, Texas."

"Where do you work during the day and do you have a family?"

"I work at the Phillips 66 plant in Baytown and, no, I am not married. No family."

Both Matt and Garcia were surprised when John became enraged with that answer. "Okay, asshole, I know that is bullshit. You all have families; mothers, fathers, brothers, sisters, nephews, nieces, etc. Where are they?" John demanded.

Garcia hesitated, but could see this guy meant business. He gave enough information about his family so they could easily be located, which was really all John cared about. Garcia understood that as well.

"Tell me about your gang, Los Surenos. Everything!"

Again, the man hesitated, but realized that he didn't have a choice. It was better to give him some information willingly than to let the guy beat it out of him.

"We are Los Surenos del sol, a part of Los Surenos, Texas, although we do not have much to do with them. Our battalion is based in Pasadena. We have about two dozen members. I am captain dos in command."

"Who is the leader?"

"It is Colonel Sylvester Flores."

"Where do you meet?"

He tried to get by with a response of, "All over," but John's intensity told him he'd better be more specific. "Usually at the cantina on Highway 3 and Fairmont."

"How does the gang operate?"

"Excelente, Sr. Flores, has many connections in Mexico. They give him jobs to do. He assigns them to us, and we do them."

"What kind of jobs?"

"It depends. Mostly, it is going after hombres who owe money. Sometimes we grab their trucks. We might have to rough them up a bit. Sometimes we break into their homes. Once in a while, it involves their families."

Matt and John looked at each other. "What about murder?" John snapped.

Garcia's eyes flashed. "We have been known to take people out. Although I have never done so."

"Now, what about us, Carlos? Why have you and your friends been after us and our families?"

"Señor, please believe me when I tell you this," the prone man pleaded. "I do not know." He could see the anger building in John's face and was quick to add, "Excelente has a contract with a group in Mexico, which I believe is the Zetas cartel. We do what they ask and are paid well. We do not question what they ask. The money is too good, and there are many others who would do the work if we refuse or fail. All I know is that the Zetas believe that Travis Nelson is still alive. They want to know where he is. It only makes sense that his family would know where he is. That is all I can tell you. I do not know any more."

The building vibrated as another airliner screamed into the sky directly overhead. John considered what he had just heard. This man was broken, and he was probably telling the truth. There was no reason he would have to know any more than he had told them. It was better, in fact, if the minions like him did not know.

"You had better be telling the truth, Carlos, because we know where you and your family can be found. We can play pretty rough ourselves. Let's set one thing straight, and you'd better pay attention. Travis Nelson was killed and blown up in Durango over two years ago. No-one in our family knows any different. If we wanted to, we could not help you. Is that clear? Tell your leader to stay away from our families or you all will be very sorry."

"Yes. I understand," he replied, and then decided to ask, "And what will you do with all this information I have given you?"

Carlos waited. There was no response. He then heard the door to the warehouse open and slam. The padlock clicked outside. Another plane rumbled over and shook the hell out of the place. He was alone.

28.

The scantily-clad young lady opened the bathroom door and picked her way through the darkness of the bedroom. She approached the bed and carefully began to slip back in. It was 3:00 AM; she still had plenty of time to catch some sleep before morning. She was exhausted. It had been an active night so far, and she had a few bruises to prove it. All in a night's work. She wondered if he was finally asleep. She quickly got her answer.

"Hold it there, Missy. Don't bother to get back in. You're done for the night. Gather your things and go. Devon will see you out the door," a husky voice ordered from the darkness on the other side of the bed in a tone that left no opportunity for equivocation or debate.

The girl hesitated, but she'd heard a lot of stories about this guy. He could be rough in the sack, and when he was done, he was done, out you went. There was no time to snuggle or at least decompress until the sun came up. She rummaged around and found her things scattered about the room. It was tough to see. It would serve the bastard right if she switched on the light. She had also heard he had a temper. She didn't want to find out if that was true. She went back into the bathroom and put herself together as best she could. As she left his bedroom, she tried a sexy, "See ya, sugar," but heard only snoring in return. Once again, she had an impulse to slam the door but had sense not to do it.

When she walked down the stairs of the townhouse, a young black man was sitting in the kitchen, flipping through a Penthouse magazine and drinking coffee. Without a word he got up and walked into the foyer, where he disarmed the alarm and let her out the front door. It was the middle of the night. Good luck finding a taxi.

Just a few hours later, Dwight Lamar began to stir as the bright sunshine crept in through the large window onto his king-sized bed. In fact, he lay there awake a good fifteen minutes before the alarm went off at 7:00 AM. One of the benefits of being in the financial industry was that no-one started early. His SETUP office opened its doors promptly at 9:00 AM, but unless he had a specific meeting, he didn't show up until 9.30 AM or so. As a matter of fact, he had a breakfast meeting that morning. He looked around the moderately sized bedroom of the townhouse he occupied in the newly revitalized Freedman's District just west of downtown. It would do for a while, but he had already planned to move out as soon as his lease was up.

The place had three levels, with a garage at the street and most of the living space (kitchen, dining room, and living room) on the second. There were two bedrooms on the third floor. There was no view or special pizzazz about the place, but it served his purposes at this point. IKEA furniture had been placed around on the advice of the same interior decorator that had helped him design the new and larger offices for the housing authority. This townhouse was where he lived, but definitely not where he entertained business associates. Since he knew that no-one from his work would ever visit here, he let his guard down a bit and purchased a few articles of African art. He still always observed his strict rule about trying not to look too "black" to his business associates.

Now that he had SETUP up running, and well on the way to actually being profitable, he had slowly and gradually been able to take some personal liberties on his own behalf. The fact that he always kept his private life separate from the office made it easier to carefully upgrade his lifestyle without being too obvious. One of his first moves after the first six months was to move his younger step-brother, Devon, down from Sparta to live with him in Houston. Devon was the only one of his siblings who had not accumulated a long rap sheet with the local police and had actually been able to hold a job for more than a few weeks, even if it was only Walmart. Devon was also bright, if still totally unsophisticated to the ways of big-city life. He was anxious to learn, and idolized his big half-brother who had become such a success in Houston.

Devon became a personal assistant, chauffeur, bodyguard, and pussy hustler. As soon as he could get away with it, Dwight would put Devon on the SETUP payroll. To start, he was just the boss's little brother in from the country. His job was to do whatever was asked and stay in the background. In a convoluted way, Dwight was pleased that he was doing something nice for a family member.

That morning, he rose when the alarm went off. He was standing by the mirror in his bathroom when he noticed a pair of black mesh pantyhose draped over the tub. They startled him for a moment, and then remembered he had a woman there last night. He had already put her out of his mind. Leaving that stuff behind was disgusting. He made a note to tell Devon not to bring that one around again, whoever she was.

He dressed in gray slacks, a blue button-down shirt with a red striped tie, and a navy blazer with gold buttons. He slipped into his Bass penny loafers and was out the door. Had he been heading straight to the office, he would have worn his usual conservative dark suit, white shirt, and wing tips. His meeting that day was not with finance people, and he could get away with being just a bit sportier. He also was still reluctant to use Devon to drive him to work. A chauffeur was a bit much for a start-up Housing Authority CEO, even if it was only your own brother.

That morning, however, was different. He tossed Devon the keys, and they were off in his company-leased Buick Le Sabre. They headed north up I-45 and got off at Greenspoint near the big airport. Devon pulled up to the drop-off at the main entrance to the Wyndham Hotel. Dwight got out, entered the hotel, and went right to the restaurant. He hadn't been introduced to the person he was to meet, but his own reputation around the city was growing rapidly. He was becoming recognizable. As he walked in, a man in the back of the room immediately stood, waved, and beckoned him over to his table. The man was richly dressed in an obviously expensive dark suit with a bright-yellow tie. Probably approaching sixty, he had neatly slicked-back graying hair. His pallid skin helped to set off his striking gray eyes. You might have placed him as an SVP or senior executive with BP, Shell, or one of the other energy giants.

Dwight smiled, shook his hand, and took a seat across from him. As he spread his napkin on his lap, an attentive waiter filled his coffee cup. The man performed the standard ritual of business card exchange as he slipped his card across the tablecloth and was slightly surprised when Dwight did not do the same. The man's embossed card said simply: "Peter Butler, Mediterranean Investments." Dwight began the conversation with the usual general pleasantries. In particular, he asked where the man lived and was told that he resided back east but had a Texas office. He assured Dwight that he was licensed to do business in Texas. If this meeting turned out to have any potential at all, Dwight would vet the man thoroughly through his own sources. So far, all he was trying to do was to get a feel for him.

They both ordered breakfast and discussed a gamut of business issues from politics, to interest rates, and the like. Dwight was impressed. The fellow came across as very knowledgeable and sophisticated. They then had a long, two-coffee-cup-refill discussion about the Houston real estate market. As it turned out, both men were especially bullish on the prospects. Oil was here to stay, one way or another. People were still rushing to the Sunbelt. There were excellent investment possibilities. After almost two hours, Dwight decided he would take a shot with this guy, who seemed to be the real deal.

"Peter," he began in a serious tone, "I have just met you, but you come highly recommended. I would request your confidence on a matter, if I may do so."

The man looked flattered and readily agreed.

"As I am sure you are aware, I am the CEO of a partnership between Harris County and the City of Houston."

Again, the man nodded.

"It is very early on, but large projects take long lead times. I am planning to spearhead a major real estate development in this city. I will need a very large piece of land and a lot of help. I have been told that you are the type of person that may be able to work with me."

There was no hesitation from across the table. "Absolutely, Dwight. I'm your man."

29.

Dwight was perched amid boxes and general disarray in his office once again, which seemed to be the rule rather than the exception for him. His organization had grown so fast that in less than one year, they were in the middle of their third move. This one, he was sure, would be the last for a while. It had all the potential to get him where he felt he needed to be. A housing authority, by mandate, had to be accessible to the groups of people who used the services it offered. A high-rise penthouse suite, which would have delighted Lamar, just would not cut it. SETUP had to be located where a steady stream of basically poor folks could walk in off the street. He also was ever mindful that the more affluent his surroundings, the more suspicion he would arouse from the watchdogs at the city, county, and especially, HUD. His game was to create an ironclad image of an efficient and austere organization that provided clean and wholesome quality housing for low income people.

After starting in a cramped space under the freeway, he had worked hard to cultivate the respect and support of his board of directors, who were exceedingly pleased with his early success. As the largest users of office space in the entire Houston area, both the city and county were perpetually involved in the space sub-leasing business. As it turned out, one-time adversary Henry Francesca told him about a unique and quaint older two-story building on Lamar Street in the Midtown district, just west of downtown. "Lamar St." Dwight loved the address.

The vacant structure was under a long-term lease controlled by the city. The floor plan was ideal, with large, open spaces on the first floor offering direct access to foot traffic off the street. There was a large area in the back for the paper shufflers and clerical staff. Lamar couldn't believe his luck when he discovered that upstairs there was already a nicely appointed wood-paneled conference/board room and a large executive office.

This arrangement was perfect for the HA's business, and Lamar could finally have the large office he deserved. Anyone would agree that since the upgrades were already in place, it would be senseless and expensive to tear them out. Accepting the existing improvements was preferable to spending lots of cash to re-create an office from scratch. In effect, he was saving money by moving into the upscale place "as is." In addition, the building shared half a city block with its own adjacent parking lot, a dream in the congested city.

Workers were still scurrying about and the incessant smell of fresh paint was everywhere. Dwight was oblivious to all the commotion around him and was concentrating on a binder on his desk. He was studying the proofs for the first annual report brochure that the Southeast Texas Unified Partnership would produce. Dwight believed that an exceptionally attractive and well-done piece would assist him when he sold his agenda for SETUP down the line. The impressive brochure was printed in vivid colors with a glossy finish, to exude a high level of professionalism. Lamar met with several graphics arts firms to find one that would produce a superb brochure up to the standards that he expected, and also would "work" with him on the price. The cost of what he had in mind was realistically much more than SETUP should have paid, but Dwight didn't care. The company he selected gave him a very low-ball "firm" quote, which for all outsiders seemed to be the cost of the brochure. At the apparent price, it appeared that Dwight had negotiated one heck of a deal. What was not so obvious was that Dwight had verbally agreed to fund any overruns or owner changes from a completely different pocket. In fact, the final brochure ended up costing three or four times the $2,500 Lamar bragged about.

As he flipped through the pages, he glanced up at a beaming figure standing in his doorway trying very hard to avoid a painter's ladder being dragged by. He leaped up and moved around his desk. "Henry, Henry! Good to see you. Glad you could make it. Please excuse our mess. We are trying to get set up here as soon as possible so our customers do not miss a second of our service." He grabbed board member Henry Francesca's hand and led him away from his disorderly office. "Please follow me. They are waiting for you down the hall." They entered the large board room where a photography crew was set up.

"I am glad I was able to help you get in this building," the state senator said. "Do you think it will work out okay?"

"Henry, it is going to be perfect. Excellent access to foot traffic off the street, and the parking is phenomenal. We couldn't be happier. And many thanks to you!"

"Glad to help, Dwight," he responded with a smile.

"By the way, once we are settled, I'd love for you to come by and meet

Mateo Gomez, our brand-new human resources director. If I am not mistaken, he is one of your constituents and lives in your district."

"Really?" *And I was afraid to have an African American here? He has done a great job bringing in and assisting Latinos.*

"Okay. I brought in the photo crew from Alpha Graphics. I want our first annual report to be perfect and after looking at the photos you supplied, please excuse me, but I just wasn't happy with yours. They somehow did not bring across the professionalism and public spirit mindedness that you represent. That is why I asked you to come by. This team will do a quick shoot for you in our new board room. Does that sound okay? Oh, by the way, I will make sure you get a complete set of prints and proofs."

"Yeah, sure, Dwight. Thanks. I never did like that other picture," Francesca replied, as he straightened his tie and did his best to screw up his best public spirit look.

Dwight snickered to himself as he closed the door and walked back to his office.

A few months later SETUP was fully operating in their new location on Lamar Street. Dwight had just returned from lunch at Tony's with two of his board members, Eloise Quimby, who was a member of the Houston City Council, and Leroy Boden, a Harris County commissioner. Both were very complimentary about the first annual report brochure that Lamar had issued. Not only did they like the professional presentation, which included flattering bios on each of them, but they were particularly pleased to see that the HUD examiner had given SETUP an "above standard" rating.

Dwight Lamar liked to leave nothing to chance and believed in staying in close touch with his board members outside their formal meetings. He needed to know exactly how they felt on certain issues to head off any problems he might encounter with his strategic plan. He never wanted them to take a vote where he did not know the result beforehand. It had been a very pleasant and fruitful lunch at one of the priciest restaurants in the city, which the public reps thoroughly enjoyed. Dessert and wine included, of course, on Dwight's tab.

His voicemail messages included one from the editor of Houston Horizons magazine, a popular quarterly that featured trendy articles on local lifestyle, restaurants, and personalities. Lamar returned the call, and the editor apologized that he had been voted runner-up for their annual Bayou City Person of the Year Award. It had been very close, but the winner was an elderly lady who was active in the battered women's movement and donated four acres for the construction of a new housing facility. The selection committee felt that as a life-long Houstonian she deserved an edge, since he had come to town fairly recently. Runner-up was a fine honor in itself, and there would be a nice write-up on him in the issue due out next week. Dwight assured the editor that he was extremely pleased to have been considered and was looking forward to reading the article.

Dwight knew that except for one fortuitous event, the magazine would never have given him a second look. The magazine didn't care that his company had started off well. A part of Dwight's overall plan was to boost his image in the local community, especially by participating in civic-spirited activities. The downtown YMCA had a mentor program where business leaders got involved with disadvantaged teens once or twice a month. Participants met with groups of youngsters at the Y and sometimes gave them a sure-to-be-boring tour of their business. Astros or Rockets games were much more popular. Sometimes they just met for pizza.

Lamar correctly calculated that the mentor program would be an easy way to earn some community service points. With no wife or family, his nights and weekends were free anyway, and African-American business leaders were especially desirable in this program. What he had not planned on was that one of the youngsters, Brian, an eighteen-year-old African-American boy from the Fourth Ward, would bond with him. The kid's story was depressingly typical: single-mother home, food stamps, in and out of school, juvenile offenses, drugs, petty theft, etc. It wasn't hard for the normally standoffish Lamar to relate to this kid. He had been there himself. Dwight drove him home on several occasions and even sat with him a few times on the playground watching pickup basketball. Brian idolized him, and he actually felt good at the same time.

On a late Thursday afternoon, Dwight was thinking about heading home when his cell phone buzzed. He was surprised to hear that an HPD officer from the Gangs Division was calling. The officer told him that there was a crisis underway over on the east side. The SWAT team had been deployed, and several blocks were cordoned off. The issue was that two local youths tried to rob a convenience store at gunpoint in broad daylight. The attempt had been thwarted, but now the kids were trapped inside holding the elderly Philippine proprietor hostage. They were threatening to kill him during a standoff over the past couple of hours. The police were planning to storm the store very shortly. The HPD hostage team had gotten nowhere. One of the kids asked for Dwight and gave the cops his cell phone number. It was Brian. Dwight did not hesitate and had Devon immediately drive him across town, where he was escorted through the police cordon.

Police hostage negotiators are normally reluctant to let private citizens get involved, but the store owner was elderly and had a heart condition. Time was running out. They might have to move on the store very soon. Dwight was their last chance.

Crouching behind a phalanx of HPD blue-and-white patrol cars about a half-block from the store, an officer handed Dwight his cell phone with Brian on the other end.

"Brian? Brian? Can you hear me?" Dwight spoke into the phone in a normal conversational and unexcited tone of voice.

"Who is that?" came an instant high-pitched, agitated reply. "It's me, Brian, Dwight Lamar. What in the heck is going on?"

"Is that you, Mr. Dwight? How can I be sure it is you? I know those cops will try all kinds of stuff to trick us."

Dwight thought for a second. "Okay, Brian, don't we both agree that Dwight Howard on the Rockets sucks? We just had that conversation last week, didn't we?" There was no response. "Brian, didn't we?"

Finally, "Yeah. We did. It is you. Can you help us?"

"Good. Sure, but if you and your friend don't come out of there pretty soon, unarmed, a hundred police may come in after you. I'll try to not let that happen, but I won't be able to stop them if they start to move. Here is what I want you to do. Very slowly open the door to the store and toss all your guns out onto the street. Then, I want you one at a time, your friend first, to walk slowly out with your hands behind your head. When you get to the middle of the street, lay down on your stomach and do not move. Have you got all that? We will keep talking until you come out."

"Will you make sure nothing happens to us?"

Dwight's reply was cautious but hopeful, "No, Brian, I am sorry I can't do that. As far as I know, no-one has been hurt. That is so much better than if someone has been shot. I will assure you, though, that I will help you get the top lawyer we can find. That's the best I can do. Do we have a deal?"

There was silence. Then, "Give us a few minutes."

"You better make it quick. I can't hold back these police forever."

Five minutes passed, and the officer pointed to the watch on his wrist and then held up two fingers to indicate the minutes until they went in.

With the sweat beading on his forehead, Dwight tried again. "Brian?" And then louder, "Brian?" Silence.

Finally, after what seemed like forever: "Okay, Mr. Dwight, we're coming out. I am going to toss out our two guns, one at a time."

"Great, Brian. I knew you'd come through. Way to go, pal." There was a huge perceptible feeling of relief all along the police cordon as the first pistol clanked out onto the street.

The incident, of course, was the lead story on all the nightly television news shows. It even made the banner on the Chronicle the next morning. Dwight Lamar, of course, was hailed as a superhero, role model, and outstanding citizen. Oh, and what about his promise to the young man now behind bars? Dwight did dutifully call a good criminal defense attorney on his behalf. Beyond that, he hoped he never heard anything from that little punk ever again.

30.

Dwight Lamar was raised in the poverty of East Texas and then spent several years in college and working in New Orleans. He had grown to enjoy all the advantages of a big city and soon decided that Houston's West Loop, or "Uptown," offered the most appealing opportunities for him, both business and personal interest-wise. That area extended on either side of the western portion of the 610 freeway that circled the CBD at a radius varying from seven to ten miles from downtown. The West Loop was everything that the East Loop was not. The West Loop featured the world-renown, upscale Galleria shopping complex, exclusive restaurants, dozens of Class A high-rise office buildings, and an ever-growing number of fashionable condominium towers.

On the east side of the city, the 610 Loop was entirely industrial, commercial, and dominated by the massive bridge that crosses the Houston Ship Channel. The West Loop is home to a number of business and athletic clubs, including the Q, which boasted the largest membership and most extensive training facilities in all of Uptown. Despite his busy schedule, Lamar recognized that staying fit and looking good was absolutely necessary so that he always presented a vigorous physical appearance. Now in his mid-thirties, he had to be careful that a steady stream of rich and expensive business lunches and dinners did not accumulate around his waistline. Regular workouts were a part of his routine since his days at PMM.

He found that a membership at the posh Q health club in the West Loop suited him just fine. The large, free-standing facility was frequented mostly by younger executives on the way up. The old guard of wealthy water buffaloes stayed cloistered in their exclusive clubs, where they liked to recline in the men's lounges and compare bank accounts. As a new "boy" in town, such places were off limits to him, at least for the present. Dwight was not interested in sitting around and discussing his background or future plans with the business movers and shakers of the community, where an odd comment here or there could come back to haunt him. He appreciated the value of schmoozing, but he wanted to call the shots. He liked the relative anonymity of the Q, where he could actually exercise for his health and not be compelled to also cultivate his business. He had also been able to negotiate a special half-price, limited-benefits membership for Devon, and he worked out there religiously on Monday, Wednesday, and Friday mornings.

It was a Friday morning at the Q, and after changing into his workout gear, Dwight entered the main exercise room heading for a treadmill. His attention was elsewhere, however, deep in an analysis of potential real estate sites, when someone struggling to carry a huge stack of towels bumped smack into him. Dwight, who was sturdy and strong, remained erect and unfazed, but the towel carrier tripped and lost the load right in front of him. Normally, Dwight was impatient and had a low tolerance for such inefficiency, especially when it involved a low functionary. He started to rebuke the careless "idiot" when he noticed a shock of lustrous blond hair and a pair of shapely female legs sprawled on top of the beaver lodge of white linen. For once, he held his tongue.

He didn't know quite what to think as he stood watching the young lady in question squirm around and do her best doggy paddle to regain her feet. Always an admirer of a striking female form, he enjoyed the show, as did several of the other young men working out nearby. Finally, the very flustered young lady regained her feet.

"Oh, sir, are you okay? I am so sorry. I just grabbed too many towels and couldn't see where I was going. Please forgive me."

Dwight did not immediately reply, but continued to take the measure of this stunning young woman whose front "headlights" in the standard white "Q Staff" sleeveless tee shirt beamed brightly. He noted her well-developed upper body and black spandex tights that left very little to the imagination. He found himself intrigued by her sparkling-blue, pleading eyes. She was the total package, and he would have forgiven far more than a mere bump from a stack of towels. He flashed his best smile. "I am fine. No problem. Actually, I am sure it was probably my fault, anyway. I was daydreaming about business and wasn't paying attention." That statement in itself was remarkable. Dwight Lamar apologizing for anything almost never happened. "Don't think a thing about it. Err ?"

Her smile blazed back. She reached up towards the name tag on her left breast. "Pam. I'm Pam."

"Sure, Pam. I am Dwight, by the way." Their eyes met for an instant and he moved on towards the treadmills as she began picking up towels.

Pam had been working at the Q for a while now and despite the towel smash-up, felt comfortable among the young people who worked there. Despite her habit of letting her mind wander at inopportune times, she learned a lot about physical fitness and personal training techniques. This job was okay for a while, but with a four-year degree from Sam, she knew she could probably do much better. It was always tough for kids just getting out of college to jump right into a lifetime profession unless you were an engineer, nurse, or something. She had enjoyed her criminology classes and had some vague thoughts about maybe pursuing something along those lines.

Finding a good job was an area where her father could have helped. Travis would have tried, of course, to bring her into his company. That just would not have worked. Once they settled that issue, he would have had plenty of ideas and contacts for her. Yes, he had been a rotten father, especially to her mother and brothers, but after all, he was her father, and she loved him. Maybe someday she could talk to him about a job.

Dwight knocked out two miles on the treadmill and decided to do a little free weight lifting before he took a shower and went to the office. He walked over to the barbells and sat on a lift bench while he caught his breath. A barbell was already set at one hundred and twenty-five pounds, which was about right for him. He wiped his brow with a towel. Devon suddenly appeared. "Okay, bro. As soon as you're ready, I'll spot for you. Okay?"

Dwight nodded and was about to lay down on the bench when a thought struck him. "No, Dev. I don't need you to spot for me, but here's what I want you to do." He pulled his brother close and spoke softly into his ear. Devon listened carefully, smiled, and took off across the room.

Two minutes hadn't passed before Pam Nelson strolled up to the bench.

"Hi, Dwight. I understand you need a spotter for a few bench presses. I am happy to do it, but after what happened earlier, I am not sure you should trust me."

"Pam, don't be silly. I appreciate your help."

Dwight lay down on his back on the bench and reached up with either hand to firmly grasp the bar that sat in the "Y" brackets. He took a deep breath and lifted the bar upward and off the support. Pam stood facing him where she could snatch the bar if he got into trouble. It may have been his imagination, but having that gorgeous woman just inches away from his face gave him special inspiration that morning. He easily knocked out three reps of ten, which was something he had never done before. After Pam helped him replace the bar into the brackets, he was still breathing hard when he sat up and wiped the sweat from his face.

"Dwight, that was just great!" Pam encouraged, just as she had been trained to do with clients when they worked out.

"Thanks, but it took some effort. Say, how long have you worked here at the Q?"

"I guess it has been about six months." Perhaps sensing the guy might just be about to put some moves on her, she looked up at the big clock on the wall and quickly added, "Whoops! I've got to give a training session in five minutes. I gotta run. Anytime, Dwight."

"Sure, thanks, Pam. I'll see you around," he replied, as he admired her stunning butt walking off.

Later, after the workout in the car heading to the office, Devon remarked, "That was some babe you worked with today. I can tell you kind of liked her. Do you want me to set her up for one night this week?"

Dwight considered what his little brother asked for a moment before responding. "Devon, you are a piece of work. You are coming along, but Houston is not Sparta, Texas. You just can't walk in and get a woman like that on the spot. Pay attention to me. I'll explain to you later what we will do."

Any additional thoughts concerning Pam Nelson's delicious body were quickly extinguished when the boss walked into the SETUP office. Although he was hardly an affable and personable manager, Dwight liked to convey visibility to his staff. He made it a part of his daily routine to greet the clerks and accountants that worked for him. He was concerned about any issues or problems they had, because problems among the troops could spell problems for the entire organization if not corrected. He really didn't give a rat's ass how cute the receptionist's new baby was, but he made it a big point to give the impression that he did.

It was a little different among his key staff members that he kept to a precious few. James Luken ran the daily operations and knew how Dwight wanted things to function. He was loyal to a fault, and was not beyond pre-serving Dwight's image at the expense of a little white one now and then. In return, Dwight made sure that the man was well compensated. There were a few others that he relied on, but there was no-one who had the big picture. Each key player, by design, only knew so much.

After glad-handing downstairs, Dwight was anxious to sit down at his desk and get to work. Once he had established the basic work flow of the housing authority, which was rooted in providing quality housing for poor folks, he had more free time to begin to craft strategy for his end game. The beauty of his position was that while a housing authority is by and large a pretty bland and lackluster entity with a very limited mission, it really didn't have to be so limited. Under the thumb of HUD, it was, in most cases, difficult to accomplish much beyond vouchers and basic shelter. In this case, however, SETUP had been created as a unique joint venture between two very powerful and competitive entities, the City of Houston and Harris County. The creators of this exceptional vehicle fully expected it to accomplish things above and beyond normal HA humdrum. Dwight recognized this situation, and would never have taken the job without it. He also anticipated that once he was up and running, as long as he was very careful, he would be able to pick and choose what path the organization took. Neither ponderous bureaucracy would be able to control him. If anything, like the clever child and his parents, he could play one against the other. In fact, he would be preaching to the choir when he presented his grand plan for the partnership. So long as he did his job, he fully expected almost everyone who really counted would jump on his bandwagon.

A stack of reports and studies all concerning the Houston market was on his desk. Among them were detailed analyses by the highly respected international Urban Land Institute. Colliers, Grubb and Ellis, Delta, Altos, Green Street, Jones Lang LaSalle, and several other real estate firms. He had personally met with several of the leading commercial brokers in the city. He analyzed the Greater Houston Partnership (Chamber of Commerce) urban growth projections. He even talked with the Real Estate Research Center at Texas A&M University. On weekends, he had Devon drive him all over the area. He was a quick study and after only a few months, he felt he knew more about the Houston real estate market than most of the local so-called experts.

Dwight needed a site for a major project. The site, however, had to fit certain specific criteria. Most importantly, it had to lay within both the jurisdictions of the city of Houston and Harris County, which was a very tough nut to crack. There were wonderful sites southwest in Ft. Bend County, where things were booming, or even north in Montgomery County, where the Woodlands Development was prospering. He knew he could hardly expect support from his board for anything outside of the city and county.

As Dwight pored over the data, he almost chuckled to himself. What he was seeking was the right piece of land that could be supported by the experts, but even more importantly, accepted by his two powerful constituents, but, strangely, not one that necessarily worked in the end. That would be nice, but he had to home in on their strong preferences first and then sell the potential and feasibility. Oh, and the price had to be right – right for him, that is.

Dwight's vision was that his little group would be the driving force behind a large, decade-long, multi-phase, multi-use development with affordable housing at the heart. He understood that planners have learned that pure concentrations of affordable housing by themselves make for very bad results. Just look at the millions of substandard public housing authority units around the country. For balance, a development must also include some upper-scale, market-rate housing. There would also be a lot of senior units as well. Single-family lots would be developed and then re-sold to whatever quality developers and builders could be attracted.

He fully expected that once the development got rolling, his role would be much diminished, if not totally extinguished, which suited him just fine. His focus was on the front end, not the long-term. His name for the project came to him one night as he lay in bed: "Destination Diversity." He loved it, and knew his directors would as well.

All the reports were piled up on the right side of his desk. After much debate and reflection, he boiled down the possibilities to three tracts of land, which he noted on a yellow legal pad. It was time to decide. He easily crossed out one, but it took several minutes for him to eliminate another. And there it was, finally. He had selected the site for Destination Diversity. He turned his pad over and got up and went to the restroom. When he returned five minutes later, he flipped the pad over and re-read his notes. Now he was satisfied. The choice had been made. Now to acquire it.

Careful to pick up his personal cell phone, no emails or speed dials, he typed a number starting with area code 212. On the third ring, the connection went to voicemail. Dwight frowned and quickly hung up. This message was too important to leave on a recorder. Before he could replace the phone in his pocket, it buzzed with an incoming call. It was the number he had just tried to call. He hesitated, but decided to answer.

"Yes?"

A man's voice responded, "Please forgive me. I was not alone just then. I have been expecting your call."

Dwight was succinct. "Crispus Attucks. Pull the trigger."

"Got it." Click.

31.

For all the years he lived there, Peter Butler never tired of the view from his twentieth-floor apartment on Central Park West and 97th. The Jacqueline Kennedy Reservoir and swatch of greenery were almost surreal in the otherwise sea of concrete and steel. Born overseas, he arrived in New York as a teenager. During those early days, as Pjeter Bodi, he lived with his immigrant parents and sister in a third-floor tenement walk-up deep in Brooklyn's Bedford-Stuyvesant neighborhood. Almost everyone he associated with, including friends and neighbors, were fellow Albanian nationals who struggled just to get by and rarely ventured far outside of their native group. In fact, they followed their own code of ethics and rules brought over from the homeland, which often trumped NYC's idea of what was appropriate and proper.

Pjeter was bright enough to make it through high school and somehow ended up working as a porter at the infamous Plaza Hotel next to Central Park. The world-wide reputation of that hotel had long made it "the" place to stay for well-to-do travelers who visited New York, often several times a year.

After a while, Pjeter began to recognize repeat Plaza guests and made a habit of learning names and offering pleasant greetings as they arrived and departed at the front entrance. In particular, an older gentleman from Beirut, who was bent on getting as much of his wealth out of his war-torn country as soon as possible by purchasing real estate in the United States, took a liking to Pjeter. When he was not on duty, Pjeter often drove the man around the city.

During one of those excursions, Pjeter met the New York real estate broker who was searching for properties for the Lebanese gentleman to buy. As time passed, Pjeter became more involved in the property search, and the buyer from Beirut began to rely on him for advice. Pjeter was surprised one day when the man informed the broker that he expected Pjeter to be in the commission split on all his deals, or he'd find someone else. Pjeter was off and running. He obtained his New York real estate license and built a successful brokerage business through the years. Early on, he realized he was uniquely positioned to become a conduit for offshore cash to funnel into the United States. Oh, and Pjeter Bodi became Peter Butler along the way.

In order to find suitable assets for his offshore investors, Peter did not limit himself to New York City. He scoured the entire country, including the Sunbelt, where he did several deals. He was familiar with Texas, and had even a licensing arrangement there through an intermediary, who, for a modest cut, basically let him trade under his Texas license. It was easier collecting brokerage commissions if you could flash a local license number.

His deals were structured in different ways. Sometimes he was a pure broker with a percentage commission for his services. In others he was part of the buy-low, sell-high arrangement. He kept a sharp eye on the marketplace and weathered several real estate downturns. Hurricane Katrina, a devastating experience for most, turned out to be a windfall for him. After the storm, New Orleans real estate was virtually being given away. At that, there were few takers. The classic dilemma is that during those bad times, real estate gets very cheap, but no-one has any money or maybe the balls to invest. When things improve, everyone wants in and prices skyrocket.

With Mayor Ray Nagin's help, Peter nailed some terrific investments at rock-bottom prices for his clients, who were not tire kickers or long due diligence types. All they cared about was making lots of money quick. Peter Butler was referred to Dwight by the ex-mayor as a man who had cash, connections, and could keep his mouth shut. If things worked out okay, someday Dwight might return the favor with some financial consideration for his old Crescent City Tulane friend.

On the condition of strict confidence, Dwight authorized Peter in a terse coded conversation to initiate the purchase of an unremarkable tract of land in the southeast corner of Houston and Harris County, not far from the NASA complex. The land was just over two hundred acres in size and had a cash asking price of $5,000,000. The seller was a land trust held by several elderly heirs who were anxious to get rid of it and enjoy some cash before they passed on.

Butler's offer was especially attractive because it was a full-price, all-cash deal and with a quick closing date. No lenders, no feasibility, etc., made it a seller's dream. There was little time allocated for feasibility or environmental studies, which might delay or kill the deal. Closing was conditioned only on Peter's group receiving clear title.

The land was mainly just scrub and brush that had not seen any visible active use for decades. In fact, a truly prudent buyer would have questioned why such a sizable tract at such a good price was sitting vacant within the traditionally hot Houston real estate market. For the transaction to work, Peter's investors would rely solely on Dwight Lamar's private verbal assurances that a purchaser would emerge in the short-term willing to acquire the tract from them at a much higher price. Nothing was in writing. When the purchase was complete in a few weeks and the deed was recorded, Peter was to confirm that fact to Dwight with a similar coded phone call.

Peter's investors for this deal were extremely aggressive and relied exclusively on his recommendation. After all, they had made a lot of money through him, and everyone was pleased. Still, they could be a pretty rough bunch. He shuddered to think what might happen the first time one of his deals fell apart. He wasn't anxious to find out. He gave kudos to Dwight Lamar for finding a tract that could be picked up on the cheap, but Peter was an experienced commercial real estate pro, and fully recognized there must be a serious issues with the tract for it to trade at such a low price.

On the other hand, he did take comfort that if Lamar's deal should happen to crater, his group's relatively low buy-in price should let them recoup most, if not all, of their cash on the open market. Personally, he stood to double-dip by earning commissions coming and going. The key, of course, was to act quickly and quietly. The land would be purchased by a trust, ultimately owned by his investors, but untraceable back to them. There would be no traceable connection or link to Lamar or Peter's investors. A transaction of this size would not go unnoticed by the Houston real estate community, but the city was used to big deals. Five "mil" was really not all that much.

Peter arranged to meet with his clients the next day in Brooklyn. He'd pitch it hard and see what happened. This one would take a lot of nerve, but he'd seen them do similar deals in the past. If they happened to pass, he had several other buyers to approach. The next morning, he took the subway, an old habit from when he was young, and was at their brownstone by nine thirty. It took him about an hour to describe the deal. There were several questions, but by noon it was done. They loved it. They called their attorney to draw up the proper trust documents to acquire and hold the property. He'd have them next week. Peter made plane reservations for Houston.

As he walked down the steps of the brownstone, he decided he'd earned an upgrade. He hailed a cab, and an hour later he was home in his office. He called his local broker contact in Texas and asked him to prepare a commercial real estate contract on the proper Texas Real Estate Commission forms. Peter gave him all the details. The local guy was thrilled with the prospect of a referral fee. Peter reminded him of their understanding to keep the deal strictly to himself.

When Peter awoke the next morning, he had an email with the contract attached. After reading it, he called his clients to say he would bring it by to be signed by their lawyer as attorney-in-fact. He also would need an earnest money check payable to Stewart Title Company for $25,000. By noon, with signed copies of the contract and earnest money in hand, he called the Texas guy and asked him to make an appointment with the selling broker for late the next day. Bright and early he would be on United Airlines headed for Houston. He would go nowhere near Dwight Lamar. It was bad luck to calculate your commission before closing, but he knew a hundred grand plus was coming. What a country!

******

After all the excitement over the past few weeks, Matt was happy to settle back into a routine. It was time to begin to develop his consulting business. Little Gail was fine and had no lasting effects from what she'd been through. They left the Surenos thug tied up in the warehouse but were sure he'd get away. They had tossed his stiletto on the concrete just inside the building on the way out. Neither brother was into killing, although John could have made an exception for that guy. The idea, though, was to let him get back to his group and spread the word that they did not know anything about their father. They hoped the gang would now stay away from them. Nonetheless, Matt had hired a security guard for both his home and office. It was better to be safe than sorry. John headed back to Lorton to see what trouble Harvey had cooked up.

Matt made up a two-sheet marketing brochure to use when he called on potential clients. It wasn't much, but at least it gave him something to talk about when he went prospecting for investors. He made a couple of appointments with some of his friends in the city to get the word out. He dropped by and had coffee with a few of them. They agreed that his game plan made sense, but already had their own staffs and couldn't use what he had to offer. They were pleased to catch up with him, though, and expressed condolences over the loss of his father.

After the first week of using up a little shoe leather, he had no prospects and nothing to show for his efforts. He wasn't down just yet, but a little self-doubt flickered that maybe there wasn't such a big need out there after all. He was discussing things with Diane one afternoon when she tossed out an idea. She had just seen an article in the Houston Business Journal featuring a wealthy elderly lady who made a gift of some land to the Riverbend Women's Shelter. Riverbend had grown to the point where they needed more space. The site was on Route 288 south of downtown, not far from the Medical Center and NRG Stadium where the Texans played. Matt began to get excited. Here was an inexperienced non-profit organization about to leap into real estate for the first time. It was exactly the type of deal that made sense for him to chase.

"Mom, that sounds interesting, but I suppose they already have their ducks in a row with a development team." The old negative Matt surfaced for just a second. "But I suppose it wouldn't hurt to call them and find out. Got any idea who runs Riverbend?"

Diane tried not to smirk but didn't succeed. "Yes, as a matter of fact, I do, and so do you."

"Really? Who is it? I hope it is not somebody we did business with during dad's days. Some of them are still pretty unhappy with us. Stop the charades. Who is it?"

"How about Jeanne Jensen? You remember Jeanne, don't you, Matt?" she snickered.

Matt jerked upright in his chair. "Are you kidding me? Jeanne Jensen! Wow. I haven't thought much about her since high school. I didn't know she was even in town. I remember she went back east to school. Bowdoin, Tufts, or somewhere like that. I guess she is the executive director over there. I am not sure that is a good thing or not. Just because you go to high school with someone doesn't mean they even remember you, much less want to do business with you. She sure was cute, though, and really smart. I think she was captain of the cheerleaders in our senior year. I'll have to think about calling her sometime."

"Think about it? Matt, what is wrong with you, son?" his mother cajoled, knowing exactly what his problem was even after all those years. "Am I mistaken, or didn't you take Jeanne to the senior prom?"

Matt could not hide the shade of crimson that flushed across his face.

"No, you are quite correct. I did take Miss Jensen to the prom in our senior year, and that is precisely why I am not sure she will even talk to me."

32.

The world was still reeling from the tragic and cataclysmic events of the previous September, when a ragtag group of Al Qaeda zealots had rammed the Twin Towers in New York and Pentagon in Washington with high-jacked airliners. The United States had been turned upside down and still hadn't fully adjusted by the following spring when Matt Nelson was preparing to graduate from high school. He was excited about next fall when he would follow his father and grandfather to Texas A&M, but he was not concerned about all that just yet. His immediate problem was getting a date for the senior prom.

He had dated several girls over the past few years, but he had his mind set on asking one particular person that he had secretly harbored a crush on since freshman year. The problem was that irrespective of the fact that she was a stunner and one of the most popular girls in the senior class, she had been going steady with the same guy during their entire time in high school. Her boyfriend, by the way, was not just any guy. He was captain of the football team and stood well over six feet and tipped the scales at about two fifty. Rickey Flowers played linebacker so well and with such abandon that he had received a full scholarship to Texas Tech. Matt, who also played football, although not nearly with the proficiency of Rickey, got along well with him. Flowers had a short temper on occasion and was very possessive when it came to his girlfriend, Jeanne Jensen. Despite his infatuation, Matt would never have considered asking her out, except that Rickey was a year ahead of them. He had already graduated and was some five hundred miles away up on the north plains in Lubbock, Texas, at Tech. Matt was friendly with Jeanne, who was in his Advanced Latin class. In fact, she even dropped a hint to him that it was a shame she would be sitting home for the senior prom.

He was in his father's study, where he hoped to get a little privacy from his insidious sister. He dialed and re-dialed Jeanne's number three times, pushing the button down before the call went through. His heart was pounding and sweat beaded on his brow. He was just about to give up on his fourth try when an incoming call actually rang on his phone. Good! He'd try again later. Unfortunately, maybe not. There was a click and a lively voice answered, "Hello?"

Oh, no, what do I do now? That is her! Maybe I should just hang up?

"Hello?" she repeated, and was considering hanging up herself when Matt finally screwed up his courage.

In a quaking voice he managed. "Hello, Jeanne? Is that you?"

"Matt Nelson! Hi, Matt. How's it going? I thought that might be you calling; at least, I was hoping it was you."

"Eh, you did? Really? Why?"

"Because I really want to go to our prom. I'd really love to go with you. What do you say, Matt? Will you take me?"

Matt could not believe his ears. The most popular girl in school, the captain of the cheerleaders, a real knockout, *had just asked him to the prom.* Matt may have been flustered, but it didn't take him long to reply. "Sure, Jeanne, I'll go with you, Err..... I mean, I'll take you to the prom."

"That is great. I couldn't imagine staying home. We'll have a great time."

His euphoria aside, Matt's realistic perspective began to return. "Jeanne, I do have one question. What about Rickey? Aren't you two still going together?"

"Oh, him. Yeah, sorta; but he doesn't own me. He is a million miles away in Lubbock." And then the infamous kiss of death comment, "What he doesn't know won't hurt him."

Matt swallowed hard, but the deal was done. He was high as a kite. Now he couldn't wait to find his little brat sister and tell her the news.

The prom itself was held in the school gymnasium, as they have been since forever. Jeanne looked absolutely stunning in a slightly less than modest blue dress that was a perfect complement to her cheerleader-hewed shape. When he picked her up at her home, he noted that her parents were warm and friendly, almost as if they were pleased to see her go out with anyone other than Rickey. As he posed for pictures with their daughter, he hoped they would not leave them laying around the house where Rickey might see them someday. (Gulp.)

True to his reputation as a good provider of the physical things, Travis Nelson had sprung for a limo for them for the evening. If Jeanne missed her constant beau for the past four years or felt at all self-conscious being out without him, she hid it well. As soon as they got in the limo and drove away from her house, she slid over and snuggled right up. He was still a little nervous about the whole thing, but his inhibitions were melting fast. As the

Jersey Boys might have sung, *"Oh, what a night!"*

Matt was so taken with his good fortune to be with this gorgeous girl of his dreams that he didn't pay a lot of attention to the faces of many of his chums and classmates as he and Jeanne danced almost every dance. On the slow dances in particular she moved herself into his body, not in a particularly suggestive way but more like they had been very close for a long time. She remained bright, animated, and sparkling the entire time. It was almost as if she had thrown off the chains of being held down over the past several years. Finally, she could relax and be herself and have fun, which she surely did. Matt loved every minute of it.

After the dance, they all went to the designated restaurant, where they ate and carried on as high school seniors do. Afterwards, a dozen or more kids piled into the limo with Matt and Jeanne, and after a brief stop back at the gym to change clothes, were off to the beach in Galveston. The midnight hour had come and gone, but the night was still young. With everybody squeezed together on the ride down to the beach, a totally uninhibited Jeanne leaned over several times to plant sweet kisses on Matt's anxious lips. These acts of affection were not lost on the rest of the crowd, who let out whoops and hollers every time she did it. Matt could only wonder what might happen when they got to the beach and could wander away in the dark to the dunes.

When they reached the beach, there was already a large crowd of kids. A roaring driftwood fire was blazing and a boom box was blaring out tunes. Someone had come up with the critical missing ingredient: beer. It is important to remember that this was a crowd of high school kids, most of whom were turned on to beer, but for the most part were rank amateurs compared to what they would become a few years down the road in college. This event was still about having a good time with friends you might never see again.

Sure enough though, Matt was emboldened with a new self-confidence. He led the way, with Jeanne showing no resistance as the couple got up and moved out of the light of the fire down the beach. They found a comfortable spot in the shadows back in the dunes and just lay there on their backs next to each other enjoying the spectacular display of stars while listening to the noise of the party. Both of them had carried a "sociable" beer with them but had barely touched it.

Finally, Matt turned onto his elbows and pulled his shoulders over Jeanne, who was smiling. It was his turn to carefully kiss those alluring lips, and when he did, Jeanne reached up and embraced him with a fire that unleashed a long-suppressed hunger. It seemed as though they had finally found each other.

At just that instant, not far from where they lay entangled, a loud voice echoed over the sound of the crashing surf and party reveling. "Where the hell are they? Let me at that bastard! I'll kill him!"

Luckily, it was dark, but when Jeanne heard that voice, she untangled herself from a startled Matt, who hadn't heard anything. She sat up. "Rickey!" she uttered.

Matt had trouble switching gears, but his mind began to readjust to this new, most relevant bit of information. "Rickey?" he repeated, and then an appropriate, "Oh shit!"

By that time, Jeanne was on her feet and doing her best to rearrange her clothes so that nothing inappropriate was hanging out. She was brushing sand away as a still confused Matt scrambled up next to her. He was about to speak when he was struck from behind in the ribs by a human thunderbolt that knocked him with a "whomp" ass over teakettle into the dunes. The huge Rickey landed on top of him and began flailing with his fists. Matt tried to cover up the best he could, but the man was a monster and had gotten even bigger after a year of football conditioning at Tech. Matt didn't have a chance.

For her part, Jeanne screamed hysterically at her former boyfriend, demanding that he stop pummeling her poor date. Nothing draws a crowd like a fight, and most of the kids had seen the obviously tanked-up Rickey and his college buddies arrive looking for Jeanne and Matt. They had followed him when he struck out up the beach towards where the couple had gone. There were a number of football players in the crowd who knew both Matt and Rickey, and it took several of them to tear the snarling linebacker off Matt and get him settled down.

Matt emerged not much worse for the wear, except for his severely bruised pride. When Jeanne was sure both guys were under control and Matt was not about to be killed, she stormed off towards the bonfire. Both of her exes, former and current, were content to let her go. Beer, fighting, and sand had exhausted both of them.

An absolutely baffled Matt, who could not think of anything else to say or do, finally looked over at a much-mollified Rickey sitting there in the sand with two burly linemen standing next to each shoulder, ready to pounce should he decide to go after Matt again.

"So, eh, Rickey, how are things going up on the high plains?" Matt hesitantly inquired.

Rickey, who had already ingested his ample college boy beer ration, at first did not know what to make of Matt's question. Was he trying to taunt him? He had always liked Matt when they played together. He was friendly and straight, a nice guy. Never had a problem with him until now. "Fine, Matt. College is a blast so far," he replied, and then in a hushed voice added, "You should see those babes up there."

"No kidding?" They both smiled. One of Rickey's buddies tossed Matt a beer, which he popped open. When Matt finally tried to stand up a few hours later as the sun began to peak over the eastern Gulf of Mexico, he was unsteady. There were lots of dead soldiers strewn about the area. Rickey had filled him in all about college. In fact, he promised to set him up with a hot lady anytime he came to Lubbock. During those hours on the beach, Jeanne's name never came up. Matt assumed she had gone home in the limo, which he had dismissed hours ago.

33.

Almost fifteen years had passed since Jeanne Jensen had last seen Matt Nelson. Their lives had not intersected, and there was really no reason they should have. They had been casual friends in high school and had one disastrous date. She had gone away to school back east at Bates College, way up in Maine. When she graduated, she took a job with Prudential Insurance and moved permanently to Boston to work with health care providers. Other than returning home every so often to see her family, during the first decade or so, she was hardly ever in Texas.

Then, two years ago, for a number of reasons, she moved back to Houston and took a position as assistant to the executive director of a women's homeless shelter. She discovered that she enjoyed the work, even though it could be very depressing. At least she was doing good things for people. In fact, she performed so well that, even though she was barely past thirty, when the executive director passed away, the board promoted her to the top position. Their confidence was a tribute to her professionalism.

She loved her work at the Riverbend Home for Women, which consumed her virtually 24/7. She rarely took time off at the expense of a non-existent social life. If she wasn't involved in the day-to-day operations counseling folks, she was out hustling benefactors for contributions to keep the shelter running. She'd read about the bizarre circumstances behind the disappearance of Travis Nelson and the fall of Mesquite Development, but did not feel she knew Matt well enough to call with condolences. Their lives, which had never been intertwined, had been totally separate since high school. She had tried to convince herself some time ago that Matt Nelson was just another guy who happened to be in her high school class. Still, she couldn't explain why she picked out her favorite suit, added an extra dab of perfume, and had her hair done after he called and made an appointment to come by. She wondered if seeing any of her other classmates would make her heart flutter as it did that morning.

At 10:00 AM sharp, her assistant buzzed to say that he had arrived. It was time for a reality check. She had to bounce back to her senses. This meeting was not with an old beau. It was a business meeting with someone she happened to have known. She slapped on her game face and resolutely assumed her most professional demeanor. "Show him in."

Matt was uneasy himself as he walked into Jeanne Jensen's office at Riverbend, although he couldn't figure out why. He'd had a crush on this woman in high school, a hundred or so years ago. Big deal. Their one date had flopped big-time. He was a happily married man with two kids. She likely had a similar family situation. Put any inkling of the past aside and pitch this business deal, which he really needed.

As he walked into her neat, functional, and plainly appointed office and saw her standing there, though, all that resolve about ignoring past history stuff flew out the window. She was beaming and radiant in a perfectly tailored navy-blue business suit and a white blouse with a frilly ruffle at the neck. Her dark hair was neatly trimmed above the shoulder, and there was no way she could hide those sparkling eyes. She looked trim, healthy, fit, and desirable. Damn it! He couldn't help it. His mouth dropped open and he was at a loss for words. The best he could do was a weak smile.

Fortunately, even though Jeanne's reaction to Matt was not a whole lot different, she was better at corralling her emotions and jumped right into the business mode she was determined to utilize. "Matt Nelson," she greeted in her most appropriate professional demeanor. "It is so nice to see you again. It has been a long time. How have you been?" She offered her outstretched hand, which he shook. There was no hug, peck on the cheek, or any outward display of affection. He had no idea that, behind that businesswoman facade, she fought a compelling impulse to grab him and plant a big, sloppy kiss on his lips.

He smiled and tried to avoid her captivating eyes. He stammered, "Yeah, Jeanne. Great to see you, too. I read somewhere that you moved back here a little while ago, and that you've had a big promotion lately. Congratulations. I am glad to hear you are doing well."

And then there was a puzzling pause when both remained awkwardly silent. Neither could figure out what else to say.

Before it became embarrassing, Matt snapped back to his senses. "Well, then, tell me all about Riverbend and your plans to expand."

Wow, thank goodness for that question. Her wheelhouse. She was programmed and could talk about the shelter all day; in her sleep, if necessary.

"Of course." She brightened. "Our mission is to end the epidemic of domestic violence against women and children by stopping individual victimization and reducing the devastating impact of family violence through safety, shelter, and expert services to battered women and their children. We are committed to preventing violence by raising the level of community awareness regarding the effects of domestic violence. We are a non-profit organization that offers an array of services to women and children in need, most of whom have been victims of domestic abuse and violence. We have a full-time staff of counselors to help the people who need our services. We offer teen and parenting counseling, among others. We maintain a hotline twenty-four hours a day."

"That is a huge job. Unfortunately, I am sure you have plenty of women who need help."

"More than you could imagine, and the sad thing is that, by far, most domestic household violence goes unreported. By the time we get involved, there have been problems in the home for some time. It is very sad."

"I'll bet. I admire what you do. Now, I thought that there was also a housing aspect to your organization, isn't there?"

"Yes, it is a big part of what we do. There are two basic components of our operation that involve housing. The first is providing on an emergency basis. We have to be able to take in women and their children immediately when they need it and get them away from violence in their homes. We also have transitional housing where they can remain with us for up to one year while their family situations stabilize. We take in women whose abusive husbands, fathers, and boyfriends continue to want to have access to them. Sometimes there is an official protective court order or TRO. Sometimes there isn't. We have to be sure that the shelter we provide is safe and secure. It can take some doing."

"How much emergency and shelter housing can you provide?" Jeanne paused and then continued. "Not nearly enough. Now we have only ten beds and twelve transitional units. They stay full. We hate to turn anyone away, but often we have to refer them to other shelters. We feel badly when that happens because we are never sure if the women ever receive the help they need."

"So, now you have a site where you can expand, what are your plans for that?" Matt held his breath. He was sure Jeanne was going to say that they had all the planning, design, and arrangements all wrapped up. He shouldn't have worried.

"We were blessed recently with a gift of four acres from an elderly lady that has been one of our most generous benefactors for well over a decade. In fact, she was just given *Houston Horizon* magazine's Bayou City Person of the Year award. We are so thankful for her generosity. We hope we can increase our capacity up to one hundred units, which would be a dream. To answer your question about planning, we haven't accomplished much at all so far. I am not sure where to start. I have always worked on the services side of things and don't know much about development. I guess I have been procrastinating, but I have been so busy with the normal resident care. I need to start making some phone calls. There are some national groups and website resources that might be of help. I just keep putting it off. I needed to start on it yesterday."

Matt felt like it was about time for him to stand up and rip off his shirt revealing his Underdog outfit underneath. Jeanne's situation was a dream come true. He knew without question that he could help her complete the development. *It would be a no-brainer. A labor of love. Hold it, that is not a good way to think about it!* What he had no idea about, at that point, was whether or not that project made economic sense for him to get involved. If Riverbend's budget could not afford his consulting fee, he might have to pass.

The conversation switched over to Matt. "I am very impressed with Riverbend and all that you do. It is truly wonderful that there are people like you around to take on these difficult tasks. Do you know much about our company and what we do?"

For the second time, Jeanne looked a little uneasy. She'd read plenty about Travis Nelson and Mesquite Development, and much of it was not very good. When she thought back, though, she could not ever remember seeing Matt's name in print. It would surely have caught her attention. She didn't want to offend him, but some of it was pretty damning. "Well, you know, Matt, most of what I saw and heard was about your dad. By the way, please accept my tardy condolences."

Matt nodded, "Thanks."

"Anyway, it sure seemed like Mesquite Development was involved in some serious stuff."

"Yup. I cannot deny it. You are right on. There was some very bad stuff, which I continue to be embarrassed about to this day. I can tell you, though, that none of it was my doing. My dad ran the show with an iron fist. It was his way or the highway, which eventually, I took."

"Really? I didn't know that."

"It is true. But anyway, if we can set aside that one huge, terrible deal with the cartel, Mesquite Development developed and assembled an outstanding portfolio of affordable housing all over Texas. We had more than 4,000 units. I personally was involved from the beginning to end on most of them. It was what I did, and I think I did it well."

"I am sure you did."

"When it all blew up, the company cratered. My developing days, which I enjoyed, ended forever. That said, my mother and I scaled way down and were able to create a property management company, which has worked out well. As mad as many of our investors were at Mesquite Development and my dad, they still let mom and I keep their property management, which is pretty incredible."

"That's great, but I don't need any property management, unless you want to come by every so often and hold the hand of an expectant unwed mother whose boyfriend chased her around with a baseball bat."

Matt smiled, "No thanks on that one. What we have done, Jeanne, is set up a development consulting business targeted at non-profits just like you, who know your own turf backwards and forwards but don't know where to start when it comes to brick and mortar. From what you've told me, maybe we can help you add that space."

"No kidding? I am all ears. I'd be delighted if something could be worked out. Before we get too far involved, though, I have to tell you that my board gives me lots of leeway, but in something like this, I would need their consent. Honestly, several of them are older and very conservative. The Mesquite situation would have to be laid out in great detail."

"I understand only too well. Say, that wouldn't happen to be a survey of your new land back there on your credenza, would it?"

"As a matter of fact, it is."

"Here, hand it over and let me have a quick look." He also noticed, and for some strange, unresolved inner feeling, he was secretly pleased that there were no personal pictures of husband or kids anywhere in her office.

34.

The scorching Houston summer was finally beginning to burn itself out. Football season had arrived. The Aggies had already played in a nationally televised season-opening kickoff classic against the "Tigas" of LSU at Jerry Jones' monumental edifice in Dallas. Matt and Ellen had driven up for the game, which Texas A&M won in the last few seconds on a blocked punt. Matt had been an Aggie fanatic far too long to get too excited too early, but what the heck, not a bad way to start.

Baseball was winding down with but a few regular-season games left for the Astros. They were actually going to make the playoffs. Matt couldn't help thinking of Travis, who had been a big baseball fan. One would have thought that he would not have had the patience necessary for baseball, but he avidly followed the team and religiously scrutinized the box scores every morning. He would have been delighted to see his team had finally achieved success after being down for so long. The kids were settling back in school, and finally, he was starting to make progress with his consulting business. Oh, and things had been quiet on the Surenos front. Everything was just fine for the moment.

As Jeanne Jensen had predicted, it took some doing to convince her board to use Matt Nelson as a consultant for the shelter expansion, but Jeanne was persistent and would not take no for an answer. Even before they signed a letter of engagement for his services, Matt was already spending quite a bit of time with her discussing concepts, sketching preliminary land plans, talking to architects, and massaging the numbers. The job would take at least a year. His $75,000 fee was low, but this job was his first, and he needed it. Riverbend was not exactly flush with cash, and he could have easily priced himself right out of the deal.

Of course, he still had to find more work and on a bright fall morning, he headed to Midtown to the offices of the Southeast Texas Unified Partnership for a meeting to discuss a Request for Proposal (RFP) for qualified firms to provide (guess what?) development and construction consulting expertise. He expected that there would be several of the local tax credit developers on hand who were at least as curious as he was about what the new golden boy in town was up to.

He hadn't met Dwight Lamar, but he'd read and heard plenty about him since he'd surfaced as the head of the city-county partnership. The man just couldn't seem to stay out of the news. Somehow, he'd been able to free up several millions of dollars of frozen HUD funds for housing choice vouchers, almost eliminating the waiting list and backlog overnight. In reading the magazine article about Jeanne's elderly lady benefactor winning Bayou City Person of the Year, he noticed that Lamar had been selected as runner-up for the award. He had miraculously talked two gunmen out of a desperate situation in a convenience store surrounded by a police cordon with no shots being fired.

Not everyone was impressed, however. In his travels around the city, Matt called on the executive directors of both the city's and county's housing authorities, hoping they might need his services. They did not. Informally over coffee and after requesting his confidentiality, however, they expressed reservations about this interloper on their turf. The guy was pushing the envelope. It wouldn't last. While Matt respected the opinions of both men, he understood some of those comments were attributed to jealousy. Lamar had snatched away a lot of their business. Now he wanted to be a developer. Matt was intrigued to see what the man had in mind. Maybe he had a shot at landing a big fish.

Matt easily found a parking space right next to the attractive two-story building that had been faced with some intricate floral grill work very reminiscent of the Creole style so popular in the French Quarter of New Orleans. He entered the building and was directed to the elevator to the second floor by a pleasant African-American receptionist.

The board room was already occupied by several of the tax credit developers in the city. He knew most of them and, after exchanging pleasantries, took a seat in the back of the room at the far end of an imposing, immaculately polished oak conference table. He was impressed by the room's appointments: extensive wood paneling, heavy overstuffed chairs upholstered with rich fabric, and plush, dark-red carpeting. A podium had been set up in front of a white screen that automatically came down from the ceiling. There was a complete coffee and beverage service built into one corner. It was a setting more appropriate for Exxon or United Airlines than a brand-new housing authority.

A glittering, multi-color copy of SETUP's first annual report had been placed in front of each chair for perusal by the meeting attendees. Matt was flipping through the brochure when two individuals entered the room at the front. He watched with curiosity as they made sure everything was perfectly arranged, the podium was aligned correctly, and that the microphone was properly tuned. Were they expecting a housing authority director or President Obama? It was already ten fifteen. The meeting was scheduled to start at ten. The sensational man was late.

"It was already here, Mr. Nelson. That is the answer and explanation for the appointments in this room," a man's deep voice surprised Matt from behind.

Matt swiveled in his chair and saw an immaculately dressed African-American man standing there with a smile on his face. He wore a dark, expensive suit that had been tailored to the contours of his bulky but fit-looking frame. His stylish striped pink tie blended well with a light-blue shirt. His slightly thinning hair was neatly trimmed. Matt had no idea how long he had been there, perhaps studying the attendees.

"Excuse me? I am not sure I understand what you mean," a confused Matt responded.

"I know what you are thinking. Most folks who have come in here are surprised by the beautiful table, paneling, and so forth. Their next question is always, how did a brand-new housing authority pay for it all? The answer is, of course, we didn't. All this was already in place when we moved in. In fact, it would have cost us a bundle to down-scale, if you will. I am always interested in doing things as efficiently and inexpensively as possible."

Matt quickly caught his drift, if not particularly buying his explanation. "That makes perfect sense to me. You must be Dwight," Matt replied, offering his hand, which the man accepted and shook firmly.

"Yes, that is me, Matt. Now I must get this show on the road. We are already behind schedule. Here I am running at the mouth about efficiency, and I can't even conduct my own meeting," he responded, as he walked towards the front, where one of his assistants stood to one side at virtual parade rest.

How the heck did he know my name? We have never met.

Dwight Lamar moved smartly to the podium, introduced himself, and greeted the fifteen or so people who gathered with a warm smile. He spent the first ten minutes describing the background of SETUP and the unique partnership that had been established between the City of Houston and Harris

County. So far, he had enjoyed total support from both organizations. He invited everyone to review the annual report in front of them, which they could also take with them. He noted that there were extensive bios of all his directors.

He went on to explain that, while SETUP was first and foremost a housing authority, it had been created with some additional objectives in mind. Unlike most HA's, he was starting brand new, and had zero stock of actual housing units. The city and county had dozens of properties and thousands of units under their control. After having staffed his "back room" and being assured that their housing choice voucher program was up and running, his next step was to create some actual housing on the ground. He planned to do that in two steps. The first would involve the development and construction of some individual projects, and then there would be a larger land development. All these plans, of course, were strictly conditioned upon the advice and consent of his board.

Matt could barely believe what he was hearing. This guy thought he was superman. A project or two, maybe, but a community land development? He must have an ego a hundred miles wide. Yet again, this is Texas, the home of big plans. He was not surprised to see other developers in the room with puzzled looks.

At that point, Lamar nodded, and his trusty assistant circulated around the table handing out thick packages to each of the attendees. Lamar then took several minutes to explain to the crowd that he knew full well that his in-house group was totally unprepared and incapable of tackling any of these brick-and-mortar projects alone. They needed a lot of experienced professional help, which was the reason he had called the meeting today. In front of them was a Request for Proposal (RFP), which was an invitation for qualified development firms to submit their credentials and ideas with the ultimate objective of becoming Dwight Lamar's and SETUP's development consultant. It was a very detailed document, and a response would take some time to prepare and submit. Lamar hoped that all the developers on hand would respond to this wonderful opportunity. He did point out that the deadline for submissions would be January 1st, allowing about ninety days to respond. He expected that several other firms not represented today would also respond. Selection would be on a competitive basis.

Once the RFP responses were received, he and his staff would evaluate them first to ensure the firms were qualified. After that step, proposal merit and cost would be considered. He introduced his two assistants, who would be available 24/7 to answer questions during the preparation process, or they could also call him directly. He then opened up the meeting to questions from the stunned audience.

Matt didn't know what to think. The idea of getting a consulting contract of this size was a dream. The first obstacle he would have to tackle was simple: should he even bother to respond? Matt knew this business very well. It was not exactly the same as the tax credit business, but there were many similarities. Government regulators hid behind every bush, or so it seemed. The city, county, and HUD, throw in a lender or two, and there was the recipe for a nightmare. He had seen it before. He wondered if Lamar would be able to navigate his new ship through all those treacherous waters. There was no question that he clearly conveyed the distinct impression he could.

There was a potential roadblock that could knock Matt out of the game before he started considering the nuts and bolts of a response. Matt would bet his next set of Aggie football tickets, a real treasure to him, that on about page ten of Lamar's RFP there would be a very simple question: "Have you or anyone in your organization ever been banned from participating in government-sponsored or related programs?" A yes response to that question would almost certainly render his submission null and void in the starting blocks. With the fall of Mesquite Development, even though he had resigned before it officially cratered, he had been president for three years. He had been advised by TDHCA not to ever try to apply for tax credits on his own again. While that directive was personally disappointing, he knew his punishment could have been much more severe. They could have even pressed criminal charges against him for his involvement. He and Diane had been fortunate enough to rekindle their management company, but he had just seen what a time Jeanne Jensen had in getting him approved. Like it or not, his reputation within the development community had been significantly soiled by the Mesquite disaster.

A good lawyer might be able to interpret the basic question in such a way that Matt could technically answer no. He himself had not been banned in writing, and his present company was only recently organized and had nothing to do with Travis's Mesquite. Such an approach, however, would be really pushing it. He would have to get that situation cleared up beforehand, if he decided he wanted to proceed.

There were other issues. The scope of work Dwight Lamar had outlined was huge, if he ever got it off the ground. While Matt was more than qualified to tackle the land development deal as far as expertise was concerned, in order to do so, he would have to add several professionals to his staff, which currently consisted of a single person. He would be willing to do so only if he were absolutely sure the SETUP projects would go forward. All that bureaucracy scared the heck out of him. All that said, the RFP could lead to a fantastic piece of business. He would have a long discussion with his mother, who, while short on actual business experience, had excellent instincts.

Beyond all the very practical aspects of the situation, there was something else that was nagging at Matt. He had been unfairly banned from all future access to the business that he loved by association with his father. A part of his reluctance to join John's group was his innate hope that somehow, he could get back into development. He was chomping at the bit to do so. A magic carpet had suddenly been waved in front of him, and yet he was still reluctant to try to jump on it. He knew the odds of him being picked were small, but what would it hurt to try? Why wasn't he anxiously grabbing this opportunity? Then, it hit him—Dwight Lamar. There was just something about the man that rankled Matt, even though he had just met the guy an hour ago. He couldn't put his finger on it. Maybe it was that age-old Matt Nelson showing through. Once burned, maybe I-don't-want-to-get-on-the "roller-coaster attitude" again?

35.

Matt and Ellen had a great holiday with their two little ones who were at ideal ages for Santa and all that goes with him. Unfortunately, Matt's hesitation to jump aboard the Aggies' gridiron express after that early impressive win turned out to be prophetic. There was no college football spectacular playoff spot or even major bowl game for the team from College Station. It was business as usual with a ho-hum invite to the Independence Bowl in Shreveport against Louisiana Tech, of all schools. Even though that game was fairly close to Houston, Matt could not gather up enough enthusiasm to buy tickets. Matt not following his Aggies? That just didn't happen.

After talking the matter over with Diane at length, he decided to make a hard run at the SETUP RFP. In a follow-up phone call, Lamar had been reassuring up to a point. Obviously, the man had checked him out extensively before he ever walked into the RFP conference. Lamar told him flat out that the negative aspects of his association with Mesquite Development would not be held against him. Moreover, it was a definite plus that he'd been responsible for the excellent properties in that portfolio. The SETUP lawyers reviewed his circumstances and could find nothing in the extensive litigation records relating to Matt's association with Mesquite Development. After all, he was never a principal or in ownership. On balance, Lamar was encouraging, and was looking forward to receiving Matt's submission.

Again, Matt was puzzled at his own attitude and was beginning to have self-doubts. What was the matter with him? Did he have a death wish? The door was wide open, and he still was reluctant to walk in. Lamar mentioned to Matt that SETUP would probably award a consulting contract for his first project or two, but hold off on the major development deal until both sides made sure the arrangement worked. As long as things looked good, the big one would follow. Matt considered that decision good news, since it meant he would have more time to staff up.

Ten responses were submitted by the first of January, and Dwight wasted no time in reviewing them. He was anxious to get a shovel in the earth. Four were from local Houston groups, three came from other parts of Texas, and three were from large national firms. One of the national firms immediately dropped out when it was announced that the large contract would be held in abeyance. Four of the respondents, including two in Houston, were eliminated as being not qualified to carry out the requirements, including a small single-family detached home builder. Five firms were deemed qualified and moved on to the next stage. Dwight notified each that they would have one more opportunity to sharpen their pencils and submit a "best and final" price proposal. Matt had been expecting as much, but still had to do some deep soul-searching to come up with his best shot.

Representatives of the five remaining contending firms were back in the conference room in mid-February. SETUP planned to announce their decision as to the best and final bids and which firm would be awarded the contract for the first two projects. Competition is at the heart of the construction business. If you were in the game, you wanted to win. Despite a lot of nervous chatter, tension and anticipation permeated the room. Matt was no exception, and Diane did her best to calm him down, but her words fell on deaf ears. Dwight's assistant stepped in twice to say that his master—er, boss—would be in shortly. Matt wondered why there was a delay. Lamar was already a half an hour late. They weren't still trying to decide, were they?

Finally, the poised and confident man strode in, looking immaculate as always. He smiled at no-one in particular and took his time moving to the podium. He reached in his suit pocket, put on his cheater glasses, a rare indication of vanity, and shuffled the files in front of him.

"Okay, folks. We have made a decision on the development consulting contracts,'" he unhurriedly announced.

Matt was surprised he said "contracts." There was just supposed to be one for two projects now, with the big one later. Was that just a slip? It wasn't.

"I want to thank everybody in this room who took the time to respond to our Request for Proposal. If you made it this far, it means that we determined that your firm was qualified to complete the work. We had a difficult job choosing among several excellent proposals to select winners."

There, he said "winners." He used plural again.

"In the end, it came down to price. As you know, my organization is owned by the citizens of the city and county, and I'm duty-bound to make the best deal I can for them at the least cost. I take my public trust very seriously, so here is what I have determined."

You could have heard a pin drop. In fact, Lamar's trusty assistant actually dropped a ballpoint pen. He turned red as he stooped down to retrieve it, but no-one noticed.

"I am going to extend a construction development consulting contract to Mr. Punjab Patel of Taj Mahal Consultants from Beaumont. "

That was it, the room broke up. The losers jammed their iPads into their briefcases and slammed them shut. There were several audible murmurs. The selected winning firm was generally regarded in the industry as poorly qualified and willing to do anything for a buck. Everyone wondered how it had gotten this far. They should have expected something like this. All that wasted work on the RFP.

Lamar saw that he was about to lose the audience and spoke up to get their attention. "Gentlemen, if you please. Wait just a minute. I have more." It took a moment, but the crowd settled down again.

"Thank you," he responded, and then took his own sweet time to continue to shuffle the papers in front of him for what seemed like an eternity. He even looked at his watch. Perhaps he had a luncheon engagement. "SETUP is also going to award a contract to Mr. Matt Nelson at Mesquite Consulting. We decided to award each of those two firms a single project to start and then decide, based on performance, who gets the larger development contract sometime in the future."

Matt was speechless. That slime ball! He'd changed the rules of the game not once, but twice, since the start of the process. He'd sliced the pie very slim. That was unfair. Unethical.

Matt's arm shot up, but he didn't wait to be called on. In an obviously agitated voice he asked, "Sir, that was not what we bid on. Our numbers were not based on a single small project but at least two, where there are economies in staffing and overhead. I don't understand."

Lamar peered down calmly from the podium at him. He waited until Matt was quite through and then answered serenely, "Mr. Nelson, once you receive our award letter later today, you will have a full week to decide whether or not to accept it. In the event that you are not inclined to do so, I believe there are several other firms still in this room who are eager to have another chance."

Matt was about to go back at the pompous idiot when he felt a jerk on his sleeve.

"Hush up, son. You just won a contract. Sit down and shut up," his mother scolded as she yanked him back into his seat.

Matt just sat there in a daze and barely acknowledged one of his friends from another firm who looked over at him as he walked out and said, "Good luck, Matt. I am not sure if you won or lost."

It took Matt a few days to simmer down, but after he thought things through, he concluded he was lucky to have grabbed any piece of the pie, even a smaller one than he'd expected. He was really in no position to be picky. He would have to add two more people to his consulting staff, and before taking any salary himself, he'd be lucky to break even on the revenues produced, which would be $200,000 from Jeanne's and SETUP's contracts. He reviewed and signed SETUP's letter of engagement, trying hard to shove his concerns aside. He was anxious to get to work.

He arranged a contract kickoff meeting in early April. He met with Lamar at the SETUP offices to go over the first new construction project. Matt was a brooder by nature and was still sore about the way things had gone down with the RFP, but he was determined not to let a bad attitude affect his work on the actual project. He would be continually optimistic and professional in the presence of Dwight Lamar. After all, the man was paying him $10,000 per month for his advice.

If Lamar even remembered Matt's display of sour grapes at the contract award conference, he gave no outward indication. His manner was formal and businesslike in a way that left no question who was the boss. Through a local real estate broker, SETUP had entered into a purchase contract for a seven-acre tract of land on the city's north side. Dwight had already selected an architect on his own and had a preliminary land plan on his desk. The architect was also hard at work on a set of initial drawings. The project, "Bluebird Acres," would have 246 apartment suites arranged in twenty-four two-story walk-up buildings.

This information took Matt aback for a minute for a couple of reasons. First, he was very familiar with the architect Dwight selected and knew the firm had done mostly small commercial projects. He didn't know if they had any multifamily experience. His own choice would have been someone who had a proven track record of having designed several successful apartments. Second, 246 units on seven acres would make for a very high-density and congested property with over thirty-five units per acre. The residents would be crowded and crammed together. He would have hoped and expected that Lamar would have consulted with him before making such key decisions, especially the architect, which was critical. He could see already, though, that Dwight was far past those choices, so he decided to keep to himself on those points.

"Do you know the architect, Matt?" Lamar asked. Matt replied that he was familiar with them. "Good. Call them and get over there as soon as you can; this afternoon, if possible. You need to be looking over his shoulder."

Matt nodded. *I hope I am not too late already!*

"Now, about the site. You need to look over the contract and the title report. I have HUD ready to fund the purchase next Monday. Make sure it all looks good to you. The environmental report will be ready in a couple of weeks. Okay?"

Monday? Three days from now. No environmental! This guy is on a fast track to failure.

Nonetheless, he replied, "That doesn't give us much time. I'll do my best."

Lamar ignored Matt's comment and continued to issue orders from on high. "Sure. Next week I will introduce you to the general contractor. I haven't quite made up my mind yet."

Holy shit, he's already chosen a builder! Matt could remain silent no longer. "Dwight, I understand you are anxious to get some units in the ground, but don't you think you are rushing things a bit? I really thought you and I would work on these critical items together and make the best decision for SETUP that is possible. I thought I was bringing my expertise in these areas to the table. I have been developing in this town for several years, and I think I know the players very well."

Lamar remained silent until Matt finished. It was clear that he had heard him loud and clear but had little intention of altering his decision-making process. "I understand your concern, Matt, and I do value your input. I expect you to stay up on what we are doing and advise me accordingly. I will take your comments into consideration and then decide what is best for the organization. Please keep in mind that from your perspective as an outside contractor and non-principal, you are not necessarily aware of all the factors that go into every decision. Now, let's talk about a few more general items."

Matt couldn't wait to hear what would pop out of this man's mouth next. He sat back and was all ears.

"First, I did not mean to ignore your concern that you expressed at the conference about my awarding two contracts instead of one. I had my own reasons, and that is the way I decided to do it. I also understand that some-one like you, who has had extensive experience in development but recently fallen on hard times, has to be very concerned about the bottom line. Frankly, it was a stretch for us to select you given that you are just getting into the consulting business and are just now staffing up. I cannot afford to make a mistake, especially with these first two projects."

Matt took it all in and wondered, *Fair point on just starting as a consultant, but the "hard times" has no bearing on where we are today. Okay, so just why did you hire me then?*

If there was one thing about Dwight Lamar, he was quick on his feet and could change directions in an instant. "I think over time you will discover that, if anything, I am a fair and reasonable man. Given that you are experiencing substantial start-up costs at the moment, I have already authorized your first contract payment, which you may pick up today before you leave. It is for $20,000, twice the agreed amount. That should help you out some to get started. We can adjust for it down the line. Also, I am a realist, and understand how complex construction development can be, especially how difficult it is to forecast all expenses some eighteen or so months out at the start. In that regard, I want you to know that as we approach the successful conclusion of the development period, if you discover that your costs have run significantly higher than you planned, I will be amenable to receiving change orders from you for additional compensation. How does that sound? Is that agreeable to you?"

Matt could have fallen out of his chair. No-one ever offers or even leaves open what he had just discussed. Damn right that extra draw would come in very handy right now. He had taken the contract based upon a bare bones fixed fee totaling $125,000. Lamar seemed to be leaving that maximum fee open and subject to renegotiation. Either the guy was so new at all of this or was just plain ignorant of normal business practices, which Matt seriously doubted, or he had another agenda for suddenly seeming so co-operative. Matt could worry about that later. He worked up his best smile. "Why, of course, thank you, Dwight, those things are appreciated. I am sure when we are done, everyone will all be very satisfied with a fine new addition to the SETUP portfolio."

"Good. Just so you know, I have also extended the same arrangements to

201

Punjab on his project up on Mesa Road. Now, Matt, I can see it in your eyes. You are still wondering why I chose you for this job when, frankly, several other qualified firms were available who had not had the problems you had to deal with at your father's company."

Matt blinked. The man was psychic. That was exactly his question. "As a matter of fact, that thought has crossed my mind," he replied in an even tone.

"I thought so, First, I took the time to take a good look at the Mesquite tax credit apartment portfolio. It is superb. I would gladly accept any of those properties into my portfolio. I am familiar enough with what went on at your company to know that, while your father was distracted in Mexico, you were operating the business. On that score, you have an excellent track record."

Matt smiled; so far, so good.

Dwight continued, "For our arrangement here at SETUP to work well, it is critical that the people closest to me, which includes you and Punjab, are the type that I can work with. They must be seasoned, intelligent, and flexible. They must know how the world really functions, if you know what I mean. You have been through a lot and are streetwise. I wanted you on our team because I felt you would understand the critical tolerances associated with the real world; things as basic as paying a few dollars more for an item now because to wait for it would in the end be much more expensive. Or maybe rearranging a payout schedule. Am I making myself clear, Matt?"

Matt nodded. He was afraid that he did.

"Based upon what you have been through, I felt you'd understand how to get things done. I am right about that, aren't I? You are flexible?"

Matt had no clue how to answer. A sudden flashback. He felt like he was back in his father's office being ordered to sabotage a competitor's project. He'd never have any part of anything like that again. The nutty thing about all of this was the guy wanted to hire him because of his problems in the past and not in spite of them. Before he could reply, Lamar's secretary's voice broke in over the intercom. The man looked very irritated to have been disturbed, but he picked up the handset.

"What is it?" he demanded. "Oh, okay. Look, tell him I am busy. I will call him right back. He is where? About to get on a plane. Okay, okay. Put him on." There was brief pause and Dwight made sure he was turned away from Matt. He put his hand in front of his mouth and without any other greeting or explanation whispered, "Crispus Attucks," into the phone. Although it had taken several more weeks than they'd anticipated, the NASA land deal was done. The Albanian investors now owned the NASA tract. He promptly hung up and turned back to face Matt.

Matt had had time to formulate his answer, for now anyway. "Sure," was the best he could do.

Dwight nodded in a distracted way, leaving Matt to assume he had probably forgotten the question Matt just answered. Whatever Dwight had dealt with on the phone had taken him completely off his game. He had no more time for Matt, and the feeling was mutual. He was completely preoccupied. "Good. Don't forget your check on the way out," he said, leaving no indication that their meeting was anything other than over.

Matt was more than happy to get out of there. Crispus Attucks, what was up with that?

That guy was a mystery man.

36.

The ground-breaking of two construction projects by SETUP kept Dwight Lamar's already full plate even fuller. The truth was that he had very little experience in construction and development projects. He was astute enough to appreciate that fact, but still failed to appreciate the criticality of his initial choices of players, such as the architect and general contractor. He was so obsessed that the "right" contractors be put in place, who were flexible and would "work" with him, that he didn't pay enough attention to the qualifications and track records of the ones he hired. He also discovered that he could not possibly micro-manage two simultaneous development projects from his office. Construction consultants served vital roles in the process, and like it or not, he found himself relying more and more on them.

Somewhat amusingly, he found that Punjab would not hesitate to do anything he asked. Hold back a little here, a little there, hire subs of Lamar's choosing with no background checks and post office box addresses, etc. Lamar was tempted to have Punjab's guys work on the upgrades on the suite he was renting with an option to purchase in the Memorial Tower in River Oaks for his personal residence. He did draw the line there, though. That move would have been way too obvious and easy to track.

Matt Nelson, however, was quite another animal, and Dwight had to admit the man was very proficient at running and tracking his job. He issued comprehensive weekly owner reports that accounted for every nail and screw. He had set up excellent critical path schedules and never failed to answer any question from Dwight completely. It wasn't long before Matt's Bluebird was far outshining Punjab's project. Unfortunately, Matt was doing a little too well for Dwight's overall scheme of things.

Dwight became so preoccupied with the day-to-day monitoring of the construction projects that he became concerned that he might ignore the folks that made it all happen for him: his board. He needed to keep his image as the wunderkind reinforced in their minds. He continued to have self-serving board meetings and lunches and dinners where he played on the egos of the members. He got the Houston social community buzzing when he started dating the daughter of Shirley Brown Waters, an African-American congresswoman from the Fourth Ward, who had been going to Washington for almost three decades. Lamar was delighted to read in one of the local gossip columns that he and this lady were contemplating marriage. In truth, he couldn't stand the bitch, but if it made him a hot item in the local press, great.

Dwight was not all work, however. Devon had become skillful at providing female company for him on demand in several shapes and sizes. If anything, his business successes seemed to have whetted his appetite for sexual companionship. The Memorial Tower condo purchase was handled through an intermediary to ensure as low a visibility for the transaction as possible. A first-class, twenty-fourth-floor, three-thousand-square-foot suite in one of the city's swankiest high-rises still might look a bit much for a lowly housing authority ED. Dwight was gradually getting to the point where he would not worry as much about who was watching him, but he was not out from under the microscope yet. He was still concerned about all the government audits and bureaucrats that constantly surrounded him. In fact, he decided to keep his townhouse in Midtown for a while. He could more easily entertain a variety of women there without being noticed. There would have been buzzing if those ladies showed up at his new high-end address.

There is something about the male ego that makes the prohibited or unobtainable more interesting and desirable than if it were easily obtained. Dwight Lamar worked out at the Q several times a week and had gotten chummy with the luscious Pam Nelson. They'd had several health-drink breaks together and even a lunch one day at the Q's snack bar. Dwight's interest in the girl was heightened when he discovered that she was Matt's sister. Although he knew eventually his name would cross between Matt and Pam, he never mentioned to her that Matt worked for him. He had tried everything he could reasonably think of to get her to go out with him, but she would only openly flirt at work. Her resistance made her even more desirable and a bigger challenge. He decided to try another approach.

Pam spotted for him on the free weights, and they were sitting at the snack bar over fruit juices.

"Pam, I know since I met you here some time ago, you mentioned that this job was just sort of a placeholder for a while until you found something better."

"Yep. It is fun to be here in a young, healthy environment, but I do sometimes feel like I am wasting my life. I really didn't spend four or so years at Sam just to fold towels."

"What would you like to do? Have you given it any thought?"

"Oh, yeah, a bunch. I dunno, maybe something in criminology, police work. I am just not sure."

"Really? Have you ever thought about the finance industry and maybe some aspect of marketing services?"

"No, not really. What do you mean?"

"Actually, I am thinking about my company, the Southeast Texas Unified Partnership. It is called SETUP for short. We are a public housing authority but also much more. I am the executive director. We are growing very fast and need to get the word out about us. From what little I know about you, there could be a fit. You would be involved in calling on clients and the people we do business with to let them know about us. What do you think?" He had pitched it as a marketing rep. What he really had in mind was a personal assistant.

Pam chuckled, "Why, how nice of you to think of me. I am not sure I am qualified to do something like that."

"I think you are, and you never know until you try. Tell you what. After I shower and change clothes, I'll leave you my card. We are in Midtown on Lamar Street. Just drop by sometime. I'll show you around and introduce you to our team. Bring a resumé."

"Team" always sounded good.

"Great, Mr. Lamar, I'll do that. You know, it does sound pretty exciting."

I think so too, babe, he pondered as he watched her firm butt swish back and forth as she strolled off towards the workout floor.

******

Sometimes it is wise to be careful what you wish for because you just may end up getting it. Punjab Patel and Taj Mahal Consultants were so flexible and easy to deal with that Lamar worried they would surely trip up in front of a HUD auditor or other watchdog. It had taken Lamar a number of years to become skillful and subtle enough to "cook the books" and divert funds in such a way that was difficult to uncover. He avoided doing anything more than once or twice and never established recurring patterns. Punjab was like a warm puppy, anxious to please his master at all times. He was the complete opposite of Matt Nelson, who approached every expenditure like it was his own last nickel, which was an admirable trait but an increasing problem to

Lamar. Punjab had come by the office late one afternoon to discuss a problem on his project. The project was limping along in the early stages and definitely suffered from the presence of "flexible," but not especially, qualified subcontractors. The issue of the moment was that the roofing subcontractor had steadfastly refused to purchase his roofing materials from the source that Lamar had directed Punjab to use in East Texas. The roofer had given the project a guaranteed price, and he needed to purchase the material as cheaply as possible from his own sources. Lamar's supplier was many thousands of dollars higher, and the increased price came right out of the roofer's pocket. This situation was not unusual. This problem was not unique, and the typical approach was to fire the sub and bring in a new one, even though construction progress would inevitably suffer. The complication with this guy was that he had the balls to be very upset and would not go away quietly. There was also the matter of his having certified on HUD forms that he was paying his workers at the mandated Davis-Bacon wage rates, which he was not. If Punjab did not cave on the materials purchase, the roofer was threatening to go to his lawyer and blow the whole thing wide open.

For the first time, Punjab was worried. It was true that he was flexible, but he was not stupid. A Davis-Bacon claim would expose his whole project and every trade that had worked on it. It could mean big trouble. He had tried everything with the roofer, including a lucrative "contract cancellation fee," but the man was adamant and would not budge. Lamar spent enough time with Punjab to make sure he had exhausted every reasonable avenue out of this dilemma, which he surely had. He told Punjab not to worry, he would take care of the problem. Just go out and find another flexible roofer who would be ready to move on the job in about two weeks. A relieved Punjab thanked his boss profusely, bowed, and was whistling a merry tune as he bounced out of the SETUP office. Lamar shook his head as he watched the man sashay out.

As Lamar had gradually configured and constructed his domain in Houston, he increasingly relied on locally-available resources to satisfy his various requirements. In doing so, he recognized that every so often, there was no substitute for muscle. At first, as was the case with the goofball in Gulfton, he merely contacted his Beaumont guys. Problem solved. Still, he was on the lookout for someone closer and more reliable when a hammer was necessary. As luck would have it, a "rent-a-cop" security guard who worked at his office provided a lead. Lamar directed his office manager to get a direct phone number, taking the security guard out of the loop and with no idea who, if anyone, followed up on his suggestion. Keep everyone in the dark by going double-blind. Each link in the chain only knows his closest contact, no-one above or below. No-one would be able to trace things back to SETUP or him in particular. Lamar was always astounded at what little scrutiny was put into vetting security guards. It seemed like almost anyone would qualify; sometimes the shadier, the better.

Lamar asked his trusted office manager, James Luken, to arrange for another intermediary in a double-blind arrangement with dead ends. The arrangement notwithstanding, Lamar was curious about who would actually do his dirty work. After doing a little digging, he discovered that the muscle-on-demand was the local chapter of a national Hispanic gang, the Surenos, with close ties to drug cartels in Mexico. That information gave him pause, and he thought long and hard about doing business with those folks. In the end, what he needed most was a reliable source to get the job done, no questions asked. Luken assured him that his contact had met with two of the key lieutenants of the gang, and was assured that their work was quick, efficient, final, and always done in complete confidence.

Dwight Lamar had no way of knowing that Luken's contact had met with none other than the doubled-down loser duo of Rico Corona and Carlos Garcia, both of whom had just botched big jobs for the gang's cell, earning them severe dress-downs by the gang's leader. In better times, the two would have simply been eliminated, but the gang was desperate for cash-producing business. Both Corona and Garcia were on notice to come up with something soon, or they'd better blow town. Excellency's patience was wearing thin.

Both men had been scouring the area for additional business when the word got around about the SETUP job. They had no idea or really cared who the ultimate client was and jumped right on it. Lamar, of course, knew who he was dealing with, and the more he investigated their reputation for Mafia-like tactics, the more he liked it. In the end, an organized national and international gang should be able to perform better than some local sloppy hit man. Also, the gang angle might be useful in further covering up tracks back to him. He decided to give them a try with Punjab's problem.

37.

Rudy Maranavich had signed up for the bidders' list with Taj Mahal Consultants, but never expected to ever get a job from them. There was something about Punjab Patel's attitude at the bidders' conference for the eastside apartments that bothered him. The man seemed much more obsessed with getting a rock-bottom price than the quality and capability of the subcontractors. In fact, he was surprised when Patel called and told him he had been selected to provide the roofing for the project. You'd have to be crazy in that business to turn down a large contract, so Rudy set aside his reservations and grabbed the job.

Roofing, of course, is not a trade that moves on site right away. The basic building framing structures have to be completed first. Based on that timing, Rudy was able to monitor progress of the project before it would be ready for him. He was not impressed, and again wondered about pulling off the job. His granddad and his dad had built the company based upon performance and keeping their word. Rudy was not about to welsh on a commitment.

Finally, the first of twenty-four two-story buildings had been decked with plywood and were ready to be dried in with roofing. Rudy's crews moved in and knocked out the work with underlayment and shingles in a single day. It was a few weeks before the next building was ready. Again, Rudy's team did their job quickly and efficiently. Unfortunately, this pattern dragged on for several more buildings. Rudy was put out, and Patel was no help. A contractor assembles and pays crews based on work being ready. You can't expect a crew to sit around and draw wages only once every three weeks. Also, Rudy bought out the entire job's worth of shingles and underlayment. He was sitting on a large outlay of cash; which he would not have done except he had gotten a good price.

The erratic and snail's pace progress of the project cost Rudy a bunch. He would be lucky to break even on the entire contract. Then, to make a bad situation completely untenable, Punjab called and ordered him to purchase the last third of the roofing materials for the project from some supplier he had never heard of in the Piney Woods. It was likely a middleman broker of some sort. Rudy "hit the roof," and it was lucky that he and Punjab did not come to blows in the site construction shack. He would have walked away right then and cut his losses, but he had already bought all those shingles. He had to complete the job or he was stuck with them. Those issues aside, Punjab still owed him a substantial amount for work he had already completed and then, the man had the balls to ask him to fake some paperwork for HUD. Maranavich had never done business that way, and he wasn't going to start. His word had always been his bond. With no other choice, Rudy decided to talk to his attorney.

It had been a long day and, with that Taj Mahal stuff, had also been an exhausting week. Rudy sat at his old, battered wooden desk in the office portion of the warehouse just off the north 610 Loop that had been the company's headquarters for almost twenty years. It was getting dark outside, and all of his men had gone for the day. He was going to have dinner at a barbeque joint with his lawyer, who had worked for his dad for many years and was as much a friend as counsel. Perhaps he'd have some good ideas about Punjab Patel.

He sat back on his squeaky chair and looked at the picture of his six grandchildren. Those kids were shooting up. Hell, he was already in his late sixties himself and not getting any younger. Maybe it was time for him to cash in his chips and think about taking it easy. Climbing roofs was no fun. He'd had his share of falls, but that was when he was young. No telling what would happen if he took a header at this age. He smiled when he looked at the picture of his wife of thirty-five years. She was still a looker in his mind. He'd better not let her get wind of retirement thoughts. She would push him into it in a minute. He checked his watch, it was almost six thirty. Best he get over to the restaurant. Just as he was about to get up, he heard a noise from outside near the loading dock. All his crew had left, but he'd told them to leave the gate open. He'd lock up when he drove out. Maybe a piece of sheet metal was rattling in the wind. His place was pretty old, and probably needed a new roof, which made him smile again. He'd check it on the way out. He flicked off the buzzing office fluorescents and opened the back door to the loading dock where there were steps leading down to his pickup. He shut the door behind him and turned to twist the key to set the lock. As he did so, two figures emerged out of the shadows and moved in behind him.

One grabbed him high and the other low. Together, he was twisted to the floor with a thud. For an older man, he still had lots of lean, sinewy muscle and he gave them a tussle as he struggled to break free. They were just too overpowering, though, and gradually they dragged him to the edge of the loading dock where there was a large, mobile vat of simmering and steaming black roofing tar, ready for the next day's jobs. Rudy's eyes got big, and terror filled his heart as he saw the tub of hot, acrid goo. Despite his resistance, the two men were able to hoist him up enough that they could launch him head-first into the boiling pot. His screams were muted and his struggling quickly stopped as his head sank beneath the surface. The men watched as life left this unfortunate man. Only a single leg was above the surface. It twitched for a few seconds and then was still.

Dwight Lamar was, of course, very concerned that his money with Surenos had been well-spent, although he could hardly call anyone to confirm things. He did not want to look interested in the fortunes of some roofer. He happened to walk through the employee lunchroom where there was a TV on. A reporter was live on the scene of a gruesome unfortunate industrial accident. It seemed a man had slipped and fallen into a vat of molten tar. As hard as he tried, Dwight Lamar could barely restrain himself. *Tar. Tar. Finally, some justice in the world. Now they know what it is to be a tar baby. Chuckle! Chuckle! I kind of like these guys' style.*

******

Between the Riverbend job, Jeanne, whose association he was enjoying, perhaps too much, and the Bluebird project, which he was enjoying not at all, Matt Nelson had all he could do to keep up. He realized that he still needed to get out there and hustle some more business. He had hired some additional staff, and he really needed to get them involved with the day-to-day so he would have time to do some selling. Unfortunately, the Bluebird project had so many problems that he found himself devoting almost his full attention to that project alone.

The Punjab job and the Bluebird were very similar with two story walk-up buildings. It didn't take Matt ten minutes after meeting the general contractor and the on-site job superintendent to determine that they were blatantly unqualified to take on a project of that size and scope. He never would have hired them, but his reports in that regard to Dwight Lamar fell on deaf ears. Although he did his best to paste on a happy face while on the site, it was clear that there was no love lost between the superintendents and Matt's people. Success on a large construction effort requires teamwork, which was sorely lacking in this case.

It was a little after 7:00 AM and Matt was already in his office trying valiantly to clear off the top of his desk. As he shifted through a stack of mail, he came across an invoice from Corinth Monitoring Services for $1,500 in reference to "Services performed on the Bluebird project." Matt had no idea what it was about, especially since it was billed directly to his company, Mesquite Consulting Services. Matt was strictly a hired hand on the project. No job invoices were incurred, billed, or paid through him. He set it aside and, a little after 9:00 AM, he called the accounting person at SETUP who handled all the payables and receivables to ask about the mysterious invoice. The man who answered seemed to have an idea about it, but quickly advised him to speak directly to Mr. Lamar about "that one." His concern rising, he immediately called the big man himself.

"Good morning, Mr. Nelson," Dwight answered in a cool, formal, and businesslike voice, almost as if he had been expecting the call.

"Hi, Dwight," Matt came back and got right down to business. "I received an invoice this morning billed to my company for $1,500 from Corinth Monitoring Services for Bluebird. What should I do with it?"

"Pay it, Matt."

"Pay it? What is it for? I don't pay project bills. I have never heard of that company," Matt responded, his irritation rising.

"Corinth is a special audit and inspection service we use on all our jobs."

"I have never seen or heard of anything from them. Where am I supposed to get the money to pay it?"

"I believe your monthly project consulting draws are up-to-date. Are they not?"

"What? Out of my fees? Why should I do that? If this Corinth whoever-they-are really earned this money, it should be paid by the project, not me."

"There are reasons why this invoice must be accounted for in this manner. I told you at the start of the project that if you feel shortchanged at the end, submit a contract change order for me to consider. In the meantime, pay that invoice. You'll have to excuse me. The mayor is on the other line. Bye, Matt." *Click.*

Matt sat there with the invoice crunched in his hand. He was just about to rip it to shreds when he decided to keep it. There was no way he was going to pay it, but it might come in handy later. He decided to give it to his analyst, Aaron Schwartz, to see what he could find out about Corinth Monitoring Services. He was steaming. The nerve of that guy and his exalted attitude. Bend over and kiss my feet and, while you are down there, shine my shoes! There was a limit, and Matt was just about there. He had a brief chat with Diane, but he just couldn't see continuing on with the Bluebird project. Not only would he not compromise his principles, but he could see the project having many issues, which might well come back to further sully his already-struggling reputation.

38.

Matt decided to sleep on his decision to terminate his SETUP contract over the weekend, but the events of Saturday absolutely convinced him that he had no choice but to get out as quickly as possible. He was sipping coffee in their breakfast room while scrolling through the Houston Chronicle on his iPad. He looked forward to watching Rusty's Little League game at 10:00 AM. His cell phone buzzed. Aaron Schwartz was out on the Bluebird site. There was a problem, apparently a big one. Matt kissed Ellen goodbye and hustled out the door.

As Matt drove up to the construction site shack, Aaron jumped out of his own pickup where he had been waiting. Normally, he would have been in the construction trailer office having coffee with the superintendent and construction crew. Matt turned off his engine and Aaron climbed in. He looked stressed.

"So, what's up?"

"Plenty, Boss." Aaron insisted on calling Matt "Boss." Matt had finally given up trying to break him of that habit. He really liked the kid, who was bright and a very quick study. Matt's original plan had been to keep the young man in the office crunching numbers, but being short on staff, Matt needed him out in the field and reviewing the work in place. It was immediately apparent that Aaron had an aptitude for the business and began to notice things even old pros missed.

On Bluebird, though, Mesquite's already-strained relations with a contractor not of their choosing rapidly turned icy. The construction crew refused to give any respect to the skinny college kid just out of Rice. "Here's the deal. They have laid out the framing for building two and are ready to start, but when I measured it, I noticed that their plumbing grounds coming up from the slab are off by six inches in some places and as much as a foot in others. When they start to go up with the framing, the plumbing will not match the suite floor plans. That's not good, is it, Boss?"

Matt frowned. It sure wasn't good. It was an absolute recipe for leaky plumbing later on. "Wow. That is really a big miss. You know, Aaron, when we reviewed the plumbing ground piping before they poured the concrete slabs, we specifically told them it was not laid out right. I have it here in my construction notes. It sounds like they just poured the slabs without adjusting the piping. That is a major problem. What are they telling you they are going to do to fix it?"

"Not much, really. The super says the framers and plumbers can make some adjustments along the way to adjust for the misalignments. Once everything is covered up, inside the walls, no-one will ever know."

Matt rolled his eyes back. He could not believe what he had just heard. "That is bull crap. There will be leaks everywhere. The only fix is to demo the slab, yank out the plumbing, and re-set everything correctly. Very expensive, to say nothing about the construction time lost."

"That is what I tried to tell them, but they wouldn't listen to me. According to my quick numbers, about $1,515,000 should fix the problem. I don't suppose that is in the budget."

Although the number was shocking, Matt had to smile. The kid was amazing. "Okay. Let's go in there and do battle. I have an idea we won't make much headway, but we have to let them know exactly what we think."

"I'm right behind you, Boss."

Dwight Lamar sat in his office on Monday morning reflecting on the Bluebird situation. The call from Matt Nelson on Friday had not been unexpected but was nonetheless troubling. Lamar had misjudged Nelson, whose troubled past he expected would make him ready to do anything to land a contract. At the same time, SETUP could buy some competent expertise with the "flexibility" he required. Punjab fit that bill, but Nelson didn't. It wasn't working, and he just didn't see how he could keep him on the job any longer, which was a shame because the man really did know his stuff when it came to brick and mortar.

Now a new issue had cropped up on the Bluebird project. The general contractor and his field superintendent asked for an emergency meeting with him this morning. According to the contractor and his superintendent, the Nelson firm had staffed the project with new, inexperienced, and unqualified people who were totally unfamiliar with normal construction practices and tolerances. Over the weekend, their rep had made a big deal over some kind of plumbing issue, which the contractor did not feel was a major problem. Lamar winced, though, when they told him that the Nelson kid had said the fix was somewhere around a million dollars. He felt slightly better when the contractor assured him they could make some easy adjustments and no-one would ever know the difference.

Lamar was no construction guy, but he was also not stupid. He knew that the cost to fix a problem like this one would come right out of the general contractor's pocket, since he agreed to a fixed-price, guaranteed-maximum contract. He reminded the contractor of that fact, and that he was also still on the hook for any warranty problems after construction was finished. The contractor acknowledged those issues and reiterated his intention to stand behind his construction work. Those promises aside, Lamar was still not comfortable, in no small part because he grudgingly acknowledged that Matt Nelson knew his stuff and could very well be right. On the other hand, there was not another million bucks around to throw into the project, and the construction delays would hurt his credibility with the board. He decided to go with the general contractor and verbally approved his "fix" for the problem. On his way out, the contractor took one more parting shot at Matt Nelson, whom he said should have picked up this potential problem long before it ever showed up.

Nelson had called twice while he was meeting with the general contractor and left voicemails demanding that they meet immediately. Of course, it had to be about this plumbing thing. Lamar asked his secretary to call Mr. Nelson and arrange for a meeting around 10:00 AM on Tuesday, the next day.

At the appointed hour, Matt walked into Dwight Lamar's second-floor office. The typically outwardly calm, cool, and in control Lamar was disturbed. He expected Nelson to be loaded for bear. He, however, always avoided direct emotional confrontations in business dealings. It was possible that this meeting could get hot. That sort of wrangling was beneath him. To avoid an uncomfortable scene he would later regret, Lamar knew he must seize the initiative. Surprisingly, when Matt walked in and sat down, he looked composed and calm.

Outward appearances notwithstanding, Matt jumped right into it. "Dwight, we need to discuss a couple of things. Now, the project…" he began. Before he could get any further, Dwight picked up a letter and handed it across his desk.

"What's this?" Matt asked as he took the letter and began to read. He was silent for a minute or two as he read and then re-read what had been handed to him. He took a moment to let it sink in. "So you are firing me for cause? Is that right?" Matt whispered in a tone that couldn't hide his astonishment.

"I am afraid so, Matt. I am truly sorry things didn't work out. I knew when we started that your organization was thin, but I decided to take a chance, and you let me down by sending unqualified people out there. It has cost me, my group, and potentially HUD, a lot of money, to say nothing about construction progress. Your gross and wanton lack of attention to detail was very surprising. I gave you a chance and you let me down. It is too bad."

Matt was seething inside but would not give this ogre a chance to see his emotions take over. Matt replied to the ridiculous assertions and personal innuendo in a calm and calculated voice. "Number one, that is total and complete bullshit. Both you and I know it. Number two, you never gave me a chance, but do you know why I wanted this meeting?"

"Why don't you tell me now, Matt?"

"Because, Dwight, I was going to hand you my resignation."

Lamar's eyebrows arched slightly. "Really? Then at least we can agree on that much. Oh, and by the way, since I did terminate you for cause, your fee immediately stops, which if I have calculated correctly means that since I overpaid you, you now owe us money. Please see to it that it is paid promptly."

Matt would have exploded had he stayed another minute. He was out the door before the man had finished. Lamar watched him go. Dismissing him was the correct move. Lamar had already called Punjab and told him to take over Bluebird. The only question left was whether or not he should contact Surenos about the arrogant Mr. Nelson.

Matt had gone to see Dwight Lamar with the sole intent of terminating his contract. Now that the deed was done, he was neither relieved nor satisfied. The man had beaten him to the punch once again. It wasn't even lunchtime, but he was tempted to call it a day and hide out in some raunchy ice house and fire down longnecks for the rest of the day. No, he was not the type of person to drown his problems in alcohol. He really needed to talk this one out with someone. Diane would have been fine, but she was his mother. While she was spot-on in her intuitive approach to many things, she was still his mother and would defend him to the hilt.

Ellen was a wonderful, devoted, caring wife and mother who had already put up with enough of his antics lately. She would be happy to talk to him about anything, but he really wanted to try to avoid getting her too involved in his business dealings. Raising a family was a huge job on its own. He opened his phone and speed-dialed John, who always had time for him. John would surely have some interesting takes on Dwight Lamar. The call went to voice-mail and then he remembered that John was on an assignment somewhere in Africa. He didn't leave a message.

With the list just about exhausted, he found himself heading down Route 288 south and within a few minutes, he pulled into the Riverbend parking lot. He noticed that Jeanne's 4Runner was there. He was pleasantly greeted by the receptionist, whom he had gotten to know over the past months. He had been there many times working on the expansion project. Almost always, he showed up having made an appointment; just dropping by was a little unusual. The receptionist said Jeanne was on the phone but should be off shortly. After a few minutes, she smiled, and Matt walked into Jeanne's office.

For someone who liked to keep things neat and tidy, her desk was awash with correspondence, reports, and forms. She saw him walk in and greeted him with a warm, "Hi, Matt, what a surprise. Sign any big contracts lately?" she teased, having no idea what he'd just been through.

He grinned at that. "Well, I happened to be nearby and thought maybe I'd grab you for lunch, that is, if you don't have plans?" he asked apologetically.

A doleful look came over her face. "Oh, no. Of all days, I was finally able to get a hair appointment, and she could only squeeze me in over the lunch hour. Just look at this mess. I am swamped."

"Hey, that's okay. I should have called. Another time. I'll call you later so we can get together to discuss the kitchen schematics." He surrendered meekly, trying desperately to hide the hurt in his voice.

"Yeah, sure, I am so sorry. See you," she said, as he walked out of her office and left the building.

It had started to rain, so he hustled to his Suburban and was about to back out when he noticed a figure standing next to the vehicle. It was Jeanne.

"Matt! Open this damn door before I get soaked."

He immediately pressed the button and she jumped in. "I thought you had things to do?"

"I do, but they'll keep. You looked like you especially needed a friend today, and I didn't want to let you down. Besides that, I'm hungry. Where to?"

How did she know what I was thinking? Damn, she looks good today.

39.

Houston has thousands of restaurants. Matt picked a small Italian place in the Rice Village shopping center a few blocks from the Rice University campus. The place was right out of central casting, with red checkered tablecloths, Chianti bottles with dried dribble candle wax, and a wall mural of villas clustered on the Adriatic Sea. The rain had intensified outside and helped the little place take on an intimate feel. There was no hesitation when the portly, balding waiter with a black cummerbund and threadbare tux asked about drinks. Two sips of wine and, for the first time in many weeks, for whatever reason, Matt began to relax and unwind.

In her business, Jeanne had to be a good listener. She had heard some horrible tales from dozens of battered women. It had become a part of her makeup, and she was anxious to hear about Matt's dealings with Dwight Lamar. She knew of him by reputation, which, by most accounts, was impeccable. The man had worked wonders since he'd arrived in the city. His face was always on TV and in the news. In fact, he seemed almost too good to be true. Although she had learned to be cautious about what she accepted as true from the women she encountered daily, she had heard an interesting story about Dwight Lamar. It came from Louisiana and his having fathered a child in New Orleans with an unwed young woman. Her ladies loved to gossip. There could be something there, or maybe not.

Matt described the entire SETUP story to Jeanne, including how Lamar had selected him from among several other more qualified firms. Intriguingly, he apparently picked Matt because of his father's problems and not in spite of them. Well aware of how hard she had to work to get Matt's company approved for her project, she was amazed. Matt described the problems with the construction and how the man refused to listen. Dwight Lamar was a peculiar sort with an almost regal bearing, who could do no wrong in his own eyes.

Matt stopped mid-sentence and took an extra-healthy slug of the house Chianti. Jeanne saw moisture begin to well in the corner of his eyes. She grabbed his hand and squeezed it.

"What's the matter, Matt?" she asked softly.

He sniffled and smiled. His ruddy complexion gave away his embarrassment. "I'm sorry, Jeanne. It just hit me that in many ways, he is just like my father. How do I get myself mixed up with these obsessed tyrants? What is it? Fool me once, shame on you. Fool me twice, shame on me?"

Jeanne smiled. "Hey, stop beating yourself up so much. You drew a couple of short straws, but were smart enough to get out each time. Say, is there a bigger picture with this guy, or is he just a two-bit hustler? The dollars he is playing with are not small. Both those first two projects will be in the twenty-million-dollar level when they are all done. There is no telling how big his land development project might get."

Just at that point, the grinning waiter arrived with two plates piled high with steaming pasta. Matt had gone for the chicken Parmesan and Jeanne for the cheese ravioli. After setting the meals down, the waiter asked if there was anything else they needed. He was just about to issue the standard "bon appétit" before he disappeared when Matt looked up at him and asked, "Now, Mario, you did have the chef go extra light on the garlic, didn't you? I might have to kiss someone later!"

At first the man looked perplexed and concerned, but the joke finally sank in. He laughed and was gone.

Across the table, however, after hearing his gag, Jeanne sat there with a bemused and then questioning expression on her face.

Matt saw it and was quick to disclaim, "Oh, oh, Jeanne, that is a standard joke in my repertoire. I always say that when I eat Italian." Unconvinced, she smiled, looked down, took her fork, and began to enjoy the scrumptious meal. They ate in silence for a few minutes, lost in personal thoughts.

All of a sudden, Matt realized that Jeanne had hit upon something that had been nagging him, but he hadn't focused on. What was this Dwight Lamar's end game? Even though he had achieved spectacular success so far in a very short period, that would not go on forever. The government was often slow and ponderous but ultimately, they always caught up to you. Surely, Dwight Lamar knew they would. He was extremely calculating, every move made after careful consideration. SETUP was indeed a unique entity, but he would not be given free rein indefinitely. The city and county had never gotten along in the past, and there was no reason to believe the honeymoon would last. An executive directorship could hardly be expected to deliver the keys to the kingdom. What was he really up to?

Again, Jeanne added a little fuel to the fire. "This guy may not be a bricks-and-sticks expert. By the way, Matt, how is that? You taught me that term." Matt grinned and touched her nose with his finger.

"If he planned to stay in the game long-term, I would certainly think that he would be a lot more concerned about the quality of the housing he is building, especially with the first two projects. Don't you think?"

"I hadn't looked at it that way, but it would explain a lot. He really doesn't care because he may not be around when the real problems hit. Even then, he can blame people like me and the general contractor. Very interesting. It also looks like he is tapping the projects and diverting cash. That may come out, but it could take years. Again, though, he has positioned himself with scapegoats. He always seems to insulate the throne room from association with the rabble."

Matt was on a roll, and didn't even realize it when he nodded to the waiter about a second bottle of wine. "There was a rather odd thing I noticed during one of our meetings in his office."

"Really, what was that?"

"Well, we were in a heated discussion, and the phone suddenly rang, which it never does when you are in his office. He has his royal guard strictly trained not to disturb him when he is in conference, under penalty of guillotine, I guess. This call had to be very important for him to take it with me there. The strange thing was that all he ever said into the phone was 'Crispus Attucks.' No hello or goodbye. Zippo."

"Huh? You mean like the Boston Tea Party slave that was killed?"

"Oh, yeah. So that's it. I knew I'd heard that name in history, but I couldn't place it until now."

"That is really strange, but it must be important to him in some devious way.""

"Oh, my gosh. Jeanne, it is almost four. I have ruined your day."

She smiled, "No, Matthew, not in the least, but I guess I should be getting back."

After declining the waiter's offer to keep their three Chianti bottles as souvenirs, Matt paid the check, and they stepped out into the falling rain. It looked like Matt had grabbed Jeanne's hand, but it might have been the other way around. Either way, there was no resistance offered. Perhaps the wine buzz made them slightly wobbly.

Once in his SUV, Matt was about to make a left turn out of the parking lot when Jeanne stretched her arm across his chest and pointed right.

"That way, Matthew. I live two streets down on the right."

Matt hesitated. He looked over at her with damp hair but a still radiant expression on her face. They looked deeply into each other's eyes as the rhythmic drops beat on the vehicle's roof. It had become impossible to hide the smoldering desire that lay dormant for decades but now had blazed to life. He drove off in the direction as instructed.

40.

It wasn't too late when Matt pulled into his driveway. In fact, if he was lucky, he still might get to say good night to the kids before Ellen put them down. There were so many thoughts racing around through his head that he would welcome almost any distraction. Dwight Lamar. Fired. Quitting. Lunch. Jeanne. Jeanne. . . In fact, he was almost relieved to see his sister's car sitting in the driveway. He remembered hearing something about Pam taking the kids to the Houston Zoo on her day off. When she was around there was no lack of conversation, and he really didn't want to have to sit across the dinner table and chat with Ellen tonight. Not tonight. He pulled into the garage, but decided to walk around and go in the front door when he noticed that Pammy had left her parking lights on. No surprise there.

As he approached her car, though, he could hear his sister's voice yakking on her cell phone. Apparently, while sitting in the driver's seat with the window open, she was depressing the brake with her foot, which made her lights flicker. He couldn't help but hear her talking.

"Yes, we are all fine. Mom and Matt have made the management company work, and you know John, he's just the same, off chasing bad guys. But what about you?" she prattled on. Suddenly, she looked up from admiring her nails and saw her brother approaching. Panic set in. "Oh, eh… Muriel, gotta go now! Talk to you soon. Bye!" she exclaimed, flipping the tiny cell phone shut and quickly opening the car door. "Oh. Hey, Matt! Where've you been?"

Leave it to Pam to innocently ask the one question he had no intention of answering. Ignoring her, he quickly changed the subject. "So, what's Muriel up to these days? Did she ever find a job?"

"Who? Oh, yeah, Muriel. No, not really, but she's waiting on tables, but she's still looking," an obviously distracted Pam responded as she stepped out of her car. When her feet hit the driveway a small, shiny metal object slipped out of her grasp and bounced onto the pavement. Matt reached down and picked it up. "Where did you get this, Pam?" he asked as he held up a tiny, cheap, metallic-blue cell phone, what the detective novels refer to as a "burner."

"Oh, that. Thanks," she replied, as she snatched it abruptly out of his hand. "I lost my cell phone and I grabbed that thing at Walmart until I can get to the AT&T store."

Matt arched his eyebrows and smiled. You never knew what to expect from Pam. As they walked towards the house together, a Guns and Roses melody erupted from the pocket of Pam's jeans. Matt recognized it as the ring tone of her usual cell phone. He didn't even bother to ask. You never knew what to expect from Pam.

Matt did luck out, perhaps for the first time all day. Rusty and Gail were still up. He was able to hear all about their trip to the zoo with Aunt Pam. Rusty was big on elephants, and Gail was fascinated by the huge, sleeping gorilla.

Once they were off to dreamland, Ellen fixed Matt a sandwich and poured the three of them a glass of wine as they sat around the island in their kitchen. Matt was hardly interested in more wine but graciously accepted it with a weak smile. He had to be very, very careful. He knew wives could sense things about their husbands, and he did not hide his guilt well. Thank goodness for the diversion of tropical maelstrom Pamela.

Matt figured it was best if he took the lead. He didn't want any of those, so tell me about your day? leading questions.

"El, you are not going to believe this, but I had an appointment with the regal Mr. Lamar this morning. We have been trying our best, but he has proved to be impossible to work with. He keeps changing the deal and skinning us back every time we turn around. He is also doing some things that I just don't like. I do not think he is completely aboveboard."

Ellen had heard most of this from Matt in the past, but it was all new to Pam, whose antennae went to maximum alert.

Matt then realized that Pam probably didn't know what he was talking about.

"Sorry, sis. You know that I have started a consulting arm of our company. It has been tough to get it going but we did win what we thought was a nice contract with a group called SETUP, which is a partnership between the City of Houston and Harris County. We were helping them with a construction project for the Bluebird apartments. Anyway, the head of SETUP is Dwight Lamar, who has not been there long but has become very well-known around the city. He was second in man of the year, or something like that. He was in the news helping out with a robbery on the east side. Do you know who I am talking about?"

224

"As a matter of fact, I do. He works out at the Q." Pam decided not to volunteer anything more until she saw where this discussion was going. Lamar never let on that he even knew her brother.

"Really? Well, as I said, it has been a rocky relationship at best, so finally, after talking it over with mom and my staff, I decided that even though we are desperate for business, I intended to march in there this morning and resign. Enough is enough."

"Intended?" Ellen questioned. "You didn't resign? What made you change your mind?"

In spite of himself, Matt couldn't help but raise his voice several octaves. "Hell! I didn't change my mind! The jerk handed me a letter of termination for cause when I walked in the door. The guy is incredible! There are problems on that job, but they are not our doing. I have continually reported them to him and he has ignored me. What an ass."

"Oh, Matt, that is terrible. I am sure you are much better off not dealing with a man like that," Ellen sympathized as the consoling wife.

For once, Pam remained silent, not sure whether to pile on Lamar or not.

"Thanks. I know you are right. I suppose he will badmouth us even more in the community, but the more I worked with him, the more I am convinced he is ultimately up to no good. If I went to the city or county with what I have seen, they would back their golden boy in a minute. I have no real evidence of anything. He is very cagey. It would only look like sour grapes from an incompetent contractor. What we...err, I...can't figure out is what his end game is."

Now Pam was really interested. "What do you mean, Matt?"

Here's the thing. If you really want to make a big score somehow, being the executive director of a housing authority is not the way you'd do it. I am sure his salary is quite generous based on his position, but really not all that much. You can gain prestige and power to a point, but there are so many regulators around you that you can't breathe. Beyond all that, I am certain that the honeymoon between the city and county will end sooner rather than later. Their own housing authorities are upset with him. They shoot at him every chance they get. His power is bound to be reduced when it does. He has to have something in mind in the short-term. I just don't know what."

"Do you have any idea?" Pam asked.

"No, I really don't. Executive director of an HA? That is hardly in the league with hedge fund managers or corporate raiders. I did overhear him say one very curious thing one day when I was in his office."

Both women leaned in close.

"He answered the phone, but before he turned away from me, as I think about it now, he may have opened one of his desk drawers and looked at something. I then heard him speak two words into the phone and then hang up. No greeting, no goodbye. Nothing else " He hesitated.

"Come on. Stop the fooling around! What did he say? Tell us!" Ellen ordered.

"Okay, all he said was 'Crispus Attucks.' That was it."

"Huh? You mean like the slave who was the first person killed in the Revolutionary War at the Boston Tea Party? That dude?" Pam asked.

Matt smiled. "Well, at least you paid attention in history class," he mocked.

She ignored his demeaning jest. "What do you think that could have meant? Any idea?"

"No, not really. Say, you said this guy works out at your gym. How well do you know him?"

Pam hesitated, but then chose her words carefully. "Oh, I have just seen him around. I might have spotted for him on the free weights. Not much." She conveniently omitted that he had been trying to go out with her for months and she'd had lunch with him a few times, or that he had offered her a job, and she had visited his offices in Midtown, or that as of right then she had not told him no yet.

Matt listened and accepted what his notorious sister said, but was quick to add, "Look, I really don't trust this guy. Stay away from him. He is bad news. It will all come out someday. This family has had enough strife for a while. Steer clear of him. Do you hear me, Pam?"

Pam smiled, "Of course, big brother."

After one more glass of wine, it was after 10:00 PM and getting late. Matt and Ellen thanked Pam for having taken the kids to the zoo. After looking in on them, she grabbed her keys and was out the door.

Matt was absolutely drained, but after Ellen cleaned up in the kitchen, she suggested that they go right to bed. She knew (or thought she knew) what a tough day he had endured. As bushed as he was, Matt said he wanted to catch what was left of the news and maybe Jimmy Kimmel, who was supposed to have Donald Trump on. Ellen was a little surprised, but didn't argue. She told him she would read in bed for a while and would be waiting for him when he got there. Matt offered her a feeble smile as he plopped down by the television. That was exactly what he was afraid of. He'd already begun to sweat.

41.

Pam took the job at the Q knowing it would only be until something else came along, although she had no idea what. The Q worked out very well for both her and the club. She was among the most popular members of the staff, especially among the young, testosterone-charged male executives who frequented the place, Dwight Lamar notwithstanding. Although the position Lamar had described to her seemed interesting on the surface, the man was such a creep that she could never seriously consider it, especially since she was sure it was just another thinly veiled attempt to get into her pants. The man was clearly obsessed with controlling everything and everyone that mattered to him.

It couldn't hurt to look, though, and she decided to visit SETUP's offices on Lamar Street in Midtown. The ever-calculating emperor had James Luken show her around the building and introduce her to several employees as if she would be joining SETUP soon. Included on the tour was the marketing department, where she would be working, which just happened to be a vacant office right next to the big boss. Although Mr. Lamar had been too busy to show her around when she arrived, he was able to clear his calendar for a leisurely lunch at Brennan's just down the street. Despite his continuous suggestions and less than subtle encouragement, Pam limited her alcohol consumption to one glass of obviously expensive chardonnay. She had planned on graciously declining his job offer outright during lunch, but the man would not accept no for an answer. Finally, expecting that she might otherwise never escape from the restaurant, she said she would sleep on it and get back to him next week.

After the unpleasant meeting with her brother just one day after his lunch with Pam at the swanky restaurant, Dwight Lamar had given up ever hearing back from her about the job. Despite Matt's name never coming up in conversation with her, he was sure they'd already discovered the connection on their own. Still, the man who prided himself on avoiding the unexpected was genuinely surprised a few days later, when Pam accepted the position. In fact, since the Q did not need any notice, she could start the following Monday.

On the Saturday before she was to start her new job, Pam met her best friend and tried-and-true confidant, Muriel, for a drink at a Mexican restaurant in the Montrose. It was the same place, ironically, where a few years back she had met Pablo, who was the man of her dreams for almost six months, a record for a Pam relationship. She needed to bring Muriel up to speed on the conversation with Matt and Ellen a few days earlier and tell her about her new position. Dwight Lamar was obviously bad news, but you had to admit he was a fascinating character. His domineering personality was a huge turnoff, but the guy was into some interesting stuff. Perhaps if she could get a little closer to him (not too close!) she could figure out his end game plan. Sure, it was a nutty idea, meaning it fit Pam quite well. Anyway, it sure beat folding towels and deflecting perpetual come-ons from married thirty-year-olds.

Pam was already well into her first margarita when Muriel elbowed through the crowd to her table. Their waiter somehow knew the high sign and like magic, Muriel had a "frozen, no salt" placed in front of her.

"So, Mur, I was meaning to ask you. When I called yesterday, you couldn't talk because you were already on a call from Numbia? Who were you talking to, and where the hell is that?"

Muriel acted as if she hadn't heard the question and sucked up her first draw of the light, sweet, green, tequila-spiked liquid. When she was done, she replied, "Wow. That hit the spot. No, it was Namibia, which I think is in Africa but I am not really sure."

"Yeah, all right, then. Whom do you know who lives in Namibia?"

"I don't know anyone who *lives* there."

"Cut the crap, woman! How is John doing? I hope he is safe and staying out of trouble."

After another generous slurp of margarita, Muriel gave her a sheepish grin. "He only called me because he was on some sort of stakeout and was bored out of his mind."

Pam rolled her eyes. "Sure, sure. Say, what would you say if I told you I am thinking of changing professions?"

"I'd say holy shit! What is she up to now? Okay, out with it. No. No. Wait a second. Let me get another one of these. I think I am going to need it," she exclaimed, pointing to her empty glass.

"I am insulted that you would take my professional career advancement so lightly. I will have you know that I have been approached by the almost man of the year in Houston, a bona fide hero, and extremely successful high-level executive, to join his firm in a marketing capacity."

"Oh, does Nolan Ryan want you to feed, water, and muck out the stalls for his horses?"

"I am not going to dignify that comment with a reply. No, Mr. Dwight Lamar, with whom I am sure you are familiar, has offered me a prestigious, high-paying, very responsible position with his company."

"Is that the dude that plays for the Rockets?"

"You are impossible. No, my Mr. Lamar is the executive director of the Southeast Texas Unified Partnership. SETUP, for short."

"Ah, ha. Finally, you said something that makes sense!"

Pam went on to tell Muriel all about the company and how well it was doing. Even though she had not spent one day there and had serious reservations about the boss, she found herself selling the place to her friend. They had several exciting projects underway. It was a ground-floor opportunity. She explained about her tour of the facilities, how nice all the people were, and the large size of her new office.

After about five minutes of listening to the rant, Muriel put her hand in the air. "Okay, okay, Pam, hold it! Hold it! Stop!"

Pam finally simmered down. "What?"

"Come on! You are out of Sam less than one year and this guy is going to give you all this stuff? He is after one thing, and I hope you know it!"

Pam could not hide her huge grin. "Of course, I do. What do you take me for, a young executive? Now, let me tell you what I really have in mind."

Well into subsequent margaritas, Pam finished telling Muriel all about her conversation with Matt. "I just need to know what this man has up his sleeve, and not up his boxers. I should have a good vantage point to find out. I will be around him every day. He is bound to slip up sooner or later. I have always been intrigued by detective and undercover work." Muriel tried to suppress a giggle, but they both laughed at Pam's choice of words. "So, Matt is all for you doing this. Right?"

"Of course not. He has no idea that Dwight Lamar offered me a job."

"Let me guess the rest, Pam. Not only does Matt not know about this harebrained scheme, but I am sure he told you to stay as far away from this psychopath as possible. Somehow, in your twisted little skull, that makes the whole thing appealing. Right?"

Pam looked incredulous. "How did you know that?"

******

Pam had been on the payroll at SETUP for a week. If she thought she'd been bored at the Q, she realized how exciting that was compared to reading through a few feet of loose-leaf binders of regulation manuals. While she saw Dwight every day and usually managed to have a cup of coffee with him in the morning when he first came in, for the most part, he was too busy to give her much time. He had so far conducted himself very appropriately and had made no moves or suggestions that would smack of impropriety. Was it possible that she was disappointed? Her office was right next to his and she could easily study his habits and movements. He arrived fairly late each morning, close to 10:00 AM, after his workout, she supposed. His office was locked tight until he arrived. No-one, not even his secretary, ever violated his personal domain unless invited. Once again, taking advantage of the previous tenant's upgrades, Dwight had his own restroom within his office, so he did not have to leave even for that necessity. He had scheduled lunch meetings every day that often lasted late into the afternoon. It did seem, though, that he almost always returned to the office just before quitting time to be assured everything was secure. She was surprised he did not burn the midnight oil there. If he worked late, apparently it was at home.

Dwight promised her that once she got a feel for the organization and what it was about, she could begin to contact and make calls on some of their clients and customers, although he never really specified who they were. He did tell her that an important part of her job was to assist him in the preparation for board meetings, including attending them and looking good. She was sure he meant eye candy. On a couple of occasions, he sent her to deliver packages to board members at their offices. They could have used a messenger service but, by going to their offices, she could get to know them and maybe schmooze a little. Yeah, sure. When she walked into Henry Francesca's office, he did everything but invite her to sleep with him during the first ten minutes she was there. What a creep.

Most of her first few days were spent with time on her hands. She didn't know if the big man would ever get around to letting her into his confidence. He just wasn't close to anyone. She drew a hard and fast line against sleeping with him, but if she had to do some extended flirting, it came with the terri-tory. So far, he didn't seem to care if she was there or not, almost as if the fun for him was overcoming her resistance to be hired. Once she was on board, the fun was over.

It didn't take long for her to realize if you wanted to get near Dwight Lamar, his younger brother, Devon, came with the package. Devon was about her age and, to that extent, they had a lot in common. Born and raised in deep East Texas, the young man had been green around the gills when his brother first brought him to the big city. He was a fast learner and now was firmly ensconced as his brother's driver, gopher, personal assistant, bodyguard, and pussy provider. Pam and Devon immediately hit it off.

Most of the time, if his master did not need to go somewhere, Devon had little to do, so he tended to hang around the company lunchroom. Devon was a pleasant sort who was much more personable than his older brother. While they shared the same mother, their fathers had been numbers one and five in mom's "husbands" line-up.

Devon was as close to Dwight as anyone. Perhaps he could shed some light on where the exalted one was headed. She made it a point to chat with the young man whenever it could be done without being too obvious. They grabbed burgers every so often for lunch. They chatted about a wide range of topics common among young people from Houston: sports teams, concerts they'd attended, styles, dress, and their friends. Coming from completely different parts and socioeconomic levels of Texas, their backgrounds were widely divergent and mutually fascinating. Pam and Devon bonded in an awkward way.

There was the one unspoken topic between them, which concerned them both. Namely, that Dwight was determined to get Pam in his bed. Right or wrong, Pam felt she could handle that when the time came. At first, Devon was okay with it, although as he got to know Pam and began to fall for her himself, his brother's obsession became increasingly troubling to him.

It didn't take Pam long to figure out that cracking the wall around Dwight Lamar's inner sanctum was going to be a long-term project, if it were possible at all. During that mysterious phone call, Matt saw Dwight glance down at something in the top drawer of his desk. If only she could sneak a peek, perhaps it might provide a hint about Crispus Attucks. She had casually dropped the name to Devon, who had no special reaction.

It was Friday morning, and Pam had just gotten back from the University of Houston where she delivered a package to Kathy Barnes, one of SETUP's directors. That woman was a pill. She sure didn't number Dwight Lamar among her friends. It was almost noon, and the office had emptied out for lunch. As she walked towards the marketing department, she noticed that Dwight's secretary was not at her desk and probably had taken an early lunch.

Impulsively, she stepped into the outer office. She knew that Dwight and James Luken were still in the conference room with some HUD people. Her heart began to pound in her chest. Dwight's door was open. This was her chance. The meeting in the conference room would surely break up at noon, but she might have a few minutes to look around until it did. Should she dare? If he came back, she'd have no good excuse for being in his office, which was normally always locked.

Without giving herself a chance to second-guess, she was in his office all alone. She was totally vulnerable. Anyone might wander in: his secretary, Devon, Mr. Luken, or even Dwight himself. She had to act fast.

She moved around the back of his big wooden executive desk and tugged on the lowest drawer on the left. It would not move. Locked. Shoot! She felt the sweat dripping on her brow, and then heard a noise outside the office. She froze. No-one entered. It must have been co-workers passing by in the hall on the way to lunch.

Quickly, she tried all the other drawers one at a time. None would budge until she came to a small one on the upper right. It looked like it would open; the pull-out writing surface had been extended over the drawer. She needed to push it in before she could see into the drawer below. She grabbed the knob and it stuck for a second, but then it slid in with a thud. Again, she heard voices. Oh my gosh, the meeting was breaking up! Dwight would be back in there in a few seconds. She glanced down at the inside of the drawer and saw scribbling in black ballpoint on a small yellow pad. There seemed to be four names:

Crispus Attucks, Frederick Douglas, Sojourner Truth, Peter Butler

She had no idea what they meant, but scrawled them down with a pen on the skin of her bare arm.

Dwight was going to appear at any moment. She struggled to pull the wooden surface extender back out to leave it the way she found it, but it wouldn't budge. There was no time to continue to fool with it. 100% full-alarm panic set in when she heard Dwight's voice as he said goodbye to the HUD people. He must have been standing right in the doorway to the outer office. What explanation could she give? What could she possibly say? She was in deep trouble.

She quickly glanced around and spotted a closed door. His bathroom! It was her only chance. Screw the desk. Maybe he wouldn't notice the difference. She bolted across the carpet just as he entered the outer office. She ripped opened the door and threw herself in, just managing somehow to quietly close it as the man walked in.

Safe for the moment, Pam huddled and shivered in the dark in that tiny little space, struggling not to be completely overcome by fear. And then it got worse. Coffee! Coffee! She prayed he had gone light this morning and did not have to use the restroom before he went to lunch. If he pulled open the door, he'd find her immediately. She prayed this was not his one day without a luncheon engagement. Had he already noticed the closed extender on his desk?

She was very concerned that her own pounding heart would give her away as she listened to him moving around the office. Then it was quiet for a moment. Had he left for lunch? Maybe she'd made it? Her hopes were quickly dashed when, to her horror, she saw the handle on the bathroom door start to turn. She closed her eyes, held her breath, and thought sure she would burst. And then, nothing happened. The door didn't open. She heard the door to his office slam shut. Did he leave? Or was he still in his office? It would be just like him to act like he'd gone but still be standing there waiting to pounce when she came out.

42.

Dwight Lamar hesitated before reaching for his coat and heading off to his luncheon with Ed Smith, a senior vice president at Shell and one of his most influential directors. He walked slowly across his office and grabbed the doorknob to his private restroom. He was about to yank the door open when he impulsively thought better of it. Instead, he abruptly turned around and left, making sure to lock his office door on the way out. His secretary was still at lunch, but she should be back shortly.

Devon was waiting at the curb in his shiny new Buick Park Avenue. They were off downtown for a lunch in the Shell executive dining room on the top floor of One Shell Plaza. Dwight looked around the car and was actually less than impressed with the immaculate just-off-the-showroom-floor vehicle. He had made a lot of progress, but he still had to be careful not to attract too much attention to his personal tastes and lifestyle choices. He couldn't wait to get that Mercedes, which he deserved. Maybe in about six months.

He was back in his office by 3:00 PM after an excellent lunch with Ed Smith, who, like him, was a man who had class and liked big deals and large projects. Dwight updated him on the "excellent" progress of the two apartments he had under construction. He was proud that both would come in on time and within budget. Needy folks were already lining up to rent units. The oil company executive was duly impressed. So much for the important business of the day. Now for that other matter.

When Dwight finally managed to get rid of those irritating HUD people, who just loved to chitchat on government time, Devon was waiting for him outside his office. The kid was very disturbed. He was making progress adjusting to life in the big city but had a long way to go. He let too many things bother him, especially in this case, Ms. Pamela Nelson.

Dwight never let others know exactly what he was thinking, and correspondingly strove to ensure that he missed little that happened around him. He was aware of the attraction his half-brother had developed for his newest employee. In fairness, he supposed, that was almost to be expected. She was a stunner; but the kid had to learn to better control his emotions. When Devon was not on a specific job for Dwight, which was a lot of the time, he was to watch out for any problems within the office. Dwight set up a special set of "security" cameras within the building that few employees knew about. Devon was responsible for monitoring them.

In this case, even if Devon had not told him he had just seen the young lady on a camera snooping around his office, he knew immediately that something was amiss. He noticed that the surface extender in his desk was not the way he'd left it. She must be hiding in his bathroom. He was about to open the door and deal with her right then when he realized that the matter would be better handled discreetly. If she didn't know she'd been seen, he would have an advantage over her, and he did not want to draw a lot of attention to an incident in his office. Dwight was a control freak to the core. It would have been demeaning for others to see that someone had violated his inner sanctum. He was, of course, curious why she had tried to look through his things, although most likely she had been put up to it by her brother, whom he axed. He was confident she hadn't seen anything that would have made any sense to her, her brother, or anyone else.

His grand scheme was taking shape and making progress towards his ultimate objective. He simply could not let an intrusive young woman jeopardize all that. Sadly, from a physical perspective anyway, it had become necessary to eliminate her after being there only a short period. It was regrettable that her brother's ire over his contract had come into play so soon. Few of the employees would find it unusual that she left. She was known to be a flighty girl who had trouble sticking to anything very long. Everyone at SETUP would remember her as a lovely person they never had a chance to get to know. During her brief stay she gave every indication of becoming a great member of the team and had no problems with anyone. Deliberately avoiding his office phone, Dwight picked up his cell and made the necessary arrangements. Meanwhile, down in the break room, Devon was almost in tears. Dwight did not mention Pam to him, but he had a pretty good idea what would happen.

Pam crouched in that tiny room for about fifteen more minutes before screwing up the courage to open the door. The big bad wolf might be sitting right there with fangs bared, but she realized that if she waited much longer, Dwight's secretary would be back at her desk. She had to chance it. Slowly, she turned the handle and inched the door open. There was no explosion. The office was empty. He had gone off to lunch. She was safe for the moment.

Gradually, her breathing eased. She gave a fleeting thought to pulling out the extender the way she'd found it but decided not to press her luck.

After checking to see the coast was clear in the outer office, she darted out and ran into her office. She grabbed her purse and the little two-frame photo set of her niece and nephew, which was the only personalizing of the place she had done. Seconds later, she was down the stairs and out to her car. She didn't expect to be coming back.

Although it was not even 1:00 PM, she drove straight home to her apartment, locked the door, took a hot bath, and jumped under the covers. She was still shaking like a leaf. The ordeal had exhausted her mentally and physically. She finally dropped off into a deep sleep. When she began to stir, not sure of where she was, panic started to set in again. After a few seconds, it faded when she realized she was home and safe. Her clock radio said it was almost 10:00 PM. She'd been out for almost ten hours and it was now dark outside. As the cobwebs began to clear, she reflected back over the horrible events of the day and just how close she'd come to getting caught by that awful man. What had she been thinking by going in there? She rolled out of bed and wandered into the kitchen where she fixed a cup of chamomile tea to help settle her jittery stomach. She had no appetite.

As she sipped from the brimming cup, she felt the need to talk to someone about all that happened and unload it from her mind. That someone was not Muriel, at least not yet. In her distracted state, she could not go to her best friend, whose sarcastic approach to most everything just wouldn't sit well with her at that moment. Matt was out of the question, since he'd lectured her about going anywhere near the man and she'd promptly ignored him. Then it hit her. Why not? She fished down in her purse and found another of those cheap Walmart throw-away phones. She'd memorized the number and codes by heart.

It took a while for the call to connect. A woman's voice answered. "This is Alice calling for Fred," Pam replied.

At least two minutes went by before a man's voice came on the line with a curt, "Fred."

"Fred, this is Alice with the Economist Magazine. I am calling about renewing your subscription."

"When does my subscription run out?" the man asked in a cold, disinterested tone.

"May," she replied.

Almost instantly, the man's voice transformed as if by miracle from cold and distant to warm and friendly. "Hey there! How are you doing? It is so good to hear your voice."

The protocol over, she found herself close to tears. Out it came, all about her nasty day and how she'd almost been caught. The man listened patiently. Strangely, once she had dumped it all to him, she felt much better. Her spunk was returning.

"Tell me about this guy, Dwight Lamar. I don't think I ever met him."

"He is new to Houston. I think he came from Beaumont, New Orleans, or somewhere over that way. He is now a big deal here. He is the executive director of a housing partnership between the city and county. He is in the news all the time. He is building two low-income apartment projects. Matt was helping him on one of them, but he fired him."

"Matt is the best there is. Do you know why he would do that?"

"Something about a big problem on his project, which Matt says is bull. He was about to quit anyway. He thinks the guy is skimming money, and also has some big scheme up his sleeve. Lamar is very sneaky and calculating. Stupidly, I was trying to get close to him to see if I could get a hint. Boy, did that backfire!"

"But you told me you did see something peculiar. What was it?"

"Just some strange notes on a piece of paper in his top desk drawer. Matt had heard him whisper 'Crispus Attucks' on the phone and, sure enough, I saw that name written on that paper."

"That is the Revolutionary War slave, I think. Hmmm? Was there anything else?"

"Yes, yes, there was." Pam hesitated and frowned, "Oh, no. Shit. Shit. Shit."

"What is the matter? What else was written there?"

Pam was so frustrated she thought she might cry. "I know there were four names, but I can't remember them now. I scribbled them on my arm with a ballpoint, but when I finally got home the first thing I did was jump into the tub and soak for a while. I am sure I rubbed it all off. What an idiot I am! All that stuff, and I don't even have anything at all. I just can't do anything right."

"Don't be so tough on yourself. You were very brave, although extremely foolish, to do what you did. It is amazing you found out anything. Oh, by the way, did you check your arm to see if there is anything left that you can read?"

"Well, I guess I should do that. Hey, great news! It is very smudged, but I can read some of it. The first name was Crispus Attucks. It is gone, but I know that was what it said. The second one is also hard to read. It looks like "F las; I can't read much. The third one is better, I think it says "Sojo...... ruth, or something like that. The last one is still pretty clear, Peter Butler, I think."

"Well, that is better than nothing. I'll have to think about them and maybe do a little research on my own, although Peter Butler seems to ring a bell. We can talk in a few days, but we need to cut this off or we'll be pressing our luck. Are you sure you're okay?"

"Yeah. I feel much better now. See you, Fred."

"Later, Alice." Click.

She flipped the cheap phone shut and tossed it into her trash. She needed to pick up a few more of them. She was much relieved after the phone call, but it was almost 11:00 PM. She had just slept for ten hours, so bed was out of the question. Her body craved exercise, so she put on her sweats, nothing too fancy for a midnight run, grabbed her trusty little can of mace, and headed out the door to Hermann Park, which was just a few blocks away. A couple of miles and she should be fine.

43.

In addition to magnificent mazes of urban congestion, Houston was also blessed with numerous beautiful green spaces, including Hermann Park, a four-hundred-and-fifty acre reserve woven between the mammoth Texas Medical Center complex and the Rice University campus. One of the most used public parks in the city, Hermann boasted extensive amenities, such as an eighteen-hole golf course, the Miller Outdoor Theater, the Mecom Fountain, Museum of Natural Science, and Houston Zoo. An impressive likeness of old Sam Houston sat proudly on his majestic mount welcoming visitors at the north entry. Miles of well-lit, and constantly-patrolled walking and jogging paths threaded through the grounds. Sometimes, first-time visitors had trouble adjusting to a peculiar situation there. The park bordered on one of the most extensive complexes of hospitals and medical facilities in the world, including the city's primary charity hospital. As a result, there was an incessant wailing of ambulance sirens both day and night. The cacophony of medical emergencies was in sharp contrast to the tranquility of the oak tree-laden Rice campus just to the west.

Pam lived in a high-rise complex just a few blocks from the park. After the troubling events of the day and her virtual collapse into bed, her body now craved the release an invigorating run would bring. She threw on her running gear and jogged from her apartment as she had done hundreds of times in the past. It was a short distance over tree-lined sidewalks and across Hermann Drive to the park entrance. The trails were well-lit at night but, as Pam moved along, she pondered whether a run at that hour was a good idea. She assumed there would still be plenty of folks out. There always were, but not now. The place was deserted.

Her spirits lifted, though, when an HPD black-and-white cruised slowly by as she ran along near the golf course not far from the zoo grounds. She planned to continue straight on the main park road until she reached Cambridge Street, which bordered on the medical center. She would turn around and head back, having run about two and one-half miles by the time she arrived back home. That route kept her mostly on brightly-lit paths.

As Pam moved in and out of shadows along the fairway of the first hole of the golf course, she noticed the flashing lights and heard the blaring siren of an ambulance rushing some poor soul to Ben Taub Hospital. The park was eerie enough at night. That racket didn't help. Perhaps the distraction of that wailing vehicle caused her to miss the ominous, dark figure that silently slipped out from a huge live oak tree as she jogged past and sprinted after her. Suddenly, she sensed motion from behind and glanced back over her shoulder. To her horror she saw a huge black blur barreling at her just a few steps away. Her rotten luck that day apparently was not over yet. She was in a spot where there were no other runners, police cruisers, or even emergency call boxes. The attacker had picked the most secluded place on her run where the street was lined by thick brush on one side and the chain-link fence of the zoo grounds on the other.

Panic stricken, Pam could not react before a powerful hand grabbed her right shoulder from behind. The grip hurt as steel-like fingers closed on her sweatshirt. Instinctively, she reached to her waist for her mace canister, but her hand got there an instant too late as the attacker's other hand knowingly slapped over hers. He was wise to the mace and tried to seize it before his prey could. Ironically, it was that very action that saved her for the moment. By reaching for the mace, the aggressor could not control her as well as if he had used both hands to wrestle her down. The mace ripped loose from her belt, disappeared into the darkness, and was gone. At the same time, though, she was able to slither out of the stranglehold just before a second attacker materialized out of the gloom and reached out to grab her arms.

Two of them. I'm in deep, deep trouble!

She was free for a split second and had to move fast. She bolted into the street and across to the other side, where the chain-link fence protected the zoo enclosure. There was no time for thinking or planning. She was operating on terror-driven impulse as she dashed along the fence back towards the way she'd come. Luckily her excellent conditioning enabled her to sprint at a good pace. Unfortunately, her assailants were no slouches either. They split up. While one chased her across the street, the other ran back perhaps a hundred yards or so and then crossed over so they had her trapped between them along the zoo fence. She was praying she could outrun them, but, just as she thought she might, her heart fell. A dark figure emerged out of the black directly ahead. Where was her cellphone? She had messed with those stupid burner phones and left her real cell at home in her purse. Great!

She quickly concluded that there was no choice but to fight as hard as she could. She would start with a swift kick between the legs of the first asshole who came close. Seeing that it was no use to keep running right into the guy up ahead, she stopped and grimly prepared to make a stand. With one attacker closing from behind and the other in front, she was boxed in. Fight she would, but still frantically searched for any other alternative.

Out of the corner of her eye, she spotted a gate in the zoo's chain-link fence. It must have been a rear access for zoo maintenance. Was there any way she could squeeze through? Her hopes evaporated. A drooping chain and padlock were visible between the two sections of gate. With nothing to lose, she ran towards the gate, which was securely chained, but there was a small gap of a few inches showing between the two sides. Could her foot fit in that space? There was no time to decide. Praying for a little luck, she leaped just before she reached the fence, grappled the chain-link with her hands and somehow inserted her foot on top of the chain in the small gap. She levered herself up and over the top and fell with a thud on the other side. She was momentarily stunned as she hit the pavement.

Her pursuers arrived in seconds and watched her scramble up and disappear into the thick vegetation at the rear of the zoo enclosure. Unfortunately, if she could jump the fence, so could they. Once again, her advantage was fleeting.

The undergrowth and foliage inside the zoo compound were dense and jungle-like. Everything was pitch-black. As she bumped, stumbled, and crawled along through the thick smelly, scratchy stuff, she could hear her pursuers right behind her. There was nowhere to hide and nothing to fight with. She was desperate, and had to keep going. She knew eventually she had to come out inside on the zoo grounds somewhere. If they caught her in that thick spot, those guys could kill her, and no-one would find her for days. She had to keep moving.

As she blindly struggled and fought her way forward in the dense under-growth, she took a step, but, unexpectedly, there was nothing but air under her foot. Emptiness. She teetered, wavered, and then lost her balance, flailing, desperate to grasp limbs, sticks, or anything to keep her from falling. Unable to right herself, she lost all control and tumbled down into a black abyss. Her last thought, just before slamming into something hard below and losing consciousness, was that she wished she'd worn her sexy running outfit for when they found her body.

44.

It was unusual for the Southeast Texas Unified Partnership to have a special meeting of the board of directors, but Dwight Lamar called for one on the basis that the information he was about to present was so important it could not wait. Secretly, he was getting a little concerned about the incidents involving both Nelsons and wanted to accelerate his timetable. The next regularly scheduled meeting was still more than sixty days off. He had to lean hard on Alpha Graphics to complete his presentation materials, but they were able to satisfy him with the handouts, a video, and the PowerPoint presentation they produced. The topic was "Destination Diversity," which was to be SETUP's signature major development project. He needed a consensus of directors on board to proceed with the important business ahead.

A key aspect of this development, of course, was the location of the project. There are many factors to consider. It absolutely had to be in either the city or the county, hopefully in both. The site had to offer all the right roadway access, surrounding infrastructure, environmental certifications, and much more. Ideally, he wanted to purchase around two hundred acres, which was going to be a difficult task. Very few tracts of that size with those qualifications were available.

In order to best approach this problem and convey the strict impression that everything was always at arm's length and impartial, Lamar interviewed three of the leading commercial real estate firms in the city: CBRE, Cushman Wakefield, and Jones Lang. All were thoroughly familiar with the Houston market. They were also aware that eventually SETUP would be looking for a piece of land, since Lamar talked to them about the Houston market shortly after he took over. All of them wanted an exclusive representation agreement with SETUP, but Lamar refused. Each knew what he needed, and he would be pleased to sign a purchase contract with whomever brought him the best and most appropriate site. The three firms were hard at it and had come up with several potential properties to consider. Lamar had worked with them to reduce the possibilities down to three, one of which was located in southeast Harris County and was owned by some offshore group.

The first site, which was brought in by CBRE, was located in far northwest Harris County in an area that was pancake flat, open prairie and rice fields. There had been tremendous population growth in that direction for several years. Infrastructure and road access would not be a problem.

The second site from Cushman Wakefield was located in the northeast, near the Hardy toll road, not far from the Houston airport. This one was more congested than site number one, but had several advantages.

The third site was located in southeast Harris County near Ellington Air Force Base and not far from NASA in Clear Lake City. Jones Lang, who had found it, was quick to point out that it was the only one that was also technically within the city of Houston and Harris County. Even though Dwight Lamar had worked closely with each brokerage firm to pare down their alternatives, he "professed" absolute neutrality. He would let the board make the choice.

The seven directors took a few minutes before the meeting started to peruse the glossy package of brochures, maps, charts, and graphs that had been left in front of them. Chairman Hobby called the meeting to order and turned things over to Dwight Lamar, who looked especially dapper that evening in his dark suit and pink tie. This was to be his moment.

"Good evening, everyone," he began as he surveyed the group to get an initial reading of their moods and disposition. Henry Francesca was beaming. Ed Smith and the preacher, Edward Pike, returned his smile. The others were attentive and seemed anxious to hear what their bright ED had to say. The exception, of course, was Kathy Barnes, who scowled and refused to acknowledge him while pretending to be fully preoccupied with the material in front of her.

"So far, thanks to all your kind assistance, the good Lord, and a whole lot of good luck, SETUP has been able to accomplish quite a bit during our short existence. More people in the city and county are receiving the housing help they critically need than ever before. We have two new beautiful apartment properties online that are almost full." He paused a second to let that sink in. "Now, we are on the precipice of a quantum leap in the interest of our citizens to whom we are committed to assist in a new and dynamic way. No longer will the income-disadvantaged among us have to be relegated to less affluent neighborhoods where crime abounds. We are about to embark upon a project that will be the harbinger of the future. Yes, Destination Diversity will introduce a new concept in communal living, where everyone is truly treated as equals. The project will consist of multiple, high-quality, integrated neighborhoods, restaurants, shops, banks, parks, and amenities for the income-disadvantaged. The centerpiece will be a gushing circular fountain surrounding a fifty-foot obelisk with a bronze plaque listing the names of all those who had the foresight to make this wonderful idea happen. Destination Diversity will offer lifestyles no different than we find in the West Loop, Memorial, and Galleria areas today, with the difference being that our folks—yes, I said 'our folks'—can afford to live there. We will offer an exciting mix of ethnic and social backgrounds that blend seamlessly into a harmonious setting. And I might add that such an undertaking has only been possible with the unique creation of this wonderful city-county partnership. Now, sit back and enjoy this fifteen-minute video, which will fill you in about Destination Diversity. When it is over, we can then get into some of the critical decisions we need to make so this incredible concept becomes a reality."

As the lights dimmed, Lamar took another quick inventory. He certainly had their attention. Even Kathy Barnes had gone from negative to perhaps neutral. As the video ended and the lights came back up, Dwight would have been amused, but he was happy that Henry Francesca did not break out into applause, which, for a moment, it appeared the Dumbo might. Dwight entertained several questions, most of which he had expected and prepared for.

As soon as there was a lull, he promptly moved on to the real business at hand: picking a site. As Dwight's minions flashed exhaustive data on the screen for each of the three possibilities, Dwight described them in detail. The price, he cautioned, was certainly very important, but should not necessarily be the final determinant. The range of prices for the roughly 200-acre parcels were all in the $15,000,000 to $17,000,000 range, which calculated out to about $75,000 per acre. Their packets were stuffed with expert reports, charts, and pages of statistics; much more, as Dwight had intended, than any of them could have digested in such a short time. The group took a fifteen-minute break after Dwight was through describing the options. He was surprised to observe that the directors hardly moved from their seats except to discuss the parcels among each other. The discussion resumed and finally, after an hour, Dwight felt it was time to call for a decision and a vote.

"Okay, everyone, here is what I would like to suggest. I believe you all need to vote for the site you feel is best, although I am convinced that any of them would work quite well. As you know, large real estate transactions are fraught with complications even after they go to contract. Nothing is certain even then. I would like to propose that we, as a group, rank the three of them in order of priority one, two, and three. We will then pursue them in that order. If number one busts out for some reason during the due diligence period, then we can go right to the next one and not lose any time. Does that seem acceptable?" There were nodding heads from the directors.

"I think that approach makes sense, Dwight," the ever-pensive Shell Oil director, Ed Smith, commented. "I know you are trying to stay neutral, but certainly you must have a favorite. Some of us board members would like to know which one you are leaning towards."

Dwight smiled; this was working out better than he could have imagined. He paused and pretended to reflect on the question as several directors leaned forward to hear his answer.

"Well, as I said before, there has been a lot of work just to get to this point. I truly believe that any of them will work just fine, but if you really pushed me, I guess I would say that I lean slightly towards the airport site, Number Two." Dwight wondered to himself how Peter Butler was going to react when he heard about that preference before the board, which wasn't the one owned by the Albanians. He would go ape shit.

In any event, the vote was cast with the airport site being ranked first by a six-zero-one abstention vote (Kathy Barnes, of course). The NASA site was second, and the northwest prairie site was last. A resolution was made, seconded, and dutifully recorded in the minutes. Somehow, Dwight Lamar had personally evaded the decision-process and, in fact, had added some misdirection away from where he knew the actual purchase would end up.

It had been a good night. Almost all the directors thanked him and complimented him on the fine job he was doing as they filed out. Dwight continued to be amazed at either his luck or his skill at manipulating these regimented bureaucrats. They had just authorized him to purchase a $15,000,000 or so parcel of raw land, and it never occurred to them to approve the basic development itself! In truth, Dwight didn't care much about that. The land was the thing. Hey, Destination Diversity might even work. Who knew? On to more important things. He wondered who or what Devon had rounded up for him tonight. He felt good. It was too bad about the Nelson woman. It would have been great to score with her tonight.

Dwight Lamar knew it would happen, and he was not disappointed. It did take two days, but not only did Peter Butler contact him that evening, but had flown into town and demanded that they meet immediately, even though it was already past 8:00 PM. Lamar knew why he was there and had no intention of avoiding the man, but they could not be seen together at all costs. He understood that Butler's Albanian clients could be quite ruthless and had no desire to incur their wrath. The consummation of this deal absolutely required cool heads and a steady hand. The boat could easily be rocked over. He had Devon call Butler and tell him to take a room at the Airport Holiday Inn on JFK Boulevard, no fancy digs. Dwight would meet him in his room at midnight.

When Dwight knocked on the door to Room 203, it was pulled open almost immediately. Peter Butler was standing there in an obviously agitated state. He had alcohol on his breath and had consumed most of a six-pack of Coors Light while waiting for Dwight to show up. The two men made interesting contrasts. Dwight Lamar was soft-spoken, reserved, calculating, and almost impossible to read. Peter Butler, on the other hand, was stressed, demonstrative, loud, and an open book. Dwight had an idea of the pressure the man was under and realized that he owed him an explanation about recent events. Besides that, he had some critical business to negotiate with Butler and his clients. The uncertainty they now felt was part of Lamar's overall plan. He wanted to keep them guessing, up to a point. As of the moment, if the deal went south, he had zip out of pocket, but they could easily blow several million bucks. In their place he'd be nervous too.

First things first. Butler grabbed Dwight and just about pulled him into the motel room. Dwight was not used to such treatment, especially from those he felt were mere functionaries. His eyes glared at the taller, silver-haired man who was obviously at least half-drunk. To his credit, Butler immediately realized his mistake and quickly tried to make amends.

"Sorry, Dwight. I didn't mean to drag you in like that. Please accept my apologies. I am a bit put out at the moment. My guys have been calling me from Brooklyn almost every hour wanting to know what is going on. I need to tell them something. They have their own contacts down here. When they heard that not only did your group put another tract under contract, but you actually told the directors that you favored the other site, they went nuts. They are damn upset at the moment. You told me over the phone to buy Crispus Attucks, which was the NASA site. Please, please don't tell me I screwed up

247

and bought the wrong one. Was the airport tract really Crispus Attucks? Tell me I bought the right one. We even confirmed it. What the hell is going on, Dwight?"

Dwight stared at him for a moment and actually enjoyed watching the rude jerk stew in his own juice. He considered telling the idiot that he did screw up, but the pressing business overshadowed a little more fun at Butler's expense. He finally answered in a slow monotone, "Yes, I expected them to be upset."

Butler could barely hold himself back. "What the hell does that mean? We have five million bucks at risk. We jumped in on your say-so and bought a lousy piece of dirt we know nothing about! Those guys are pissed, and they can play rough. I am not sure I want to get on that airplane and go home tomorrow."

"I would recommend that you do, Peter. As far as I can see, this deal is perfectly on track. Those people should not be worried at all."

"How the hell do you figure that?"

"Easterners, especially New Yorkers, are always impatient. They are short-tempered and always like to worry about everything. Down here, we do things a little more slowly. Apparently, the information your people got assumes that one, we will close on the other tract, which I can assure you we will not, and two, that I personally want that other tract, which I most certainly do not. I remain in full control of what is happening. Did it ever occur to you smart boys that it may not be in my, or even our, collective interests to run straight at the NASA tract? As things stand now, I am on full public record of wanting the other site. If something should blow up on our arrangement, I will have some protection. Your guys may not give a shit about that, but I sure do. As long as we can come to some agreement on the post-closing distribution of cash, SETUP will buy your tract for $15,000,000, which, if I did my math right, is a profit of some ten very big ones. It will take from thirty to forty-five days for me to turn down the airport contract for any number of reasons; title, environmental, etc. I really don't need much of an excuse. We will move right on to your tract in good time. That is the way it is going to be. If the bozos in New York don't like that, too flippin' bad. And, oh, by the way, you purchased the right tract."

The light had gone on in Butler's semi-inebriated brain. Suddenly, he felt much relieved. What Lamar had said made perfect sense and had never occurred to any of them. All they saw was him welshing on their deal. The truth was, the guy was calling the shots at this point. "Okay, okay, Dwight, that does make sense. In fact, it makes perfect sense, even for us. What is another month or so? I will explain it to them. I assume they will understand before I lose any teeth—or worse."

"Good, Peter, but now here is the really tough part, which your guys knew was coming. Based upon all the regulators around me, I absolutely cannot put anything in writing. I cannot even consider it. You purchased the tract on my word. Nothing is written down. You did your part so far and I am prepared to do mine, as long as we can agree on a few more things. Certainly, it should come as no surprise to your boys that they are going to split the excess cash with me."

"Of course. You might be surprised to find that despite their somewhat primitive ways, they are in the end very honorable, if for no other reason than they expect to do repeat business, which is possible, is it not?"

"Yes, certainly, as long as everything goes well. SETUP is just getting started."

"So, what do you want, Dwight?"

Dwight had pondered this question over and over. The deal died without him, but the same was true about the Albanians. He had absolutely no reason to trust them, but to pull this thing off, he must. There didn't seem to be much choice. If they chose to screw him, at least he would live to fight another day. He concluded that he was better off not getting greedy. It killed him that he had to bow to these beasts, but it just made sense to do so.

The problem was, when SETUP purchased the NASA tract, the $15,000,000 would be transferred to the seller, which was the Albanian partnership. He could not dare to be in line when that cash disbursement was made to them. After they recouped their original $5,000,000, they'd be $10,000,000 ahead. He had to trust them to then send his portion to a numbered Switzerland account that he had set up. If they thumbed their noses at him, he would be out of luck. For a man who didn't trust anyone, this was a difficult move. Was there honor among thieves?

"Half of the profit, $5,000,000, is what I get in total, but $2,500,000 of that is wired to where I say, before we actually sign the closing papers. We don't close until I have the $2,500,000 safely deposited in my account. The rest comes immediately when your boys get their money. That is just in case you forget my address when the funds come rolling in. It, at least, will fund the army I hire to come to Brooklyn."

In spite of it all, Butler chuckled. He wasn't sure what his investors would do, but he knew that was the kind of demand from Lamar they had been expecting. The cash *before* the closing part was a surprise. "Fair enough, Dwight. I'll see them tomorrow night when I get back to New York. I'll let you know."

"Nope, Peter. You get them on the phone right now. We settle this tonight, before I leave.

I'll be sitting in my car in the parking lot. I will be back up in thirty minutes."

Butler's face assumed a forlorn look. "Okay, Dwight, I'll do my best."

Dwight left. He came back in thirty minutes later and was greeted by a thoroughly drained go-between who had downed another brew while Dwight was gone.

"So?"

"Well, it took me quite a while to explain the confusion over the tracts. I think I got them comfortable about that. I explained to them that I thought you were firm on $5,000,000 and they did go for that, finally, but no cash before close."

"Deal-breaker. Contact me if they reconsider," Dwight spat back and got up to leave.

"Hold on! Hold on! I'll call them back." Dwight stood there while Butler pressed his speed dial and spoke quietly into the phone.

"Dwight, how about $500,000?"

"Bye, Peter."

More discussion. "Okay; okay, Dwight, you get your $2,500,000 just before closing."

"Deal," Dwight said, as he sank down and sat on the bed. "Hey, Peter, have you got one more beer left?"

45.

Perhaps fate was at work that evening when Pam unexpectedly "dropped in" to the zoo. She'd visited many times with Rusty and Gail, who could not get enough of the place and were especially fascinated by the gorillas. Pam told them about King Kong, Fay Raye, and the antics of that monstrous and violent brute who smashed humans every chance he got. She was quick to add that the story was made for a movie. Unfortunately, Kong's bad manners on the screen set an unfair example of gorilla behavior and conveyed a common misimpression about them. Sure, there have been documented instances of these robust and muscular animals attacking and killing humans, usually by biting with their powerful teeth and jaws, but such incidents are extremely rare. While aggressive behavior by gorillas is common, it is usually directed towards other gorillas during mating or male domination encounters.

The Houston Zoo was justifiably proud of their newly refurbished habitat that featured seven gorillas divided into two troops from the African lowlands, where they lived in dense rain forests. The zoo had created a bars-free habitat for these animals who could be observed from above on an elevated walkway. At first, Rusty and Gail clung closely to Aunt Pam as they peeked down at the massive, hairy creatures only a few feet below with no protection in between. Not only were the gorillas the kids' favorite, they had become the signature attraction of the zoo. Great care had gone into the design and construction of the facility to replicate the natural habitat, while ensuring absolute safety to both watchers and the watched.

Houston Zoo officials had done their best to learn from a tragic event at the Cincinnati Zoo involving a young boy that fell into the gorilla enclosure. A 450-pound male grabbed the youngster's hand and, even though the animal seemed to be exhibiting protective and non-aggressive behavior towards the child, zoo authorities decided to destroy it. The gorilla was shot and the boy rescued unharmed. Houston officials were determined to make sure such a tragedy could never occur in their habitat. Alarms and cameras were positioned along the elevated walkway to closely monitor every inch of space on the ground. Unfortunately, it never dawned on the enclosure designers that anyone would ever approach the compound through the dense bamboo and other vegetation in the rear. They apparently had not met Pamela Nelson.

Pam tumbled and fell down fifteen feet next to a steep wall and slammed into the earth strewn with rocks, logs, and small bushes. She was knocked out cold by the impact and was lucky not to have been killed. She narrowly missed jagged boulders just a few feet away. She ended up sprawled in a crumpled heap behind a brush pile that obscured her from the security cameras. The shaggy local folks, however, were immediately aware that the young lady had come calling.

Bongo, who tipped the scales at a quarter-ton, was the dominant male in his troop. He enjoyed this distinction for one primary reason: he was the only male in the troop. He never had to do battle with competitors for the favor of the two females who shared his enclosure. Male gorillas are often compelled to do battle royal with other males to achieve dominance. They often bear the scars and wounds of the fighting necessary to determine "who gets the girl." In that respect, Bongo had drawn the long straw. He had all the food and water he could ever need, along with two lovely ladies at his beck and call—well, sort of. In any event, he had never displayed unusually aggressive behavior towards anyone, including his keepers. Bongo was happy with his situation.

Just to show how difficult things can be even when you are a product of privilege, however, Bongo's life was not without anxiety and discomfort, to the extent that he was almost continually harassed by his two ladies, both of whom thought they should be the main apple of his eye. There was an uneasy truce among the two females, but at times, instead of fighting with each other, they tended to take out their frustrations on poor Bongo. Nice guy that he was, Bongo had nowhere to run.

Pam lay motionless as the morning rays began to filter through from the eastern sky. She was dreaming about the screech of an ambulance siren when she felt something poking at her side. Instinctively, she brushed it away, but it soon returned. Now it felt like a hand was trying to roll her over. "Stop it!" she murmured. "Leave me alone." That seemed to work, and the jostling stopped. She also dreamed of an utterly awful smell, kind of like what you'd find in a horse's stall before it was mucked out. Yuck! These disturbances were enough to gradually rouse her. Her eyes felt like they'd been glued shut, but slowly she peeked them open and tried to focus. She blinked several times but could not register what she saw or where she was. Two huge, black, gleaming orbs on an enormous, flat, black, glistening face with monstrous nostrils was staring at her with intense curiosity. She was totally confused. Nothing made sense at first. Her mind was still a muddled mess.

Slowly, she began to recall the events of last night. She wondered if she had been captured and, now *wait a minute; that's not a man, it's, it's an ape! It's a freaking ape! "Mommy!"* she shrieked, and tried to scramble away from the massive, hairy, black creature. She had two problems when she tried to move. The first was her right leg hurt like hell. She probably fractured it when she fell. The second problem was that the gorilla was holding her wrist with his big, black paw.

"Help! Help!" she gulped and cried, having no idea where she was or who might possibly hear. She trembled, and was certain the monster was about to have her for breakfast. Then she looked directly into his eyes and was sure she had totally lost all sense of reality. The big monkey didn't look mean at all. In fact, he seemed to have a curious look of sympathy and understanding. Was that possible? He did not appear to be fierce or about to smash her around. He just calmly stared at her while she quivered and then, after a few moments, with his other hand, he gently reached for her blond hair, which he draped across his thick, ebony fingers. He examined it with bewilderment. Pam was not ready to ask him to run to Starbucks for her, but she began to relax a little.

The slight reason for optimism, however, was short-lived. Just when Pam began to think there may be some way out of this predicament, all hell broke loose. Out of nowhere another huge, black creature appeared, thumping its chest, growling, and kicking up dirt everywhere. To make matters worse, the new arrival was headed directly at Pam, who could not move. The animal got close enough that Pam could smell the hot, foul breath and see the gnashing white teeth. At the last instant her big friend ambled between them and swatted the other gorilla back with his massive arm. He also held forth with a blast of gorilla language and did a little growling and thumping of his own. The other animal, which was much smaller, snarled, but backed away and disappeared.

When the dust cleared, her black knight looked down at Pam, once again with a bemused expression. She could think of nothing to do but smile. What she didn't know was that Bongo's steady girlfriends had no use for this new female interloper. Pam was horning in on their man. Bongo, so far, was protecting his newly found "whatever."

Jonas Edgerton was the first of the gorilla keepers to arrive that morning.

He was the senior and most seasoned member of the primate team. He and Bongo had been together for seven years. He and the massive creature had bonded long ago. Jonas had been extremely upset over the Cincinnati incident that resulted in an innocent magnificent animal's demise. While it was probably the right decision given the safety of the boy, he lived in fear that a similar incident could occur in his habitat. He knew that their protocol would probably be the same; destroy the animal if there was any threat at all to the safety of a human. He prayed he would never have to make that decision.

He immediately knew something was up in the habitat that morning. Esmerelda, one of Bongo's wives, was on the warpath. He could hear her loud screaming as he walked up to the compound. At first he didn't see anything on the security monitors, but when he stepped to the rail of the walkway, he did a double take. He rubbed his eyes to make sure they weren't deceiving him. There was Bongo, sitting calmly, holding the hand of a person who, judging by the long, blond hair, must be a woman.

He forced himself not to panic. He had to first determine if the woman was alive. He called out, "Hey, you in there, lady. Are you okay? Please speak to me!" There was no reply, although Bongo did look up and seemed pleased when he heard the voice of his good friend.

"Hey, you, down in the habitat. Are you okay?" he desperately tried a second time. If she didn't respond, he'd have to get the 30.06 rifle and get ready to destroy the animal, his pal. He would also have to call the zoo director and put everything on full alert.

Silence; but then, "Are you calling me?" a woman's voice weakly drifted up from below.

"Yes. Yes. Are you hurt? What is the animal doing? Can you tell? What is your name?" he urged.

"Pam, I'm Pam. I am okay, I think, except I may have broken something when I fell. So far, he hasn't hurt me. In fact, I think he is protecting me from the other one. Please get me out here Please. Hurry!"

Jonas was extremely relieved that Pam was alive. In the middle of this horrible predicament, it was as good news as he could have expected. He now had one chance to save the girl and maybe Bongo, too. If it didn't work, both of them would probably be killed, and he would be arrested. What he was about to attempt was strictly against emergency procedures, but he had to give it a try.

"Okay, Pam. Don't worry, I am going to get you out of there safe and sound (gulp, I hope). Your friend there is Bongo. Normally he is pretty even-tempered, and not at all aggressive. He seems to be protecting you from his girlfriends. Now, can you see the wall just behind you? There is a small door there, which opens from the outside. I am going to go around on the outside and slowly open it. Once I get it open, I am hoping Bongo will let you crawl over to it and get out. Do you think you can make it?"

"Yes, I will make it as long as he lets me go. He is still holding my wrist."

"Okay. We need to give it a try. He and I have known each other for quite a while. I hope I can convince him to release you. I am heading over to the door right now."

"Okay, okay. Please hurry," Pam wept.

Jonas disappeared. He first went by the office and grabbed the 30.06 rifle, which he loaded by slipping several shells into the magazine. He then hustled through the paths to the maintenance door. He used his keys to unlock it. He then chambered a round and took the safety off the rifle. Slowly, he opened the metal door. The last thing he would permit was an escaped gorilla. If Bongo made any attempt to approach him, he would shoot to kill. Also, if the animal made any aggressive moves towards the woman, he would likewise immediately shoot. The door was open, and the animal and girl were about fifteen feet away.

The gorilla looked at him with innocent curiosity. "Hey, Jonas, how you doin' this morning?"

Jonas spoke in the firm but steady and even voice he'd used with Bongo over all those years. "Morning, Bongo. I see you have a new friend there. I have come for her. I want you to let her go, and she will move over to me. You just stay right there, okay?"

The muscular giant took in everything Jonas said, although it was impossible to determine if he understood any of it. He continued to regard the keeper with a contented and relaxed expression on his face, almost as if he wanted to show off his new discovery to his friend.

"Okay, Pam. Very slowly, see if you can begin to crawl towards me."

Pam took her cue and twisted to begin. For the first time the gorilla, who had been entirely placid up to then, suddenly showed emotion. He began to smack his teeth and emit a low growl. Pam closed her eyes and stopped trying to crawl. He still had her hand. This reaction was what Jonas had feared.

Bongo just didn't want to lose his newfound plaything. Jonas had no choice. He raised the rifle and took a good sight picture directly on the animal's heart. He inserted his finger into the trigger guard.

One more try. "Now, Bongo! Let her go," he ordered with a louder and more assertive tone. Pam squirmed and, by some miracle, the beast dropped her arm and remained still as he watched her crawl slowly to the door. She moved about halfway, and Bongo hadn't made any move to stop her. Jonas prayed he wasn't getting ready to charge. She was almost there when the animal's expression changed to one of almost admonishment, like he'd been a bad boy. Jonas began to relax and smiled at the antics of the ape. He was going to pull it off: save the girl and the gorilla.

Not quite so fast, Tarzan, because suddenly, out of nowhere, an agitated Esmeralda came charging in for all she was worth like a freight train, straight at the still-open access door. She flew by Bongo so quickly he had no time to get in her way.

Jonas tossed the rifle aside, grabbed Pam's sweatshirt and hauled her through. He slammed the door shut and leaned all his weight against it. The jealous female smashed it very hard from the other side, but somehow Jonas hung on and the door remained fast. Sweat poured down his face. Pam lay at his feet; she was a mess.

46.

The broker from Cushman Wakefield was very upset. He had just come from a meeting with SETUP's attorney about the closing of the land parcel near the airport that the board had approved for purchase. The seller's lawyer and that snake, Dwight Lamar, were also present. After the board meeting, a sales contract had been drawn up and promptly executed by both parties. The agreement called for a thirty-day feasibility period, during which time the buyer, SETUP, was permitted to do additional investigations of the property to make sure everything was in order. SETUP had posted an earnest money deposit of $100,000 in escrow with the Charter Title Company. After thirty days, SETUP would lose those funds if it backed out of the deal.

Twenty-nine days had elapsed without anything happening, and then, suddenly on the thirtieth and last day, Lamar instructed his attorney to notify the title company that SETUP was canceling the contract. While SETUP didn't really need a reason to cancel, the proffered excuse was that a critical feeder road, which Destination Diversity needed, would not likely be constructed by the City of Houston for some time. Lamar had checked with one of his board members who was on the city council and confirmed that to be the case. The broker was extremely pissed. He knew deals bust out all the time, especially, it seemed, when a very large commission was at stake, but it seemed to him that Lamar was bailing for a very thin reason. Little did he realize how right he was.

As upset as the Cushman Wakefield agent had been, his Jones Lang contemporary was just as sure there was a Santa Claus when Lamar called him and told him he was prepared to sign a contract on their NASA property, provided it was still available.

Coincidentally, it was and, within two days, a purchase and sale agreement was executed by Lamar and the seller. The earnest money transferred over to the new contract. Lamar was sure the Albanians' local mole had reported to them that he was a man of his word and the proper site was now under contract.

The feasibility analysis on the second tract was proceeding smoothly, and it looked like this site would be purchased by SETUP for Destination

Diversity. A significant issue did crop up, however, that required Dwight's immediate attention. Dwight was well aware that any property he acquired, especially one involving HUD, would have to undergo a comprehensive environmental assessment. Such studies involved research into every prior use of the property, and exhaustive physical testing of the grounds. Any inkling of contamination could kill a deal.

In the Houston area, with oil and gas so prevalent, special care is always taken to ensure there are no old contaminated wells present. It is not unusual to have pipelines that crisscross everywhere, but old drill sites are another problem. Lamar knew about this potential problem and hired a reputable local environmental assessment firm to perform a preliminary study of the NASA tract. Sure enough, the company discovered that there was indeed an old, abandoned oil well on the north end of the site. The mere presence of an old well does not necessarily condemn a site and remediation is often possible. The biggest problem for Lamar was time. Such a problem could take months or even years to resolve. HUD would eventually commission their own study, which typically took many, many months to complete. He simply could not afford to wait.

Lamar decided to be proactive and arranged lunch with the owner of the environmental assessment firm, who was an older gentleman close to retirement. After requesting that their conversation be kept confidential, Lamar discussed the well site on the tract. During the preliminary chitchat, Lamar noted that the man was hoping to retire soon on Galveston Island and had found the perfect beach house, although it was priced too high for him to consider. Lamar innocently suggested that through SETUP he had made lots of contacts on the island. Maybe he could help somehow. The matter was dropped, but not forgotten by either man.

The environmental man pointed out to Lamar that the scope of his study on the NASA site called for a brief physical inspection and only a few test samples taken. He wasn't sure if the problem well was even out there at all. He went as far as to suggest that if someone were to go out there one night, remove the top sections of pipe, pour some concrete, and backfill a few feet of dirt, his team would probably never see it. There would be no physical well on his report.

Lamar smiled and thanked him. It was, therefore, a mere coincidence that the final environmental report was clean, and the guy retired to Galveston

258

shortly thereafter. Ten bags of concrete cost Lamar around fifty bucks, although the beach house help was a bit pricier. Overall, it was "well" worth it.

Dwight Lamar had one final steep hill to climb before he could actually close on the land. He really didn't care very much about what happened after the closing. He needed to arrange for $15,000,000 cash to purchase the site. Eventually, most of the development funds would come from HUD, but it was unlikely the government would actually fund until their own one-year-plus timetable environmental review was acceptably complete. Lamar couldn't wait, and didn't want to face the potential well issue all over again. His plan was to approach the city and county to put up $2,000,000 each out of their own general funds and then negotiate a short-term acquisition loan from a local bank. With the high visibility of the transaction and excitement over Destination Diversity, the governmental entities fell all over themselves wanting to throw money at the deal. Lamar could hardly believe it when the city decided to contribute not the $2,000,000, he asked for, but $2,500,000. The county blinked, but promptly followed suit.

With $5,000,000 cash already in the deal, it was no problem to get a short-term loan of $10,000,000 from Ken Underhill at Texas Enterprise Bank, who, ironically, had been Travis Nelson's former banker. Banks were always under pressure to make community-related loans. In just the few months since the board had approved the purchase, Dwight Lamar had the site acquisition ready to close. When it did, he would personally become several million dollars richer.

It was the middle of the week, and the lawyers were scrambling to arrange all the paperwork so the land closing could take place on Friday at the offices of the Charter Title Company. Dwight felt especially good that morning riding to the office. He'd stopped working out at the Q after Pamela Nelson disappeared. He felt it was better if he stayed away from there.

Devon pulled smartly up to the front door of the SETUP building in Park Avenue. Dwight waited while Devon got out and opened the car door for him. He avoided making eye contact with his half-brother, who was clearly troubled by something. Dwight had to open the front door of the building himself, which he found a bit inconvenient, but was pleasantly greeted by the attractive receptionist behind her desk in the front waiting room. He smiled and nodded to her. He was sure she'd be a tiger in the sack but had wisely kept his distance. He turned and noticed three or four African Americans sitting there waiting to meet with his staff for help with finding housing. He deliberately walked over to shake each of their hands and exchange pleasantries. They all seemed impressed that this obviously important man had taken time to say hello.

The lobby security guard in his neat, dark-blue uniform had already called the elevator, which he held open. The man came to attention as Dwight entered the elevator and actually threw up a salute just as the doors closed.

Dwight stepped off on the second floor and nodded to several members of his staff as he passed by their offices. Each person returned his acknowledgment with a smile. His secretary had just returned from the lunchroom with a steaming cup of coffee with three creams and two sugars, just the way he liked it. She had been buzzed by the receptionist down below that Mr. Lamar was in the building.

She stood next to her desk and greeted him warmly as he unlocked and entered his office for which only he had the key. After giving him a moment to get settled, she entered and placed the coffee carefully on the blotter on the right side of his desk. She also left a few pieces of correspondence and phone messages in his inbox while glancing to make sure his outbox was empty. After asking him if there was anything else he needed, she promptly returned to the outer office.

Dwight sipped his coffee and, after debating whether or not to send it back for another cream, glanced at the phone messages. Sure enough, there was another one from Kathy Barnes, the SETUP board member at the University of Houston who had consistently proved to be a thorn in his side. She'd called several times, and he ignored her. He was sure she wasn't calling with good news. He smiled. He was just about to the point where he could stop kissing those people's asses as he had done for so long. On balance, though, he had no complaints; things had worked out well in Houston. Dwight Lamar was truly master of all he surveyed. He was comfortable in his position, especially now that he was being accorded the respect he deserved. In many ways, it was a shame to leave, but he knew he must. His plans were coming together right on schedule, but he must not get complacent. Once he made his move a lot would quickly unravel. He did not plan to be sitting there when all that began.

He was still concerned about the snooping of the Nelson girl and was irritated that his attempt to eliminate her had failed. As far as he was able to determine, she was still in the hospital. Somehow, she had evaded the goons he sent after her, but at least she had been seriously injured in the process. He didn't see how she could possibly link the attack to him. Moreover, while she might have seen the code names, he doubted she could connect them to the properties. Even if she did, that in itself would still be a dead end. Just forget her. He had no intention of commissioning any more "wet" work. He was too close to his final objective.

As he tied up loose ends, the one difficult problem he could not acceptably resolve was what to do about Devon. The kid had made enormous strides since he showed up from the Big Thicket. He had been incredibly helpful and efficient on a day-to-day basis and would do anything Dwight asked without hesitation. And, wow, did the kid excel in hustling pussy! Despite all his super work, though, one thing held Devon back: that damn Nelson girl. Dwight always kept his personal activities very private, but at times he had to include Devon. Still, he didn't think the kid knew about the hits he had ordered. In the case of the girl, he was sure Devon figured out who had hired the thugs in Hermann Park. The young man had become very sullen and withdrawn since that happened. He thought about the range of options for Devon, which ran from taking him along to sending him home to Sparta to eliminating him and what he might know. Killing the kid would be unfortunate, but maybe necessary: all because of that nutty girl.

47.

Pam Nelson had been through plenty, both mentally and physically, in a short time. She had been rushed that morning from the zoo down the street to St. Luke's Hospital, where emergency surgery was performed on her horribly fractured leg. It was not surprising that she began to have nightmares about screaming ambulance sirens and large, hairy animals. Her family rallied around her, with someone remaining at her bedside 24/7 for the first several days. Her leg healed nicely, but she just didn't want to be alone.

At first, the onset of nighttime and shadows caused her to tremble in fear. Even John flew over from Virginia to help out. Although they were anxious to hear the details of her ordeal, Matt, John, and Dianne decided not to press her until she was ready.

They met with zoo officials, who were extremely concerned about keeping a lid on the matter, if at all possible. Publicly, all they would say was that Pam had been injured in a fall on the zoo grounds. They would give no other details. The event had happened so early that there were no other visitors in there who might have witnessed something. Their stonewalling had been successful in keeping the incident away from the news people. John Nelson, however, was extremely upset with their closed-mouth policy. He needed to know more and demanded details.

Everyone began to feel better when, after a few days, Pam's characteristic spunk gradually began to return. Slowly her "groove" came back, especially when the doctors told her she could go home soon. A bit of her mischievous nature flashed when she looked at John, sitting next to her bed, and with a deadpan face announced that her friend, Muriel, was on the way over. Did he remember Muriel? John blinked, turned scarlet, and promptly made an excuse to leave, something about checking a parking meter. What John didn't know was that Muriel had told Pam that she was meeting John for drinks later that afternoon.

A few hours later, Muriel had come and gone. Matt was in the guard seat next to his sister, whose disposition had improved markedly after gabbing with her girlfriend. He wondered if that might be a good time to ask her what really happened at the zoo. He was just about to broach the subject when there was a knock at the hospital room door. Matt looked around and saw a slightly built African-American man in his early twenties standing there wearing a white shirt with a blue tie and dark pants. He was not wearing a sport coat, but had a bouquet of flowers and a box of candy with him. Matt thought he looked vaguely familiar.

Pam was delighted. "Devon! Hey, it's nice to see you. What's up? Thanks very much for coming. Come in here. I want you to meet my brother, Matt."

Devon did not move. "It's okay. I just wanted to know how you were doing. I miss you at work. Here you are," he said, stepping forward and handing her the flowers and candy.

Pam gushed, "Oh, how sweet, Devon. Thank you very much. You are a really nice guy." She gave him a quick kiss and a hug.

"That's okay. I am glad you're doing better. I got to go. My brother doesn't know I am here. Bye, Pam. See you around." He was out the door and gone. Matt hadn't had a chance to say hello or goodbye.

"One of your co-workers at the Q, I guess?"

Pam was definitely feeling better, because instead of going to pieces, which had been a frequent practice lately, she switched into her old standard evasive mode. "Well, not exactly."

"I know I have seen him around, but I don't go to the Q very often. Where would I have run into him then? Wait a minute! Now I remember. He is Dwight Lamar's chauffeur and gopher. Isn't he? Oh, no, Pam... don't tell me that you, you took that job at SETUP that he offered? I would ask you if you are nuts, but I already know the answer!" Matt snapped back, completely forgetting for a moment that his sister was in a hospital bed.

Pam was close to tears and could only offer a weak nod and almost inaudible, "Yes."

"After all I told you about that slime ball, why in the world did you do that?"

"B-Because I thought maybe I could get close enough to find out what he was up to. I was just going to stay there a few weeks. The Q will always take me back. I want to be more than a towel folder, you know."

Matt just shook his head. She was one incredible person. There was nothing to be gained by berating her here in the hospital. He might as well find out what she had learned. "So, Miss Mata Hari, what did you find out? That he likes lettuce on his tuna sandwiches?"

"No, smart ass." She was really returning to form. "I saw a handwritten list on his desk that said Crispus Attucks, F las something, Sojo ruth, and Peter Butler. Do those names mean anything to you?"

Matt thought about it. "No; except for Crispus Attucks, which I told you about before, they don't."

"I guess I need some more work on my spy stuff. I jotted the names on my arm, but I took a bath and most of the writing wore off. That's why I am not sure about two of the names. After all, I was so nervous after hiding in his bathroom."

"Huh? What? I am afraid to ask you to explain."

Matt sat there and listened for the next half-hour as Pam took him through the horrible events of that day and night. At times, he wanted to hug her until she broke and at others, he wanted to hit her over the head. If he didn't know Pam, he would have thought she was making it all up. Now he understood why the zoo people did not want the details to get out. Her attackers must have given up when she fell into the habitat. They probably left her for dead. Automatically, he thought of the Surenos, who had been quiet for some time. Based on her sneaking around Dwight Lamar, that guy would have a good reason to try to take her out. At first, he couldn't conceive that a person in that position would stoop to such tactics, but after thinking it through, he convinced himself that Lamar just might turn to something like that. If Lamar ordered the attack, it probably left the Surenos out, since it wasn't likely they would work together. The bottom line was, somehow, she was safe and would be staying with Diane for a while. Maybe they could control her that way.

He thought about those names. What did they mean? Dwight Lamar never did anything by chance. It was too bad she had lost the rest of them. Peter Butler seemed to be the odd one. It just didn't fit. Deep down, he had a nagging feeling that he had met a Peter Butler, but probably so had everyone. It was a common name. He couldn't wait to talk to John, as soon as he took care of that "parking meter." Matt kissed his sister and told her to get some rest. Her mother would be in around six. He reassured her he was not mad and loved her very much.

Pam was tired, but her pluck and energy were fast returning. After Matt left, she was dozing when she heard a strange buzzing on the table next to her bed. She ignored it at first and then realized it was the Walmart burner phone in her purse that her mother had brought over to the hospital from her apartment. She stabbed her hand into her purse and fumbled to answer it. She was about to say, "Hello, this is Pam," when she remembered just in time. "Err, Alice here."

"Hang on for Fred." She waited for what seemed like hours but was only a minute or two.

"This is Fred."

"Fred, this is Alice; about that subscription to the Economist."

"Alice, I am still thinking about it," and then a complete change in tone. "Hey, how are you?

I know we just spoke a few days ago, but I have some information for you."

Pam had to fight back the tears for so many reasons. She took a deep breath and told perhaps her biggest whopper of all time. "I am fine." Sniff. Sniff. She had zero intention of telling him about the past few days.

"Are you sure? You don't sound so good."

"No. No. I'm okay. It must be the long-distance connection." Sniff.

"Well, I know who Peter Butler is."

In spite of herself, Pam's heart leaped. "Who is he?"

"I met with him a couple of times in Houston and once in New York. He is a heavyweight real estate broker who has access to a lot of offshore clients from Eastern Europe in places like Albania and Hungary, where you would not think there was a lot of extra money. We never sold any tax credits to them, but we talked about it a lot. I believe his company is called Mediterranean Investments."

Pam panicked. Her mother walked into the room.

"Gotta go! Gotta go! Bye," she nervously whispered into the phone as she flipped it shut, much to her mother's look of surprise.

"Pam. You don't have to hang up just because I'm here. Who were you talking to?"

Pam looked at her mother and the tears that she had been holding back all day suddenly erupted in torrents. "Oh, Mommy! Mommy!"

48.

After the wayward child was released from the hospital, she returned to her old self. In fact, she even picked up on Muriel's terrible gorilla joke. *Pamela goes to the zoo and gets a little too close to the gorilla cage. Before you know it, a hairy arm reaches over the fence and pulls her in. She is with the gorilla for a while, and he is pretty rough with her before she is rescued. A week later she is still in the hospital, bandaged from head to toe. Her best friend comes in to see her and is shocked to see her in such bad shape. Not knowing exactly what to say, the friend asks, "Pam, is that you? Are you hurt?" There is a pause. Finally, Pam replies, "Yes, it's me, and damn right I'm hurt. He don't call, he don't write. He don't text..."* Well, anyway, Pam was feeling much better, and got around awkwardly on crutches. She agreed to stay with her mother until she fully recovered.

Her brothers showed up at noon, and, just like old times, Diane made lunch for her kids. Matt had filled in John on Pam's escapades. John was concerned about the attack before she fell into monkey city. Nothing had been reported to the police. He planned on remaining in Houston until he was sure that the situation was under control (and for no other reason?). The four of them sat around the breakfast room table munching on peanut butter and jelly and "gorilla" (grilled) cheese sandwiches while sipping iced tea.

It was John's first chance to hear things directly from the source. "So, you saw those four names written in longhand on his desk?" John queried the amateur sleuth.

"Yes, actually, they were written on a piece of paper in the top left-hand drawer of his desk under the wooden extender. They caught my eye because of the Crispus Attucks name, which Matt had heard him whisper over the phone."

Matt cut in, "Since we talked about it in the hospital, I've done a little research on the names or pieces of names that you could remember. As far as I can determine, at least three of them refer to famous slaves through history. Crispus Attucks was supposed to have been the first person to die in the Revolutionary War, during the Boston Tea Party. I think the second was Frederick Douglass, an abolitionist and famous orator after the Civil War.

The third has to have been Sojourner Truth, a woman slave in New York in the 1830s who espoused women's rights. I have no clue about Peter Butler. That name does not appear on any slave lists. My guess is that these names are code words for something."

John scratched his chin. "Yeah, you may be right; but slave names? Where do we go from here?"

Pam beamed. "No problem. That's easy. Peter Butler is a commercial real estate broker from New York City. His company is Mediterranean Investments. We should check him out first, don't you guys think?"

John and Diane were used to Pam's "helpfulness" in almost any matter, which often came from right field, but Matt stared at her in amazement. His mouth dropped open. "Where in the hell did you come up with that? You didn't mention it when we talked at St. Luke's."

Pam tried to act cool, but her reddish hue gave her away. "I don't know. Maybe Dwight mentioned it to me or something."

Clearly agitated, Matt was about to pursue the line of questioning when Diane spoke up. "Hey, guys, take it easy on your sister. She has been through a lot and has had a bump or two on the head."

Matt backed off and let it drop, but John picked it up from a different angle. "Let's hold it for a second and see if we can figure out what this guy is doing. Matt, from your dealings, you are pretty sure he is already skimming money out of the housing authority, one way or another. Do you think that is his ultimate goal?"

"Maybe, but I doubt it. He is extremely cagey, devious, and smart. He has got to know that with all the government bean counters around him, sooner or later that penny-ante stuff will come to light. No. I think he is somehow lining up a big hit and then will immediately vaporize."

"That could be," John replied. "Does he have any big deals planned soon?"

"He sure does," Pam chimed in. "Destination Diversity. SETUP is buying two hundred acres of land for a long-term development. The land purchase is supposed to close very soon."

"Bingo!" Matt yelped. "I'll bet you my next paycheck that must be it. The Butler broker connection fits in there somewhere. A good piece of land that size could trade in the $10,000,000 to $15,000,000 range. That is a big enough deal. I'll bet he has arranged a directed sale where he grabs a part of the proceeds off the top. That's it. I just know it."

"But if that is his game, wouldn't that be easy to trace? All these deals go through title companies with the recipients of every penny of the proceeds disbursed for all to see. Even some empty sham corporation would stand out in that case. He couldn't hide that."

"Maybe that is where Peter Butler comes in. I'll bet they have some under-the-table deal. I am going to check him out right away. He should be easy to find. Also, I am going to look at the sales history of that parcel they are about to buy. It might be interesting to see how much it has appreciated over the last three years since his majesty took over at SETUP."

"That sounds good, Matt, but I am still worried about the attack on sis, here. We need to get to the bottom of that. After what happened in the office, I just have a gut feel that Dwight Lamar arranged the attack. He probably felt she was sniffing too close to his big end game. Even a cool operator tends to get nervous and over-eager as the big day approaches. How could we check that out?"

"Well, you know, the zoo had to report the incident to the police, but they really did not know anything about the attackers, who were long gone when they found me with my buddy, Bongo," Pam reminded them. "I was already so upset that I can't tell you much about the attackers except that there were two of them, and I was lucky to jump the fence, or they would have had me. Sorry, John, I just can't be much help. I have seen enough of Dwight Lamar to know he plays everything close to the vest. He never tells anyone everything about what he does. He is a master of deceit. He uses intermediaries and sets up blind allies. He is very cunning. I can think of only one possible source who could know a little more about him."

"Who's that?" John asked.

"Devon, his brother, chauffeur, and general gopher. He even came to see me in the hospital." Pam paused for dramatic effect. "But Bongo didn't!"

Despite the seriousness of it all, the four of them looked at each other, and together they roared with laughter.

******

Dwight Lamar remained impassive on the exterior, but he was in an upbeat mood. Even though there'd been a few bumps in the road lately, overall, things were progressing well towards the final consummation of his long-term scheme. The lawyers were furiously working to prepare all the documentation for the NASA site closing next week. The county and city were making the arrangements for their collective $5,000,000 to be disbursed to the title company, and Texas Enterprise Bank was finalizing all the loan documents so they could add their $10,000,000 swing loan proceeds to complete the funding needed. Dwight spent many hours with the officers and lawyers of all three entities answering questions and reviewing legal papers.

Despite all this activity, however, something was nagging at him, which was very unusual because he normally possessed the unique ability to compartmentalize and set aside any extraneous issue that popped up. For some reason, this matter was different. It was that letter he'd received last week from that woman in New Orleans from so long ago. It had come to his office in a handwritten envelope addressed to him and marked "personal." Luckily, none of his employees opened it before it reached his desk. With the volume of poor people that moved through his office in a normal week, it was not unusual for him to get odd pieces of mail.

It was from Karen, whom he had conveniently put out of his mind. She had been a comfortable facilitator for a while, but when he left, that relationship was toast, as far as he was concerned. The last time he'd seen her she was strung out on drugs, which was a shame, but not his problem. He was not that surprised that she was finally trying to contact him. He had expected she would hit him up for money long before this. From the tone of her letter, she was still very much down on her luck. No surprise there, but the troubling part was that she claimed that after he left, she had a child, his child, making him a father.

His immediate inclination was to dismiss the whole thing as a grandstand play by a distressed druggie to extort cash. Obviously, she was just attempting to target a high-profile, successful person with dirt. That had to be the case. The practical side was that he was going to be leaving Houston soon anyway. He was sure she'd never be able to reach him after that. While the matter still irritated him, he was able to satisfy himself that the woman offered no real threat. He didn't dwell on the unlikely possibility that she was telling the truth. A boy, no less.

49.

Matt and John weighed their alternatives regarding Dwight Lamar, wondering if it was worthwhile to pursue him at all. Pam's attack was different. There was no question they had to get to the bottom of that situation. As to the slippery executive director, maybe they should just forget everything and rack up Matt's experience to poor judgment. Still, Matt brooded and did a slow burn when he thought about how the man terminated his contract for ridiculous and unfounded reasons. As if that act wasn't enough, the brazen SOB bad-mouthed Matt and Mesquite all around the business community. By doing so, he had effectively killed any chance of Matt obtaining new contracts. Before this SETUP contract, Matt was always able to at least get in front of potential clients. Now he couldn't even get appointments. The matter became clear; they would aggressively go after the slimy crook.

Matt confirmed his suspicions that Peter Butler and Mediterranean Investments had crossed paths with Mesquite Development Company. In fact, he discovered that his father had talked to Butler and probably met him at some point. There was no record, though, that they had ever done any business together. He reached back on his bookcase behind his desk for Travis Nelson's old Rolodex file, which had come in handy while prospecting for his consulting business. He readily found Butler's card stapled in the file. There was a chance the number had changed, but when he dialed, it went right through. After three or four rings, the recorded voice of Peter Butler asked the caller to leave a message. Matt did.

As Matt hung up, he reflected back on the old days when Travis Nelson ran every aspect of the company with drive and bravado. It was in situations like this one when Matt missed his father the most. Once you discounted the lack of overt affection for his family, the man was an absolute genius at running the business. Matt wondered how Travis would have handled Butler. As far as Matt knew, the man was a major-deal real estate broker from Manhattan. Just because his name was on a piece of paper in Dwight Lamar's office, did not mean he was necessarily in on anything illegal or illicit. On the other hand, he could not discount that possibility. If only his dad were here for some direction.

His reverie was interrupted when his phone rang with a New York 212 area code showing. Butler was returning his call. "Matt Nelson. How are you, sir?" an enthusiastic voice with a distinctive back east tinge bounced out of the phone. "Peter Butler here. You know, I am not sure we ever actually met. I had lunch down there with your father at Tony's, I think. I do know that he was singing your praises and made it very clear that if we struck a deal, I'd be dealing mostly with you, in whom he had total confidence. By the way, very sorry to have heard about all that. I'll bet you miss him."

"Yes, Peter, we certainly do," Matt replied, somewhat humbly as he found himself suddenly choked up.

"What's up? Are you looking for some folks to buy a chunk of tax credits? I might have some sources."

"Actually, no, Peter. With Travis gone, we are no longer in that business."

"Oh, okay. Then how can I help you?"

"The reason I called is that we are now in the development consulting business. I know that you are, or at least have been, active in Houston in the past. I am looking for contacts with anyone who might need help putting together a deal for a fee. Most likely a non-profit or governmental entity. Of course, if a referral of yours pans out, I would make it worth your while. Are you still active down here? When was the last time you did a deal here?"

There was a pregnant silence on the line for several seconds, and when Butler finally responded, all the enthusiasm was out of his voice. "Nope, I haven't done a deal in Houston, or in fact, anywhere in Texas, for a long time, maybe six, seven years or more. I am always willing to look at a deal, but just haven't seen much from your neck of the woods for a while. I haven't even been down there in like forever. I need to come down and get some of your famous barbecue. Say, I'll keep my eyes open about that consulting referral deal. Look, I gotta go. I have an appointment I am already late for. Bye, Matt."

The guy obviously didn't want to talk. "Hold on just one more second, Peter. Do you still work with all those middle-European investors?"

"Nope. I sure don't. Those boys can be pretty hard to please and very un-understanding at times. See ya." Click.

Matt had been around long enough and had dealt with enough brokers through the years to be convinced that the man was not telling the truth, which was unusual in itself, if he had done a deal in Matt's market. Most brokers are not shy about trumpeting their successes. If Butler was in on the SETUP site purchase, chances are he would have bragged about it to someone like Matt; unless, of course, there was something shady about the deal.

Matt's next call was to the broker at Jones Lang, who handled the sale of the NASA tract to SETUP. As expected, the man there took refuge in "professional ethics," and since Matt was an outside person, flatly refused to give him any information about his seller client.

Title companies in Texas provide the central point for almost all real estate closing transactions. Since, in general, the title insurance rates in Texas are very high and the real estate market is so robust, there are many title companies in the state, all of whom are perpetually clamoring for business. During his career, Matt had used several title companies, who still considered him a potential source of additional business and someone to whom to be nice. A small favor was never out of the question. It only took him a few minutes during a call to a closer at the Stewart Title Company to obtain some of the relevant information he was looking for about the prior sales history of the NASA tract SETUP was about to purchase. After a little research by the title company contact, Matt knew the names of the buyer, seller, and brokers of the last sale of the property, as well as the sales price of that sale. Additionally, he also found out what SETUP had agreed to pay now. There was a very healthy difference.

While he was talking to Stewart Title, John walked into his office. They were going to run out for a burger. John sat down facing his brother, who concluded his conversation and hung up. "Johnny, listen to this. The NASA tract, which is about 200 acres that Lamar's group is buying for Destination Diversity, last sold two and a half years ago for $5,000,000. That is actually a little on the cheap side based on the market, unless it had some warts or major flaws. The seller was a local Houston family and the buyer was a Texas limited partnership, with all the papers signed by lawyers to make sure the real buyer remained anonymous. There was a local Texas broker, though. I have his name right here."

"Whoa, Poncho. Stop right there. Let me guess the big one. SETUP is paying, say, $10,000,000 for the same dirt now less than three years later. The seller doubles his money. Am I close?"

"Sorry, man. You are way off. How about $15,000,000. The seller, whoever it is, bags ten million big ones. Not a bad profit. What a country!"

"You are kidding me! That is surely enough incentive to tweak even

Dwight Lamar's radar. Do we have anything to tie him to the previous sale three years ago? Or even maybe indirectly through Peter Butler?"

"No, I talked to Butler, and he claims he hasn't been anywhere near Texas for many years. I am going to chase down this other agent. Maybe he can give us an idea if Butler or his company were involved. Maybe he even shared a commission with him."

Matt found the man's number and placed a call. The very courteous lady who answered the phone advised him that the man he was trying to find had left the company a few years back. She had no contact information on him at all. Another dead end.

Matt was frustrated. "We have all this juicy stuff that smells so bad, and yet there is nothing we can point to that directly implicates anyone."

"Welcome to my world, Matt. On the other hand, we have not discovered anything that rules them out, either. The glass is still half full."

With time on her hands "between engagements," Pam limped into the office. She would be going back to the Q, but obviously not until her leg had completely healed. In the meantime, she showed up occasionally at the management office to help her mother with odd jobs, which seemed to Matt more like gossip sessions. But he had to remember: "she has been through a lot." Catching both her siblings, there was the perfect opportunity for an update on things, which they readily gave her after extracting her blood pledge that she would keep the info to herself.

"We seem to be stuck because we really can't tie Lamar to the seller of the site or to Peter Butler, and the guy who was the local broker representing the seller is among the missing. Am I right?" she asked. "What is that guy's name?"

Matt nodded his head in agreement with her statement. "The local broker's name on the first sale was Eli Apple. I suppose you know the dude."

Pam lit up, smiled, and got that mischievous grin on her face that they all had learned to dread. "Eli Apple, huh? Be back in five minutes with your information," she teased on her way out the door, fishing out her cell as she hobbled along. Matt and John looked at each other with blank stares.

It was only four minutes later when she returned to Matt's office and collapsed on his couch. She wore a big Cheshire cat smirk.

"Well?" Matt asked.

She took her time to respond, obviously enjoying the ability to toy with her brothers. Finally: "Eli said he misses me. He was worried that something bad had happened to me. He heard a rumor that I was..."

"Damn it, woman! Out with it!" John was about to blow a gasket. Still, she looked over at him in no particular hurry.

Matt added tersely, "Don't forget, John, she's been through a lot."

"Okay. Eli Apple happens to work at the Q with me. He gave up full-time real estate a year or so ago, but he keeps his broker's license up to date and yes, he knows Peter Butler very well. Peter uses Eli's Texas license so he can participate in commissions here as an out-of-state broker. Eli doesn't have to do much more than make sure his name is spelled correctly on any of Peter's clients' contracts. It is found money for Eli and, oh yes, Peter and his clients did purchase the NASA tract three years ago. Eli also spoke to me under the strictest confidence. Butler had called him not an hour ago demanding him to keep his big mouth shut."

"Then, why would he tell you of all people?" John asked.

Pam took a deep breath. "The things I do for the team. Tomorrow night, seven thirty. I think we're going to the new Harry Potter movie."

50.

Lamar assumed his best professional demeanor as he walked into the large conference room on the eighth floor of the Charter Title Company offices on Westheimer in the West Loop near the Galleria. It was almost 10:30 AM. The closing had been scheduled for 9:00 AM, but he knew there would be nothing but paper shuffling and last-minute nitpick changes for the first hour at least. Also, he knew that he was the key to making this deal work. He would enter when it was convenient for him.

Gathered around the table were Ken Underhill and a female assistant from Texas Enterprise Bank, a representative from the city of Houston Comptroller's office and his attorney, their counterparts from Harris County, the seller's attorney, SETUP's (the buyer's) attorney, the Jones Lang real estate broker, the title company closing agent, and several minion helpers. An impressive array of pastries, cookies, and beverages had been set out on a table at the end of the room. To Lamar's slight annoyance, most of the people verbally greeted him, but none rose to shake his hand other than Ken Underhill. They were all still buried in the mountains of paper spread around the table.

The title company agent advised Lamar that she was almost through working up the closing statement figures for his review. Oh, and most critically, she mentioned that fifteen million dollars had been wired into her escrow account. It is always an encouraging sign when the money is already in escrow.

Lamar sat down next to his lawyer and proceeded to look important. Devon, who accompanied Dwight up in the elevator, presumably to open doors for him along the way, headed straight for the pastries. Lamar's attorney opened the bank loan agreement to page 168, and showed Lamar a typing error, which said "calandar" instead of "calendar." Dwight let the man prattle on over the importance of his having caught this egregious error. Lamar noted the comment and sat back for a minute to reflect on it. He then whispered to his lawyer in a voice that could easily be heard by anyone in the room that while the error was substantive, he would live with it, this time. Ken Underhill looked relieved.

Perhaps an hour later, the closing agent declared that everything was in order, and they could start signing documents. This announcement was the moment Dwight Lamar had been waiting for. He very slyly, but purposely, caught the eye of the seller's lawyer across from him and nodded slightly. In this case, the seller didn't have a lot to do other than to sign the deed and collect his money. The man, who had been watching Lamar like a hawk since he arrived, acknowledged Dwight's gesture. Dwight got up and excused himself from the room and was gone for at least thirty minutes.

When he finally returned, everyone looked up. They had been waiting, and some were getting antsy. It was almost lunchtime. Despite this obvious sense of irritation caused by his delay, SETUP's executive director was completely at ease and relaxed as he sat down again next to his lawyer. All the interminable negotiation and laborious document preparation was finally over. Everything was ready. All Dwight had to do was sign the documents and the NASA tract would belong to SETUP. Of course, he would also personally become $5,000,000 richer. Dwight had every reason to be relaxed.

He had everyone's full attention as he picked up his pen. The lawyer opened the first document and pointed to the little red sticker arrow where he was supposed to sign. At just that very moment, the conference room door burst open and in walked Henry Francesca, local hotshot state senator, board member, and Dwight's' new best friend. The small-time political hack glad-handed the whole room. With him was a photographer to capture the moment when Dwight Lamar took the first bold step to make Destination Diversity become a reality.

If he was put out by the distraction, Dwight hid it well. He was able to conjure up and maintain a pleasant expression through multiple photo flashes. When the slide show ended, instead of promptly executing all the dozens of documents as the final step in the long process to close the transaction, he hesitated and put down his pen. He whispered something into his lawyer's ear, and they both stepped outside. There were murmurs around the table. Something was up.

Perhaps ten minutes later, the lawyer returned to the room alone. He stood next to the door and solemnly addressed the now-agitated group. "My client has asked me to inform you that it will not be possible for SETUP to complete the purchase at this time." A loud collective groan rose from around the table. "It has come to his attention that there are very important matters that remain unresolved with respect to the environmental suitability of the property. It seems a preliminary environmental report reflected the presence of an abandoned oil well. The final report from the local firm, however, did not cite this serious impediment. As you are all aware, the Department of Housing and Urban Development is currently in the process of completing their mandated environmental study, which is expected to be available within the next six to twelve months. Mr. Lamar did not feel that he could put the city, county, and Texas Enterprise Bank funds at risk at this time. He asked me to reiterate that he is still sold on the site and would like very much to pursue it, so long as the HUD report proves to be acceptable. He also understands that his action, at this time, may result in the earnest money deposit being forfeited and paid over to the seller. While that is unfortunate, it is far preferable to putting several million dollars possibly in jeopardy. He regrets that this decision became necessary, but feels that his first obligation is to protect the collective interests of the citizens of the city and county."

The people in the room were shocked. Stunned. On some level, the reps of the city, county, and bank, while disappointed, were nonetheless relieved that a potential gross error would not be made. The Jones Lang broker let loose with a loud, "Shit!" and then, "Double shit!" The seller's lawyer remained silent, but his face clouded into a distant and vindictive look. He slammed his briefcase shut and was muttering under his breath as he rushed from the room. A confused Henry Francesca asked if anyone wanted to go to lunch, on him. The title company agent would go. She hoped to scrounge something out of this otherwise disastrous day, and the bankers were in. Bankers are always hungry.

51.

Even though it was only mid-day, Dwight had Devon take him straight home to his high-rise apartment in River Oaks. After what he had just done, it was best that he remain out of the public eye for a while. While his reluctance to close was a shocker for virtually everyone, his espoused reason for reneging left a big enough cloud of smoke that the city-county team on the buyer's side would probably end up regarding him as a hero. Once again, Dwight Lamar, demonstrating amazing foresight and incredible business acumen, saved his stakeholders from a potential huge mistake.

Even though he worked hard to stir up the excitement for Destination Diversity and a few folks might be disappointed by the delay, no-one felt the compelling need to rush as much as he did, albeit for his own selfish reasons. The deal was not dead, and indeed the NASA site might yet be purchased. A lot of lawyer's fees had been wasted and possibly an earnest money deposit forfeited, but that was the cost of doing business. Some frustration but no real angst, at least around Houston.

There was, of course, the not so small matter of the seller, the Texas limited partnership owned anonymously by the New York Albanian investors that Peter Butler had put together. Those people were choking on their grape brandy right about now. That crowd was not happy. Peter Butler had impressed upon him that they were short-tempered and could be violent. The broker had an almost impossible job to calm them down when Lamar appeared to be choosing another site. It was only after the airport site was rejected and their site actually went under contract that they settled down. They closely tracked the deal's progress right up to the moment when Dwight balked and refused to sign the papers with some lame excuse about an environmental study. Hell, they had jumped on the property in the first place on his assurances alone that the sale would fly through. They barely gave the tract a second look. Now, what was this crap about?

The Albanians' predicament had quickly become far more serious and complicated than just another delay. The price of poker had jumped through the roof. From the start, everyone knew there could not be a paper audit trail of any kind out of the closing leading to Lamar. To protect himself, he had insisted on the double-dare arrangement. Thieves had agreed to trust thieves. The agreement was after recouping their initial investment of $5,000,000, Dwight Lamar and the Albanians would split the profit of $10,000,000 evenly. Each would get $5,000,000. In theory, that arrangement sounded very simple, but to pull that off, a great deal of trust had to be worked into the mechanics. An interesting footnote is that neither side, Lamar nor the Albanians, had ever trusted anybody in the past. Why would that change now?

Dwight played his side of the deal like the deceitful maestro that he had become. Naturally, the Albanians were extremely reluctant to advance half of Dwight's profit to him before the deal was signed, sealed, and delivered. On the other hand, being kindred souls of sorts, they understood Lamar's concern that once the closing happened and all the money came to them, they could easily thumb their nose at him and walk away. He would be "SOL." Grudgingly, they sent half the cash he was to receive after closing just before the deal actually closed. They sent the money fully aware that if there was another hiccup, and closing didn't happen, they'd be out another cool $2,500,000. The idea was to closely monitor the closing progress and not wire Lamar's money to Switzerland until the very last second, just before the closing happened. Dwight carried out his role perfectly so that the Albanians' attorney was satisfied enough that the closing was imminent to okay the wire. The closing was virtually done. All it took was Lamar's signature, and he had pen in hand. Dwight left the room and called to confirm the funds were in his account and never returned. He had his cash and was gone. At that point, it was checkmate and game over.

Lamar had been convinced from the start that the middle-European fellows, if left to their own devices, would give him a wink and a nod, but not a red cent of the $15,000,000 once it was disbursed to them by the title company. His antics in not initially recommending their site to the board definitely did not help things. Too bad, little government bureaucrat. See you later. What are you going to do, sue us? Pass the Rakia. Let's do this again sometime. In order to ensure he wouldn't get totally shafted, Lamar demanded that half of the cash be deposited in a numbered Swiss bank account controlled by him just seconds before the closing was completed. To make this happen, the Albanians would have to dig into their own pockets for those funds. If all went as planned, the money would be refunded right back to them by the title company. With all the negotiations done, documents reviewed and approved, and all the money on hand in escrow, everything would be a hairsbreadth away. The fifteen million big ones should have gone zinging over the wires to the Albanians within the hour. Unfortunately, Dwight Lamar had other ideas.

Even if the Albanians had an honorable intent to pay him the $5,000,000, Lamar reasoned there was plenty of incentive for them not to do so. They certainly knew he had zero legal recourse against them. Any hint of protest or whining by him could easily tip off unwelcome scrutiny from the powers that be. In fact, the act of actually paying him would only reconfirm their own guilt. They did reside in the United States and were not immune to domestic litigation. The last thing they wanted was a nasty lawsuit from Texas. If he played his hand well enough to get the $2,500,000 into his account, he would be satisfied.

The question came down to whether he should collect his half and then close on the land, or just walk away. If he closed, the disbursements would be made and $15,000,000 would be sent to the Albanians. Maybe they would send him the additional $2,500,000, although he sincerely doubted it. At that point, his side—the city, county, and bank—would be out $15,000,000 against a tract of land of questionable value with perhaps fatal development deficiencies. He would personally be positioned right in the center of a potential maelstrom of future problems, some of which were certain to surface. Should all the facts come out, any court in the land would quickly convict him of graft and corruption. If he suddenly left the city, eyebrows would be raised, and ultimately, accusations would fly. It would only be a matter of time before the magnificent extent of his deceit would come to light. Was it worth gambling on an unlikely additional $2,500,000 against these inevitable adverse consequences? He thought not.

Clearly, it would be best for him not to close the sale. He had no interest in hanging around to see if the crazy deal would actually work. With the grand deal on hold, he could then cut and run. He could walk away not having overtly shafted the city, county, or the bank, none of which had invested or lost any money. The bank loan was never disbursed and the government entities still had their investments. The only cash out of pocket by anyone was his $2,500,000 wired by the unsuspecting Albanians. Strangely enough, despite having orchestrated a monumental deceitful scam, Dwight Lamar had somehow preserved his local good standing. Only the Albanians had been stiffed. Too bad for those fellows.

Sure, if he were the guys in Brooklyn, he'd be pissed too. Yet, if their rage ever subsided and they thought things through, there was still a reasonable chance they could come out okay. They still owned the site, although they now had invested $7,500,000, instead of only $5,000,000. Within the next year or so, if the HUD environmental report came back clean, the Albanians might sell the site to someone for $15,000,000. Should that happen, those ungrateful folks could thank Lamar going away for only half his agreed split and leaving $2,500,000 on the table. They could reap a $7,500,000 profit instead of only $5,000,000. Maybe he would mail them an invoice for the half he had foregone? After all, they were honorable. Ha! Ha!

Dwight Lamar had tiptoed his way into a big payday, but he clearly understood that Peter Butler's group would not lick their wounds and go home. He was absolutely sure they would be after him with a blood lust very soon. Although he enjoyed the regal niche he had created in the Bayou City, he had always known it would not be permanent and had been planning his exit for some time. At least having refused to close on the NASA land, it would be difficult for any local folks to associate his expeditious departure with misdoings on that deal. As far as anyone knew, no money ever changed hands. He could not imagine that Peter Butler would traipse into his boardroom and demand a closing because Dwight had been a bad boy. He had also covered his tracks on a few other inappropriate things that might come to light someday. His only significant open issue was what to do about his half-brother. He wasn't sure how much Devon knew, but he just could not take any chances with the kid. Remorse was not a word that Dwight Lamar used often, but it did creep into his plans to completely close the loop in Texas.

Peter Butler had been calling him repeatedly since he walked out of the closing. Brooklyn was in a frenzy. When Dwight walked out and sent his lawyer back in with regrets, the seller's lawyer bolted out and called the Albanians in Brooklyn. Only minutes before he had told them all was okay for them to deliver the first half of his cash to Switzerland, which they did. Lamar confirmed that the sweet $2,500,000 was in his account at the Swiss bank and, with that wonderful news, he immediately transferred all of it to an account of a shell corporation he had set up at a bank in the Bahamas. The timing had been perfect.

Months ago, he had researched the group and studied how they operated when it was time to throw their weight around. He was sure they had few qualms about taking swift and final recourse with anyone who dared to cross them. He was now number one bad actor on their list. Even though he still had his love nest townhouse in Midtown, he stayed very close to his River Oaks high-rise, which came with formidable security. Devon was armed, and he called his Surenos contact to follow him around for protection at a distance for a few days whenever he left his apartment.

A day later, in order to best complete his plan, Lamar boldly decided to buy a little more time from the angry mob in New York to make his exit. Peter Butler was surprised when after six ignored voicemails, Dwight Lamar's number flashed on his phone. He was not subtle or discreet. "Lamar! What the hell are you trying to pull? The deal was all but done and you backed out after my guys sent you your half. Do you know how ripshit they are right now? If they didn't need me, I'd already be shoes-up in the East River by now. These guys play for keeps. They are not nice. You crossed them and they don't like it one bit. They trusted you and you screwed them. It was about the worst thing you could possibly have done. Of course, it is not only the money, but the way you did it that made them see red. What the hell made you do that, you asshole? I told you about these guys. They play rough."

Lamar patiently let him rant, ramble on, and get everything off his chest. There was little Butler was telling him he was surprised about or didn't expect. In their position, he would have been equally as upset. "Whenever you are through, Peter, just let me know, and I will speak," he responded in a low-key and calm voice.

Peter went on for another five minutes or so and finally decided to let Dwight speak. "Okay, okay, what the hell is going on?"

"Number one, Peter, the deal is not dead."

"What the hell are you talking about? Everyone walked out of the closing. The escrowed funds were returned. You said everything had to wait for the HUD study, which could be a year away. What is up with that crap?"

"I am sorry, Peter, but it did strike me that if that HUD study does come back with a problem, I would be right in the gun sights of everyone. You all would be long gone, and I'd have some cash, but I would be facing some stiff heat and possibly even an indictment."

"Dwight, if you think the Albanians really give a shit about what might happen to your ass a year from now, you're nuts!" Peter snapped back.

"Oh, I have no doubt about that, but I am a little concerned about my ass going forward; and, guess what, Peter? Now I have some of their money. Maybe they should be a little more concerned about my health."

"Lamar, I can't believe what I'm hearing. You have some monster-sized balls. These boys will kill their grandmothers over milk money!"

"Good for them but listen to me, if you can. With a little more time, I am sure I can work with the HUD environmental team and head off any problem. An adverse report does not necessarily mean a site is unacceptable. It usually just means remediation is necessary. When I get a feel for the problem, if there is one, I can fix it, and then we have a green light to close. In that case, my coast is clear."

"And what if the HUD report is fatal?"

"You are correct. That is a possibility. In which case, your boys paid $5,000,000 for a site that is worth less than $15,000,000, maybe only about $10,000,000, which doesn't sound too bad to me. Don't forget, though, if I don't make this work, I don't get a dime."

"Hold it, asshole. You just stole $2,500,000 of our money!"

"Peter, I always told you if this happened I would give it back."

"When the hell did you ever say that?"

"Peter, how much beer had you drunk that night at the airport hotel?"

"Then you will give them their two point five mil back?"

"Of course; but not if they are going to hunt me down with thugs and Uzis. In fact, I'll even do this for your lovely pals. Due to this minor inconvenience, I will agree to take less on my end. Instead of a final two point five, I'll take a million less, one point five. There, I've sweetened the deal for them. All I need is a little more time. How could they not go for that?"

"And you'll send back the two point five right away?"

"Sure, Peter."

"I'll go to them, but I am not optimistic. They are still seeing red. They just don't trust you."

"Then maybe it is best if we give them a couple of days to calm down. Maybe reason will take over. Let's talk on Friday."

"I can only take it to them." CLICK!

Sure, Peter. Sure, Peter. They would never talk again.

52.

Matt and John knew that Lamar planned to close on the land at Charter Title Company shortly. While it was not strictly their personal business, they feared that a horrible mistake involving the city and county was possible, and they were the only ones who could prevent it. They had to contact someone in authority about what they suspected. Time was critical.

They looked over the list of SETUP board members for anyone they already knew or could approach. No name jumped out from the group that collectively thought Dwight Lamar was infallible. After talking briefly with the attorney who had represented Travis Nelson and Mesquite Development in days gone by, they arranged to meet with Leslie Glazer, an Assistant District Attorney, at her office downtown on Franklin Street.

Ms. Glazer was pleasant enough, given that she spent 100% of her time trying to bring bad people to justice. She was dressed in a conservative navy business suit with a white blouse. The brothers judged she was in her late thirties. Her dark hair was neatly trimmed and she wore tortoise shell-framed glasses. Her desk was neat and orderly, but her small office was otherwise piled high with case files. She was a very busy person and got right to the point. "Okay, gentlemen, what can I do for you?"

Matt took the lead. "First, Ms. Glazer, thank you for seeing us on short notice, but this is a matter of some urgency. I will try to sum things up as much as possible. I am sure you are aware of the Southeast Texas Unified Partnership, SETUP, where Dwight Lamar is the executive director."

She nodded. Who hadn't heard about him?

"SETUP has announced plans for a project called Destination Diversity to be developed on a site in Clear Lake near NASA. The land is under contract and is scheduled to close shortly."

Matt had to begin to tread carefully. As recognizable as Dwight Lamar had become in the city, his own father's troubles were also well known. Leslie Glazer knew all about Travis Nelson. In fact, she was probably intrigued on that basis alone when Matt called to meet. "I guess what this all boils down to is that we have uncovered information that leads us to believe that the pending land purchase by SETUP is not on the up and up. It very well could be a directed sale and an inflated purchase price."

Glazer's eyebrows rose as she made notes on a yellow legal pad. "What makes you think so?"

"We have discovered that the executive director of SETUP, Mr. Lamar, had contact with the broker for the current seller of the site when they purchased it two-plus years ago."

"That is interesting, Mr. Nelson. Please continue."

Matt hesitated and looked over at John. There was a bridge to be crossed here, and it was a dangerous one. If they started discussing how they knew what they'd discovered, it could come right back to bite them, especially if they were wrong, and there was very little they could actually prove. Matt could talk about his contract with SETUP, but that would not have played well.

John piped up to add a little smoke screen and, hopefully, convince the lady there was some fire there too. "Ms. Glazer, there is a lot more to this story, which, at this point, is technically insufficient to be used as evidence in a court of law. On the other hand, based upon our experience and knowledge of the situation, it just doesn't smell right. If the closing were not imminent, we wouldn't have wasted your time today. Perhaps you have sources that could at least look into the situation."

It would have been easy for Leslie Glazer to shrug her shoulders, curtly thank them for wasting her valuable time, and usher them out the door, but she didn't. Instead, she thanked them for coming in and promised to see what she could find out about the matter.

Later that afternoon, Matt was in his office working on some design revisions for Riverbend. John was sitting on the couch nearby after just hanging up from a one-hour call with Harvey, back in Virginia. The brothers now felt a little embarrassed about the meeting with Leslie Glazer. They were so carried away with Dwight Lamar that they hadn't stopped to think how little hard proof they had that the guy was up to no good.

Matt's phone buzzed. It was Leslie Glazer. Matt put her on the speakerphone.

"Okay, gentlemen," she began in a very businesslike and lawyerly tone, "After our meeting this morning, I made a few calls to see if I could learn anything about the transaction we discussed. I did learn a lot. First of all, you would be interested to know that the land closing for SETUP happened yesterday."

"Damn!" Matt could not help himself. "We're too late."

"Maybe not," Leslie replied over the speaker. "The closing was never completed."

"No kidding. Why not? What luck."

"Perhaps; but if you are looking for a smoking gun in Mr. Lamar's hand, you'd better keep looking. According to the report I received, the deal was all but closed. Fifteen million dollars was in the title company escrow account, and all that was left was for the papers to be signed. Even all the lawyers were happy. Why didn't it close? Because your bad guy got up from the table and refused to sign. Something about an environmental issue. That move does not square with someone hot to trot because he has a bone coming his way. Dwight Lamar singlehandedly killed—or at least delayed—the deal."

John and Matt looked at each other in disbelief.

Leslie continued, "Now let me pile on while I've got you down. I also talked to a couple of the directors. Most of them think Dwight Lamar invented sliced bread. Aside from that, they told me that the site under contract was independently selected by a vote of the board and not by Lamar. As it turned out, they did select the site he favored, but it was not the Clear Lake site. Lamar wanted a site near the IAH airport. It was only after that site busted out that they settled on the NASA tract. I haven't met this Dwight Lamar, but maybe I should. If he can let the board pick the site, then lose his favorite site, and stop a closing the way he did and still have no good up his sleeve, he must be Harry Houdini reincarnated. Sorry, guys, I just don't see it here."

"And, Matt, I hate to add this part, but I guess it is my job. In my conversations, I was told that Mr. Lamar terminated you from a contract with SETUP. I fully understand that there are always two sides to such things, but by the same token, there are those around here that would say that gives you an ax to grind with the man, if you get my drift."

Matt did a slow burn and, perhaps fortunately, was still lost for words. "Yeah, okay, Ms. Glazer. Thanks for looking at it. Bye."

"Sure, anytime. I guess that's why I am here. If something else should come up, do keep me in the loop. Goodbye."

******

Dwight Lamar sat there serenely as Kathy Barnes finally had her say. The professor had left several calls that Mr. Lamar had not returned. Now there he was, sitting right in front of her. It didn't matter that Lamar had called a special board meeting on short notice because he had pressing matters to discuss. She was going to unload on him.

"Mr. Lamar, at the university, I have a couple of students who are residents in the Bluebird Acres Apartments, your first newly constructed housing authority units. The students have told me that the living conditions you have created are sub-standard. The roofs leak, the toilets overflow, and crime is already a problem on the site. This property is brand new and should be SETUP's signature facility. How do you answer these allegations, Mr. Lamar?"

As Lamar looked around the room at the board members, it became immediately apparent to him that no-one had any more interest or concern about his answer than he did. His reply was simple, stoic, and to the point. "Professor Barnes, I certainly regret any problems perceived or otherwise that our residents might have. On the other hand, if only one or two of the several hundred folks who reside at that property have problems, my guess is that we are doing well." He looked away from and intentionally ignored the professor, who was about to launch her next salvo. He directed his eyes towards Chairman Hobby. "Sir, I asked that you all come here this evening and take time out of your personal schedules and private time so I could address certain items which I believe are very important to this organization. May I do so?"

Chairman Hobby nodded in the affirmative. Professor Barnes let out an audible groan that could be heard across the room.

"First, I know you all have heard by now that the long-awaited closing on the NASA site did not happen yesterday. In fact, at the last minute I opted to put it off for a while longer. There are some possible environmental issues which have not, in my opinion, been sufficiently addressed. As we all recognize, the Department of Housing and Urban Development is our partner in all our endeavors. It is our solemn obligation to be certain that we always meet and exceed their requirements. In any event, I remain hopeful that the NASA site will one day soon blossom into Destination Diversity." There were smiles and nods of appreciation from almost everyone.

"Unfortunately, as much as I deeply regret it, Destination Diversity will have to move ahead under the leadership of someone other than myself. Yes, ladies and gentlemen," he paused for dramatic effect, "This evening I am tendering my resignation from my wonderful position as executive director of the Southeast Texas Unified Partnership."

There was a hush in the room. You could have heard a pen drop, which, by the way, Henry Francesca did.

"I have thoroughly enjoyed my stay as your director, but I have determined that it is time to move on. We have accomplished much, and there is still much to do. I am always distressed on rare occasions such as occurred tonight when comments about our housing being less than perfect reach me."

Henry Francesca looked across the table at Kathy Barnes with daggers in his eyes as if she alone was responsible for driving the prodigal son from home.

"No, I am not sure where I will go or just what I will do. Just be assured that I will be involved somewhere helping the poor and indigent improve themselves. I would like to thank everyone here, and I mean everyone," he actually gave a furtive glance in the direction of the professor, "For the support you have always given me. Thank you all," he concluded in an uncharacteristically soft and humble voice. It was a masterful performance.

Henry Francesca was beside himself. He was losing his African-American Hispanic. He addressed the chairman, "Mr. Chairman, with due respect to the wishes of this fine gentleman who stands before us and has accomplished so much for our entire community, I would like to request that you hold his tendered resignation in abeyance, but do not accept it, until we have had a chance to meet with Dwight individually and perhaps convince him to rethink his decision. This matter is such a surprise and shock to us all. Would that be acceptable?"

The chairman looked at Dwight, who smiled.

"Certainly, Mr. Chairman, if that is what the board wishes. Sure, I'd love to talk to you all. Just one condition, Henry; please, not this evening. I am just too torn up to think rationally." *And I have a plane to catch to London in a couple of hours.*

53.

As far as Devon knew when he dropped his brother at International Terminal C at Houston's George Bush Intercontinental Airport, Dwight was getting away for a much-needed vacation. Dwight hadn't told Devon where he was headed or when he would return, but as always, Devon was confident that his brother would be in touch. He had no inkling that when Dwight said, "Goodbye, Devon. Good luck," at the curb, they would never see each other again.

Dwight went right to the British Airways Executive Club Lounge and ordered a Courvoisier to sip while he waited for his 9:30 PM departure for London Heathrow. He was in an exceptionally good mood. All the loose ends had been, or would be, tied up soon. He had informed James Luken at SETUP that he was taking an extended vacation and to just take over while he was gone. He smiled when he thought about his phone conversation with Peter Butler, the poor slob. He threw out a bunch of crap about giving the two point five back. Not in a zillion years! Everything had fallen into place. He had a fat bank account and was leaving Houston as a conquering hero. He still had to continually duck the Albanians, but he really wasn't sure how far afield their muscle extended. You didn't want to walk past them on a street in Brooklyn, but a worldwide manhunt was surely out of their league. Still, he would take every precaution. Long live the king.

The twelve-hour flight arrived in England mid-morning. Dwight Lamar walked off the plane feeling refreshed after traveling comfortably in the first-class cabin. He collected his luggage and then took a cab into the city, where he spent two days wining, dining, and relaxing. The following morning, he took a taxi to London's Gatwick airport and bought a ticket with cash on the Norwegian Shuttle to Gardermoen Airport in Oslo, Norway. Had there been another option, he would not have chosen such a cheap economy airline, but the trip was short, so he endured the inconvenience.

After arriving at Gardermoen, he went to the Avis counter and paid extra to rent a comfortable American full-size car. He then drove to the Grefsen area of Oslo, where he located the real estate office he had been in contact with over the past few weeks. The fully furnished apartment the agent had selected suited his purposes perfectly, and he signed a one-year lease on the spot. He found the local Walmart equivalent, where he purchased the basic necessities for a two-week stay.

Several times during those days, he suppressed brief pangs of regret for not bringing Devon. He hated doing these menial chores himself, but he did what he must. He rented a mailbox at a local post office so that he had a mailing address. Over the next two weeks, he attempted to make his presence known and be as openly visible as possible to the local folks in the area. Of course, that task was not especially difficult for a black American in a country where fair skin and blond hair proliferate. He dined out every night and visited and re-visited enough bars so that some of the sharper barmaids knew to have his Courvoisier ready when he walked in.

It wasn't very long before Dwight felt the need for female company. Now he really missed Devon. Somehow, the local women were not as impressed with his charms as they should have been. Nonetheless, without too much trouble, he was able to find the local red-light district. Problem solved. He told his neighbors that he was an electronics salesman from the US who traveled all over Europe. He would be gone a lot. Up to that point, he had made no attempt to hide his true name. He intended to leave a trail.

It didn't take Dwight long to conclude there wasn't much about the people or Scandinavian lifestyle that appealed to him. Socialism was not for someone who believed in a superior lifestyle consistent with the trappings of wealth. He had no regrets the day he departed. He hoped he'd sown enough seeds that anyone looking for him would conclude he had settled in Oslo. He planned to keep the apartment indefinitely, but would never return.

To that point on his trip from Houston, he tried to make his tracks somewhat difficult, but not impossible, to follow. He wanted it to look like he was deliberately being evasive. It was time to really cover his tracks. After dropping his car at the Oslo airport, he was tempted to board the semi-luxurious overnight ferry between Oslo and Copenhagen. There was usually minimal passport control between co-operating European Union countries, but still there would be a record of his having been on board. Instead, he took a smelly, diesel-reeking, crowded bus to Kristiansand on the southern Norwegian coast. After enduring a long, uncomfortable ride, he was happy to finally arrive at the seacoast village. It took a few inquiries and the flashing of cash to find a fishing boat to take him across the North Sea to Denmark. His trail of breadcrumbs was now over. It was critical that he keep his movements as invisible as possible. After a few hours of nausea on rough, bouncing seas, he was dropped at a small town on the Danish coast. Once again, he had to endure an atrocious, crowded, smoky bus ride to Copenhagen, although after his recent shipboard experience, it didn't seem so bad.

His research indicated that with green American dollars you could buy almost anything in Copenhagen. It didn't take him long to procure a new US passport, Louisiana driver's license, and a few credit cards with his likeness under the name of "Ashton Jeffers," his new alias. The purpose of this move was to create a red herring across his trail for anyone trying to follow him. He chuckled to himself, since that particular metaphor fit his present circumstances. He had no intention of using that name forever, but it would provide some cover until the Albanian threat cooled down.

After all the discomfort of the trip from Oslo, he finally got relief in cushy first class aboard a Lufthansa flight to Johannesburg, South Africa. Although he'd heard delightful things about South Africa, he never left the Jo-burg airport and was on the next Delta jumbo flight to Mexico City, with still one leg to go. A final ten hours in the air on COPA transported him to his new home, the dual island nation of St. Kitts-Nevis in the West Indies. Despite first class the whole way, when he finally touched down, Dwight Lamar never wanted to see an airplane again.

******

Back in the Bayou City, Matt and John licked their wounds after the abortive attempt to get the DA interested in their suspicions. Dwight Lamar's actions were perplexing at best, but Matt was still sure the deceitful crook had somehow fashioned a big kickback to himself. What else could it be? But, why in the world would the guy back off at the last second? No money changed hands. How could anything have slipped into his pocket? He thought about Peter Butler and wondered if Dwight's abrupt change of heart had surprised him. Dwight Lamar was cagey, and prone to making last-minute moves that surprised everyone. He'd love to talk to Butler, but was sure Butler would not talk to him again.

For the moment, the two brothers set Lamar aside and decided to pursue Pam's attack, which was also likely a blind alley unless they could somehow sweat it out of Devon. According to Pam, Dwight Lamar had two residences.

One was a swanky high-rise apartment in River Oaks. The other was a more modest townhouse in Midtown where he liked to "entertain" young ladies. Devon was usually at Dwight's beck and call, but sometimes he spent the night at the townhouse. John felt they should probably visit the townhouse some dark evening. If both Lamar and Devon happened to be there, they would come back another time. On the other hand, if Devon was alone, perfect. Even if neither were home, they might discover something inside that would be worthwhile.

After dropping Dwight at the big airport, Devon decided to grab a bite at a hamburger joint on North Shepherd on the way back to the townhouse. Dwight told him the lease on the high-rise apartment was over and to stay at the townhouse from now on. When Devon finally arrived, it was already past 10:00 AM. He flipped on the TV and put on a porno movie from Dwight's collection. Dwight had not left much stuff in the townhouse when he moved to the high-rise. Devon expected he would be asked to haul a bunch of it back when Dwight returned.

After cracking a beer, he finally relaxed a little. Unfortunately, he could not stop thinking about Pam Nelson. She seemed glad to see him at the hospital. It was too bad her brother was there, and he had to bug out. Maybe he'd even try calling her now that Dwight was out of town. They still had her cell phone number at work. He must have dozed off in the overstuffed chair because he never heard the two dark figures who crept up the stairs behind him.

54.

No so long ago, Matt Nelson turned down the chance to work full-time with his brother on clandestine operations. Upon further review, here he was, dressed in black at 1:00 AM, cruising up and down West Gray in Mid-Town checking out activity at Dwight Lamar's townhouse. Matt had butterflies in his stomach as they rolled past the place the first time. John was his usual stoic self. If he had any nervousness, it didn't show, but Matt was so jittery that he almost blew it by jamming on the gas when John told him to look straight ahead and act normal when they passed an HPD black-and-white going in the opposite direction. Matt had not even seen the cops. Fortunately, the police officers did not notice them, either.

On the third pass a few minutes later, John ordered Matt to pull over to the curb about a half-block from the townhouse. Both brothers stared intensely at the driveway, which was lit by a security spotlight over the garage. To their amazement, as they looked on, two dark figures with stocking masks over their heads moved stealthily through the shadows in the bushes of the unit next door. They slowed as they approached Lamar's well-lighted driveway and then, one at a time, sprinted past the garage door and disappeared around the corner to the main entrance to the townhome.

Matt couldn't figure it out, but John knew exactly what was happening.

"Well look at that, Matt. Someone is trying to beat us to the punch. Either that or Dwight is having a costume party and we weren't invited. Let's go crash the festivities." He was about to leap out of their vehicle but hesitated. "Matt, don't take this the wrong way, but we were not expecting any rough stuff on this op. It was supposed to be an intelligence-gathering mission. Those guys who just went in there have changed the whole deal. It could get nasty. Please, stay right here and be ready to call 9-1-1 if you don't hear from me in five minutes. Got it?" he instructed, as he looked over at his desk-jockey brother.

Matt's reply was swift and to the point. "Asshole!" he replied, as he opened his door to get out. John smiled. He knew what Matt's reaction would be before he even asked.

With John leading the way, the twosome ran quickly to the driveway and around to the front door, which had been left unlocked by the first two intruders. John pulled out his Glock and slowly opened the door. Matt was not armed. They eased into the small foyer and could hear sounds on the next level above them where the kitchen and living room were located. There was the sound of heavy steps, but no apparent scuffling or struggling.

"There you go, little guy. That should do the job. Sweet dreams," a voice echoed down the stairs to where they crouched. There was silence and then an excited voice. "I think someone is coming. Quick, out the back way. Now!" A drumbeat of loud footsteps followed from up there.

That was enough for John, who took the stairs two at a time and burst into the living room, rapidly aiming with his Glock in all directions. Matt followed and stood just behind him. They both spied the body of a young black man slumped in a big easy chair. Devon! Ignoring the body, John moved cautiously forward towards the kitchen where there was a rear door. He began to relax a little bit. It looked like whoever had been here had run out the back way and was long gone. Matt moved, approaching the chair where Devon lay still.

John took a deep breath and turned slowly, looking back towards Matt and said, "We're too late. They're gone…" His observation was a bit premature as a dark, masked figure hurtled out of the bathroom and grabbed his arm, slamming it down on the counter and causing him to release the gun, which went spinning down onto the tiled kitchen floor. John reacted like a cat, reaching around and bear-hugging the assailant, who was at least as tall as him and very strong.

The two grappled, knocking the kitchen table over and falling to the floor, where they continued to struggle. The man was able to slug John fully in the jaw, which left him stunned, and then seized the chance to scramble for the Glock, which was only a few feet away. John recovered enough to grab him by the waist and flip him over just before his fingers reached the weapon. John was on top and tried his best to apply a chokehold under his neck. Unfortunately, the man was a bull and kept moving just enough to not let John get a good grip.

Just about the time Matt saw John being taken down by the dark figure, he heard the wailing of police sirens from outside. Someone, probably a neighbor, had heard the scuffling and called the cops. He took a step away from Devon to help John, but was unceremoniously leveled from behind by another black figure who slammed a heavy piece of African art onto his head. Matt dropped like a rock into a heap on the floor. The second person then ran to help his cohort, whom John had just about choked into submission. With John on the floor and totally occupied with the first man, he was virtually defenseless when the other man gave him a swift swat directly on the side of the head with the same piece of art he had used on Matt. John had no choice but to release his grip and tumble over himself. His last vision was of a very clear yellow number thirteen tattooed on the man's wrist.

John was still groggy when a uniformed HPD officer appeared up the stairs from down below with his service weapon drawn. He commanded John to lie flat and put his hands behind his head. John was barely able to do so. Matt began to stir as well and was given the same instructions. It took a couple of hours and a trip down to the central station at Reisner Street to get everything sorted out. Finally, the police bought the story about the other intruders, and that Matt and John did not knock themselves out. John was also able to produce his license to carry in Texas. The biggest problem was poor Devon, who was still breathing, but barely, when the police arrived. He was rushed to Ben Taub Hospital, where he was listed in a critical condition. He had been shot up with drugs. A bunch of drug paraphernalia was also found at the scene. It had been made to look like the kid had overdosed in a big way.

John did not buy any of that. After seeing the Surenos trademark, he was convinced they had walked in on a set-up to kill the kid and make it look like he had overdosed on his own. Dwight Lamar was not to be found anywhere. Attempts to contact him about the scene at his house and his brother were unsuccessful. No-one had seen him. At the SETUP office, they only knew that he was on vacation. No-one knew where or when he would be back.

For John, now any question about Lamar and Surenos working together was moot. There was a very good chance that Mr. Lamar had tried to silence the only person that could possibly shed any light on his shady activities. That person just happened to be his own brother. Nice guy.

During his difficult recovery, it was to Devon's advantage that he had never gotten into drugs. Ironically, Dwight's pulling him out of Sparta prob-ably saved him from that fate. It was a touch-and-go battle for a few days, but the odds turned in his favor. He pulled through. After literally taking their lumps, John and Matt were anxious to interrogate the young man about his brother, although it didn't seem quite right to sweat or "wash" it out of him.

As far as they could determine, Devon was probably an innocent lackey in the whole thing. They could threaten him with horrible legal consequences if he didn't rat on his brother, but there was also a good chance he would just clam up. Another possibility was to convince him that bro Dwight had arranged the overdose hit that almost killed him. When he was eventually discovered, it would have looked like he had done himself in with an overdose.

They were still stymied until in strolled Mata Hari, whom they had desperately tried to keep as far away from all this as possible. She insisted she was going to visit Devon in the hospital. After all, hadn't he been thoughtful when she had gotten hurt? You didn't have to be Dr. Ruth or have a PhD to recognize that the young guy was smitten with her, although Pam didn't seem to notice. Such things happened to her all the time. Thank goodness she rarely reciprocated. On those occasions when she did encourage a male admirer, inevitably, after a brief period, she became bored and ducked out of the relationship.

Regretfully, both brothers reached the same conclusion. Perched there checking out her manicure was the answer to their dilemma. Fully well realizing they were probably making a big mistake, but with little alternative, Matt and John decided to capitalize on Devon's crush on their sister. Of course, she agreed in two seconds. Even under the sway of Pam Nelson's deep-blue eyes, golden hair, and Sports Illustrated swimsuit edition figure, getting Devon to turn on his brother was a tall order. A few weeks passed, and there was still no word from Dwight. At first Devon showed little concern by Dwight's silence. He had been so faithful and was certain Dwight would turn up very soon.

As Devon began to feel better, though, Dwight's silence began to trouble him more and more. Pam added to the young man's concerns by telling him that John and Matt, who had saved him, were convinced that Dwight was never coming back and had even set up the hit on him. For the first time, Devon had serious doubts about his brother. Bills were piling up. The mortgage payment notice for the townhouse came, as did the gas and electric bills. Dwight usually handled all those things. Devon was running out of cash. Dwight always paid him or just gave him money when he needed it. His paychecks from SETUP had been stopped per Mr. Luken's orders. He was almost broke. Dwight had better be back, and soon.

Pam discovered the hard and painful way that she wasn't very good at sneaking around people to get information. Getting a man to bare his soul, well, that is quite another question. She genuinely liked Devon and enjoyed his company. She knew he wanted a lot more than just being friends, but he was also realistic enough to know that would never happen. In the end, he was just thrilled to have such a terrific person paying attention to him. The fact that she bought him several meals didn't hurt either. She even hinted that if Dwight didn't return, she might be able to find him a job, possibly at the Q. He liked that idea.

One evening, they were sitting in the townhouse watching Game of Thrones. After knocking off a six-pack of Landshark, Devon just simply caved in. He finally accepted the fact that his brother had ditched him and wasn't coming back. He had been on the shady side of things for so long, he was amazed to discover that in Pam's world, not everything was secret and mean-spirited. He had little awareness that such a life existed. Maybe now he even had a path in that direction. He crossed the bridge, and now decided that he just had to unburden himself of the things he had been carrying for such a long time. Pam was all ears.

He went to great lengths to explain that Dwight did his absolute best to keep as much as possible away from him and never consulted with him about anything before it happened. He always structured things such that people in the chain were kept apart. Each knew one little piece, but only he knew the end game. The only time Dwight was ever the least bit vulnerable was when, after a long day, he settled back and had a couple of nips of Courvoisier, his favorite cognac. Every so often, those shots loosened him up and made him feel like he needed to talk, or more likely, brag, at how smart he was. What good is it to put one over on a person if they never realized it? In these private late-night sessions, he talked and preached to Devon. Occasionally, he would tell him things that he'd never mention during the day.

As Pam opened another beer for him, she gently asked what kind of things his brother talked about. Once he got moving and on a roll, it all came tumbling out. "Dwight bragged about how he would send phony invoices from his own private shell companies to his contractors to be paid out of construction funds. He was amused that one of his hand-picked contractors, Punjab, paid them like clockwork, but Matt Nelson refused. He saw what a piece of crap Punjab was building and realized that Matt was very good, but he really didn't care. He had misjudged Matt's desperation for a contract, and then had to fire him before he got too involved. He had the SETUP directors eating out of his hand. He manipulated the vouchers so more Hispanics would get them just to win over one of the directors. Every move he made was to woo them over and give him a green light to operate the way he wanted.

"Chiseling a few bucks here and there was bad enough, but there were also some really horrible things." Devon paused, and Pam wondered if he would continue. "He told me how there was an Asian greaser from somewhere in Houston who barged into the office one day and demanded a voucher for his mother. Dwight saw to it that guy was bludgeoned to death one night at a roadhouse near the Barker-Cypress Reservoir. Another time, he needed to look good for HUD so he had an innocent inspector framed for stealing stuff from a tenant's apartment. On the Punjab job, a roofer would not co-operate and threatened to turn him in to HUD. That guy ended up in a vat of hot roofing tar." Pam cringed at that one. "Again, I am not sure, but I think he used that Mexican gang from Pasadena to do his dirty work."

He reminded Pam that these were all stories from a half-drunk Dwight. Maybe they weren't even true. He had no firsthand information.

"There was only one incident that I am sure was absolutely true," he continued. His voice began to crack as he looked away to hide his doleful and watery eyes.

"What was that, Devon?"

He spoke in such a soft tone that she barely heard him. "You. Yes, Pam, that crazy day when you went into his office, I was the one that told him about it. I saw you on the monitor that we have at the guard stand on the first floor. I felt it was my duty to tell him. When I did, I saw him get a look in his eye. He asked me again about it when I drove him downtown for lunch. When you didn't show up for work the next day, I just knew he had had you killed. I was sure of it. I almost confronted him. I was totally bummed out, and he knew it. I was so relieved when I found out you were at least alive in the hospital. I just had to go and see you. Oh, Pam, I am so sorry. Do you hate me?" he pleaded, as tears streamed down his face.

She got up and squeezed into the big chair next to him. She put her arms around him and replied tenderly, "No. No, Devon. I do not." She sat there for several minutes, holding him and letting him gather his composure. She then moved back to her seat on the couch. "He was a sneaky creep. What about the Destination Diversity land? Do you know anything about that?"

"No, I really don't. He was very careful and closed-mouthed about it. I am sure he had some kind of scam worked up but, I don't know what. I was surprised when the land purchase fell through. On the other hand, if that happened, it was because Dwight planned it that way."

"And now he has disappeared. Do you have any idea where he may have gone?"

"All I can tell you is that I dropped him off at the international terminal at IAH around 8:00 PM after the emergency board meeting. He didn't tell me where he was going or when he'd be back. He only said it was for a vacation."

"So, you had no inkling before you took him to the airport that he was leaving?"

"Nope. He did tell me to stay here from now on. He had ended the lease on the River Oaks apartment. That was the way he usually acted. I never had any notice about things anyway. I didn't worry too much this time at the start, until I almost got drugged to death. There was one thing that was a little strange."

"What was that?"

"Dwight Lamar never lifted a finger in his recent life that he didn't have to. I drove him, opened doors, brought him coffee, covered his butt, the works. That's why I was surprised he would leave the River Oaks apartment without telling me to lug all his personal crap back and forth. I mean, that was my job. I expected to do that when he got back. After I dropped him at the airport, I took his car to the car wash before I stopped for something to eat. While I was there, I found a pink copy of a FEDEX packing slip, which may well have slipped out of Dwight's briefcase. I kept it." He reached for his wallet and extracted a pink piece of paper. He handed it to Pam. "Here it is."

Pam unfolded the paper. In the "SHIP TO" box there was an address in St. Kitts-Nevis.

Bingo!

55.

Dwight Lamar had invested huge amounts of time looking for the perfect place to relocate after his time in Texas was up. After eliminating dozens of spots all over the world, he finally settled on a tiny country in the far Caribbean. St. Kitts-Nevis is a dual island nation in the West Indies chain with the Atlantic on one side and the Caribbean on the other. These particular islands were the first to have been settled as an original British colony by Europeans over 200 years ago. He considered the fact that much British culture and tradition remains in evidence as a definite attribute, and English is the spoken language.

Together, the two islands have a land mass of just over one hundred square miles with a population of 55,000, giving it sufficient critical mass for some exposure to the modern world. Nevis itself is just a short powerboat ride across the channel from St. Kitts. The country's economy is based on tourism and, to a lesser extent, the sugar industry.

St. Kitts-Nevis also offered a unique opportunity of particular interest to Dwight Lamar. One of the oldest prevailing "economic citizenship" programs remained in effect there. Under that arrangement, anyone who makes a certain level of economic investment automatically receives citizenship. In fact, usually just purchasing a home will do it. A St. Kitts-Nevis passport also brings with it visa-free access to over 130 countries, including the entire European Union. Dwight Lamar was hardly planning to remain a hermit forever.

His new home had to be somewhere warm that was out of the way but not totally isolated. In his mind he was certainly not in exile, and still entitled to the finer things in life. This beautiful place offered a high standard of living, including the ability to surround himself with enough functionaries to ensure a comfortable lifestyle. Personal comfort aside, he could also design a residence that would afford him protection and warning if the bad guys ever showed up. He had no intention of staying there forever; probably only until his genius hatched his next scheme.

Lamar registered as Ashton Jeffers at the Four Seasons Resort. After looking around for a week or so, he decided to settle on Nevis' thirty-six square miles of tranquil beaches, rain forests, and foothills. It even had a small airport. He purchased a pleasant, older, but thoroughly modernized, home in the foothills not far from the beach. By doing so, he was well on his way to citizenship-by-investment. He chose that particular property because it backed up to a small hill and was elevated compared to the ground surrounding it. Besides the main entrance, there were two rear drives out of the property, enabling quick evacuation if necessary. It also had a large garage and barn-like utility building in the backyard. The quaint and charming stone veneer dwelling included several bedrooms and ample space for his household staff. He marveled that with today's incredible technology, he had every bit as good an access to world events and entertainment out there in the middle of nowhere as in Houston. He was pleased with the cool ocean breezes and could live with the frequent monsoon downpours. Before long he had a staff of three locals, which, in the aggregate, cost him only a fraction of what he, or really SETUP, had paid Devon.

Security was the one important issue that continued to trouble him. The locals were pleasant and happy folk, but he just couldn't see any of them gunning down an Albanian in cold blood with an Uzi, should that become necessary. He decided that problem was important enough to bring in someone from the US. Maybe he would sneak a trip back to the US, where everyone still loved him—except, of course, a few grumps in Brooklyn. He had no restrictions on travel and could move freely as he wished.

Just the same, he needed to be very cautious. During his very last "wet operation," which involved the Nelson girl, in his eagerness to snuff out that problem, he had almost decided to cut a corner and go directly to the Surenos himself. Fortunately, he did not, and worked through his usual middleman. He did, however, get the direct contact information for future use. Using untraceable satellite networking and burner phones, he called the Surenos directly. He ended up speaking to Sr. Carlos Garcia, who represented himself as the "general" in charge of the Houston cadre. Dwight had never met any of his hitmen, nor had they ever known exactly who they were working for.

The purpose of his call was for a referral of someone associated with the Surenos who could operate and function in his newly found part of the world. He needed protection, and he knew they operated all over the US and perhaps other places as well. He did not disclose his identity or location. What Dwight did not know was that the Houston Surenos gang, which had justifiably earned the reputation as "the gang who couldn't shoot straight," was all but disbanded. Even if all the assignments they had botched had gone well, the information about them fed back to the FBI and DEA from the Nelson brothers had produced so much heat that they could no longer function effectively.

Carlos Garcia was desperate for work. The call was music to his ears. Without going into great detail, he was sure there were affiliates that could provide the services the caller had in mind. It took two more conversations for Dwight to get enough confidence and arrange a meeting in Miami. Dwight flew in and met Carlos at a bar in South Beach. Without disclosing the location, he described the position in much more detail. They spent the next day together, during which Carlos admitted to Dwight that he was from Houston, although neither made the connection that Carlos may have worked on jobs for Dwight, who never told him he also was from Houston. Dwight was surprised but pleased by the man's candor. They got on well, and Dwight offered him the job on the spot. Carlos had no marital and only a few family ties, so he was free to leave immediately. Dwight agreed to meet him in Kingston, Jamaica, in one week's time and take him to a place yet unnamed. What Dwight did not tell Carlos was that there was no trial period for this job. If things didn't work out, Dwight would personally see to it that the sea turtles would be pecking the eyes out of his floating corpse in short order. Dwight understood he was taking a risk, but he had proved he was infallible, hadn't he?

After Pam had charmed Devon to bare his soul, she was tempted to play games with her brothers, but, for once, she recognized that the matter was too serious to jack them around. She did, however, extract one promise from them both before she began. They had to agree to go easy on Devon and try to help him as much as they could. That was no problem for them.

Matt and John sat there transfixed as their always unpredictable, never reliable sister relayed everything she had learned from the deceit master's brother. The smoking guns they lacked materialized before their eyes. DA Glazer had left the door open and, so long as they could structure some kind of immunity for Devon, they planned to see her again with him in tow. It was a cinch that with his information, investigations could be launched that would ultimately lead to indictments of the Teflon executive director.

On the other hand, with the star of the show gone, all that could end up being a total waste of time. They now knew without doubt that he had attempted to kill Pam and ruin Matt's company. They still did not have an answer to the big scam question. No money ever changed hands on the land and yet he had disappeared. They had to get an answer to that burning question.

The St. Kitts-Nevis discovery was phenomenal. It looked like the man who never slipped up just may have gotten a tad bit sloppy. John contacted Harvey and asked him to shake the palm trees discreetly in the West Indies to see if there was any evidence of someone resembling the "king" to have shown up over the past month or so. Harvey called back in a few hours. As a matter of fact, a man resembling Dwight Lamar, who went by the name of Ashton Jeffers, had recently arrived in Nevis. Even in that very laid-back Caribbean atmosphere, his pompous attitude had singled him out. It seems as though the man threatened to have the bartender at the Four Seasons fired because they ran out of Courvoisier, his favorite cognac. Yep. That's our boy.

John and Matt looked at each other. An operational plan was born. Matt would arrange for tickets, and John would lay out the strategy for corralling the monster and dragging him home. Pam stood there and put on the most mortified face she could muster. Her brothers tried to ignore her, which was, of course, impossible. The old Pam returned with a vengeance.

"After all I have done! You'd be nowhere without me. I found that broker. I made Devon come clean. I even had to sleep with a monkey, for heaven's sake! Where is your appreciation and gratitude?" she scolded, and then got really serious. "Do you guys know how beautiful it is supposed to be on those Caribbean Islands? Just look at me. After all that hospital time, I am white as a sheet. I need to go just to get healthy. I need to get my tan back." Try as she might, neither of them would bite. This trip could be very dangerous, and having her along would make it worse. After it was over, they would all take a vacation somewhere. Predictably, she stormed out of the room.

Often Pam's antics in similar situations were for show, but this time she was very frustrated after all she had contributed. She needed an outlet of some kind, or at least someone she could talk to who would understand. Her face lit up as she sat on the bed in her old room at her mother's house and pulled another burner phone out of her purse. She dialed the latest number, announced herself as Alice, and asked for Fred concerning his Economist subscription. There was the usual four-or-five minute pause before he came on the line.

"Hey, how's it going?" the man's voice asked from so far away. "Okay, I guess, but I am frustrated and mad at the moment."

"Well, at least you haven't changed. What's wrong now?"

"As usual, those rotten brothers are excluding me from all the fun!" Even she couldn't believe she'd said that. The man laughed heartily.

"What's new on your big deal with the housing authority director?"

"Plenty. Mostly thanks to me, we found out that he was stealing money and actually arranging hits on people, such as contractors, who wouldn't cooperate with him." She conveniently left out the fact that she had been the target of one of those hits. "He was ready to close on a large piece of land, but, at the very last minute, he walked away before any money changed hands. None of us can figure that out, and now he's disappeared, although we now know, again thanks to me, where he is hiding."

"Very interesting. Where is he?"

"In the beautiful West Indies on Nevis, where the beaches are incredible. Matt and John are going to get him, but I can't go."

"Are you sure about Nevis?"

"Yes. He is even using a phony name. Ashton Jeffers."

The line was silent for a minute or so, causing Pam to ask, "Are you still there?"

"Yes, Pa...err, Alice. I'm here. I was just thinking. I have an idea. Now listen to me."

Pam listened for a couple of minutes and when she finally hung up, the moisture that began to accumulate in the corners of her eyes had turned into full-fledged tears. That was, of course, the cue for her mother to walk in.

Diane took one look at her daughter and said, "Oh, no, who is it this time? I sure hope it's not Devon!"

In spite of herself, Pam chuckled at that thought. "No. No, but sit down here with me, I need to talk to you about something."

In less than two minutes, both women were wailing so loud they could probably be heard in Dallas.

56.

The night was steamy, but the brilliance of the millions of stars in the wide Caribbean sky provided enough light so that moving around was not difficult, even in the tropical jungle. These conditions were still far from optimal to execute an assault on an unfamiliar objective. John and Matt were hunkered down in the bushes of the thick tropical vegetation that surrounded Dwight Lamar's new lair. They'd arrived at the St. Kitts airport two days earlier and taken a powerboat across the channel to Nevis to recon the place. They caromed around the island on rented motor scooters like tourists, being very careful to avoid any chance encounter with their quarry. In the evening, they returned to the St. Kitts side and took a room at a tiny, out-of-the-way motel in Basseterre, the capital city.

Their reconnaissance did not turn up much hard data about the house, which was constructed of sturdy stone but didn't look particularly well-fortified. They were not surprised to see three or four local people milling about, attending to the landscaping and other menial chores around the place. John had a hard and fast rule of never underestimating your opposition, but it just didn't seem likely that those folks would put up much of a fight. If all went well, they'd grab his highness, who for all his bravado was probably not much of a fighter, and secure him with zip ties and blankets. They planned to use a small rented Toyota pickup to haul him under cover of darkness to the island's airport at Charlestown, where a Cessna Citation Harvey McClung had arranged would pick them up and fly them straight to Miami. It was as simple as that. What could go wrong? FUBAR, thought John. FUBAR, thought Matt.

From their hiding spot, they observed the man himself pull up and emerge from a large American car that was chauffeured by a local. He was nattily dressed in a seersucker suit but seemed to stagger a bit as he walked up the steps and through the front door, held open by another manservant of some kind. Mr. Lamar just might have had one too many.

As usual, Harvey had turned a miracle and found them handguns and a limited amount of ammunition on the island. They were semi-ancient .45 automatics, but they still worked and would stop a man in his tracks at twenty feet.

The brothers felt much more comfortable with them than with bamboo sticks, which would have been their alternative. They sat tight for an hour before getting set to go in. Hopefully, all the local lackeys had gone home by then.

The pair moved out slowly and noiselessly through the thick foliage and crouched just at the edge of an open grassy area that was seventy-five yards wide on that side of the house. John went first and darted quickly into the shadows next to the wall. After waiting for any reaction from inside and seeing none, Matt then sprinted across. The plan was for Matt to creep around the front and enter through the main door. John would head for the back and come in from the rear. As they squatted there next to the house preparing to go in, a peculiar noise filtered down through the open window just above their heads. "Ooooh! Aaaaaah! Ooooh! Aaaah! More! More! Don't stop!"

Matt furrowed his brow. "Huh? Girl. There?" he whispered to John and motioned towards the window.

John shook his head and smirked. "No. Porno movie," he responded in a barely audible voice.

Matt nodded. John motioned and at John's signal, they both moved out.

For a while it looked like this op was going to go just as planned, and maybe even easier than they dared hope. Matt moved swiftly up the steps and bolted through the half-open front door. He burst into the darkened living room, where there was indeed a hot sheets flick on the television, and there was his excellency, sitting back in a big, overstuffed chair, his tie loosened, with a drink in his hand, enjoying every bump and grind.

Matt nervously yelled, "Freeze!" just like the cops did on Law and Order.

Dwight Lamar had no reaction. For a second, Matt thought he might have been asleep. He then slowly turned his head away from the action and spoke in slow and measured tones, "You know, Matt. The one problem with this place so far is the women. I just haven't been able to find a reliable source. I guess in time I will figure it out. Oh, and welcome to Nevis. I thought maybe I'd have visitors sooner or later, but I am frankly surprised to see you. If you've come to reinstate your contract, I am afraid it is too late. I have resigned from SETUP, or haven't you heard?"

Matt seethed. Can you imagine the balls on this guy? "Sorry, Dwight, you're on your way back to Texas to face charges of embezzlement, extortion, and murder. Now, very slowly, get your fat ass up and lay down on the floor on your stomach."

After chugging the remains of his drink, Lamar again looked up. "Matt. Matt. Those are pretty strong charges. You could barely get the DA to meet with you before when she threw you out of her office. I've done nothing wrong, except perhaps not saying goodbye to everyone but, you know that is so hard sometimes. I am a pretty emotional guy."

"Maybe you should ask Devon about saying goodbye, you lousy bastard."

If mention of his brother's name was supposed to evoke a reaction, none was apparent on the man's face.

John then moved into the room and stood next to Matt. "I've cleared all the other rooms. No-one else is here. Now let's get lard-ass dressed up for his trip. Move, Lamar!" John commanded.

Lamar still did not move from the chair. "We have not been formally introduced, but I am assuming that you are 'John-Boy,' the hotshot cowboy from Virginia. We have been watching you for two days since you arrived. Did you enjoy your little outing yesterday on those cute little scooters? Welcome to Nevis. I guess I should say I hope you enjoy your time here, but I don't think you are going to, which is a shame because it is a delightful place."

John was pissed, and stepped forwards to grab the asshole when a deep, Hispanic voice broke the silence behind them. "Both of you drop those little toys right now and get on the floor. I am six feet away from you and have my Uzi on full automatic. You'll both be dead before you can say "puta." Now! Do it."

John looked around slowly to see a dark man pointing the barrel of an Uzi right at them. John motioned to Matt, and they both dropped their weapons.

For the first time, Lamar had a little inflection in his voice. "Next time, John-Boy, be sure and check the hurricane room that all these houses have. You must have missed it, which, maybe in this case, was lucky for you. You are still alive, for now. Say, gentlemen, I believe you may have already met Carlos, my head of security. He is from Houston."

Carlos snarled, "Hobby Airport. You bastadas!"

Matt and John had been tied securely at hands and feet using their own zip ties.

They were sitting on the rough dirt floor of the corrugated metal outbuilding to the rear of Lamar's house. John kept apologizing to Matt over and over about letting him down. Matt got so tired of hearing that, he told his brother to shut up. It was pretty obvious that unless they figured out something quickly, their return plane tickets home would never be used.

Both their captors were killers of innocent people they didn't even know back in Houston. What chance did they have way out here in the middle of nowhere when they were hated? Not much. John decided to buy some time, even at great personal cost.

"Carlos, do you remember when we waterboarded you in that warehouse?" As if Carlos could ever forget that humiliation. "We laughed at how you cried like an old woman!"

The insult of all insults! That was all it took. Carlos was incensed. He walked over and gave John a hard kick in the ribs. The man was furious. John had insulted him where it hurt the most, his pride. Lamar stood there watching it all with a bemused smile on his face. As many times as he had set up rough stuff, he had hardly ever witnessed it.

Carlos left the building but returned shortly with a full bucket of water. He pulled over an old piece of plywood and shoved a log under one end. With a wicked smile on his face, he walked over and grabbed John by the shirt and dragged him and threw him on the plywood. Despite John's attempts to resist, Carlos was able to tie a rough hemp rope around his chest and under the plywood to keep him still. Enjoying every second, he threw a filthy cloth that had been used to check engine oil levels on a dipstick over John's face. John was already coughing. Matt was screaming for him to stop.

Carlos paused with the bucket right over John's covered face. "Watch this, Mr. Lamar. Let's see who the puta is!" He slowly poured the water on John's face, who immediately went into a coughing, wheezing, and blowing frenzy. Carlos laughed as John's pain worsened.

Everyone was so intent on watching this macabre ritual that no-one noticed a tall, graying, still rather distinguished-looking white man in his early sixties who now stood at the door of the building. He was, in fact, very white, like he hadn't been out in the sun very much, if at all. He wore tan pants, a flowered Hawaiian print shirt and a panama hat. He had on sandals, which if one looked closely, revealed that he was missing a little toe on one foot. He addressed the group in a stern, no-compromising voice of authority.

Carlos heard him and looked up. He glared at the non-threatening-looking old man.

"Who the hell are you, old fart?"

Matt could not believe his eyes. He must be hallucinating. It couldn't be.

No way. Could it be?

"I said put down that bucket!"

Carlos decided to comply. He threw it down and moved aggressively towards the intruder, who calmly reached into his pocket and pulled out a small revolver. There was a thunderous bang, puff of smoke, and pungent smell of cordite in the confined space. In the blink of an eye, a red dot appeared in the middle of Carlos's forehead, causing him to halt in his tracks and collapse stone-dead on the dusty floor.

In the meantime, the smelly cloth had fallen away from John's face and he had been able to spit out most of the water. That was horrible; worse than he could have imagined. It made him delusional. Right now, for instance, he was sure he was looking directly into his dead father's face.

57.

Perhaps it was telling that Travis Nelson went first to Matt to cut him free of the zip ties with his pocketknife rather than his younger son, but no-one took much notice. All three of them were overcome with emotion. Despite the bloody thug that lay on the floor right next to them, the threesome melted into a hug session that was unprecedented in the Nelson family. While Matt had at least worked closely with his father for several years, John and the old man had been estranged virtually from the time he graduated from high school. None of the past meant anything right then, however, as the unexpected reunion became a signature moment in their collective lives.

John literally came up for air, and when he finally settled back for a moment, still delighted to see his father alive, he suddenly realized that his highness had disappeared. In all the action following Travis's dramatic grand entrance, Dwight Lamar had slipped away. John tried to struggle to his feet.

"Oh, shit! That bastard Lamar has run off. We need to catch him right away. There is no telling what kind of an escape plan he has set up. The SOB probably has a submarine parked offshore. Let me up."

"Relax, son," Travis assured. "He won't get far. You may not realize it, but there are some other folks who want him as much or even more than you do."

Before Travis could say more, three figures emerged out of the night into the building. There were two very burly-looking men with buzz cut hair wearing dark tee shirts and jeans and heavy work boots. Even in the poor light of the shed, their pale skin helped enhance the network of tats burnt on their bulging biceps. One wore a short, black beard, and although the other did not, his thick stubble made it obvious that he hadn't shaved in some time. Clearly, this pair were not locals or typical tourists enjoying a Caribbean holiday. Both wore scowls on their faces that threatened to wake some of the frequently discussed West Indian ghosts.

Dwight Lamar had always demanded immediate and full attention to his personal whims. Well, he had now reached the ultimate in that regard. The deposed monarch was strung between the two men, who had tied his wrists and ankles and then strung him over a bamboo pole. They summarily dropped him on the floor with a thud. The unfortunate fellow's face looked as if he'd been "nudged" a time or two by his new pair of menservants. Both eyes were bruised and blackening, and his forehead had a large gash and was bleeding. Despite it all, after being dumped in the dust, he continued to mumble, "I will negotiate. I will negotiate," to anyone who would listen.

Matt and John looked on with amazement and curiosity. It was Travis who spoke. "Matt, John, I'd like to introduce my friends, Sali and Edi, who just happened to be down here in St. Kitts-Nevis from Brooklyn catching some rays on the beach. Their families are originally from Albania in eastern Europe. It seems as though your friend here, Mr. Lamar, had agreed to do some business with their family, and surprise, surprise, things didn't quite go as planned. They are of the opinion that Mr. Lamar just might owe them a few dollars.

"Now John, I can understand how much you want to bring this turd to justice back in the States, but I am not sure you want to take on my friends who have other plans for him. I can assure you he will not be able to buy any life insurance ever again. So, what do you think?"

John got it very quickly. The king was doomed. The Albanians would never let him go. In fact, their justice for him was actually much more assured that dragging him through the US criminal justice system, where the slimeball just might pull off another miracle. John was not about to take on his father's mean looking friends. "Dad, I get the distinct sense that Matt and I have more than accomplished what we set out to do down here. Good riddance."

"Great. Now let's get out of here before any authorities show up. We have a lot of catching up to do, and I don't have much time."

With that, Sali and Edi grabbed the ends of the bamboo pole after each giving the king one more swift kick in the ribs and disappeared with him into the night.

Travis took his sons back to a cabana suite at the Four Seasons. As they walked in, they were surprised once again at who was sitting on the bed: their smug little sister, with a definite I-just-showed-up-you-guys look in her eyes. Pam was prone to pop up almost anywhere, but they were even more surprised to see their mother present in the room as well. Unlike her daughter, she openly broke down when they walked in. She'd never, ever thought she would see her entire family back together again in one room.

As if surprises would never end that day, Travis Nelson walked over to her, gave her a big hug and a kiss on the lips. Diane grabbed him and held on tight. Amazingly, he made no attempt to resist; in fact, he seemed to be enjoying it.

After a few minutes, when the shock of the gathering began to wear off just a bit, Travis Nelson, as he always had, took over the proceedings. Everyone was anxious for him to explain. "You all know how thrilled I am to see you but if I dwell on that, I'll never get around to explaining things." John and Matt could not believe their father was getting choked up as he spoke. His eyes were actually glistening. "Anyway. Please do not ask me where I am now living. There is no reason for you to know, so if you're ever pressured, you all can honestly say that you don't know. I am comfortable, but it is nothing like Texas.

"Since it has been a few years now since all my troubles went down, in a weak moment, when perhaps I was fortified with some alcohol, I decided to try to contact Pam, on the strict condition that she would not breathe a word of it to anyone. Well, I have had a few conversations with her, and I believe she has kept it to herself." He looked over at his daughter, who was beaming, and even took the opportunity to stick out her tongue at her envious brothers. Everyone cracked up at her antics.

"Pam told me about this Dwight Lamar guy, whom I'd never heard of, but that you, Matt, had done some business with him and were suspicious he was up to something big. Naturally, that piqued my interest. I spent a career in Houston and, as hard as it is where I am to get Astros scores, I don't have a lot else to do. In a call she mentioned Peter Butler, whom I did know."

Matt broke in, "So that is how she knew the name and that he was a broker from New York?"

Pam smiled.

"Yes, I am sure of that. Anyway, although I never did any direct business with Peter's clients from Brooklyn, I did have dinner with Edi and Sali's father, Bujar, one time when I was in New York. We got on well, and although we didn't strike a deal, we promised to keep in touch. The entire family was originally from Tirana, the capital of Albania. They were able to emigrate from their country to Brooklyn in the late 1990s after the communist state capitulated. When Pam mentioned Peter Butler, who was born Pjeter Bodi, by the way, I felt it was likely that the Albanians were somehow involved, probably as passive investors."

Matt and John nodded, following their father's reasoning. "So," he continued, "With time on my hands I contacted Bujar, who at that point, was ready to tar and feather poor Peter Butler. It seems that your friend, working through Butler, had convinced the Albanians to purchase a site in Houston that he'd picked out. He promised them they couldn't lose and a big score was a certainty. Bujar's group immediately bought it, with almost no investigation, strictly relying on Lamar's say-so. Lamar assured them he would purchase it a few years down the road for a greatly increased price. They'd stand to split a very substantial profit."

Matt said, "I knew it! I knew it! What a slippery guy but, Dad, the deal never closed; the $15,000,000 was in escrow and ready to fund but Lamar walked out of the deal right at the end. No money changed hands. Why the heck did he do that? He was so close to a huge payday. I never have been able to figure that move out."

"You are right, Matt, but it shows the genius and cunning of that guy. He was smart enough to know that a high-visibility deal like that sale, with all those government entities and HUD crawling all over, would be intensely scrutinized. If a single dollar found its way to his pocket, red flags would wave and sirens would go off. By dramatically quashing the deal at the last minute, apparently to keep his company and his partners out of trouble, he earned considerable respect from the SETUP people. He was a white knight who helped them avoid a possible catastrophe. When he left Houston, he was convinced he could return at any time and be welcomed back with open arms."

"So, you are telling us he never got any cash out of the deal?" John asked.

"No, John, I didn't say that. Here is how slick he was. Even the Albanians could see how exposed Lamar would be if he signed the papers and closed the deal with only a verbal promise from them to pony up after all the cash was disbursed to them by the title company. Neither side could risk anything in writing, so Lamar was able to convince the Albanians to give him half of his share, $2,500,000, right at the last second, just before closing happened. At least then he'd have some insurance money if the Albanians happened to forget him after the closing. They sent him that half of his half, expecting $15,000,000 to be coming their way in a matter of minutes."

Matt jumped in, "I get it now. He brings everything right to the brink, and the Albanians send him two point five. He walks the deal. No-one knows any different except the Albanians, who are fit to be tied. Dwight Lamar then disappears without a trace; only, the Albanians are really mad at him."

"Right. As long as he can avoid them, he is set for a comfortable life. What he didn't plan on was the skillful work of one Pamela Nelson. When she told me about the St. Kitts-Nevis situation, my next call was to Bujar, who, at that point, would have kissed my boots. I settled for a round trip flight down here. Oh, and I did suggest to Pam that maybe we would have an impromptu little family reunion at Dwight's expense. Naturally, neither your mother nor sister wanted you guys to know about it, knowing full well that you'd both try to prevent them from coming. Something about being dangerous."

"Well, Dad, I have to admit, your timing in Lamar's garage turned out to be pretty good. Thanks very much," John said, in no way attempting to hide his sincere appreciation.

"I didn't know it until recently, but apparently you guys did your best to save my bacon in Mexico. I owe you both big-time for that. I am glad I happened along when I did also, but, you know," he said as his face broke out into a big smile, "After I watched that guy operate on you, I got to thinking. If that punishment had been available when you were young, everything might have turned out very differently." Everyone broke up at that one.

Travis told them that unfortunately, he had to leave first thing in the morning. That didn't stop them from catching up into the wee small hours. Finally, Pam gathered her brothers, and the three of them left the suite. Diane and Travis still had some of their own catching up to do without their kids under foot.

58.

The long flight from St. Kitts-Nevis had been made even longer by the collective sadness that gripped the four Nelsons. Even the normally indifferent John, who had not been in his father's presence for more than a decade, acted as if he were depressed, or at least very preoccupied. Other than banalities every now and then, the trip was accomplished in almost total silence.

Seeing Travis Nelson alive and fit was a dream come true for all of them. While the thrill of spending even a few hours with him was wonderful, it was depressing to contemplate the very real prospect that they would never see him again. What made it even worse was that after being with him in Nevis, everyone sensed that he had fundamentally changed from his glory days in Houston. For the first time, Travis Nelson openly showed that he truly cared deeply about every one of them. Those feelings were simply not apparent in the past. Wouldn't it have been wonderful to take things up again with this new man? They could only wonder and dream. If he ever showed up in the United States again, neither the FBI nor DEA would hardly give him credit for suddenly openly loving his family. He would be immediately escorted to prison, never to emerge a free man.

John and Matt still harbored a fleeting sense of failure not having Dwight Lamar in tow back to Houston, but they understood that the jerk was headed for swift and uncomfortable justice at the hands of the Albanians. The stark fact was, he was much more likely to be held accountable for his brazen acts by that group than by the unpredictable American justice system. After all, the man had somehow managed to leave Houston in good graces and even admired by many. Given competent legal counsel, with his uncanny knack for survival, it might just have been possible that he could wiggle out of real punishment in Texas. No chance of that in Brooklyn or wherever he was headed. The brothers agreed that they needed to sit down with the proper authorities, including the Assistant District Attorney, and explain all that had transpired, up to a point. Even though Dwight Lamar was a cooked goose who would never be seen in the Lone Star State again, they presumed that the police would be interested in the information relative to those specific crimes he had ordered. Investigations regarding them were certainly still open. The

Nelsons would help Devon find appropriate legal protection in order for him to share what he knew with the authorities. Otherwise, he would not have any incentive to discuss his dealings with Lamar.

Of course, the one real sensitive aspect of the story they would absolutely keep from the authorities was any mention of the presence of Travis Nelson. Their meeting was brief, and Travis very wisely gave them no hint as to where he had been living. While they yearned to know what he had been doing since that event in Mexico years ago, they would just have to make do without. He also made no promises about contacting them ever again. None of them, including Pam, had any clue how they might find him.

After returning to Houston and tying up some of the loose ends, John was anxious to get back to Virginia and see how bad Harvey had screwed things up in his absence. Before he left, though, despite all that had happened, John still wanted to make sure that the Surenos threat was dead and gone so Matt and his family could live their lives without worrying about them popping up. They contacted James Forney at the Houston DEA office to tell him Carlos Garcia was now dead, with a bit of a variation about how he died. Forney was pleased to hear about the thug's misfortune and also advised that the Pasadena Surenos cell was no longer in existence. That was good news indeed. With that reassurance, John was ready to depart for the East Coast with one more final stop. Pam, in fact, became a bit perturbed because she had arrived back from St. Kitts bursting with a lot to tell her best friend, who was somehow unavailable until the big boy jetted back to DC.

It remained to be seen what kind of consulting business Matt could drum up, but he was anxious to get back out there and try. He did continue to work on Riverbend for Jeanne, who consistently came up with additional things for him to do with respect to the new building addition. The long flight home from the West Indies had sparked one idea that Matt felt was worth pursuing. Pam had recovered enough that she was about to go back to the Q, where, by the way, she had gotten a job for Devon. By all reports, he was doing quite well. Pam had made it very clear, though, that for her that place was a dead end. She really wanted something much more challenging and yet still involved in working with people. A light went on in Matt's brain. Who did he know who possibly might need to add to staff and had a challenging job working with people? The answer was obvious: Jeanne. Was there any reason he should be careful about introducing a close family member to an old flame?

He really didn't think so.

After first mentioning the idea to Jeanne, who was very encouraging, he asked Pam about it. She was ready to go that evening at 9:00 PM. As luck would have it, with the big, brand-new expansion of Riverbend, Jeanne was very short on staff. She and Pam hit it off immediately. In fact, not five minutes after Matt had made introductions, he found himself alone in Jeanne's office. Jeanne had grabbed Pam, and was already showing her the new digs and introducing her to people. Within a week, Pam Nelson came aboard as a consultant trainee. The amazing Pam had done it once again. He had never seen her more enthusiastic about anything.

Matt was very pleased about how two of the favorite women in his life had immediately jelled. It had taken a while, but Matt had long since been able to rid himself of the guilt feelings about that peculiar rainy afternoon when he and Jeanne had that long Italian wine-soaked lunch and then went back to her condo. All the pieces for a few moments of passion followed by imminent disaster were on hand that fateful day. The desire was impossible to resist, but somehow, they did. Jeanne made him a cup of coffee, and they sat and talked for a while, and then he left. Nothing happened. Matt still carried the guilt of his desire for a while, but he knew deep down he had made the right decision (damn it!).

It was just a few days after they got back on a bright and sunshiny day when Matt pulled into the Riverbend parking lot. He noticed Pam sitting on a bench in a garden area deep in conversation with an attractive young woman close to her age. A youngster who could not have been more than four or five was weaving in and out of the bushes playing with a toy airplane. Matt walked over to say hello. When he did, Pam introduced him to a pleasant-looking lady named Karen, who was obviously a resident at Riverbend. The young jet pilot who went flying by was her son. After chatting for a few moments, Matt excused himself and went into the building to find Jeanne. As he walked into her office, she got up from her desk, rushed up to him and gave him a big hug.

The gesture caught Matt by surprise, and he could not hide his embarrassment. "What was that for? I am not used to such attention, especially before I even open my mouth."

"Sorry, Matt, if I am in such a good mood today. First of all, thanks so much for Pam. I think she is going to work out great. All the women she has met so far just seem to love her. She is so understanding. I don't think I could have found a better assistant."

"Well, that is great news, I guess; but was that enough to assault me?" he quipped with a feigned indignant look on his face.

"No, you're right. There is something else I need to show you. Look here," she said, pointing towards her computer screen, which was open to Riverbend's bank account at Houston City Bank.

Matt peered at the screen and responded, "Holy cow! Where'd that come from?"

Jeanne smiled, "We have a young lady who has been with us for a few months now who has really been down on her luck. She is a single mother with a five-year-old son. She is still struggling with her addiction, but we have seen some real progress lately. I think she is going to be fine. Her name is Karen."

Matt broke in, "I think I just met her out there sitting with Pam."

"Yes, that's her. The deposit you just saw on my screen came with instructions: "For use in the Riverbend Women's Shelter as management sees fit in the name of Karen and her son."

Matt looked down again at Jeanne's screen and, plain as day, he saw a wire transfer credit entry for one million dollars, which originated from a bank in the Bahamas.

Better Riverbend than Bujar.

About the Author

Robert John DeLuca writes on a variety of topics, both fiction and non-fiction, drawing much of his material from enriching life experiences during careers in banking, real estate, and fatherhood. He holds BA and MBA degrees from Brown University and the University of Pittsburgh respectively and served as a Captain in the USMC during Vietnam. He is the proud dad to four sons, who have delivered ten rambunctious grandchildren. Robert resides in south Texas with his wife and fifth son, Stanley, a bullmastiff.

*I would be appreciative of any feedback you have on "**Master of Deceit**," particularly reviews on Amazon and other reader websites. This book is the second of the Nelson family saga series. You'll want to check out "**The Pact with the Devil**", my first novel in the series. Two more are already in the computer just itching to jump to print.*

Thanks.

R J D

Made in the USA
Coppell, TX
28 April 2020

23176370R00187